TOEIC

全面備戰

7大題型 應考策略 + 13大情境 必備詞彙

目錄 Table of Contents

Section A

7 大題型應考策略 ⸺⸺⸺⸺ ⑪

From the Editors

根據報導，為了讓畢業生在職場具競爭力，目前有九成以上的大專院校都設有「英語畢業門檻」，而多益成績便是其中一項重要指標。許多企業徵人時亦以英語能力作為第一階段的篩選，不同工作職位有不同要求。多益成績 550 分（滿分為 990 分）是基本門檻（根據官方統計，2019 年台灣有近 35 萬人次的多益測驗考生，平均成績為 564 分）；許多公司對於基層主管的多益分數需求為 650 分；有些高階職位甚至要求多益成績須達到 750 分。對於準備進入職場的社會新鮮人，或是想在職場上更具競爭力的上班族，具備良好的英語溝通能力及國際認證多益成績之重要性可見一斑。

為了幫助考生在最短的時間內做好萬全準備，本書從準備多益測驗兩個最重要的面向切入，亦即「7 大題型應考策略」與「13 大情境必備詞彙」，不僅教您如何解題，更帶您熟悉多益測驗中常見的出題情境與必備詞彙，最後透過一回 200 題完整的模擬測驗讓您實戰演練，以零死角的方式應戰，相信讀者一定能一舉拿下高分。

本書架構與特色如下：

Section A　7 大題型應考策略

以系統化的分析與一目了然的表格破解多益的七大題型與考法，並提供精簡且切中要領的應考策略，讓您以最有效率的方式迅速掌握解題關鍵。

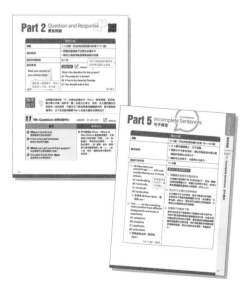

根據 ETS（美國教育測驗服務社）所公布多益測驗考試內容之 13 大主題情境分類，熟悉題目常見情境的同時，也累積該主題的相關必備單字。

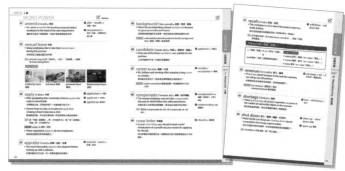

↑ 每單元扉頁即列出主題及其涵蓋內容，讓讀者即刻掌握單元方向。

↑ 每單元收錄 40-50 個主題字彙，搭配情境例句，並詳列同義字 同、反義字 反、不同詞性的衍生字 衍、延伸的相關字 關，以及 常用詞彙 和 常用片語；並適時補充相關圖示或字首／字尾等說明，讓讀者可依單字組別，有系統地背誦，迅速提升字彙量。

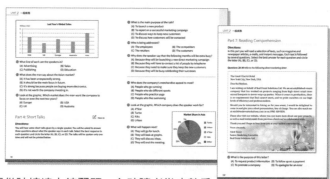

↑ 每單元末尾均提供該情境之練習題，有助讀者徹底熟悉各種情境，並理解所學詞彙能如何應用於考題中。

仿照多益測驗命題的全真模擬測驗，讓讀者做完整 200 題的試題，練習有效掌握考試速度並測試學習成效。

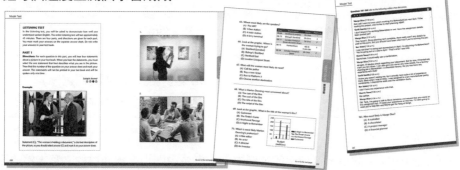

藉由本書精闢的應考策略以及符合多益出題情境的字彙，再搭配切中考點的試題練習，相信讀者必能有效戰勝多益測驗，增進職場英語競爭力。

一、 什麼是多益測驗？

TOEIC 多益測驗全名是 Test of English for International Communication（國際溝通英語測驗），這是針對英語非母語人士所設計之英語能力測驗，其測驗分數反映受測者在國際職場環境中與他人以英語溝通的熟稔程度。

二、 誰需要多益認證？

每天工作環境中會用到英語之人士，例如在企業、飯店、醫院、餐廳、 航空業以及經常要出席國際會議的專業人士。

☑ 跨國企業的員工，英語已經成為必要的工具。

☑ 欲在履歷表與學歷證件上，附有經國際肯定的英語能力檢定者。

跨國企業以及其他民營機構皆可以採用多益測驗來因應下列的需要：

☑ 招募員工時可設定應徵或報名考試之標準。

☑ 評量員工英語程度作為升等、海外受訓及開會的甄選參考。

☑ 作為英語進修課程編班標準以及檢定進修效果。

三、 多益測驗方式為何？

• 分兩大類（two categories）：聽力（Listening）及閱讀（Reading）。
• 總題數：每部分各一百題，總共二百題。
• 測驗時間：聽力部分約四十五分鐘，閱讀部分七十五分鐘，總共兩小時。
• 類型：全部為 單選題 。考生選好答案後，要在與題目卷分開的答案卷上畫卡。

第一大類： 聽力

共四部分（4 parts）。考生會聽到各種主題英語的直述句、問句、對話以及獨白，然後根據所聽到的內容回答問題。

大題	題型	題數
Part 1	Photographs 照片描述	6 題（四選一）
Part 2	Question and Response 應答問題	25 題（三選一）
Part 3	Short Conversations 簡短對話	13 組對話共 39 題（四選一）
Part 4	Short Talks 簡短獨白	10 組獨白共 30 題（四選一）

第二大類： 閱讀

共三部分（3 parts）。題目及選項都印在題本上。考生須閱讀多種題材的文章，然後回答相關問題。考生可以自由調配閱讀及答題速度。

大題	題型	題數
Part 5	Incomplete Sentences 句子填空	30 題（四選一）
Part 6	Text Completion 段落填空	16 題（四選一）
Part 7	Reading Comprehension 閱讀測驗 • Single Passages 單篇閱讀 • Multiple Passages 多篇閱讀 · Double Passages 雙篇閱讀 · Triple Passages 三篇閱讀	• 單篇共 10 篇文章 共 29 題（四選一） • 多篇 5 組文章 共 25 題（四選一）

在正式考試前，會有大約三十分鐘填寫個人資料和關於教育與工作經歷問卷的時間，因此真正待在考場內的時間大約為二小時三十分，中間不休息。

四、 多益測驗考哪些內容？

多益測驗的設計以職場需要為主。測驗題的內容是從全世界各地職場的英文資料中蒐集而來，題材多元，包含各種地點與狀況，依字母排列分類如下：

分類	內容	
企業發展 Corporate Development	• 研究（research） • 產品研發（product development）	
外食 Dining Out	• 商務／非正式午餐（business & informal lunches） • 宴會（banquets） • 招待會（receptions） • 餐廳訂位（restaurant reservations）	
娛樂 Entertainment	• 電影（cinema / movies） • 音樂（music） • 展覽（exhibitions） • 媒體（media）	• 劇場（theater） • 藝術（art） • 博物館（museums）
金融／預算 Finance & Budgeting	• 銀行業務（banking） • 稅務（taxes） • 帳單（billing）	• 投資（investments） • 會計（accounting）
一般商務 General Business	• 電影（cinema / movies） • 音樂（music） • 展覽（exhibitions） • 媒體（media）	• 劇場（theater） • 藝術（art） • 博物館（museums）
保健 Health	• 醫藥保險（medical insurance） • 看醫生或牙醫（visiting doctors or dentists） • 去診所或醫院（going to the clinic or the hospital）	
房屋／公司地產 Housing / Corporate Property	• 建築（construction） • 規格（specifications） • 購買和租賃（buying and renting） • 電力瓦斯服務（electric and gas services）	

製造業 Manufacturing	• 工廠管理（plant management） • 生產線（assembly lines） • 品管（quality control）
辦公室 Offices	• 董事會議（board meetings） • 委員會（committees） • 信件（letters） • 備忘錄（memoranda） • 電話留言、傳真訊息、即時訊息及電子郵件 （telephone, fax, text messages and e-mails） • 辦公室設備和器材（office equipment & furniture） • 辦公室流程（office procedures）
人事 Personnel	• 招考（recruiting） • 雇用（hiring） • 退休（retiring） • 薪資（salaries） • 升遷（promotions） • 退休金（pensions） • 獎勵（awards） • 求職申請表（job applications） • 徵才廣告（job advertisements）
採購 Purchasing	• 採買（shopping） • 訂貨（ordering supplies） • 送貨（shipping） • 發票（invoices）
技術層面 Technical Areas	• 電子（electronics） • 科技（technology） • 電腦（computers） • 實驗室與相關器材（laboratories & related equipment） • 技術規格（technical specifications）
旅遊 Travel	• 火車（trains） • 飛機（airplanes） • 計程車（taxis） • 巴士（buses） • 船隻（ships） • 渡輪（ferries） • 票務（tickets） • 時刻表（schedules） • 車站和機場廣播（station & airport announcements） • 租車（car rentals） • 飯店（hotels） • 預訂（reservations） • 誤點與取消（delays and cancellations）

雖然取材自這麼多領域，但考生不需要具備各個領域之專業辭彙，而是以整體一般用字遣詞之熟悉與了解為主。

五、 TOEIC 成績與英語能力參照

多益測驗的計分方式由答對題數決定，再將每一大類（聽力類、閱讀類）答對題數轉換成分數，總分在 10 分到 990 分之間。得到不同的成績代表擁有不同層級的英語能力，請參閱以下對照表。

TOEIC 成績	語言能力	證書顏色
905–990	英語能力已十分接近英語母語人士，能夠流暢有條理地表達意見、參與談話、主持英文會議、調和衝突並做出結論，語言使用上即使有瑕疵，亦不會造成理解上的困擾。	金色 (860–990)
785–900	可有效運用英語滿足社交及工作所需，措詞恰當，表達流暢；但在某些特定情形下，如：面臨緊張壓力、討論話題過於冷僻艱澀時，仍會顯現出語言能力不足的狀況。	藍色 (730–855)
605–780	可以英語進行一般社交場合的談話，能夠應付例行性的業務需求、參加英文會議、聽取大部分要點；但無法流利地以英語發表意見、作辯論，使用的字彙、句型亦以一般常見者為主。	綠色 (470–725)
405–600	英文文字溝通能力尚可，會話方面稍嫌辭彙不足、語言簡單，但已能掌握少量工作相關語言，可以從事英語相關程度較低的工作。	
255–400	語言能力僅僅侷限在簡單的一般日常對話，且無法做連續性交談，亦無法用英文工作。	棕色 (220–465)
10–250	只能以背誦的句子進行問答而不能自行造句，尚無法將英語當作溝通工具來使用。	橘色 (10–215)

六、 答題時間分配表

多益測驗須在 120 分鐘之內做完 200 道題目，考驗著應試者的耐力及應試技巧與策略。以下表列各個大題之題目難易度與考試時間分配策略，考生應先掌握「低、中階」難度的題型，然後再循序漸進攻占「高階」難度的題型。而在閱讀測驗中尤其要注意作答時間的掌控，才有機會奪取高分。

	總題數	相對難易度	時間分配
聽力 Listening	100		45 分鐘
Part 1	6	低	隨錄音播放速度
Part 2	25	低／中	
Part 3	39	中／高	
Part 4	30	中／高	
閱讀 Reading	100		75 分鐘
Part 5	30	低／中	12 分鐘
Part 6	16	低／中	8 分鐘
Part 7	54	低／中／高	55 分鐘
Total	200		120 分鐘

點讀筆與 MP3 下載說明

認識點讀筆

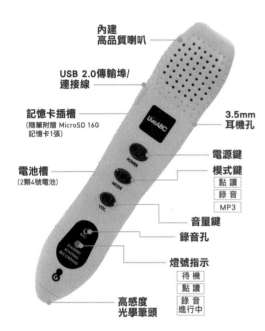

內建
高品質喇叭

USB 2.0傳輸埠/
連接線

記憶卡插槽
(隨筆附贈 MicroSD 16G
記憶卡1張)

3.5mm
耳機孔

電池槽
(2顆4號電池)

電源鍵

模式鍵
| 點 讀 |
| 錄 音 |
| MP3 |

音量鍵

錄音孔

燈號指示
| 待 機 |
| 點 讀 |
| 錄 音 進行中 |

高感度
光學筆頭

四大功能

 高科技光學點讀筆頭 內建高品質喇叭 支援USB檔案傳輸 點讀/錄音 MP3/字典 四機一體

尺寸	14.6 x 3.1 x 2.4 (CM)	重量	37.5g (不含電池)
記憶體	含 16G micro SD 記憶卡	電源	4 號 (AAA) 電池 2 顆
配件	USB 傳輸線、使用說明書、錄音卡 / 音樂卡 / 字典卡、micro SD 記憶卡 (已安裝)		

下載及安裝點讀筆音檔

1. 請至 LiveABC 首頁上方的「叢書館」，從左側分類中點選「TOEIC 多益」，找到本書後點開內容介紹頁，即可在「檔案下載」區塊下載 LiveABC 點讀筆音檔。

2. 用 USB 傳輸線連結電腦和 LiveABC 點讀筆，將下載好的壓縮檔解壓縮後，把檔案(.ecm) 複製至 LiveABC 點讀筆中的「BOOK」資料夾內，即可完成安裝。

下載 MP3 音檔

同上第一步，點開本書內容介紹頁，即可在「檔案下載」區塊一次下載全書 MP3 音檔。

開始使用點讀筆

Step1

1. 將LiveABC光學筆頭指向本書封面圖示。
2. 聽到「Here We Go!」語音後即完成連結。

Step2　開始使用書中的點讀功能

詞彙部分，點 Track 編號即播放整軌內容；點 圖示則播放單頁內容。

應考策略及練習題部分，點 TRACK 編號，即播放整軌內容。

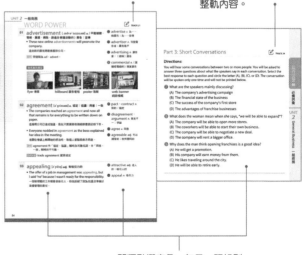

單獨點選字彙、句子、題組則
可聆聽其個別發音。

Section A

7 大題型應考策略

Section A 以最精簡、有效率的方式

以及系統化的分析，幫助您迅速掌握

多益測驗各大題的題型及應考技巧。

Part 1 Photographs 照片描述

題型介紹

題數	六題（多益考試兩百題中的第 1~6 題）
題型說明	• 6 張照片印在試題本中 • 聽完四個選項後，選出最符合照片的敘述
題目時間間隔	約 5 秒
題目範例	**錄音內容** ✏ TRACK 01 (A) The woman is talking on the phone. (B) The businessman is relaxing in the spa. (C) A guest is receiving a keycard from the clerk. (D) The bellboy is carrying the luggage. （C）鞠五

> 選項不會印在題目卷上，須聆聽錄音得知各項敘述。

> 題目卷僅會顯示相片。

應考技巧

Part 1 是考生必須要把握的拿分題型，以下歸納此大題的基本句型分析及應考技巧。

✏ TRACK 02

基本句型	範例	應考技巧
❶ 現在進行式 （be + V-ing）	The man is taking a book off a shelf. 男子正將一本書從架上拿下來。 	◆ 是照片上正在進行的動作或正呈現的狀態。這樣的句子描述占 Part 1 所有選項中至少一半以上。 ◆ 若照片中僅有一人，各選項的主詞通常一致，故要留意的是其動作描述是否與照片相符。 ◆ 照片中若有多人，則要注意個別的（the man / the woman）動作及外觀描述是否正確。

❷ 現在完成式的被動語態 （have/has been + p.p.）	Some lounge chairs <u>have been placed</u> on the beach. 有一些躺椅被放在海灘上。 	◆ 表示動作已完成，在圖片中乃呈現完成後的結果。 ◆ 常用來描述「物品」已擺放好的方式或狀態等。
❸ 現在進行式的被動語態 （be + being + p.p.）	The menus <u>are being handed</u> to the customers. 菜單正被遞給客人。 	◆ 此句型用在 Part 1 描述中常以「事物」為主詞，說明某事物正進行或呈現的狀態。
❹ 現在式 （S. + V.）	The table <u>has</u> some wine glasses on it. 桌上有一些酒杯。 	◆ 表示常態／事實。 ◆ 這類句型在照片題中大多都是用 be 動詞或 have，對整個句意的了解影響不大，因此聽的重點要放在其他名詞或（副詞）片語等上面。
❺ 現在式的被動語態 （be 動詞 + p.p.）	A statue <u>is located</u> in the park. 有一座雕像被設置在公園裡。 	◆ 題目選項中常以「物」作為主詞，描述事物所呈現的狀態。

Part 2 Question and Response 應答問題

題型介紹	
題數	二十五題（多益考試兩百題中的第 7~31 題）
題型說明	• 問題及選項皆不出現在試題本中 • 聽完三個選項後選擇最適當的回應
題目時間間隔	約 5 秒
題目範例	考生只能透過聆聽錄音內容得知題目及選項。 **錄音內容** 📝 TRACK 03 What's the deadline for the project? (A) The projector is broken. (B) It has to be done by Tuesday. (C) You should wait in line. 正解 (B)

題目範例中：Mark your answer on your answer sheet.

題目卷上僅會顯示「請在答案卷上作答」的字樣。

應考技巧

因問題及選項皆「不」出現在試題本中，Part 2「應答問題」是四個聽力單元中唯一純粹考「聽」的能力之單元。然而，此大題的題型及回答有一定的規則，只要充分了解並學會辨識關鍵字詞，便可輕鬆掌握得分。以下為您整理歸納 Part 2 的基本題型及應答技巧。

題型 1 Wh-Questions 疑問詞疑問句

出題頻率：約 40%-50%　📝 TRACK 04

範例	應考技巧
Q **When** is the bill due? 那張帳單什麼時候到期？ **A** It has to be paid **tomorrow**. 帳單必須在明天繳納。 **Q** **Where** can I get one of those gadgets? 我在哪裡可以買到那種小玩意？ **A** I brought it back from **Japan**. 這是我從日本帶回來的。	◆ 問句開頭為 When、Where 及 Who/Whose 屬低難度題型，正確選項分別找有關「時間」（如：幾點幾分、某時段或日期等）、「地點或場所」（如：國家、城市、房間、辦公室或建築物等）或「人」（如：人名、姓氏、職稱或身分關係等）的答案。

Q **Who** will pick me up at the airport?
誰會到機場接我？

A I think **David** will.
我想大衛會去。

Q **Which smartphone** would you like?
你喜歡哪一支手機？

A The one with the large screen.
有大螢幕的那一支。

Q **What** do you **think** of the speech?
你覺得那場演講如何？

A It's pretty useful.
還滿實用的。

◆ 句型為「Which/What + 名詞」時，注意聽此名詞為何。

◆ 句型為「Which/What + 助動詞」時，不理會助動詞，而抓出問句中之動詞。

Q **How** does this dress **look**?
這件洋裝看起來如何？

A I think the other one suited you better.
我覺得另一件比較適合妳。

Q **How long** have you been working here?
你在這裡工作多久了？

A About seven months now.
到現在大約七個月了。

◆ 句型為「How + 助動詞」時，同樣不必理會助動詞，而要注意聽問句中的動詞。

◆「How +形容詞或副詞」，可用來詢問金額（How much）、時間長短或頻率（How long/often）或狀態（How well/bad）等。

Q **Why** do we have to work this weekend?
我們這個週末為何需要工作？

A We have to complete the project by next Monday.
我們下週一前得完成這個專案。

Q **Why don't** we have a picnic this Sunday?
我們這週日去野餐吧！

A That sounds like a good plan.
聽起來不錯喔。

◆ 問句開頭為 Why 時，預想有關「原因」之答案。表原因之連接詞可省略不說，故須了解問題及所有選項之內容大意，亦即注意所有動詞、其時態及基本受詞等，屬較高難度之題型。

◆ 以 Why 開頭接 don't/doesn't 表提出建議時，屬於「隱藏式 why 問句」，不是要問對方原因，而是提供建議或提議，適當的回應通常是對提議表示「贊同」或「不贊同」。

題型 *2* Yes/No Questions 一般是非問句

出題頻率：約 40%-50%　　 TRACK 05

範例	應考技巧
Q **Is** the classical concert happening tonight? 那場古典音樂會是在今晚舉行嗎？ **A** No, it's been canceled. 不是，已經被取消了。 **Q** **Do** you think you'll ever leave Asia and move back to Europe? 你認為自己會離開亞洲，然後搬回歐洲嗎？ **A** I'm still thinking about it. 我還正在考慮。	◆ 問句以 be 動詞或助動詞開頭，且問句語調上揚，稱為「一般是非問句」。其回應不見得包含 yes 或 no，但不脫「是／有」、「不是／沒有」或「不確定」等範疇。 ◆ 含有表「不清楚／不確定」或「再做查詢／確認」之模糊回答，由於在邏輯上往往都說得通，因此通常會是對的選項。如：I haven't heard.「我沒聽說」、Let me check.「我查查看」、We're still deciding.「我們還要再做決定」等。
Q Could you tell me **where** you bought that shirt? 你能告訴我那件襯衫是在哪買的嗎？ **A** From the department store downtown. 在市中心的百貨公司買的。	◆ 「一般是非問句」中夾雜 Wh- 疑問詞時，即為「間接問句」，語調同樣是上揚的。此題型須注意聽中間的 Wh- 疑問詞為何，為回應答案的關鍵。
Q Tomorrow's a holiday, **isn't it**? 明天是假日，對吧？ **A** Yes, it's Labor Day! 對，明天是勞動節！ **Q** You never know what to expect from her, **do you**? 你永遠無法預期她會做些什麼，是吧？ **A** She often surprises me. 她常讓我感到驚訝。	◆ 「附加問句」看似以直述句開頭，其實是隱藏式的 Yes/No 問句，其句型為： | 主要子句	附加問句
S. + V.,	be 動詞／助動詞 + (not) + 代名詞？ | ◆ 回應亦可以 Yes/No 來回答，但同「一般是非問句」，Yes/No 二字亦可被省略。

> **附加問句的語調**
>
> 若附加問句在句尾語調上揚，通常表示說話者是真的心存疑惑。而句尾語調下降時，表示說話者並非真的想問問題，而是想尋求對方的確認。例如：
>
> • **Tom told me the truth, didn't he?**
> 　湯姆跟我說了實話，不是嗎？
>
> → 語調上揚表示說話者不確定湯姆是否真的說了實話。
>
> → 語調下降表示說話者認為湯姆說了實話，但希望對方也認同。

題型 **3** A or B Questions 選擇疑問句

出題頻率：約 5%-10%　　 TRACK 06

範例	應考技巧
Q Will you take a shuttle bus to the airport **or** go by taxi? 你要坐接駁巴士去機場還是坐計程車呢？ **A** It will be cheaper if I take the bus. 坐巴士的話會比較便宜。 **Q** Do you prefer the gray blouse **or** the black one? 妳比較喜歡這件灰色的女用襯衫，還是黑色的？ **A** I don't like dark colors, so I'll say neither of them. 我不喜歡深色，所以都不喜歡。	◆ 此題型以助動詞開頭，乍聽像 Yes/ No Questions，但有兩個不同的特點： 　① 句中多一個關鍵連接詞 or 　② 問句語調下降 ◆ 其答案選項通常有三種： 　① 二選一（可聽到題目中的其中一種選項） 　② 兩者皆選（常出現 both、either 或 whichever/whatever 等關鍵字） 　③ 兩者皆不選（常出現 neither 或 none 等關鍵字）

題型 **4** Statements 直述句

出題頻率：約 10%　　 TRACK 07

範例	應考技巧
Q It's too late to take the subway. 現在已經來不及搭地鐵了。 **A** Let's call a cab. 我們叫計程車吧。 **Q** You've been upgraded to business class, free of charge. 您已被免費升級至商務艙。 **A** Wow, is this for real? 哇，這是真的嗎？	◆ 聽到題目整個句子無（助）動詞倒裝、語調亦沒有上揚，即可辨識出為直述句題型。 ◆ 此題型的答案沒有一定的模式，須盡可能聽出句意，找出「合理」的回應，屬較高難度的題型。

Part 3 Short Conversations
簡短對話

題型介紹	
題數	三十九題（多益考試兩百題中的第 32~70 題）
題型說明	• 會聽到 13 組二或三個人之間的簡短對話 • 每組對話各有三個問題，13 組對話共 39 題 • 每題組的問題和答案選項都出現在題本中
題目時間間隔	約 7~8 秒
題目範例	**錄音內容** ✎ TRACK 08 對話錄音內容以 2~3 位男女互相交談的方式進行。有些題組會需要在聽對話的同時，另外搭配所附的圖表資訊來作答。 ***Questions 1 through 3** refer to the following conversation.* W: Mr. Adams, please take the floor. I think you should start the board meeting. M: Thank you, Ms. Johnson. Let me go ahead and say first that I am honored to have been chosen as chairman. My first motion as chairman is to create a committee whose job is to improve sales before September. In order to carry out that motion, I need a majority of you to raise your hands in agreement. W: Everyone here raised their hands. The motion is carried unanimously and will be implemented tomorrow. M: Thank you, everyone. Under no circumstances will I allow our profits to fall. 正解 1. (B) 2. (C) 3. (D)

① What is the man's occupation?
  (A) A politician
  (B) A businessman
  (C) A lawyer
  (D) A professor

② Where are the speakers?
  (A) At a furniture store
  (B) In the Senate
  (C) At a board meeting
  (D) In a courtroom

③ What does the chairman ask everyone to do?
  (A) Take the minutes
  (B) Take the floor
  (C) Nominate a new chairman
  (D) Create a new committee

常考題型與解題技巧

這個部分的題型大多以 Wh- 形式的問句為主，包括人物、地點、談論主題、談話的細節內容等。常考題型與解題技巧整理如下：

題型	常見問題	解題技巧
❶ 詢問主題／目的	• What are the man and woman talking about? • What are the speakers (mainly) talking about? • What are the speakers (mainly) discussing? • What is the conversation (mainly/mostly) about? • What is the purpose of . . . ?	主旨題（main idea）的答案常遍布於整個對話中，就算不小心聽漏了某一部分，仍有機會選出答案，屬於必要把握的送分題型。這類問題可以聽完全部對話再綜合全部資訊來作答。
❷ 詢問人物身分	• Who is sb.? • What is the man's/woman's job/occupation? • What line of work is the man/woman in? • What type of job/business does the man/woman have? • Where do the speakers most likely work?	常會詢問人物的身分、職業、工作性質或產業類別等。這類題型可從對話中所談論的關鍵字詞來掌握可能的訊息，如：若問對方訂位時間或人數，則可推斷他是在餐廳工作。
❸ 詢問行動／做法或建議	• What does . . . plan to do . . . ? • What will . . . do next? • What does A ask B to do? • What does . . . want to do? • What does A want B to do? • What does . . . suggest/ offer . . . ? • What does the man/woman recommend doing?	預先瀏覽問題時先注意題目是詢問男子或女子會如何做，或是哪一方給予另一方建議，然後仔細聆聽其陳述。 各答案選項常以動詞開頭，描述某個做法或行動，如：visit another store、cancel the appointment/ reservation、 arrange a different flight 等。

題型	常見問題	解題技巧
❹ 詢問發生的問題或擔憂之處	• What is/was the problem (with . . .)? • What is the man's/woman's problem? • According to the conversation, what is the problem? • What is wrong with . . . ? • What is the man/woman concerned about?	預覽題目時先看是詢問何人或事物的問題點,若無明確指出時,亦可從答案選項中找尋蛛絲馬跡。聆聽對話時,若有 The problem is . . . 或 I'm (a bit) worried because . . . 等字眼便很可能是答題的關鍵處。
❺ 詢問細節	• 問時間:When should (sth.) be completed? / When will (event) take place? • 地點:Where is (sth.) taking place? • 問數字或多少錢:How many people do the speakers expect for the (event)? • 問方式:How will the man/woman contact (sb.)? • 問物件:What does A give B . . . ? / What does the man/woman request?	相對於 main idea 一類的問題可以等最後再答,細節題(specific questions)是一聽到對話中提及就要馬上作答的,否則很容易會忘掉該題的答案。這類問題的辨識方式在於其答案選項通常都很短。
❻ 推論題	這類題型問句中多半含 most likely、probably、might、inferred/implied 等字眼,如: • Where does sb. probably work? • Where do the speakers most likely work? • Where most likely is the conversation taking place? • What can be inferred about the speakers?	推論型題目(inference questions)屬 Part 3 中難度較高的題型,正確答案並沒有在對話中明講。成功答題的秘訣在於聽出關鍵字詞後,能靠合理、有邏輯的思考模式推敲出答案。

題型	常見問題	解題技巧
❼ 考口語用法或句意	• Why does the woman/man say, "…"? • What does the woman/man mean when she/he says, "…"?	先瀏覽題目看是要詢問男子或女子所說，然後聽對話時仔細聆聽該句出現的地方並根據上下文推斷出語意。
❽ 圖表題	• Look at the graphic. Wh-question …?	考生應試時須一心二用，耳朵在聽對話的同時，眼睛要同時閱讀圖表的資訊內容。看到題目後先快速瀏覽圖表及相關問題，然後答題時整合對話內容及圖表所呈現的資訊來作答。

常見圖表類型列舉如下：

Table 表格

Line	Train No.	Destination	Departure Time
A	156	Willford	8:30
B	263	Harris	9:15
C	521	Willford	10:30
B	877	Bentley	12:15

Floor Plan / Layout 平面圖

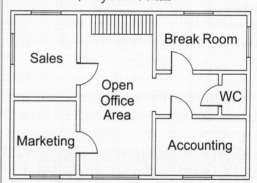

Map 地圖

Chart 圖表

line graph 曲線圖　　bar chart 長條圖

pie chart 圓餅圖

考題範例　題組 1 　✎　TRACK 09

① What is the man's occupation?
  (A) A real estate agent
  (B) A gas station attendant
  (C) A home inspector
  (D) A construction worker

② What problem does the woman mention?
  (A) The gas pipes are leaking.
  (B) There are holes in the floor.
  (C) Many cracks are in the walls.
  (D) There is a hole between the patio and doorframe.

③ How long has the woman lived in the house?
  (A) A few months
  (B) Less than a year
  (C) Less than a month
  (D) More than a year

錄音內容

Questions 1 through 3 *refer to the following conversation.*

M: This house is uninhabitable. There are gas leaks, holes in the floor, cracks in the walls—the condition of your home might be the worst I've ever seen. You were right to hire me to inspect it.

W: And what about the gap between the patio and doorframe? It's at least five centimeters!

M: Yes, and with a gap that size, it's easy to imagine small animals—worms, beetles, spiders, snails—getting inside. How long have you lived in this house, and when was it built?

W: We haven't even lived here a year! It was finished a few months before we moved in.

解析

Q1 此為題型 ❷ 詢問人物身分。關鍵句為男子說 . . . the condition of your home . . . You were right to hire me to inspect it.「妳家的屋況……妳請我來檢查是對的。」可知答案選 (C)「房屋檢查員」。

Q2 此為題型 ❹ 詢問發生的問題。關鍵句為女子所說 And what about the gap between the patio and doorframe? It's at least five centimeters!「露臺和門框之間的縫隙呢？至少有五公分吧！」，故答案選 (D)。選項 (A)、(B)、(C) 則皆為男子提到的問題。

Q3 此為題型 ❺ 詢問細節。題目問「女子住在這間房子多久了？」，關鍵句為女子說 We haven't even lived here a year!「我們住這裡還不到一年！」，故答案選 (B)。

考題範例 題組 2　　　　　　　　　　　 TRACK 10

④ What activities does the woman state she wants to do in Morocco?
(A) Hike and exercise　　　　　　　　(B) Eat and shop
(C) Watch TV and sleep　　　　　　　(D) See a movie and read

⑤ Where do the speakers most likely live?
(A) In Africa　　　　　　　　　　　　(B) In Rabat
(C) In or near London　　　　　　　　(A) In Marrakesh

⑥ Look at the graphic. Which flight did the woman book?
(A) BX021　　　　　　　　　　　　　 (B) LH045
(C) LH046　　　　　　　　　　　　　 (D) BX022

BX021	London (LGW) 07:40 a.m.	Marrakesh (RAK) 11:25 a.m.	*£200
LH045	London (LHR) 06:00 a.m.	Marrakesh (RAK) 11:10 a.m.	*£220
LH046	London (LHR) 03:15 p.m.	Marrakesh (RAK) 09:25 p.m.	*£230
BX022	London (LGW) 03:40 p.m.	Marrakesh (RAK) 07:20 p.m.	*£250

* Listed price is for two passengers.

錄音內容

Questions 4 through 6 *refer to the following conversation and flights.*

W: I just booked us a flight to Marrakesh in Morocco.

M: Morocco? Why did you choose Morocco for our vacation?

W: Well, for one, it's known for a lot of delicious food and amazing shopping. And it's really cheap! Look! This flight from London to Marrakesh is only £100 per person round trip! Plus, these hotels look really nice, and their prices are also rock-bottom.

M: Yeah, and I recall reading about an African arts festival happening in Rabat too. All right, sounds like you made a good choice!

解析

Q4 此為題型 ❺ 細節題。當男子問女子為何選摩洛哥作為度假地點，女子回應說 Well, for one, it is known for a lot of delicious food and amazing shopping.，故知女子想在那裡從事的活動為「吃東西和購物」，答案選 (B)。

Q5 此為題型 ❻ 含有 most likely 字眼的推論題。由於女子提到 This flight from London to Marrakesh . . . 可知他們是從倫敦出發，因此推論他們住在倫敦或附近的城市，答案選 (C)。

Q6 此為題型 ❽ 圖表題。關鍵句為女子說 This flight from London to Marrakesh is only £100 per person round trip! 且圖表下方備註顯示「列出金額為兩位乘客的價格」，可知女子訂的班機是兩人共兩百元的 BX021 班機，故答案選 (A)。

考題範例 | 題組 **3**　　　　　　　　　　　　　　　　　　　　 TRACK 11

⑦ What is the purpose of this conversation?
(A) Making an urgent announcement
(B) Asking for time off
(C) Inviting coworkers to a wedding
(D) Opening a new bank account

⑧ What does the woman ask the man to do?
(A) Go on vacation to Florida next month
(B) Take his kids to Disney World
(C) Tell his coworker key information about ongoing projects
(D) Help her to solve problems for important clients

⑨ What does the man mean when he says, "I know everything will go smoothly"?
(A) He wants his coworker to make an announcement for him.
(B) His absence won't cause any problems.
(C) He always needs his colleagues to help him.
(D) He wants to thank his boss for handling his pre-vacation preparations.

錄音內容

Questions 7 through 9 refer to the following conversation.

W: Hello, Simon. What can I help you with?

M: Well, my brother is getting married next month in Florida, and I was hoping to take some time off to attend. I've already filled out the request form.

W: Which dates do you want to take off?

M: I'd like to take the whole week of the seventeenth. That way, I can take my kids to Disney World too.

W: That seems fine. Just make sure you send an out-of-office announcement a few days beforehand and brief Karen on any ongoing projects you're working on. She can cover your accounts while you're gone.

M: No problem. With everyone's help, I know everything will go smoothly. It will be like I never left!

解析

Q7 此為題型 ❶ 詢問目的。關鍵句為男子說「我弟弟下個月要在佛羅里達結婚,我希望能請假去參加。我已經填好申請表了。」,故答案選 (B)。

Q8 此為題型 ❸ 詢問做法。關鍵句為女子要求男子「向凱倫說明你目前在進行的案子。你不在時,她可以替你負責你的客戶。」,原文中的片語 brief sb. on sth. 表「向某人簡要說明某事」,故答案選 (C)。

Q9 此為題型 ❼ 考口語用法或句意。關鍵句為男子說「有大家的幫忙,我知道一切會很順利的。就好像我從來沒離開過!」,故答案選 (B)「他的缺勤不會造成任何問題。」

Part 4 Short Talks 簡短獨白

題型介紹	
題數	三十題（多益考試兩百題中的第 71~100 題）
題型說明	• 會聽到 10 組不同類型的一人獨白 • 每組獨白各有三個問題，10 組獨白共 30 題 • 每題組的問題和答案選項都出現在題本中
題目時間間隔	約 7~8 秒
題目範例	**錄音內容** ✎ TRACK 12 ***Questions 1 through 3*** *refer to the following recorded message.* You have reached the Smith City branch of Television City, your first choice for televisions, computers, and other electronic products. It looks like we weren't able to answer your call. We are currently closed while we make renovations to better serve you. We will reopen on the 17th of next month with a grand reopening party, so see our website for details. Our normal business hours are 10 a.m. to 9 p.m., Monday through Saturday. If you have an urgent issue, please press star 1 and you can leave a message with your name, who you would like to reach, and what you want to say. You can also e-mail us at help@tvtvcity.com.

題目範例：

① Why is the store closed?
  (A) It's past 9:00 p.m.
  (B) It's a holiday.
  (C) It is undergoing repairs.
  (D) It went out of business.

② When will the store reopen?
  (A) On the 7th of this month
  (B) On the 7th of next month
  (C) On the 17th of this month
  (D) On the 17th of next month

③ What should you do if you want to talk with someone specific?
  (A) Call back
  (B) Press star 1
  (C) Wait just a moment
  (D) Ask for the operator

> 有部分獨白還須配合圖表來回答問題（如 p.30 的考題範例）。

正解 1. (C) 2. (D) 3. (B)

常考題型與解題技巧

Part 4常見的獨白類型包括：Announcement「公告或宣布」、Introduction「介紹或引言」、Instruction(s)「指示或說明」、Media Broadcast「廣播或電視媒體」、Voice Message「語音訊息」、Speech/Lecture「演講」等。由於部分獨白內容較長，且沒有對話情境，很容易導致考生聽著聽著就分心或漏掉重要資訊，因此以下幾項基本應試技巧務必熟練：

1. 快速瀏覽每題組的三個題目及其選項

根據問題及選項中的關鍵字，判斷獨白主題及方向。

2. 仔細聽介紹句

每一題組的介紹句 "Questions . . . through . . . refer to the following (talk type)."
會有助於進一步正確判斷主題和獨白情境。

3. 掌握問題點及作答順序

題組答題順序有七八成會依照順序問，一般來說可依序作答，但與整體內容相關的主旨題或高難度題型可最後作答，細節題則應立即作答以免遺忘相關內容。

以下歸納各類常考題型與應答技巧：

題型	常考問題	應答技巧
❶ 問主旨或目的	• What is the message/talk mainly about? • What is the (main) topic of . . . ? • What is the (main) purpose of . . . ?	屬必考題型，30 題中大約會出 3~4 題。通常可由獨白內容中多處地方聽出整體訊息並做判斷。
❷ 問說話者的身分	• Who is the speaker? • Who (most likely) is sb.? • What is sb.'s position/occupation?	問說話者本身是誰，或是問獨白中所提到之某人的身分或職業等。這類題型只要仔細聆聽說話者的自我介紹或是介紹來賓的引言，即可從關鍵字詞中判斷出答案。
❸ 問談話的對象	• Who is being addressed? • Who is the audience for this talk? • Who is the intended audience for this talk/announcement? • Who is the speaker probably addressing?	問這段獨白的主要對象是誰，通常須由整體內容和訊息的性質來判斷。

題型	常考問題	應答技巧
❹ 細節題	常見問題包括： • 人名，例：Who will (do sth.)? • 時間或日期，例：What time . . . ? / When . . . ? • 地點，例：Where is . . . located? • 物品，例：What does (the company) sell?	如同 Part 3，在 Part 4「簡短獨白」中，這類問題的答案選項同樣會比較短，一定要先預覽題目和選項，然後針對題目一聽到答案便即刻作答。
❺ 題目含 will . . . next/last 字眼的題型	• What will happen last/next? • What will the speaker do next? • What will the next talk be about?	問何事會最後或緊接著發生，或是問接下來的談話內容為何。這類題型的答案常會在獨白的後段出現。
❻ 問事件內容、原因或行動	• What does the speaker say about / want . . . ? • What problem does sb. mention? • What is the speaker doing?	這類問題問法比較沒有固定模式。務必事先瀏覽題目及選項以便聽獨白時抓出解題的關鍵字句。
❼ 問口語用法或句意	• What does the speaker mean/ imply when he/she says, "..."? • What does the speaker mean/ imply by saying . . . ?	須仔細聆聽該句於獨白中何時出現，並依上下文來判斷其含意。
❽ 推論題	• What does the speaker imply about . . . ? • What is implied about . . . ?	題目中看到 imply / infer / might / most likely 等字眼即為推論題。須由獨白中的相關訊息去推敲出合理答案。
❾ 圖表題	• Look at the graphic. Wh-question . . . ?	須整合獨白訊息及圖表資訊來答題。要注意圖表所呈現的不代表就是最後的正確資訊，有時獨白中會另外說明有變更或異動等。

考題範例 　題組 1　　　　　　　　　　　TRACK 13

① Who is the speaker?
(A) A bank clerk
(B) A cashier at a supermarket
(C) Staff for a water and electric company
(D) A receptionist from a phone company

② What's the main purpose of this phone call?
(A) To say sorry for making a mistake　　(B) To remind the man to pay his bill
(C) To remind the man to fill out a form　　(D) To thank the man for his time

③ How much will be charged in late fees if the bill isn't paid on time?
(A) $150　　　　　　　　　　　　　　(B) $25
(C) $35　　　　　　　　　　　　　　(D) $126

録音內容

Questions 1 through 3 *refer to the following telephone message.*

Mr. David Wagner, my name is Sarah from Jones Water and Electric Company. We are sorry we were unable to reach you. This message is to remind you that you have failed to pay your bill. Your account shows that you owe $154.26. Please remember that it is crucial to pay your bills promptly. This is the last time we will notify you. In two days, if you do not make the mandatory payments, your water and electricity will be shut off, and you will be charged a late fee of $25. If you already paid your bill and believe there was a mistake, please come to our office and fill out a Billing Discrepancy form. Until you complete this form and Jones Water and Electric Company has verified there was a mistake, you are still responsible for paying your bill and any related fees on time. Thank you for your time, Mr. Wagner.

解析

Q1 此為題型 ❷ 詢問人物身分。答題關鍵在於 Mr. David Wagner, my name is Sarah from Jones Water and Electric Company.「大衛‧華格納先生，我是瓊斯水電公司的莎拉。」，答案選 (C)。

Q2 此為題型 ❶ 詢問主要目的。關鍵句為 This message is to remind you that you have failed to pay your bill . . . Please remember that it is crucial to pay your bills promptly. 「此通留言係提醒您，您尚未繳納帳單……此事非常重要，請記得立即繳納您的帳單。」，答案選 (B)。

Q3 此為題型 ❹ 詢問細節。關鍵句為 . . . you will be charged a late fee of $25.「……被索取 25 美元的延滯金。」，答案選 (B)。

考題範例　題組 2 TRACK 14

④ Where is this talk most likely taking place?
(A) At Mr. Fisk's office
(B) At a festival
(C) In a department store
(D) In a factory

⑤ What does the man mean when he says, "I hope we can clarify the issue of product defects"?
(A) He wants to apologize for something.
(B) He wants to explain a situation to Mr. Fisk.
(C) He wants Mr. Fisk to teach him something.
(D) He thinks Mr. Fisk misunderstood something.

⑥ What will workers do after the finished product is placed on the drying rack?
(A) Assemble the product
(B) Paint and seal the product
(C) Test the product out
(D) Send the product to a warehouse

錄音內容

***Questions 4 through 6** refer to the following introduction.*

Thanks for taking the time to come down here and check out our operation, Mr. Fisk. I hope we can clarify the issue of product defects. First up here on the left is our receiving warehouse where shipments come in. Over there on the right is our molding area. Just past that is the assembly area. After the product is assembled, it's brought over to this room, where it's sealed and then painted. This is the room you said you wanted to inspect for production issues. Then, workers place the finished product on the drying rack. After that, it's tested over there in that small room. And last but not least, if it passes quality checks, it is sent out from our shipping room in the back. Any questions?

解析

Q4 此為題型 ⑧ 推論題，詢問獨白最可能的地點在哪裡。關鍵句為 Thanks for taking the time to come down here and check out our operation . . .「謝謝您撥空來到這裡參觀我們的運作……」，且接下來說明產品製作與出貨流程，可知答案選 (D)「在工廠裡」。

Q5 此為題型 ⑦ 詢問句意，題目問男子說 I hope we can clarify the issue of product defects. 為何意。前一句男子先感謝 Mr. Fisk 來參觀，接下來又仔細說明相關流程並說到「這是您說想檢查生產問題的房間。」，故答案選 (B)「他想要向費斯克先生解釋某個情況。」

Q6 此為題型 ⑥ 詢問做法或行動。題目問「工人將成品放在乾燥架上後會做什麼？」。關鍵句為 Then, workers place the finished product on the drying rack. After that, it's tested over there in that small room.「接著，工人會將成品放在乾燥架上。之後，會在那間小房間裡做產品測試。」，故答案選 (C)。

考題範例　題組 **3**　　　　　　　　　　　　　　TRACK 15

⑦ Who is the speaker probably addressing?
(A) A client　　　　　　　　(B) An adviser
(C) A physician　　　　　　(D) A contractor

⑧ Look at the graphic. During which month is the talk most likely taking place?
(A) January
(B) March
(C) September
(D) November

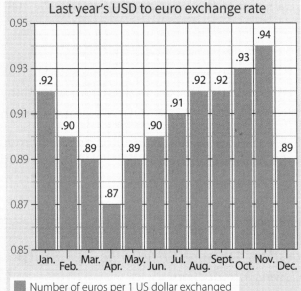

Last year's USD to euro exchange rate

Number of euros per 1 US dollar exchanged

⑨ What will the speaker probably do next?
(A) Buy euros
(B) Buy US dollars
(C) Exchange products
(D) Get a refund

錄音內容

Questions 7 through 9 *refer to the following talk and chart.*

Hey, thanks for meeting with me. I remember last year you recommended for me to buy some US dollars because the exchange rate was the best. I made quite a bit off of that advice. Well, based on how exchange rates went last year, it looks like it might be a good time to buy back some euros with my US dollars. So what do you think? This time last year it was peaking, and then it dropped sharply the next month. I think I'd better act quickly or I might regret not taking the chance.

解析

Q7 此為題型 ❸ 問談話的對象。由關鍵句「我記得去年你推薦我買一些美金，因為當時匯率是最好的。你的建議讓我賺了不少錢。」可知答案選 (B) An adviser「顧問」。

Q8 此為題型 ❾ 圖表題。題目問「這段談話最有可能發生在哪個月？」，關鍵句為「去年此時它漲到最高點，隔月又暴跌。」，圖表上顯示去年十一月漲到最高點，十二月暴跌，可知這段談話發生在十一月，故答案選 (D)。

Q9 此為題型 ❺ 題目中含 will . . . next 的字眼。題目問「說話者接下來可能會做什麼？」。關鍵句為「……看起來現在是我用美金買回一些歐元的好時機。」，而最後說話者提到「我想我最好快點行動，以免後悔錯失良機。」故答案選 (A)「買歐元」。

Part 5 Incomplete Sentences
句子填空

題型介紹	
題數	三十題（多益考試兩百題中的第 101~130 題）
題型說明	• 三十題中題題獨立、互不相關。 • 每題句子中會有空格，須從四個選項中選出最適當的答案以完成句子。 • 測驗考生的單字、片語與文法能力。
建議作答時間	12 分鐘

① All these items are painstakingly ------- with care and devotion by our in-house artisans.

　(A) handcrafting
　(B) handcrafts
　(C) handcraft
　(D) handcrafted

辨識選項是否為同一個字的變化？

→ 主詞為 All these items、動詞為 are。

② The ------- for the marketing intern position have different backgrounds and levels of experience.

　(A) symptoms
　(B) specifics
　(C) applicants
　(D) restrictions

→ 空格處為主詞，動詞為 have。

正解 1. (D) 2. (C)

基本作答流程與技巧

1. 閱讀題目選項及空格前後文

在每題作答時間不到 30 秒的情況下，若每一題都從頭到尾閱讀句子，將難以在時間內完成。故務必要先閱讀題目選項後分辨題型（詳見 p.32）。

2. 找出句子主要的主詞和動詞

此大題的句子往往很長，甚至句構會比較複雜，但有時並不需要完整閱讀即可作答。故須養成「化繁為簡」的能力，抓出句子主要的主詞和動詞，以便找出考題重點並有效解題。

3. 依題型不同對症下藥

除非空格是須了解整個句子結構或句意才能作答，否則不要浪費時間看完整個題目再作答。如基本詞性題或固定用法的片語等，看完選項及空格前後關鍵字詞後便可立即作答。對於須耗費較多時間的題目應勇敢跳過，務必先做完拿手題型，掌握基本分。

解題步驟與題型分析

瀏覽
四個選項

選項皆以**同一字（根）**
做變化

選項皆是**不同的字**

各選項為**詞性
變化**

例
(A) origin
(B) original
(C) originally
(D) originate

各選項為**動詞時
態變化**

例
(A) chose
(B) choose
(C) was choosing
(D) was chosen

各選項為**不同的
單字或片語／慣
用語**

例1
(A) admitted
(B) described
(C) ordered
(D) completed

例2
(A) due to
(B) instead of
(C) regardless of
(D) according to

各選項為**不同的
介系詞、連接
詞、副詞或（關
係）代名詞等**

例
(A) because
(B) since
(C) while
(D) although

題型 1
詞性題
（詳見 p.33）

題型 2
時態題
（詳見 p.34）

題型 3
單字片語題
（詳見 p.35~37）

題型 4
文法題
（詳見 p.38~51）

題型 ① 詞性題

詞性題屬於不用看完句子即可馬上做答的題目，只要能正確判斷詞性並具備各詞性功能及在句中位置的概念，便能輕鬆應答，是務必要掌握得分的題型。

各詞性常見結尾

	名詞 *n.*		動詞 *v.*	形容詞 *adj.*	副詞 *adv.*
常見結尾	-ance / -ancy -ence -ant -ian -ism -ist	-tion / -sion -ment -ness -ship -or / -er -ty / -ity	-ate -en -ify -fy -ize	-able / -ible -ous / -ious -ic / -ical -al -ful -ish -ive -ant	-ly -ward -wise
範例	admission		admit	admissible	admissibly
	condition		condition	conditional	conditionally
	critic / criticism		criticize	critical	critically
	expectation		expect	expectant	expectantly
	origin		originate	original	originally
	specification		specify	specific	specifically
	suggestion		suggest	suggestive	suggestively

考題範例

These survey charts and tables are _____, but unfortunately they don't fully account for our Q2 losses.

(A) inform
(B) informing
(C) information
(D) informative

解析

本句主詞為 These survey charts and tables、動詞為 are。觀察選項皆以同一字根做變化得知本題考詞性。空格前出現 be 動詞，可見應填入形容詞修飾本句主詞，故答案選 (D) informative「提供（有用）資訊的」。整句意思為：「這些調查圖表與表格提供有用的資訊，但遺憾地是它們並未完全解釋我們第二季虧損的原因。」

(A) inform *(v.)* 通知。
(B) informing 為 inform 的現在分詞或動名詞。
(C) information *(n.)* 資訊。

| 題型 ② | 時態題 |

瀏覽四個選項看到皆屬同一個動詞，但以不同形式出現，便知為考時態的題型。動詞時態依時間點不同主要分為三種：現在式、過去式、未來式。每個時間點因動作形式不同又分為：簡單式、進行式、完成式、完成進行式。各種時態搭配例句整理如下：

	現在式	過去式	未來式
簡單式	He <u>sometimes</u> writes business plans. 他有時會寫商業計畫書。	He wrote business plans <u>last week</u>. 他上週寫了商業計畫書。	He will write business plans <u>tomorrow</u>. = He is going to write business plans <u>tomorrow</u>. 他明天會寫商業計畫書。
進行式	He is writing business plans. 他正在寫商業計畫書。	He was writing business plans <u>when I got into the office</u>. 我到公司時，他正在寫商業計畫書。	He will be writing business plans <u>when I get into the office later</u>. 我晚點到公司時，他將會在寫商業計畫書。
完成式	He has just written business plans. 他剛才寫了商業計畫書。	He had <u>already</u> written business plans when I got into the office. 當我到公司時，他已寫好了商業計畫書。	He will have written business plans <u>by the time I get into the office</u>. 當我到公司時，他將已寫好商業計畫書。
完成進行式	He has been writing business plans for hours. 他寫商業計畫書已經寫了好幾個小時。（並且還在寫）	He had been writing business plans <u>for hours when I got into the office</u>. 我到公司時，他寫商業計畫書已經寫了好幾個小時。	He will have been writing business plans <u>for hours by six o'clock</u>. 到了六點，他寫商業計畫書就會持續寫好幾個小時了。

| 考題範例 |

By the time you receive this text message, it's likely that my train _____ already arrived.

(A) will have
(B) have
(C) had
(D) had been

| 解析 |

由句意可知 by the time 引導的子句在此表未來發生的事，故應使用未來完成式 will have + p.p. 的時態，答案選 (A)。整句句意為：「你收到這封簡訊時，我的火車有可能已經抵達了。」

題型 ③　單字片語題

單字片語占考題中約三成左右。這一類題目範圍廣泛，除了多背多益考試出現頻率較高的單字片語外，平時亦應多接觸英文相關的媒體報章，以增加應考實力。以下列舉多益常考變化字組及片語。

常考變化字組

• affect (v.) 影響 • effect (n.) 影響；結果；效果 • effective (adj.) 有效的 • efficient (adj.) 有效率的	• customize (v.) 量身訂做 • customer (n.) 顧客 • custom-made (adj.) 客制化的（反義詞為 ready-made「現成的」） • customs (n.) 海關
• assist (v.) 協助 • assistance (n.) 協助 • assistant (n.) 助理	• enterprise (n.) 公司；企業 • entrepreneur (n.) 企業家；創業者 • entrepreneurship (n.) 企業精神
• board (v.) 搭乘（飛機、船、火車、巴士） • aboard (adv.) 上（飛機、船等）	• hesitate (v.) 遲疑 • hesitant (adj.) 遲疑的 • hesitation (n.) 躊躇；猶豫
• certain (adj.) 確定的 • certainly (adv.) 無疑地 • certainty (n.) 確實；必然	• produce (v./n.) 生產；農產品 • product (n.) 產品 • production (n.) 產量；生產
• commercial (n./adj.) 廣告；商業的 • commercially (adv.) 商業上 • commerce (n.) 商業；貿易 • noncommercial (adj.) 非營利的	• think (v.) 想 • thought (n.) 想法 • thoughtful (adj.) 考慮周到的；體貼的
• compatible (+ with) (adj.) 相容的 • compatibility (n.) 適合性；相容性 • incompatible (adj.) 不相容的；矛盾的	• tour (v./n.) 旅行；作巡迴演出（或比賽）；旅遊 • tour guide 導遊 • tourist (n.) 遊客 • tourism (n.) 旅遊業

常考片語／慣用語

at one's disposal 任某人處置、自由運用	• With the tax break, people had more money **at their disposal**. 由於賦稅減免，人們有更多可自由運用的資金。
attribute A to B 將 A 歸因於 B （＝A + be attributed to + B）	• He **attributed** his success **to** his hard work. ＝His success **is attributed to** his hard work. 他將成功歸因於他的努力工作。

be capable of + { N. / V-ing 有……的能力	• This old car **isn't capable of** fast speeds. 這台老車無法高速行駛。 • This train **is capable of** reaching speeds above 250 kilometers per hour. 這班火車能夠達到時速兩百五十公里以上。
be exposed to 暴露於……之中	• People who **are exposed to** secondhand smoke are more likely to get cancer. 暴露於二手菸之中的人較有可能得到癌症。
be familiar with . . . 熟悉……（可接人或事物） be familiar to + someone 對某人而言是熟悉的	• Few people **are familiar with** this actor's work. 幾乎沒什麼人熟悉這名演員的作品。 • The smell **was familiar to** Helen, but she couldn't put a name to it. 那氣味是海倫熟悉的，但她無法說出是什麼。
be known for 因……有名	• This bakery **is known for** its delicious pineapple cakes. 這家烘培坊以其美味的鳳梨酥而聞名。
depend on 依賴；取決於……	• Whether you get a promotion (or not) will **depend on** your performance. 你能否升遷取決於你的表現。
distinguish between/ from A and B 分辨 A 與 B 之不同	• It is difficult to **distinguish between** Eric **and** his brother. 要分辨出艾瑞克和他弟弟很不容易。 • Maxine's original creations **distinguished** her **from** the rest of the fashion industry. 麥克辛的原創作品使她與時尚界的其他人有所區隔。
in addition 此外 （= additionally、moreover）	• We'd like to hire you for 100k a month. **In addition / Additionally / Moreover**, there will be a bonus at the end of the year. 我們想以一個月十萬元的薪水雇用你。此外，年終還將會有獎金。
instead of + { N. / V-ing 以一個取代另一個；而非 （= rather than）	• **Instead of** candy, you should eat fruit for a snack because it's so much healthier. 你應該吃水果當點心而不是糖果，因為水果健康多了。 • **Instead of** buying a new couch, we should just get the old one cleaned. =**Rather than** buying a new couch, we should just get the old one cleaned. 與其買新沙發，我們應該把舊沙發清洗乾淨就好。

keep track of 瞭解、掌握……；注意…… 的進展	• My father reads news online to **keep track of** current events. 我爸爸在網路上看新聞以掌握時事。
make up for 補償	• There is no way we can **make up for** the lost time. 我們無法挽回失去的時間。
on behalf of 代表 on sb.'s behalf 代表某人	• **On behalf of** my family, I'd like to extend our thanks to all of you. 我代表我家人向各位表達我們的感謝。 • John couldn't be here to accept the award, so I will accept it **on his behalf**. 約翰無法到場領獎，所以我將代表他領獎。
A results in B A 導致 B （= B results from A，即 B 起因於 A）	• A problem with the car's brakes **resulted in** the accident. 這輛車的煞車問題導致這起事故。 =The accident **resulted from** a problem with the car's brakes. 這起事故起因於這輛車的煞車問題。

考題範例

① Before we go into mass _____, we make a trial product to see if it works.
(A) entrepreneur
(B) hesitation
(C) production
(D) assistance

② It's just a matter of time before electric cars are the rule _____ the exception.
(A) on behalf of
(B) instead of
(C) in addition
(D) depend on

解析

① 由句意：「在我們進入大量……之前，我們製作試驗品以便觀察它是否運作正常。」可知適合的答案為 (C) production「生產」，go into mass production 為常見搭配用法，表產品進入量產階段。其餘選項 (A) entrepreneur「企業家」、(B) hesitation「躊躇」、(D) assistance「協助」皆不符合句意。

② 由句意：「電力車成為主流……特例只是早晚的事。」空格前後的名詞 rule「通例；常規」與 exception「例外」是相反的概念，可知空格處應填 (C) instead of「而非」才能使句意完整。其餘選項 (A) on behalf of「代表」、(C) in addition「此外」、(D) depend on「取決於」皆不符合句意。

題型 ④ 文法題

文法題占多益 Part 5 考題比例約四成左右。以下針對多益常考的文法重點做整理歸納及練習。

文法重點 1：代名詞

人稱代名詞

主格	所有格	所有格代名詞	受格	反身代名詞
I	my	mine	me	myself
you	your	yours	you	yourself
he	his	his	him	himself
she	her	hers	her	herself
it	its	its	it	itself
we	our	ours	us	ourselves
you	your	yours	you	yourselves
they	their	theirs	them	themselves

- **He** has a new tablet. 他有一台新的平板電腦。（主格）
- This is **his** new tablet. 這是他的新平板電腦。（所有格）
- The new tablet is his. 這台新的平板電腦是他的。（所有格代名詞）
- The new tablet belongs to him. 這台新的平板電腦歸他所有。（受格）
- David bought himself a new tablet. 大衛買了一台新的平板電腦給自己。（反身代名詞）

不定代名詞

one another (the) other(s) each other one another	- A new box of red pens has just arrived. Do you need **one**? 一盒新的紅筆剛到。你需要一枝嗎？ - We'll make one order now, and **another** later in the week. 我們現在將會下一張訂單，另一張這週晚點再訂。 - This is the main meeting room; **the others** are much smaller. 這間是主會議室；其他會議室則小多了。 - The first bus arrives at 9 a.m. **Others** come every 15 minutes. 第一班巴士九點到達。其他班次每隔十五分鐘來一班。 - The new coworkers gradually got to know **each other** (= **one another**). 新的同事們漸漸認識彼此。

all both some any none	• Most people were late to the meeting, so we can't blame them **all**. It must be a traffic issue. 大部分的人開會都遲到了，所以我們不能責怪他們所有人。一定是交通問題。
	• Pam and Jerry helped me a lot on this project, so I thanked them **both**. 潘和傑瑞在這個專案計畫上幫我很多，所以我謝謝他們兩位。
	• Most of our clients live locally, but **some** live overseas. 我們大部分的客戶住在當地，但有一些住在國外。
	• I've run out of post-it notes. Do you have **any** spare? 我的便利貼用完了。你還有任何多的嗎？
	• We interviewed some candidates, but unfortunately **none** were able to meet all the requirements. 我們面試了一些應徵者，但可惜的是沒人符合所有的需求條件。

考題範例

① After politely requesting several times that he clean up after _____, Evelyn got in Simon's face about leaving garbage all over the office.
(A) he
(B) his
(C) him
(D) himself

② Michael is a great salesman, _____ whose goal is to close all the deals.
(A) it
(B) one
(C) any
(D) none

解析

① 本題考代名詞。根據句意，空格內所指涉的人和 that 子句中的主詞 he 相同，因此應使用反身代名詞 himself，答案選 (D)。整句意思為：「在幾次禮貌性地要求賽門清理自己弄髒的地方後，艾芙琳直接質問他為何把垃圾丟得整間辦公室都是。」

(A) he 是人稱代名詞的主格。
(B) his 是人稱代名詞的所有格或所有格代名詞。
(C) him 是人稱代名詞的受格。

② 逗點後在補充說明主要句子 Michael is a great salesman，故空格處應填不定代名詞 one 代替前面的 salesman，作其同位語，答案選 (B)。整句意思為：「麥克是一位厲害的業務員，一位以拿下所有交易為目標的業務員。」

文法重點 2：介系詞

表時間的介系詞

at +（一天中的）某鐘點、某時間點 **on** +星期幾、特定的某日（包括某日上午、下午或傍晚） **in** +較長的一段時間	• The meeting starts **at** nine. 　會議九點開始。 • We'll launch the new product **in** December. 　我們十二月將會推出新產品。
before / by / no later than + 某時間點	• I'll give you an answer **before / by / no later than** 4 p.m. 　我會在下午四點前給你答案。
till / until / up to + 某時間點	• The probationary period lasts **until / up to** the 30th. 　試用期會持續到三十號。
during / in / throughout + { 某段時間 某個活動期間 **during / over** + { 某段時間 某個活動期間 **from** + 某時間點 **to/till/until** + 某時間點	• **During** my last job, I overcame many challenges. 　我在上一份工作時克服很多挑戰。 • **During/Over** the holidays, we took a trip to Japan. 　假期期間，我們去日本旅遊。 • **From** December **to** March, Jill wore her coat every day. 　從十二月到三月，吉兒每天都穿外套。
for + 一段時間 **since** + 過去某個時間點	• I've been interested in psychology **since** high school. 　我從中學時就對心理學感興趣。

表空間的介系詞

表位置： **above**、**at**、**before**、**behind**、**below**、**beneath**、**by**、**in**、**on**、**over**、**under**	• There is water dripping from the ceiling **above** my desk. 　我桌子上方的屋頂有水滴下來。
表方向： **across**、**along**、**around**、**down**、**for**、**from**、**in**、**into**、**off**、**out of**、**through**、**to**、**toward**、**up**	• If you work hard, there's a chance to move **up** the ladder. 　若你工作努力，就有機會可以在公司升職。

「藉由……工具、方法」的介系詞

with + 工具、物質、特質	• He wrote on the board **with** a blue marker. 他用藍色麥克筆寫白板。
by + 方法、手段、交通工具	• You can make new contacts **by** attending networking events. 你可以藉由參加人脈網路活動建立新的人際關係。

其他常考介系詞

because of owing to due to 因為……；由於…… } + 名詞／代名詞	• We lost the deal **because of / owing to / due to** a bad negotiation strategy. 由於談判策略不佳，我們失去了這個交易。
besides in addition to except (for) 除……之外 } + 名詞	• **Besides / In addition to** a good salary, Mandy's job gives her immense pleasure. 除了待遇不錯之外，曼蒂的工作也給了她極大的樂趣。 • Everyone **except (for)** the boss was at the dinner. 除了老闆之外，每個人都出席了晚宴。
among 在……之中（用於超過兩者的人、事、物）	• Please feel free to chat **among** yourselves until the speaker gets here. 在演講者抵達這裡之前，各位可隨意交談。
despite + 受詞 = in spite of + 受詞 儘管	• **Despite (= In spite of)** his lack of experience, Jack has performed well in his first month. 儘管傑克缺乏經驗，他第一個月還是表現良好。

考題範例

Emphasis on internal competition for higher positions has bred a sense of distrust _____ coworkers. (A) above (B) during (C) among (D) until	解析 本題是考介系詞。根據空格後的名詞 coworkers 及句意可知答案選 (C) among「在……之中（用於超過兩者的人、事、物）」。整句意思為：「為了爭取更高職位而著重於內部競爭使同事之間衍生出不信任感。」。其他選項 (A) above「在……之上」、(B) during「在某段時間」、(D) until「直到某時間點」皆與句意不合。

文法重點 3：連接詞

連接詞是用來連接字與字、片語與片語、子句與子句或句子與句子。一般分為：「對等連接詞」、「從屬連接詞」和「連接副詞」。

對等連接詞

對等連接詞： **and、but、or、so、for、yet、nor**	• They ordered a large amount, **so** they didn't have to pay the delivery fee. 他們訂購的量很大，所以不須付運費。
配對連接詞： **both . . . and、not . . . but、not only . . . but also、either . . . or、neither . . . nor**	• Vanessa is **both** talented **and** hardworking. 凡妮莎有天分又認真工作。 • The items were **not only** late **but also** damaged. 這些物品不但延遲送達還損毀了。

從屬連接詞

引導「時間」： **as、while、when、before、by the time (that)、after、as soon as、once、the moment that、until、since、no sooner than** 等	• Harry took notes **while** he was listening to the presentation. 哈利聽演講時做了筆記。 • I was out of the office **by the time** you called me. 你打給我時我已經離開辦公室了。
引導「狀態」： **as、as if、as though**	• Kevin said he was still going to take a few days off **as** he had planned to. 凱文說他還是會依照原訂計畫請幾天假。
引導「原因」： **because、since、as、now that** 等	• We'll have to extend the deadline **because/since** Francesca is on vacation. 因為法蘭西斯卡在放假，所以我們截止日得延後。
引導「結果」： **so . . . that、such . . . that、so/such . . . as to**	• The delivery was **so** heavy **that** three men had to carry it. 這批運送的貨品非常重，所以需要三個男子搬運。
引導「目的」： **so that、in order that** 等	• We've bought some new marketing software **in order that** we can increase sales. 我們已經買了一些新的行銷軟體，目的是要增加銷售。

引導「對比」： while、whereas	• **Whereas** some staff members go outside for lunch, most people just eat in the office. 一些員工到外面吃午餐，然而大部分還是在辦公室裡吃。
引導「讓步」： although、though、even though 等	• **Though/Although** the job was difficult at first, Sue eventually got used to it. 儘管這份工作一開始很困難，蘇最後還是適應了。
引導「條件」： if、unless、in case (that)、provided (that)、providing (that)、given (that)、on the condition that、only if、as long as	• **If** you see Bob, please tell him I had to go home early today. 如果你看到鮑伯，請跟他說我今天得早點回家。 • **Given (that)** that our computers are almost ten years old, we should consider getting new ones. 我們的電腦用了快十年了，我們應該考慮買新的。

連接副詞

表「推論或結果」： accordingly、as a result、consequently、hence、therefore、thus	• Demand for our product went down. **As a result**, we had to close the store for a few months. 我們產品的需求下降。結果，我們得關店幾個月。
表「反義或對照」： by contrast、however、nonetheless、nevertheless、on the contrary	• We all expected the worst at the meeting. **On the contrary**, the boss was very positive. 我們在會議上都做了最壞的打算。相反地，老闆卻非常樂觀。
表「總結」： all in all、in brief、in conclusion、in short、in sum、in summary、to sum up	• The new idea was great and the client loved the proposal. **All in all**, it was a successful meeting. 這個新點子很棒，客戶也喜歡這個提案。總之，這個會議很成功。

考題範例

The firm's partners discussed the situation thoroughly, _____ left the meeting still unclear as to the organization's future.
(A) for　　(B) once
(C) if　　(D) yet

解析

空格前提到「公司的合夥人已經徹底討論現況」，空格後提到「會議中關於組織的未來仍舊模糊不清」，由前後語意相反可知應填入表轉折語氣的對等連接詞，答案選 (D) yet「然而」。

文法重點 4：分詞構句

副詞子句簡化為分詞構句

	構成原則：
連接詞 **+ S. + V., S. + V.** （副詞子句）　　（主要子句） 改→ V-ing 　　p.p. } ,　**S. + V.** 　　　　　　　（主要子句） 改→ After 　　Before } + { V-ing ,　**S. + V.** 　　　　　　　 p.p. 　（主要子句）	1. 表時間、條件、讓步、原因的副詞子句，主詞與主要子句相同時，將副詞子句中的主詞省略。 2. 把動詞改為分詞：表主動時用現在分詞；表被動時用過去分詞。 3. 不會造成語意混淆時可省略連接詞。

- **While Jenny was** waiting for Dan to call her back, she browsed his company's website.
→ **Waiting** for Dan to call her back, Jenny browsed his company's website.
珍妮一面等丹回電，一面瀏覽他公司的網站。

- **After he was given** a full refund, the customer left the store.
→ **Given** a full refund, the customer left the store.
那位顧客拿到全額退費之後便離開了店家。

- **Since we have** no money, we can't go on a trip this year.
→ **Having** no money, we can't go on a trip this year.
因為我們沒有錢，所以今年無法旅遊。

- **Before he started** work, Phil checked his e-mails.
→ **Before starting** work, Phil checked his e-mails.
菲爾在工作前，先查看他的電子信箱。

- **Because she was** unfamiliar with the software, Janice needed time to get used to it.
→ **Being** unfamiliar with the software, Janice needed time to get used to it.
因為珍妮絲對軟體不熟，她需要時間適應。

對等子句簡化為分詞構句

	主詞相同時：
S1 + V. . . ., and (S1) + V. . . . （前後主詞相同） 改→ **S1 + V. . . ., V-ing . . .**	1. 省略 and 後面的主詞 2. 省略連接詞 and 3. 將之後的動詞改為現在分詞 V-ing

- The interviewee entered the meeting room, **and (she) smiled** nervously.
→ The interviewee entered the meeting room, **smiling** nervously.
那位面試者進入會議室，緊張地微笑著。

獨立分詞構句

獨立分詞構句是指前後主詞不同時，省略連接詞並將其中一個動詞改為分詞的情形。

連接詞 + S1 + V., S2 + V. **改→** S1 + V-ing / being + p.p., S2 + V.	主詞不同時： 1. 兩個主詞都保留 2. 省略連接詞 3. 將之後的動詞改為分詞
S1 + V., and S2 + V. **改→** S1 + V., S2 + V-ing	

- <u>Since</u> the door **was** open, we decided to let ourselves in.
- → The door **being** open, we decided to let ourselves in.
  由於門已經開著，我們決定自己進去。
- <u>Because</u> the conference **had finished** early, I had the chance to go to the bank.
- → The conference **having finished** early, I had the chance to go to the bank.
  因為會議提早結束，我才有機會去銀行。
- <u>Because</u> the printer **was broken**, staff found other ways to work.
- → The printer **being broken**, staff found other ways to work.
  因為印表機壞掉了，員工找到其他方式工作。
- My supervisor pointed to the screen, **and** his voice **was holding** my attention.
- → My supervisor pointed to the screen, his voice **holding** my attention.
  我的主管指著螢幕，而他的聲音抓住了我的注意力。
- She was reminded of her summer trip, **and** her face **filled** with joy.
- → She was reminded of her summer trip, her face **filling** with joy.
  某事令她想起了她夏天的旅行，臉上充滿喜悅。

考題範例

_____ the project, Bill could relax for the rest of the weekend.
(A) Been completed
(B) Completed
(C) Completing
(D) Having completed

解析

本題考分詞構句。選項均為動詞 complete 的不同形式，得知本句逗點前省略了與主要子句相同的主詞（Bill）；又因受詞為 project，可知應用現在分詞表主動。(D) Having completed 為分詞的完成式，符合文法故為正確答案。整句表「比爾已經完成了專案，現在週末剩下的時間都可以放鬆了」。本句可還原為：Since Bill had completed the project, he could relax ...。(C) 雖亦為現在分詞，但置入句子後表「正在完成專案」，與本句要表達的情境不合。

文法重點 5：關係詞

關係代名詞

	主格	受格	所有格
人	who/(that)	whom/(that)	whose
事物	which/(that)	which/(that)	whose（今較常用） of which（今較少用）
人、事物	that	that	✗

主格關係代名詞的用法

> 先行詞 + 主格關係代名詞 $\begin{cases} 人\ \textbf{who}、\textbf{that} \\ 事物\ \textbf{which}、\textbf{that} \end{cases}$ + 動詞

- The man **who/that** is talking to Jeff is the new IT support guy.
  正和傑夫說話的那位男子是新的資訊技術協助人員。

- This is the book **which/that** has the information you need.
  這就是有你需要的資訊的那本書。

受格關係代名詞的用法

> 先行詞 +（介系詞）+ 受格關係代名詞 $\begin{cases} 人\ \textbf{whom}、\textbf{that} \\ 人／事物\ \textbf{that} \\ 事物\ \textbf{which}、\textbf{that} \end{cases}$ + 主詞 + 動詞

- Kathy is the woman **(whom/that)** you met in the reception area.
  凱西就是那位你在接待處遇到的女子。

- It's important that you remember the things **(which/that)** Sharon tells you in the meeting.
  記得雪倫在會議上告訴你的事情是很重要的。

所有格關係代名詞的用法

> 先行詞 + 所有格關係代名詞 $\begin{cases} 人／事物\ \textbf{whose} + \text{N.} \\ 無生命物\ \textbf{whose} + \text{N.} / \text{N.} + \textbf{of which} \end{cases}$

說明 先行詞為無生命時，可以用 N. + of which，不過這種用法現今較為少見。

- We only hire people **whose skills** meet specific requirements.
  我們只雇用符合特定技能條件的人。

- This is a company **whose products** are known around the world.
= This is a company **the products of which** are known around the world.
  這間公司的產品聞名全世界。

關係副詞

when	• Last night was the moment **when** Helen decided to quit her job. 海倫是在昨晚決定辭職的。
where	• My office is just next to the café **where** we usually get coffee. 我的辦公室就在我們經常買咖啡的那家咖啡店隔壁。
why	• This market is very competitive, which is (the reason) **why** we need to plan our strategy carefully. 這個市場的競爭很激烈,這就是為何我們要仔細計畫我們的策略。

複合關係詞（wh-ever）

複合關係代名詞:**whoever、whichever、whomever、whatever**
• **Whoever** goes home last must turn off the lights. 最晚回家的人一定要關燈。 • **Whatever** he says, you should maintain a positive attitude. 無論他說什麼,你都應該要保持樂觀的態度。
複合關係形容詞:**whichever、whatever**
• **Whichever** path you take, make sure it's the right one for you. 不論你走那條路,務必確定那對你而言是對的路。 • Good or bad, we're just happy with **whatever** publicity we can get at this early stage. 不論是好是壞,在目前的初期階段,不管得到什麼樣的關注我們都會很開心。
複合關係副詞:**whenever、wherever、however**
• We'll begin the meeting **whenever** Mark gets here. 不論何時只要馬克一抵達,我們就會開始這場會議。 • **However** you want your gifts wrapped, we can do it for you. 不論您想要禮物如何包裝,我們都可以幫忙。

考題範例

This is a friendly reminder to clean all the office supplies and place them in the same drawers ＿＿＿ you found them.
(A) when   (B) where
(C) what   (D) how

解析

空格前出現的 the same drawers 表示「地方」,須使用關係副詞 where 來引導關係子句,故答案選 (B)。整句句意為:「提醒您,請清理所有的辦公用品,並將它們放回您原來找到它們的抽屜裡。」

文法重點 6：比較級

同等比較

A + be 動詞 + as adj. as + B A + V. + as adv. as + B	和……一樣……

說明 這個句型是同等比較用法，表示比較的兩個人事物在某方面的程度相等。

- I'm disappointed that your hotel room is **as big as** mine, even though you paid less.
  即使你付比較少錢，旅館房間卻和我的一樣大，讓我覺得很失望。
- Beth swims **as fast as** Theo (does), so I don't know who will win the race.
  貝絲游得和西奧一樣快，所以我不知道誰會贏得比賽。

形容詞和副詞的 比較級 與 最高級

A + be 動詞 + $\begin{Bmatrix} \text{adj.-er} \\ \text{more/less + adj.} \end{Bmatrix}$ + than + B A + V. + (O.) + $\begin{Bmatrix} \text{adv.-er} \\ \text{more/less + adv.} \end{Bmatrix}$ + than + B	A 比 B……
S. + be 動詞 + the $\begin{Bmatrix} \text{more} \\ \text{less} \end{Bmatrix}$ + adj. + of the two	兩個之中比較……的那一個

說明 一般而言，比較級之前不須加冠詞 the，但如要表示「兩者中較……的那一個」，則須加 the 以表示特定。

- That company **is bigger than** ours (is).
  那間公司比我們公司大。
- Sarah **types faster than** Frank (does).
  莎拉打字比法蘭克快。
- Nigel is **the more productive of the two**.
  奈傑爾是兩位中產能較高的那位。

much ／ even ／ still ／ far ／ a lot ／倍數／單位詞 + 比較級 + than

- Helen is **much more experienced than** Samantha (is).
  海倫比珊曼莎有經驗多了。
- This machine copies **far less quickly than** that one (does).
  這台機器影印的速度比那台慢多了。
- Your desk is **50% bigger than** mine.
  你的桌子是我的桌子的 1.5 倍大。

the + 比較級 + S. + V. . . ., the + 比較級 + S. + V.	越……就越……
	慣用語： the sooner, the better（越快越好） the more, the merrier（越多越好）

- **The earlier** you wake up, **the earlier** you will get to work.
  你越早起，你就會越早去工作。

比較級 + and + 比較	越來越……

- We hope our relationships with our partners will continue to get **better and better**.
  我希望我們和合作夥伴的關係會持續越來越好。

S. + V. + 副詞最高級 S. + be 動詞 + 形容詞最高級 + { of the three/four/five . . . of all . . . in + 範圍、團體	

- That computer is the oldest and works **the least efficiently** of the three.
  那台電腦是三台裡最老舊且運作起來最沒效率的。

- We believe that our products are **the most impressive** in the market.
  我們相信我們的產品是市場上最讓人印象深刻的。

the last + N. + that + S. + V.	最不可能……

- Work is **the last** thing **that** I'm thinking of when I get home on Friday night.
  週五晚上回到家我最不會去想的事情就是工作了。

考題範例

The new trainees have talent, but Tim seems to be ＿＿＿ of the three.
(A) more dedicated
(B) the most dedicated
(C) much dedicated
(D) as dedicated

解析

空格後出現 of the three，可知空格應填入形容詞最高級，答案選 (B) the most dedicated「最用心的」。整句表：「新的見習生都有天分，但提姆似乎是最用心的。」

(A) 為比較級。
(C) much 在此為副詞，用來修飾形容詞原級 dedicated，有「非常……；很……」的意思。
(D) 無此用法。

文法重點 7：假設語氣

與現在事實相反

表「現在幾乎不可能或完全不可能發生的事實或願望」。

if 子句	主要子句
If + S. + 過去式 ,	S. + { could / might / should / would } + V.
f + S. + were . . .,	

- If we **had** enough money, we **would move** to a better office.
  如果我們有足夠的錢，我們就會搬到好一點的辦公室。

- If the company **were** more established, it **would be** easier to secure contracts.
  (倒裝) **Were** the company more established, it **would be** easier to secure contracts.
  如果公司更有信譽的話，就會比較容易拿到合約。

與過去事實相反

表「過去並未發生的事實、或是過去未能實現的願望」。

if 子句	主要子句
If + S. + had + p.p.,	S. + { could / might / should / would } + have + p.p.

- If Pam **had**n't **gotten** sick, she **would have finished** the project sooner.
  (倒裝) **Had** Pam not **gotten** sick, she **would have finished** the project sooner.
  要是潘沒有生病，她就會更快完成這份專案計畫。

過去的假設影響到現在的結果

if 子句	主要子句
If + S. + had + p.p.,	S. + { could / might / should / would } + V.

- If I **had quit**, I **wouldn't have** this comfortable new office.
  如果我之前把工作辭了，我就不會有這間舒適的新辦公室。

與未來事實相反

表「未來並不可能發生，或發生的機率非常低」。

if 子句	主要子句
If + S. + were to + V.,	S. + $\begin{cases} \text{could} \\ \text{might} \\ \text{should} \\ \text{would} \end{cases}$ + V.

- If I **were to move** into that apartment, I **could walk** to work in five minutes.
  如果我搬到那間公寓住，走五分鐘就能到達公司。
- If it **were to rain**, we **would move** the event indoors.
  如果下雨了，我們會把活動移到室內。

對未來某事抱持強烈懷疑時，亦可用假設法未來式，表「萬一⋯⋯的話」。

if 子句	主要子句
If + S. + should + V.,	S. + 過去式助動詞 + V. S. + 助動詞 + V. 祈使句

- If you **should hear** of any rumors regarding the merger, you **should keep** it to yourself.
  萬一你聽到任何有關合併的傳言，你應該要保密。
- If you **should see** Jason, you **can tell** him I said "hi".
  萬一你看到傑森的話，幫我跟他說聲「嗨」。

考題範例

	解析
If I hadn't taken that call, we _____ the biggest sale in our company's history. (A) would make (B) wouldn't make (C) should make (D) wouldn't have made	由 if 子句中的 hadn't taken 可判斷這是與過去事實相反的假設語氣，故主要子句的動詞應為 could/might/should/would + have + p.p.，答案要選 (D)，整句表「如果當時我沒有接到那通電話，我們就無法達成公司歷史上的最大筆交易。」

Part 6 Text Completion 段落填空

題型介紹	
題數	十六題（多益考試兩百題中的第 131~146 題）
題型說明	• 由四篇文章組成，每篇有 4 題填空題，整個大題共 16 題。 • 文章中會有空格，須從四個選項中選出最適當的答案。 • 與 Part 5 類似，旨在測驗考生的字彙、文法能力及對文意的理解。 唯題型由句子變成段落文章，且加入將完整句填入短文的題型。
建議作答時間	8 分鐘（每題至多 30 秒）

題目範例與解析

Questions 1-4 refer to the following notice.

To our valued customers,

Dear Pets is getting ready to close its doors after 22 years of business. We want to thank you for your patronage, from both you and your pets, many of ---**1**--- have become like family to us. Starting October 1, you will see many discounted prices around the shop as we start to get rid of our inventory. As of December 1, the entire stock will be put up for clearance. ---**2**--- We welcome new and old customers to join us for a final day of ---**3**--- on Saturday, December 20, from 10 a.m. to 5 p.m. We will have door prizes, refreshments, and a lively ---**4**--- of any leftover items, including shelving units and display tables, at 3:00 p.m.

Sincerely yours,
David Hodgkins

① (A) whose
　(B) which
　(C) whom
　(D) where

> **文法題**
>
> 由句構及句意可知空格處 many of ... 乃指逗點前的 from both you and your pets，故這裡的要用關係代名詞的受格 whom，答案選 (C)。
>
> 這裡須閱讀空格之前後，了解空格處與上下文關係後再進行答題。

② (A) The amount will be a flat fee of only $1.99.
(B) Be sure to be there for our grand opening.
(C) Please remember to adjust your schedules accordingly.
(D) Don't miss out on the great deals, just in time for Christmas!

句子插入題

空格前一句提到 As of December 1, the entire stock will be put up for clearance.「從十二月一日起，全部的存貨將要拿出來出清。」，空格後一句又提到歡迎舊雨新知來參與十二月二十日這個最後一個營業日。故語意連貫的選項為 (D)「別錯過這麼棒的買賣，恰巧能趕上耶誕節喔！」。the great deals 指的就是前面提到的清倉大拍賣。

 此題型常須閱讀空格的前後文，根據上下文意找出最符合邏輯及文章脈絡的句子。

③ (A) celebrate
(B) celebrating
(C) celebration
(D) celebratory

詞性題

觀察選項皆以同一字根做變化，可知本題考詞性。空格的前面是 for a final day of ...，可判斷空格處應填入名詞，故答案選 (C) celebration「慶祝（活動）」。選項 (A) celebrate 為動詞指「慶祝」、選項 (B) celebrating 為現在分詞或動名詞、選項 (D) celebratory 為形容詞，指「慶祝的；祝賀的」。

 務必利用詞性題節省作答時間，將多出來的秒數分配給須閱讀上下文才能作答的題型。

④ (A) auction
(B) expression
(C) subscription
(D) connection

單字片語題

選項中為四個不同的單字。由本句關鍵字詞「所有剩餘商品的熱鬧……，包括層架和展示桌」以及本文主要在邀請顧客來參與出清特賣，可推斷適合的答案為 (A) auction「拍賣會」。其餘選項 (B) expression「表達；表情」、(C) subscription「訂閱（費）」、(D) connection「連結；聯繫」皆不符合句意。

 若是熟悉 auction 一字常用在公開競標或拍賣等場合，便可迅速作答進入下一道題目！

Part 7 Reading Comprehension
閱讀測驗

題型介紹	
題數	五十四題（多益考試兩百題中的第 147~200 題）
題型說明	• 文章具各種題材和形式，包括廣告、書信、備忘錄、公告、即時訊息對話及文章報導等。 • 分為單篇閱讀（single passages）約 10 篇文章、每篇搭配 2~4 個問題（單篇文章共 29 題），以及雙篇和三篇閱讀（double/triple passages）5 個題組的文章，每組搭配 5 個問題（雙篇或多篇文章共 25 題）。
建議作答時間	55 分鐘（平均每題約 1 分鐘）

基本作答流程與技巧

1. 先讀介紹句

先看開頭介紹句 "Questions . . . refer to the following (article type)." 了解文章形式。常見文章類型包括：advertisement「廣告」、letter/e-mail「信件／電子郵件」、memo/notice「備忘錄／公告」、calendar/schedule「日程／時間表」、form/graph「表格／圖表」、text message chain「即時訊息對話」、article「文章」等。而雙篇或三篇閱讀題組其實就是組合任兩篇或三篇上述文章類型，而同一題組中的幾篇文章彼此之間有關聯性。

2. 看問題並快速瀏覽答案選項

面對大量文章與題目，有效掌控作答時間並正確快速解題乃得分關鍵。因此作答時應把重心放在「題目」，而非理解文章的全部內容。

3. 依問題類型決定答題順序

須了解文章整體內容的主旨題、除外題及推論題可最後作答，而僅與部分內容相關的細節題則可一邊掃描文章內容，一邊找出答案。以下歸納主要常考題型與解題技巧。

題型	常見問題	解題技巧
❶ 主旨題	• What is the (main) purpose of the (notice/memo/e-mail)? • Why was the (memo/letter) written? • Why did A write to B?	◆ 如同聽力單元的主旨題，這也屬於拿分題，因為文章大意或主旨往往從整篇內容多處可找出答案，看完整篇再答即可。

❷ 細節題	• What time does the (event) begin? • What is provided . . . ? • When will sb. begin work?	◆ 這類問題占 Part 7 的多數，問法包羅萬象，但多為 wh-questions。 ◆ 細節題一般會依文章順序出題。快速瀏覽問題和選項後，便馬上回文章中，試著將答案找出。
❸ 同義字詞	• The word/phrase ". . ." in paragraph 2, line 3, is closest in meaning to	◆ 有時一個單字或片語可有多種意思，因此需要根據該字的前後文理解其意思，然後再從選項中找出與該意思相近的字。
❹ 除外題／是非題	• What is NOT mentioned/indicated/cited/suggested . . . ? • What is (probably) true about . . . ?	◆ 要把各選項所敘述的事物全找出來，一一對照後排除錯誤的選項。 ◆ 選項與文章內容往往會用不同的字詞表達相同的意思。 ◆ 此題型亦常搭配文章中有條列的敘述，只要比對哪一項沒有在敘述中被提及，即可找出正確答案。
❺ 篇章結構題	• In which of the positions marked [1], [2], [3], and [4] does the following sentence best belong? ". . ."	◆ 題目會給一個新的句子，須把這個句子插入到適當的位置。須注意所插入的句子必須和前後句子在邏輯關係及脈絡上保持一致。
❻ 句意題	• At (time), what does sb. mean when he/she writes, ". . ."?	◆ 通常出現在「即時訊息對話」或「線上聊天討論」的閱讀題組中，須依上下文來判斷某詞句的意思。
❼ 推論題	• What can be inferred about sth./sb.? • For what kind of company/business does sb. most likely work? • Who most likely is sb.?	◆ 題目中會出現 implied / inferred / most likely 等字眼。 ◆ 答案可能不會直接在文章中顯示，而是要應考者根據內文資訊，以合理、有邏輯的方式去判斷或推敲。
❽ 整合題	• What feature do A and B have in common? • Wh-questions?	◆ 整合題型難度較高，出現於雙篇或三篇文章題組中，需要結合不同篇的內容才能回答。大多整合題沒有明顯辨識之字眼或模式。若在依循某問題關鍵字閱讀其中一篇文章無法找到解答時，便須整合另一篇文章資訊方能解題。

考題範例 | 題組 1

Questions 1-2 *refer to the following e-mail.*

● ● ●

To:	arthurbryk@houseofpanes.com
From:	edover@clifftonconsultants.org
Re:	Job status

Dear Arthur,

—[1]— I'm writing this with a heavy heart. We've been working together for many years now, but I'm afraid I'm finally going to have to call time on our relationship.

The previous job you did on our office was, to be frank, completely unacceptable. —[2]— The quality of the glass left a lot to be desired, and we were amazed when cracks started to develop in the pane after just a couple of days. —[3]—

As this is just the latest in a long line of such incidents, I'm left with no choice but to make this decision. —[4]—

Sincerely,

Eileen

① Why did Eileen write to Arthur?
(A) To admit a mistake
(B) To tell him the time of a meeting
(C) To end a business relationship
(D) To announce a new feature of a product

解析

此為題型 ❶ 主旨題。關鍵句為 We've been working together for many years now, but I'm afraid I'm finally going to have to call time on our relationship.。片語 call time on sth. 表「結束某事」，故答案選 (C)「結束商業關係」。

② In which of the positions marked [1], [2], [3], and [4] does the following sentence best belong?
"Our relationship will be terminated forthwith."
(A) [1]
(B) [2]
(C) [3]
(D) [4]

解析

此為題型 ❺ 篇章結構題。由信件第一段可知信件的目的是要結束與對方的合作關係，因此最適合的位置是在結論句重述此目的，答案選 (D)。前一句的 make this decision「下這個決定」指的便是題目句所陳述的結束關係。forthwith 意同 immediately「立刻；馬上」。

考題範例 題組 2

Questions 3-4 refer to the following online chat discussion.

Michael S.　[1:14 p.m.]
Hey, guys. I need to give you a heads-up. The paper shredder next to the copy machine is temporarily out of service. Until it's fixed, use the one next to the server room.

Selena W.　[1:15 p.m.]
Oh, let me guess. Did someone overload it again? That's happened so many times now. How hard is it to follow the rules? I can't believe I work with people this incompetent.

Trevor B.　[1:15 p.m.]
Whoa, whoa, whoa. Calm down, Selena. I'm sure it was just an accident. Nobody intentionally broke it.

Selena W.　[1:16 p.m.]
I know. Obviously, that's not the case. But even though it was an accident, it's still bad. People need to pay attention to what they're doing.

Prishna C.　[1:17 p.m.]
I have an idea. Maybe we should put a sign over the machine. That way, people will be reminded of the correct operating instructions whenever they use it.

Michael S.　[1:17 p.m.]
I like that idea. I appreciate your constructive attitude, Prishna. Can you handle making the sign?

Prishna C.　[1:18 p.m.]
Yes, of course. I'll get right on it. The sign will be ready by the time the machine is fixed.

Michael S.　[1:18 p.m.]
Great. I estimate it'll be ready in a few days. That leaves you more than enough time to get it done.

---

③ At 1:16 p.m., what does Selena mean when she writes, "Obviously, that's not the case"?
  (A) Accidents are no big deal.
  (B) Someone did it on purpose.
  (C) They don't need to work on the case anymore.
  (D) Somebody misinterpreted her meaning.

解析

此為題型 ❻ 句意題。題目問 Selena 寫 Obviously, that's not the case 是什麼意思。本句前面 Trevor 寫道 Whoa, whoa, whoa . . . I'm sure it was just an accident. Nobody intentionally broke it., 而 Selena 便回應 I know. Obviously, that's not the case. But even though it was an accident, it's still bad., 可推知 Selena 是要表達 Trevor 誤解她的意思,她並不是說有人故意弄壞機器,答案選 (D)。

---

④ When will Prishna begin working on the sign?
  (A) Right now
  (B) In a few days
  (C) When the machine is fixed
  (D) As soon as Michael gives permission

解析

此為題型 ❷ 細節題。題目問「普席娜何時會開始製作標示?」,關鍵句為 Prishna 寫道 Yes, of course. I'll get right on it. The sign will be ready by the time the machine is fixed., 慣用語 get right on it 指「馬上著手處理」,故答案選 (A)。

考題範例　**題組 3**

Questions 5-9 *refer to the following advertisement, quote, and e-mail.*

OFFICE SURPRISE ®
OFFICE EQUIPMENT RENTALS

COMPUTERS　COPIERS　FAX MACHINES
PRINTERS　TELEVISIONS　& MORE!

Office Surprise® has all of your office rental needs. Whether you need the latest, high-tech equipment, or are just looking for a temporary solution, we've got you covered. There's no need to worry!

Our equipment is available for rent by the month, week, or day. Customers can also choose to purchase the equipment they rent. The selling price of the equipment will be discounted by the amount already spent on the rental. In addition, for a limited time only, we're offering a hot deal! If you rent four or more different pieces of equipment, we'll give you $100 off of your bill.

USE OUR ONLINE CALCULATOR TO GET A QUOTE FOR YOUR RENTAL

Office Surprise® Online Quotation Calculator

		QTY.			QTY.
Printer	Monthly ($300)		Fax Machine	Monthly ($250)	
	Weekly ($85)			Weekly ($75)	
	Daily ($15)	10		Daily ($12)	10
Computer	Monthly ($700)		Copier	Monthly ($900)	
	Weekly ($200)			Weekly ($300)	
	Daily ($35)	30		Daily ($50)	30
Conference Phone	Monthly ($100)		Television	Monthly ($200)	
	Weekly ($30)			Weekly ($60)	
	Daily ($8)	10		Daily ($10)	10

Questions? Send us an e-mail at manager@officesurprise.net.

TOTAL ~~$1,800~~ **$1,700**

To: jeff.thomas@crealtech.com
From: manager@officesurprise.net
Re: Hourly Rate?
Date: May 12

Office Surprise Manager,

I'm Jeff Thomas from Creality Technology. My company is having an event next month, and we will be in need of quite a bit of equipment (I've attached the estimate your website provided for me). Your website states that equipment can be rented by the day. What about by the hour? We need a massive amount, but we only need it for the morning. Would your company be open to renting it for less than the daily rate? I think a discount of 40 percent off of my total bill would be reasonable for using it for less than half the day.

⑤ In the advertisement, the word "covered" in paragraph 1 is closest in meaning to
(A) estimated
(B) compensated
(C) appreciated
(D) supported

解析

此為題型 ❸ 同義字詞。原句中的口語用法 we've got you covered 常用來表示會「掩護、支持對方」，意同 We will support you.，故答案選 (D) supported「被支援」。

⑥ What is NOT mentioned in the advertisement?
(A) Customers can get discounted prices
(B) Customers can hire equipment by the hour
(C) Customers can get a quote online.
(D) Customers can buy what they've hired.

解析

此為題型 ❹ 除外題。詢問在廣告中沒有提到的事。選項 (A) 由 . . . we'll give you $100 off of your bill. 得知會有折扣、(C) 由 USE OUR ONLINE CALCULATOR TO GET A QUOTE FOR YOUR RENTAL 得知有線上報價、(D) 由 Customers can also choose to purchase the equipment they rent. 得知可以購買他們已租賃的設備。唯獨 (B)「顧客可以小時計算來租借設備」並未提及。廣告中只提到可以月、週或日為單位來租借，故答案是 (B)。

⑦ Why was the price altered in the estimate's bottom line?

(A) The customer had store credit with Office Surprise.

(B) The customer rented six different pieces of equipment.

(C) The customer used a coupon code from the website.

(D) There was an error in the quotation.

解析

此為題型 ❽ 整合題。題目問「為什麼報價單最後一行的價格會改變？」。第一篇廣告中提到 If you rent four or more different pieces of equipment, we'll give you $100 off of your bill.「如果您租借四種或以上不同的設備，您的帳單可再折抵一百元。」，而第二篇報價單中顯示有六種設備，符合打折的資格，故答案選 (B)「顧客租借了六種不同的設備。」

⑧ What can be inferred about Jeff Thomas?

(A) His company is having some cash flow problems.

(B) He thinks Office Surprise is being dishonest with him.

(C) He works for a large International technology company.

(D) He thinks the price would be too high given his situation.

解析

此為題型 ❼ 推論題。詢問關於傑夫・湯瑪士可推斷出何事。由第三篇電子郵件中最後一句 I think a discount of 40 percent off of my total bill would be reasonable for using it for less than half the day. 可推知傑夫認為他只租用設備不到半天，價格應該要可以打折變得更便宜，所以答案選 (D)「以他的情況來說，他認為價格太高。」

⑨ How much would the total price be with Jeff's suggested discount?

(A) $1,800

(B) $1,700

(C) $1,020

(D) $680

解析

此為題型 ❽ 整合題。題目問「以傑夫建議的折扣計算，總價會是多少？」。第二篇報價單顯示總價為 $1,700，而第三篇傑夫的信件中提到 I think a discount of 40 percent off of my total bill would be reasonable for using it for less than half the day.「我認為以租借不到半天而言，將我的總費用打六折是合理的。」，因此 1,700 x 60% = 1,020，答案選 (C)。

NOTES

Section B

13 大情境必備詞彙

Section B 根據 ETS（美國教育測驗服務社）所公布多益考試之 13 大主題情境，收錄各情境常考單字並設計大量練習題，讓您在動手做題目的同時，亦將所學字彙融會貫通。

Unit 1 Offices 辦公室

本主題涵蓋內容包括：

- board meetings
  董事會議

- committees
  委員會

- letters
  信件

- telephone, fax, and e-mail messages
  電話留言、傳真訊息及電子郵件

- office equipment & furniture
  辦公室設備和器材

- office procedures
  辦公室流程

WORD POWER

 TRACK 16

---

01 **access** [ˈæksɛs] *n./v.* 使用;存取(的方法)

- All employees are allowed access to the kitchen.
  所有員工都可以使用廚房。

- Enter a username and password to access the computer system.
  輸入使用者名稱與密碼來使用電腦系統。

常考片語 have access to + N. 有機會或權限能接觸……

- We have access to up-to-date information through a computer database.
  我們透過電腦資料庫可以取得最新的資訊。

常用詞彙 access code 通行碼

衍 accessible *adj.* 易接近的;可使用的

---

02 **administration** [ədˌmɪnəˈstreʃən] *n.* 行政;管理

- Collect your new ID card from administration.
  請到行政部門領取你的新識別證。

衍 administrative *adj.* 管理的;行政的

衍 administrate *v.* 管理;治理

衍 administer *v.* 管理;實施;提供

---

03 **aisle** [aɪl] *n.* (貨架間或成區座位之間的)通道;走道

- Every afternoon, a cleaner comes to clean the aisles and spaces under the desks.
  每天下午會有一位清潔人員來打掃走道與桌子下方的空間。

常用詞彙 aisle seat 靠走道的座位(靠窗的座位則稱為 window seat)

---

04 **attachment** [əˈtætʃmənt] *n.* 附件;附加檔

- I've included a full price list as an attachment in this e-mail.
  我已在這封電子郵件的附檔中附上了一份完整的價目表。

說明 可指任何文件的「附件」,而 e-mail attachment 則特指「電子郵件的附加檔案」。

衍 attach *v.* 附加;伴隨

---

05 badge [bædʒ] *n.* 名牌；識別證

• Visitors to the office must wear a visitor's badge.
進入辦公室的訪客一定要佩戴訪客證。

說明 現在有越來越多公司的 ID badge「識別證」同時具有上下班刷卡及門禁卡的功能。

圖 identification *n.*
識別證（簡稱 ID）

06 board meeting 董事會議

• A final decision on the company's future is expected at next month's annual board meeting.
下個月的年度董事會議預計將對公司的未來做出最終決定。

說明 board 指「董事會；委員會」。

關 boardroom *n.*
會議室

07 board of directors 董事會

• Bill was elected to the board of directors after twelve years in management.
在管理階層任職十二年之後，比爾入選董事會。

說明 可簡稱為 board，是公司決策的最高管理單位。

關 board of trustees
（大學）董事會

08 briefing [ˋbrifɪŋ] *n.* 簡報

• The manager gave new staff a quick briefing before they were introduced to the CEO.
經理在新員工們被介紹給執行長之前，先向他們做了一段簡報。

同 summary *n.* 總結；摘要

同 report *n.* 報告

關 overview *n.* 概況

關 conference *n.*（正式）會議；討論會

09 brochure [broˋʃʊr] *n.* 小冊子；指南

• There are brochures on display at the front desk, in which visitors can read about the company.
櫃檯展示了一些小冊子，訪客可以在其中讀到公司的相關資訊。

同 pamphlet、
booklet *n.* 小冊子

關 leaflet *n.* 傳單；單張印刷品

10 bulk mail 大宗郵件

• We will get a better price if we send in bulk mail.
如果我們以大宗郵件的方式寄出，會拿到比較優惠的價格。

說明 形容詞 bulk [bʌlk] 指「大量的；大批的」。

關 printed material、
printed matter
印刷品

關 postmark *n.* 郵戳

11 business trip 出差

- The boss is away on a business trip this week, but you can leave a message with his assistant.

  老闆本週出差不在，但是你可以留言給他的助理。

  說明 因出差而由公司給付的「差旅費」可用 business trip allowance 或 travel allowance 表示。

12 colleague [ˈkɑlig] *n.* 同事；同僚

- Melissa sometimes goes for dinner with her colleagues after work.

  梅麗莎有時下班後會跟同事一起吃晚餐。

同 coworker *n.* 同事

13 committee [kəˈmɪtɪ] *n.* 委員會；全體委員

- The committee was set up by the management to find out why the company was not making progress.

  管理階層組了一個委員會來找出為何公司的營運沒有進展。

  說明 committee 指「委員」時為集合名詞。

  常用詞彙 executive committee 執行委員會

同 board、commission *n.* 委員會

關 delegation *n.* 代表團

14 correspondence [ˌkɔrəˈspɑndəns] *n.*

通信；往返書信；一致；調和

- We are still in correspondence with several suppliers and will choose the most suitable one soon.

  我們仍在與幾家供應商聯繫中，很快就會選出最適合的一家。

衍 correspondent *n.* 通信者；通訊記者；【商】客戶

衍 correspond *v.* 與……一致；與……通信（後面常接 with）

15 document [ˈdɑkjəmənt] *n.* 公文；文件

- Kelly puts all important documents in a file in one of her desk drawers.

  凱莉把所有重要文件放在書桌抽屜的一個檔案夾中。

衍 documentation *n.*（總稱）文件

16 donate [ˈdonet] / [doˈnet] *v.* 捐贈；捐獻

- The company donates money to a local children's charity once a year.

  該公司每年捐款一次給當地的一家兒童慈善機構。

衍 donation *n.* 捐贈物；捐款

衍 donor *n.* 捐贈者

17 **executive** [ɪɡˋzɛkjutɪv] *n.* 經理主管級人員 *adj.* 執行的；行政的

- She is now a senior executive after years of working her way up through the company.

  她多年來在公司裡逐步晉升，現在是資深主管。

  說明 executive 作名詞時，還可以指「行政部門；行政官」，如「行政院」就是 Executive Yuan。

  常用詞彙 chief executive officer 執行長（簡稱 CEO）

衍 execution *n.* 執行；實行

衍 execute *v.* 執行；履行

---

18 **extension** [ɪkˋstɛnʃən] *n.* 分機號碼；分機電話

- The company's number is 555-4939, and you can reach me directly on my extension, which is 156.

  公司的電話是 555-4939，而你可以直接打我的分機找我，分機是 156。

  說明 可讓分機之間互打的「內線」叫做 internal line。

同 extension number 分機號碼

---

19 **forward** [ˋfɔrwəd] *v.* 轉寄

- Please forward me that e-mail with the quote from Star Supplies.

  請將有星空供應商報價單的那封電子郵件轉寄給我。

  說明 收到 forwarded mail「轉寄的郵件」時，郵件主旨的開頭會以 Fwd 或 Fw 的簡稱顯示。

---

20 **get the hang of sth.** 掌握做某事的方法

- This new software is tricky to figure out, but with a bit more practice I think I'll get the hang of it.

  這個新軟體有一點難搞懂，但我想我多練習一下就能掌握訣竅。

  說明 hang 在此指「訣竅；做法」的意思。get the hang of 之後常接 N. 或 V-ing。

同 get the knack/feel of sth. 抓到做某件事的訣竅

---

21 **ink cartridge** （印表機的）墨水匣

- The printer is out of ink, so we need to order a new pack of ink cartridges.

  印表機沒墨水了，所以我們需要訂一盒新的墨水匣。

  說明 cartridge [ˋkɑrtrɪdʒ] 指「（可換裝的）墨水筒；筆芯」。

關 inkjet/laser printer 噴墨／雷射印表機

關 toner、toner cartridge （雷射印表機的）碳粉匣

22 junk mail 垃圾郵件

- We need an e-mail server that is good at identifying junk mail and moving it to a trash folder.
  我們需要一個能有效識別垃圾郵件並將其移至垃圾匣的郵件伺服器。

  說明 junk 是「廢物；垃圾」。junk mail 起初是指廣告推銷信件、傳單等實體的垃圾信件，在電子郵件盛行後也用來稱垃圾電子郵件（junk e-mail）。

同 spam *n.* 垃圾郵件

23 minutes [ˈmɪnɪts] *n.* 會議記錄

- The boss asked her assistant to take the minutes of the meeting, so that she'd have a record of everything that was said.
  老闆要求她的助理做會議記錄，以便保有所有討論事項的記錄。

  說明 minutes 作「會議記錄」解時，須用複數。

  常考片語 take/keep the minutes 做會議記錄

同 meeting record/ minutes 會議記錄

關 agenda *n.* 會議議程

關 detail *n.* 細節；詳情

24 photocopier [ˈfotəˌkɑpɪə] *n.* 影印機

- If the photocopier isn't working, check if the paper has loaded correctly and that there is enough ink.
  如果影印機故障，檢查一下紙張有沒有放好，以及墨水夠不夠。

同 copy machine 影印機

關 enlarge *v.* （影印）放大

關 reduce *v.* （影印）縮小

25 projector [prəˈdʒɛktə] *n.* 投影機

- The meeting room has tables and chairs, plus a computer and an overhead projector.
  會議室有桌椅加上一台電腦，以及一台吊架式投影機。

同 overhead projector 吊架式投影機

衍 project *v.* 投影；投射（光線等）

關 laser pointer 雷射光筆

26 punch in 上班打卡

- Employees have to punch in when they arrive in the morning, and punch out when they leave.
  員工早上到公司時必須打上班卡，而離開時必須打下班卡。

  說明 punch [pʌntʃ] 有「用力擊；用力按」之意。這個片語還有將資料「鍵入」電腦或資料庫中的意思。

同 clock in、punch the clock（上班）打卡

反 punch/clock out 下班打卡

27 put through 轉接電話

• Please hold for a moment while I put you through to our IT support department.

請稍等一下，我幫您轉接到電腦技術支援部門。

圓 direct、transfer v. 轉接（電話）

28 receptionist [rɪˋsɛpʃənɪst] n. 櫃檯人員；接待人員

• The receptionist should be friendly and welcoming, as he/she is the first point of contact that visitors have with the company.

櫃檯人員應該要友善好客，因為他／她是訪客與公司的第一個接觸者。

衍 reception n.（旅館、大機構的）接待處

關 front-desk clerk （飯店等的）櫃檯人員

29 recipient [rɪˋsɪpɪənt] n. 收件者；接受者

• The internal business e-mail had multiple recipients.

這封內部的商務電子郵件有多位收件者。

反 sender n. 寄送者

衍 receive v. 接收；收到

關 reply v. 回覆

30 replace [rɪˋples] v. 取代；代替

• Many factory worker jobs are being replaced with robots.

許多工廠工人的工作正逐漸被機器人取代。

常考片語 replace A with B 用 B 來取代 A；把 A 換成 B

圓 substitute v. 取代

衍 replacement n. 取代；替代物

31 resolution [ˌrɛzəˋluʃən] n.（會議等的）決議

• The office took a vote and the resolution was passed by a 70% majority.

公司進行了投票，以七成的多數成員同意通過該決議。

說明 resolution 除作「決議」解外，亦可指圖片等的「解析度」，如 high-resolution「高解析度的」。

常考片語 pass a resolution 同意／通過某決議

• The board passed a resolution authorizing the construction of a new headquarters.

董事會通過決議要興建興建一個新的總部。

衍 resolve v. 決議；下決心

32 **set up** 成立；安裝；設定
- John is leaving the company to set up his own business.
  約翰要離開公司自行創業。

- 同 establish *v.* 成立
- 同 arrange *v.* 安排
- 關 setting *n.* 設定；（戲劇、故事的）背景

---

33 **shareholder** [ˈʃɛrˌholdə] *n.* 股東
- The shareholders would like to know how the business plans to adapt to a changing market.
  股東想要知道公司打算如何適應多變的市場。

- 同 stockholder *n.* 股東
- 關 shareholding *n.* 股權；持股
- 衍 share *n.* 股份；股票

---

34 **staple** [ˈstepl] *v.* 用釘書機裝釘
- You should staple all those papers together so that you don't lose them.
  你應該把那些紙張用釘書機釘好，才不會弄丟。

  說明 「將……釘在一起」可說 to staple . . . together。

- 衍 stapler *n.* 釘書機
- 衍 staple *n.* 釘書針

---

35 **state** [stet] *v.* 陳述；說明
- It clearly states in the contract that employees must keep company information private.
  合約裡面明確說明員工必須將公司資訊保密。

- 同 describe、explain *v.* 解釋；描述
- 衍 statement *n.* 陳述；聲明

---

36 **stationery** [ˈsteʃəˌnɛrɪ] *n.* 文具；信紙（皆不可數）
- Every three months, the company will order new stationery such as pens and paper clips.
  公司每三個月會訂購像是筆與迴紋針之類的文具。

辦公室常見文具或用品

binder clip 長尾夾

post-it note 便利貼

glue stick 口紅膠

folder 文件夾

correction tape 修正帶

Scotch tape 透明膠帶

paper clip 迴紋針

stapler 釘書機

37 stock [stɑk] *n.* 存貨；庫存；存量

同 inventory *n.* 存貨

- It looks like we don't have that size here, but I'll check if we have it in stock.
  看來這裡沒有那個尺寸，但我會查查看庫存還有沒有。

說明 另可指「股票；股份」，與 share 同義。

常考片語 in stock 有庫存；有現貨
out of stock 無庫存；缺貨

- Unfortunately, that item is out of stock, but we'll have more next week.
  很遺憾，該品項沒有庫存了，但我們下週會進貨。

38 stockroom [ˋstɑkˏrum] *n.* 儲藏室

同 storeroom、
supply room、
storage 儲藏室；倉庫

- We need to throw out some old items to make space in the stockroom for the new ones.
  我們需要丟掉一些舊品項，以便挪出一些儲藏室的空間來放新的。

39 subject [ˋsʌbjɪkt] *n.* 主旨

- Please write "Office Assistant Application" in the subject of your e-mail.
  請在電子郵件的主旨欄寫上「應徵辦公室助理」。

說明 信件中主旨欄常會出現 Re:，意思是 regarding 或 in regard to「關於」，亦指本信「主旨」。

40 supply room （供應必需品的）補給房；儲藏室

- Can you check if we have any more receipts left in the supply room?
  你可以去看一下我們的儲藏室裡還有沒有多的收據嗎？

41 swipe card 刷卡卡片

- Keep your swipe card in your pocket at all times, as you'll need it to get in and out of the office.
  隨時把你的刷卡卡片放在口袋裡，因為你進出辦公室都會用到。

說明 swipe 是將卡片「刷」過機器的動作。隨著科技進步，許多刷卡設備都具有磁感應功能，但 swipe card 仍被沿用來稱呼這種兼具保全和出缺勤控管效能的卡片。

42 take the leap 大膽地放手嘗試做某事

- The company finally seems ready to take the leap into the online world.

  公司似乎終於準備好大膽邁入網路市場了。

  說明 leap 作名詞指「跳躍；躍進」的意思。

同 make the leap 勇敢嘗試

---

43 tidy up 收拾；整理

- The boss commented that my desk was looking a little messy, so I decided to tidy up.

  老闆評論說我的桌子看起來有點凌亂，所以我決定要整理一下。

同 clean up 使整齊；使整潔

---

44 vendor [ˋvɛndə] *n.* 賣主；供應商

- There is a hot dog vendor behind the office building if you're looking for a quick snack.

  如果你要找簡便的零食，公司的大樓後面有一家熱狗小販。

  常用詞彙 street vendor 街頭小販
  online vendor 線上賣家

衍 vend *v.* 出售；販賣

關 vending machine 自動販賣機

---

45 voicemail 語音信箱

- He didn't pick up the phone so I left a message on his voicemail.

  他沒接電話，所以我在他的語音信箱中留了一則留言。

  說明 亦可拼為兩個字 voice mail。而存在語音信箱中的「語音訊息」則是 voice message。

---

46 workstation [ˋwɝkˏsteʃən] *n.* 工作區

- I'm looking for Mike but he's not at his workstation. Have you seen him?

  我在找麥克，但他不在他的工作區。你有看到他嗎？

PRACTICE TEST

Part 1: Photographs

 TRACK 17

Directions:

For each question in this part, you will hear four statements about a picture. When you hear the statements, you must select the one statement that best describes what you see in the picture. Then circle the letter (A), (B), (C), or (D). The statements will not be printed below and will be spoken only one time.

(A) (B) (C) (D)   (A) (B) (C) (D)

Part 2: Question and Response

TRACK 18

Directions:

You will hear a question or statement and three responses spoken in English. They will be spoken only one time and will not be printed below. Select the best response to the question or statement and circle the letter (A), (B), or (C).

③ (A) (B) (C)

④ (A) (B) (C)

⑤ (A) (B) (C)

⑥ (A) (B) (C)

Part 3: Short Conversations

 TRACK 19

Directions:

You will hear some conversations between two or more people. You will be asked to answer three questions about what the speakers say in each conversation. Select the best response to each question and circle the letter (A), (B), (C), or (D). The conversation will be spoken only one time and will not be printed below.

7 What is the purpose of the woman's call to the man?

(A) To ask him to check his e-mails

(B) To invite him to a meeting with the CEO

(C) To ask him to fix her computer.

(D) To inform him of a problem

8 What does the man plan to do?

(A) Send the e-mail again

(B) Print the attachments

(C) Speak to the IT guy

(D) Photocopy some documents

9 When will the woman get the documents?

(A) Tomorrow morning

(B) This afternoon

(C) Tonight

(D) Just now

INVENTORY LIST—STATIONERY & EDUCATIONAL SUPPLIES

ITEM #	DESCRIPTION	LOCATION	UNITS (PER PACK)	QUANTITY
SP7076	Early Readers (Books)	Aisle 1, shelf 1	x5	10 units
TR8765	Pencils (HB)	Aisle 2, shelf 1	x10	50 units
SY4545	Colored Pencils	Aisle 2, shelf 1	x10	20 units
XZ3124	Markers	Aisle 2, shelf 1	x6	10 units
AH9787	Colored Paper	Aisle 3, shelf 2	X100	3 units

10 What is the woman's occupation?

(A) Principal   (B) Secretary

(C) Deliveryman   (D) Publisher

11 What does the man say about the books for kindergartners?

(A) They are not kept in the stockroom.

(B) They are too hard for kindergartners.

(C) They are no longer in stock.

(D) They take longer to arrive.

12 Look at the graphic. How many new kindergarten books does the woman need to buy?

(A) 5   (B) 10

(C) 50   (D) 90

Part 4: Short Talks

✎ **TRACK 20**

Directions:

You will hear some short talks given by a single speaker. You will be asked to answer three questions about what the speaker says in each talk. Select the best response to each question and circle the letter (A), (B), (C), or (D). The talks will be spoken only one time and will not be printed below.

⑬ What problem does the speaker have?

(A) She doesn't know where the marketing department is.

(B) She doesn't know what is inside the box.

(C) She doesn't know who a delivery belongs to.

(D) She doesn't know how to place an order.

⑭ What does the speaker mean when she says, "I signed for a delivery"?

(A) She put a sign up in the lobby.   (B) She sent out a delivery.

(C) She signed up for an activity.   (D) She provided a signature.

⑮ What will the speaker do next?

(A) Send the box up to marketing   (B) Return the box to QuickPrint

(C) Wait for a call from Mr. Johnson   (D) Give out the brochures to visitors

Room	Seating Capacity	Facilities
Reception area, 1st floor	4	Water cooler
Room A, 1st floor	5	Projector
Room B, 2nd floor	10	Projector, Coffee maker
Room C, 5th floor	12	Whiteboard, Photocopier, Coffee maker

⑯ Who most likely is the speaker?

(A) A cleaner   (B) A secretary

(C) A receptionist   (D) A company director

⑰ What is implied about the upcoming meeting?

(A) It will be casual.   (B) It will be important.

(C) It will be brief.   (D) It will include lunch.

⑱ Look at the graphic. On which floor will the meeting be held?

(A) In the reception area   (B) On the 1st floor

(C) On the 2nd floor   (D) On the 5th floor

Part 5: Incomplete Sentences

Directions:

A word or phrase is missing in each of the sentences below. Four answer choices are given below each sentence. Select the best answer to complete the sentence. Then circle the letter (A), (B), (C), or (D).

⑲ In order to track working hours, employees are given a special card so that they can punch _____ every day.

(A) back
(B) on
(C) in
(D) at

⑳ If we _____ out of stock of ink cartridges, we would need to order some more from our supplier.

(A) are
(B) is
(C) was
(D) were

㉑ Mr. Lee _____ for an important business trip to Shanghai last Monday.

(A) left
(B) was leaving
(C) leave
(D) leaves

㉒ There has been a lot of _____ between the company and the tax office.

(A) correspondent
(B) corresponding
(C) correspondence
(D) corresponded

㉓ The executive committee passed the _____ with a vote of five to one in favor.

(A) recipient
(B) resolution
(C) receptionist
(D) requirement

Part 6: Text Completion

Directions:

Read the text below. A word, phrase, or sentence is missing. For each empty space in the text, select the best answer to complete the text. Then circle the letter (A), (B), (C), or (D).

Questions 24-27 refer to the following notice.

NOTICE TO ALL STAFF

Our administration department has noticed a great increase in the amount of ---24--- being produced in this office recently, which has led to rising costs for ink and paper. This notice is to let everybody know that we will no longer automatically replace ---25--- in individual printers. The decision has ---26--- by the directors that, once the ink has run out on your personal desktop printers, the ink will not be replaced. ---27--- Desktop printers that are no longer in use will be donated to the local junior high school. Thank you for your understanding and remember to think before you print!

24 (A) swipe cards
   (C) printed matter

   (B) voicemails
   (D) board meetings

25 (A) ink cartridges
   (C) shareholders

   (B) junk mail
   (D) stock

26 (A) made
   (C) been made

   (B) make
   (D) be made

27 (A) Instead, the ink will be replaced for you so you can carry on printing.
   (B) Rather, your printing needs will be handled by the central administration team.
   (C) However, you will be able to use your swipe card to enter the building.
   (D) Nevertheless, you will still be able to forward your junk mail to our department.

Part 7: Reading Comprehension

Directions:

In this part you will read a selection of texts, such as magazine and newspaper articles, e-mails, and instant messages. Each text is followed by several questions. Select the best answer for each question and circle the letter (A), (B), (C), or (D).

Questions 28-30 refer to the following letter.

Dear colleagues,

It is with some sadness that I am informing you all of my decision to leave the company after ten memorable years. This is a subject that I have been thinking about for a while, but yesterday I finally took the leap and informed the board of directors of my decision to resign. It wasn't an easy decision, but I decided that the time was right for me to spend more time with my young family.

As I will be away on my final business trip for the company next week, I may not have the chance to say goodbye to you all in person. However, I am happy to give you my personal e-mail, which is sally.taylor@tmail.com. Charles in HR has my address if you need to forward any mail that may arrive for me by post.

Finally, I would like to thank everyone for making my time here so pleasant and I hope to see you all soon.

All the best,

Sally

28 The phrase "took the leap" in paragraph 1, line 3, is closest in meaning to
  (A) jumped over
  (B) took control
  (C) changed one's mind
  (D) made a decision

29 What is NOT mentioned in the letter?
  (A) The date she will be leaving
  (B) Her decision for leaving
  (C) How long she has worked there
  (D) Her personal e-mail address

30 What is implied about the letter writer?

(A) She has elderly relatives.

(B) She needs a break from traveling.

(C) She has children at home.

(D) She doesn't like her employer.

Questions 31-35 refer to the following e-mail and instructions.

To:	allstaff@elt.com
From:	toby@Qcopiers.com
Re:	Installation and use of new photocopier

Dear ELT Staff,

Q-Copiers are very pleased to be your new vendor and servicing company of your brand new ADX4009 photocopier. Yesterday, our team visited your office to set up the new machine and it is now ready to use.

We think you will be pleased with the many excellent features of the ADX4009, which include the ability to copy color as well as black and white, the capacity to produce bulk mail as well as individual documents, and various options to staple and finish your photocopies. The ADX4009 is also one of the most user-friendly machines and you will have no trouble getting the hang of it. To help you, I am attaching a brief summary of the instructions and access codes for you to punch in when you want to make copies.

We will be servicing the photocopier every six months and Rob Lane in your Administration Department is the person responsible for the day-to-day operation of the photocopier. So, if you have any problems, you can call him on extension 203.

Best Regards,

Toby Smart
Sales & Servicing Manager
Q-Copiers Inc.

Company: ELT Inc.
Installation Date: January 3rd
Model: ADX4009

BASIC INSTRUCTIONS FOR USE

1. Photocopier will usually be in standby mode, so you will not need to turn on the power.
2. Ensure paper trays are full. Stocks of paper can be found in the supply room where the stationery is kept.
3. Place your document(s) face-up in the paper feeder (for multiple pages) or lift the lid and place your document on the glass face-down (for single pages).
4. The menu screen will guide you through the steps for photocopying. Here you will select paper size, number of copies, color, and printing options, and position of staples.
5. Press the green "Copy" button.

ADDITIONAL INFORMATION

- If pages get stuck, contact extension 203.
- If the resolution of your copies is not adequate, please call a member of our servicing team on 1-800-555-992.
- Check your employee badge for code, or see table on the right.

Department	Code
Administration	0985
Marketing	0986
Sales	0987

31 What is the main purpose in writing the e-mail?

(A) To sell the company a new photocopier

(B) To send instructions for use of new photocopier

(C) To introduce a photocopier supplier

(D) To tell people about various photocopiers

32 What is NOT mentioned in the e-mail?

(A) The number of people that installed the machine

(B) The features of the new machine

(C) The model number of the machine

(D) The name of the vendor company

㉝ What are the code numbers on the instructions?

(A) Telephone extensions

(B) Model numbers

(C) Maximum number of copies

(D) Access codes

㉞ In what month will the photocopier next be serviced?

(A) January (B) March

(C) June (D) July

㉟ What is the access code for Rob Lane?

(A) 0986 (B) ADX4009

(C) 0985 (D) 0987

Unit 2 General Business
一般商務

本主題涵蓋內容包括：

- contracts 契約
- negotiations 談判
- marketing 行銷
- sales 銷售
- business planning 商業企劃
- conferences 會議
- labor relations 勞雇關係

WORD POWER

TRACK 21

01 advertisement [ˌædvə·ˈtaɪzmənt] *n.* （平面媒體、電視、廣播、網路、路邊及會議活動的）廣告；宣傳

• These new online advertisements will promote the company.
這些新的廣告將能推廣該公司。

說明 常簡稱為 ad、advert。

衍 **advertise** *v.* 為……做廣告；為……宣傳

衍 **advertiser** *n.* 刊登廣告者；廣告客戶

衍 **advertising** *n.* 廣告業；（總稱）廣告

關 **commercial** *n.* （廣播或電視的）商業廣告

常見廣告類型

flyer 傳單　　billboard 廣告看板　poster 海報　　web banner 網路橫幅

02 agreement [əˈgrimənt] *n.* 協定；協議；同意；一致

• The companies reached an agreement and now all that remains is for everything to be written down on paper.
這幾間公司已達成協議，現在只需要將每個細節書面記錄下來。

• Everyone nodded in agreement as the boss explained her idea in the meeting.
老闆在會議上解釋她的想法時，每個人都點頭表示同意。

說明 agreement 作「協定、協議」解時為可數名詞，作「同意、一致」解時則不可數。

常用詞彙 trade agreement 貿易協定

同 **pact**、**contract** *n.* 契約；協定

反 **disagreement**、**argument** *n.* 意見不一；爭論

衍 **agree** *v.* 同意

衍 **agreeable** *adj.* 可以接受的；欣然贊同的

03 appealing [əˈpilɪŋ] *adj.* 有吸引力的

• The offer of a job in management was appealing, but I said "no" because I wasn't ready for the responsibility.
一個管理職的工作機會很吸引人，但我拒絕了因為我還沒準備好承擔管理的責任。

同 **attractive** *adj.* 迷人的；吸引人的

衍 **appeal** *n.* 吸引力

04 billboard [ˋbɪlˏbɔrd] *n.* 廣告招牌

- The company paid a lot of money for the advertisement to be shown on billboards around the city.
  公司花了一大筆錢在市內各處的廣告看板上張貼廣告。

🔗 bulletin board
佈告欄

05 boardroom [ˋbordˏrum] *n.* 會議室

- A video conference with our New York office will take place in the boardroom on Wednesday.
  和紐約分公司的視訊會議將於週三在會議室舉行。

說明 boardroom 通常是指較高級的會議室、董事會會議室。

🔲 council chamber
董事會會議室

🔗 meeting room、
conference room
會議室

06 brainstorming [ˋbrenˏstɔrmɪŋ] *n.* 腦力激盪

- We need to do some brainstorming to come up with ideas for products that will excite our audience.
  我們需要做些腦力激盪，以便激發出一些能讓觀眾興奮的商品點子。

常用詞彙 brainstorming session 腦力激盪會議

🔀 brainstorm *v.* 集思廣益

07 campaign [kæmˋpen] *n.* （有商業或政治目的的）活動 *v.* （為達某特定目的而）從事、發起活動

- We're introducing a promotional campaign that will target new customers as well as existing shoppers.
  我們將推行一種能同時鎖定新客群與既有消費者的促銷活動。

- Women have been campaigning for fairer pay in many work industries.
  在許多行業中，女性一直在發起活動來爭取更平等的薪資。

常用詞彙 ad campaign 廣告宣傳活動
　　　 promotional campaign 促銷活動

🔀 campaigner *n.*
（政治或商業）活動的發起者

08 collaborate [kəˋlæbəˏret] *v.* 合作（+ with）

- When two companies collaborate there are many challenges, but the possible rewards are big.
  兩家公司合作時會出現許多挑戰，但可能獲得的報酬也會很高。

🔲 cooperate *v.*
合作（+ with）

🔀 collaboration *n.*
合作；協同運作

SECTION B 必備詞彙 | UNIT 2 General Business 一般商務

09 **collapse** [kə`læps] *n./v.* 崩塌；瓦解；失敗；倒塌

- The 2008 economic collapse of the US and western European economies was linked to too many unpaid loans.
  二○○八年美國與西歐洲經濟體的崩潰與許多未清償的貸款有所關聯。

- The business collapsed because it couldn't keep up with its competitors.
  該企業因為無法與競爭對手並駕齊驅而倒閉了。

圓 destruction *n.*
破壞；毀滅

---

10 **commercial** [kə`mɝʃəl] *n.* （廣播或電視的）廣告 *adj.* 商業的；營利的

- It's time to consider using YouTube commercials to promote our product.
  是時候考慮用 YouTube 廣告來推銷我們的商品了。

- Planners hope the new department store will turn this part of town into a popular commercial area.
  籌劃人員希望新的百貨公司會將鎮上的這一區變成受歡迎的商業區。

反 noncommercial
adj. 非商業的

衍 commerce *n.* 商業；貿易

衍 commercialize *v.*
商業化；商品化

衍 commercially *adv.*
商業上；貿易上

---

11 **competition** [ˌkɑmpə`tɪʃən] *n.* 競爭；角逐

- Small grocery stores are going out of business because of strong competition from large supermarkets.
  因為來自大型超市的激烈競爭，小型雜貨店正紛紛倒閉。

衍 compete *v.* 競爭；對抗；比賽

衍 competitive *adj.*
競爭性的

衍 competitor *n.* 競爭者；對手；敵手

---

12 **consumer** [kən`sumɚ] *n.* 消費者

- Computers became a consumer item in the early 1990s, and soon most people had one.
  電腦在一九九○年代早期成為消費品，很快地大部分的人都有一台。

常用詞彙 consumer item/goods 消費品；民生物品；日用品

反 producer *n.* 製造者

衍 consume *v.* 消費；購買（產品）；攝取（食物）

衍 consumption *n.* 消費；消費量

13 contract [ˋkɑntrækt] *n.* 契約；合同

- We signed a huge contract that will see us supplying a client with 3D printers and related services for the next five years.

  我們簽了一筆鉅額的合約，將在未來五年內為一位客戶供應3D印表機與相關服務。

衍 contractor *n.* 立契約者；承包人；承包商

---

14 demonstrate [ˋdɛmənˏstret] *v.* 示範；證明

- The investors asked the young businessman to demonstrate how his product could be used.

  投資者要求那位年輕商人示範他的產品要怎麼使用。

同 show、display *v.* 展示；展出；顯示

衍 demonstration/demo *n.* 證明；示範；示威遊行

衍 demonstrator *n.* 遊行示威者；示範者

---

15 direct marketing 直效行銷

- Direct marketing is moving away from paper-based advertisements toward electronic ones.

  直效行銷正逐漸從平面廣告轉換成電子廣告。

  說明 又稱為 direct mail「直接投遞給個人的廣告信件」，即一般常說的 DM。

關 online advertising 線上廣告

關 telemarketing *n.* 電話行銷

關 e-mail marketing 電子郵件行銷

---

16 distribution [ˏdɪstrəˋbjuʃən] *n.* 分配；配銷；流通

- More channels of distribution should equal a higher volume of sales.

  更多配銷通路應該就等於更高額的銷售數字。

  常用詞彙 channels of distribution（商品的）銷售途徑；經銷通路

同 spread *n.* 流傳；普及

反 gathering *n.* 收集；聚集

衍 distribute *v.* 分發；配送

衍 distributor *n.* 銷售者；批發商

---

17 downsize [ˋdaʊnˏsaɪz] *v.* 縮編

- The company had to ask 10% of its staff to leave because they were downsizing.

  該公司因為要進行縮編，必須讓一成的員工離職。

同 reduce *v.* 縮小

衍 downsizing *n.* 縮減開支

---

18 efficiency [ɪˋfɪʃənsɪ] *n.* 效率；效能

• Better communication, organization, and time management will increase our efficiency.
更好的溝通、組織與時間管理將能增加我們的效率。

衍 efficient *adj.* 效率高的

衍 inefficient *adj.* 效能差的；效率低下的

---

19 enclose [ɪnˋkloz] *v.* 把（公文、票據等）封入；附上

• Shane enclosed the letter and price list in an envelope and sent it to the customer.
尚恩把信件與價目表封入信封裡，然後寄給顧客。

反 disclose *v.* 使顯露；公開

衍 enclosure *n.*（信函的）附件

> 字首 en- 可表「進入；在……之內」

en（進入；在……之內）＋ close（封起來）

⬇

enclose 把……封入；附上（把東西放進去再封起來）

其他同字首單字
• enforce 加強（en＋force「力量」）
• entitle 給……頭銜或資格（en＋title「名稱；頭銜」）

---

20 enterprise [ˋɛntɚˌpraɪz] *n.* 事業；企業；公司

• This project is a joint enterprise between a German and a Korean company.
該企劃是關於一家德國公司與一家韓國公司的合資企業。

衍 enterpriser *n.* 企業家

衍 enterprising *adj.* 富有創業精神的

---

21 entrepreneur [ˌɑntrəprəˋnɝ] *n.* 企業家；事業家

• Many young entrepreneurs see big possibilities in new technology.
許多年輕企業家都看到了新興科技極大的可能性。

 本字源自於法文。

同 enterpriser *n.* 企業家

---

22 expand [ɪkˋspænd] *v.* 擴張；展開

• They're looking to grow the business by expanding in foreign markets.
他們期待透過擴展海外市場來壯大公司規模。

同 enlarge *v.* 擴大

反 shrink *v.* 萎縮；變少

衍 expansion *n.* 擴展；擴張

衍 expansive *adj.* 遼闊的

23 firm [fɝm] *n.* 公司

- We hired a small engineering firm to help us on this project.

  我們雇用了一間小型的工程公司來幫我們進行這個企劃。

說明 firm 作形容詞時指「結實的；堅固的」。

同 company、corporation、enterprise *n.* 公司

---

24 franchise [ˈfrænˌtʃaɪz] *n.* 連鎖企業；（製造商授與店家的）經銷權；加盟店

- The franchise consists of more than 3,000 stores across the country.

  該連鎖企業由全國三千多家分店所組成。

常用詞彙 franchise organization 特許加盟組織

衍 franchisee *n.* 經銷商；加盟者

關 chain store 連鎖商店

---

25 from scratch 從頭開始

- We lost all the files when the server crashed, so we have to start again from scratch.

  伺服器掛掉的時候我們遺失了所有檔案，所以我們必須從頭開始。

說明 scratch 作名詞時可表示「起跑線」。本慣用語以字面的「從起跑線開始」之意引申指「從頭開始；白手起家」。

同 from the ground up 從零開始

---

26 headquarters [ˈhɛdˌkwɔrtɚz] *n.* 總部

- Several big bosses are coming from headquarters to check up on us today.

  今天有一些高階主管要從總部過來查看我們的工作情形。

說明 常簡稱為 HQ。

衍 headquarter *v.* 設立總部

衍 headquartered *adj.* 以……為總部所在地的

關 branch *n.* 分公司；分支

關 division *n.* （機關、公司等的）部門

關 department *n.* （行政、企業等的）部門

SECTION B 必備詞彙 | UNIT 2 General Business 一般商務

27 hold [hold] *v.* 舉行；舉辦
- The company holds monthly meetings to make sure everyone is up-to-date with what's happening.
  公司每個月都會開會確保大家知道最新狀況。
- Meetings in this office are held weekly.
  辦公室每週都會舉行會議。

[說明] hold 指「舉辦」時常用被動式，另外，常見的意思還有「握住；保留；保有」等。

同 conduct *v.* 引領；帶領；實施

---

28 issue [ˈɪʃu] *v.* 發布；核發 *n.* 問題；爭議
- The company issued a warning to employees that sharing company secrets would result in being fired.
  該公司對員工發出警告，表示分享公司機密將遭致開除。
- How to protect the environment is an issue that many big companies face.
  如何保護環境是許多大公司面臨的問題。

[常用詞彙] social issue 社會議題
pressing issue/problem、urgent issue/problem
急迫問題

同 announce *v.* 公布
同 publish *v.* 發布
同 controversy *n.* 爭議

---

29 launch [lɔntʃ] *v.* 開辦；產品上市 *n.* 產品發表會
- The company proudly launched its new range of cars.
  該公司自豪地推出新車款。
- The world is going to get its first look at the company's latest product at tomorrow's launch.
  全世界將能在明天的發表會上首窺該公司的最新產品。

同 start、introduce、commence、inaugurate *v.* 開始
同 go to market 產品上市

---

30 lengthy [ˈlɛŋθɪ] *adj.* 長時間的；冗長的
- We expect talks between the companies to continue for a lengthy period of time, as there are many things to discuss.
  我們預期兩家公司的會談將持續一段很長的時間，因為有很多事情需要討論。

[說明] 通常置於名詞前修飾。

同 long、overlong *adj.* 長的；過長的
反 short、brief *adj.* 簡短的
衍 length *n.* （時間的）長短；期間；（距離的）長度

31 **market** [`mɑrkɪt] *v.* 銷售 *n.* 市場

- There is a debate over whether marketing fast food to children is ethical or not.
  對兒童推銷速食是否道德存在著爭議。

常用詞彙 market value 市價；市值
market research 市場研究

同 merchandise、sell
v. 銷售；販賣

衍 marketing *n.* 行銷

關 mart *n.* 市場；商業中心

32 **merchandise** [`mɝtʃənˌdaɪz] *n.* 商品 *v.* 買賣；經營

- After the concert, fans can buy the band's merchandise such as t-shirts and hats.
  演唱會之後，樂迷們可以購買該樂團的 T 恤、帽子等商品。

- We merchandise the product online.
  我們在網路上販售那個商品。

同 goods、product *n.* 商品；產品

衍 merchant *n./adj.* 商人（的）；零售商

33 **negotiate** [nɪˋgoʃɪˌet] *v.* 談判；協商

- We're trying to negotiate a better deal than the one they suggested.
  我們試著要協商出一個優於他們原本建議的交易。

衍 negotiation *n.* 談判；協商

衍 negotiator *n.* 磋商者；交涉者

34 **offer** [ˋɔfə] *n./v.* 報價；出價；提供；提議

- The car salesman said that this offer was available for a limited time only.
  那名汽車銷售員說這個報價只在一段限定時間內有效。

- Chain stores can offer large discounts because of the volume they sell.
  因為大量販售，連鎖店可以提供大筆的折扣。

說明 offer 作名詞時，除了可指「提供；提議」外，在議價中是指「出價」，而 special offer 就是指「特別的價格；特價供應」的意思。

同 propose、suggest
v. 提議

同 proposal、suggestion *n.* 提議

35 **potential** [pə`tɛnʃəl] *n.* 潛力 *adj.* 有可能的；有潛力的

- This market may be small now but it has potential to be big in the future.
  這個市場現在也許很小，但在未來有擴大的潛力。

- We're looking at potential locations for a new store.
  我們正在關注新分店的可能地點。

囘 capability *n.* 能力；才能

衍 potentially *adv.* 潛在地；可能地

---

36 **productive** [prə`dʌktɪv] *adj.* 富有成效的；有生產力的

- Our workers will be more productive if they are healthy and happy.
  我們的員工如果健康又快樂，生產力就會更高。

- The chair ensures the time spent in the meeting is productive by following an agenda.
  主席保證只要遵守議程，開會所花的時間就會是有成效的。

囘 constructive *adj.* 建設性的

反 unproductive *adj.* 沒有成效的；無益的

衍 produce *v.* 生產；製造；出產

衍 production *n.* 生產；製造

衍 productivity *n.* 生產力

---

37 **project** [prə`dʒɛkt] *v.* 預測；投射
[`prɑdʒɛkt] *n.* 課題；專案

- Spending for the coming year was projected at over $100,000.
  明年的開支預計會超過十萬元。

- Jeff is the leader of our new research project which will be investigating the market for wearable technology.
  傑夫是我們新研究計畫的組長，該計畫將會調查穿戴科技的市場。

囘 estimate、predict *v.* 預估

衍 projector *n.* 放映機；投影機

---

38 **promotion** [prə`moʃən] *n.* 促銷；升遷

- We should invest more in promotion so that more people understand the true benefits of this product.
  我們應在促銷上投資更多，好讓人們了解這個商品的真正益處。

- Jill will receive an improved salary and extra responsibility following her recent promotion at work.
  吉兒最近升職後，將有較佳的待遇與額外的責任。

衍 promote *v.* （使）晉升

衍 promotional *adj.* 宣傳的；推銷的

39 **recovery** [rɪˋkʌvərɪ] *n.* 恢復；復原；痊癒
- Business was badly affected by the virus, but we expect it to make a recovery in the new year.
生意因為病毒受到嚴重的影響，但我們預計新的一年就會恢復。

同 improvement *n.* 改善

衍 recover *v.* 復原；恢復

40 **release** [rɪˋlis] *v./n.* 發行；推出；釋放
- We will introduce some new features to the phone market when we release the new product next month.
我們下個月推出新產品時，將為手機市場引進新的功能。
- Disney's latest release has got everyone talking.
迪士尼最新發行的作品引起大家熱烈討論。

同 come out 出版；發行

41 **retail** [ˋritel] *n./adj.* 零售（的）
- Online retail lets customers browse a variety of products without leaving their homes.
線上零售業讓消費者不須出門就能瀏覽各式各樣的商品。
- There's a popular retail park just outside the city.
有一個受歡迎的零售園區就位在市外。

常用詞彙 retail price 零售價

反 wholesale *n./adj.* 批發（的）

衍 retailer *n.* 零售商；零售店

衍 retailing *n.* 零售業

關 wholesaler *n.* 批發商

42 **reverse** [rɪˋvɝs] *v.* 使逆轉；徹底改變 *adj.* 反面的；顛倒的 *n.* 相反；逆轉
- The company reversed its decision to open a new store due to a drop in demand.
因為需求下降，該公司推翻其開設新店鋪的決定。
- Shut the system down by repeating the same steps in reverse order.
以反序重複相同的步驟來關閉這個系統。
- Last year was great for business, but this year we suffered a reverse in fortune.
去年的生意很好，但今年我們的財務狀況卻完全相反陷入了困境。

同 switch *v.* 改變；轉換

衍 reversible *adj.* 可逆轉的

衍 irreversible *adj.* 不能逆轉的；無法更改的

43 risk [rɪsk] *n.* 風險;危險

- Most people view investing in BitCoin as being more high risk than investing in gold.
  很多人認為投資比特幣比投資黃金的風險更高。

說明 risk 亦可當動詞,指「冒著……的危險」,後面通常接 V-ing。

常用詞彙 risk management 風險管理

反 danger *n.* 危險; 威脅

衍 risky *adj.* 有風險的; 危險的

---

44 rival [ˋraɪvl] *adj.* 相互競爭的;敵對的 *n.* 對手
v. 與……匹敵

- It is stated in the contract that workers must not share company secrets with rival companies.
  合約中載明員工不得與競爭公司分享公司機密。

- Even though the two businessmen were rivals in the industry, they were friends outside of it.
  雖然這兩位商人在業界是競爭對手,但他們私下是朋友。

- We're launching a new phone to rival other products in the market.
  我們要發表一款新手機來和市場上的其他產品競爭。

同 competing *adj.* 互相競爭的

衍 rivalry *n.* 競爭;對抗

---

45 session [ˋsɛʃən] *n.* 會期;一段時間;集會;講習會

- A one hour lunch break will split the morning and afternoon sessions at the conference.
  一小時的午休時間將把會議分隔為早上與下午的時段。

  常用詞彙 training session 訓練課程
  emergency session 緊急會議

同 period、term *n.* 期間

同 conference *n.*(正式)會議;討論會

---

46 stiff [stɪf] *adj.*(競爭)激烈的;艱難的;僵硬的

- The competition in this market is stiff, as there are many well-known companies selling the same product.
  這個市場的競爭很激烈,因為有許多知名的公司都販售同樣的商品。

同 tough *adj.* 困難的

47 strategy [ˋstrætədʒɪ] *n.* 策略；戰略

- Our strategy in the negotiation will not be to start with our highest offer.
  我們的協商策略不會從最高的報價開始。

- The company adopted a risky strategy to maintain its position as the industry leader.
  該公司採取了一個高風險的策略以便維持其在業界的領先地位。

說明 後面可接 for N./V-ing 或 to V.。

同 tactics、plan、scheme *n.* 策略；計畫

衍 strategic *adj.* 策略性的

---

48 submit [səbˋmɪt] *v.* 提交；呈遞

- A final proposal regarding the merger will be submitted before Friday's deadline.
  關於併購案的最終企劃書將在週五的截止期限前呈交。

同 hand in 提出；繳交

衍 submission *n.* 提交；服從

---

49 wrap-up [ˋræpʌp] *adj.* 結束；概括總結（**wrap up** 為片語動詞）

- The producers organized a wrap-up party for everyone who had worked on the movie.
  製作公司籌辦了一場殺青派對讓每個參與電影製作的人參加。

常考片語 wrap sth. up / wrap up sth. 完成、結束某事

- We're delighted to finally wrap up a deal with Fenton Electronics and look forward to years of working together.
  我們很開心與范頓電子的交易能定案，並期待接下來幾年的合作。

關 finish、finalize *v.* 結束

SECTION B 必備詞彙

UNIT 2 General Business 一般商務

PRACTICE TEST

Part 1: Photographs

TRACK 22

Directions:

For each question in this part, you will hear four statements about a picture. When you hear the statements, you must select the one statement that best describes what you see in the picture. Then circle the letter (A), (B), (C), or (D). The statements will not be printed below and will be spoken only one time.

(A)　(B)　(C)　(D)　　　　　　　(A)　(B)　(C)　(D)

Part 2: Question and Response

TRACK 23

Directions:

You will hear a question or statement and three responses spoken in English. They will be spoken only one time and will not be printed below. Select the best response to the question or statement and circle the letter (A), (B), or (C).

❸ (A)　(B)　(C)

❹ (A)　(B)　(C)

❺ (A)　(B)　(C)

❻ (A)　(B)　(C)

Part 3: Short Conversations

 TRACK 24

Directions:

You will hear some conversations between two or more people. You will be asked to answer three questions about what the speakers say in each conversation. Select the best response to each question and circle the letter (A), (B), (C), or (D). The conversation will be spoken only one time and will not be printed below.

7 What are the speakers mainly discussing?

(A) The company's advertising campaign

(B) The financial state of the business

(C) The success of the company's first store

(D) The advantages of franchise businesses

8 What does the woman mean when she says, "we will be able to expand"?

(A) The company will be able to open more stores.

(B) The coworkers will be able to start their own business.

(C) The company will be able to negotiate a new deal.

(D) The company will rent a bigger office.

9 Why does the man think opening franchises is a good idea?

(A) He will get a promotion.

(B) His company will earn money from them.

(C) He likes traveling around the city.

(D) He will be able to retire early.

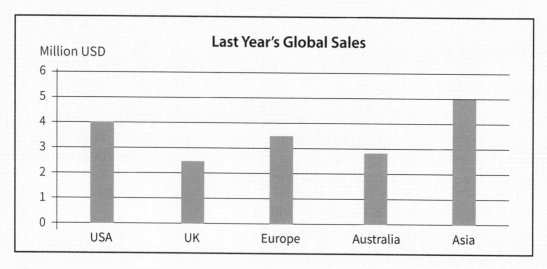

⑩ What line of work are the speakers in?

(A) Advertising

(B) Sales

(C) Publishing

(D) Education

⑪ What does the man say about the Asian market?

(A) It has been unexpectedly strong.

(B) It should be the main focus in future.

(C) It's strong because people are buying more electronics.

(D) It's not worth the company investing in.

⑫ Look at the graphic. Which market does the man want the company to focus on over the next two years?

(A) Europe

(B) USA

(C) UK

(D) Australia

Part 4: Short Talks

TRACK 25

Directions:

You will hear some short talks given by a single speaker. You will be asked to answer three questions about what the speaker says in each talk. Select the best response to each question and circle the letter (A), (B), (C), or (D). The talks will be spoken only one time and will not be printed below.

⑬ What is the main purpose of the talk?

(A) To launch a new product

(B) To report on a successful marketing campaign

(C) To discuss ways to keep new customers

(D) To discuss how customers will be contacted

⑭ Who is being addressed?

(A) The employees

(B) The competitors

(C) The retailers

(D) The customers

⑮ Why does the speaker say that the following months will be extra busy?

(A) Because they will be launching a new direct marketing campaign

(B) Because they will have to contact a lot of people by telephone

(C) Because they need to make sure they keep the new customers

(D) Because they will be busy celebrating their successes

⑯ Who does the company's merchandise appeal to most?

(A) People who go running

(B) People who do different sports

(C) People who practice yoga

(D) People who like swimming

⑰ Look at the graphic. Which company does the speaker work for?

(A) A*Star

(B) Turbo

(C) Kiks

(D) Urban

⑱ What will happen next?

(A) They will go for lunch.

(B) They will look at graphs.

(C) They will discuss ideas.

(D) They will end the meeting.

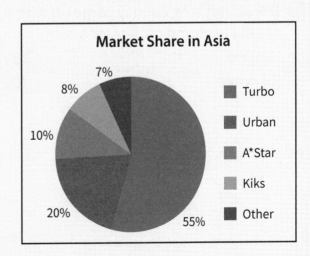

Part 5: Incomplete Sentences

Directions:

A word or phrase is missing in each of the sentences below. Four answer choices are given below each sentence. Select the best answer to complete the sentence. Then circle the letter (A), (B), (C), or (D).

⑲ We will hold a follow-up _____ after the initial brainstorming meeting to present our ideas to the Board of Directors.

(A) compromise   (B) strategy

(C) session   (D) consumer

⑳ The coworkers held a highly _____ meeting in the boardroom in which they finalized their sales strategy.

(A) productive   (B) commercial

(C) rival   (D) brief

㉑ The _____ brochure will tell you all about the services we offer, our prices, and what special discounts are available.

(A) enclose   (B) encloses

(C) enclosed   (D) enclosing

㉒ The contract was given to a large construction _____ based in Taichung, as they had the most experience with this type of building.

(A) boardroom   (B) competition

(C) distribution   (D) firm

㉓ The advertising agency came up with a TV commercial _____ would appeal to young professionals.

(A) who   (B) that

(C) when   (D) where

Part 6: Text Completion

Directions:

Read the text below. A word, phrase, or sentence is missing. For each empty space in the text, select the best answer to complete the text. Then circle the letter (A), (B), (C), or (D).

Questions 24-27 refer to the following e-mail.

To:	stern.greg@telltech.com
From:	tinaquick@tca.tw
Subject:	**Invitation to Digital Marketing Workshop**

Dear Greg Stern,

It is our pleasure to invite you to our Digital Marketing Workshop, ---24--- we are looking forward to hosting during the Technology Trade Fair in San Jose. Make time in your busy trade fair schedule to attend our informative workshop in which you will hear ---25--- and take part in discussions on how to market your products, drive traffic to your website through SEO (Search Engine Optimization), and increase sales by utilizing social media. This year, we are delighted to welcome the highly-successful ---26--- Bill Grange, who will be giving a talk on *How to Market in the Digital Age*. If you would like to attend, please click on the link below to request tickets.

---27--- We look forward to welcoming you!

Attend Digital Marketing Workshop

Kind Regards,

Tina Quick
Technology Companies Association

24 (A) which
(C) whose
(B) when
(D) who

25 (A) presentations
(C) agreements
(B) advertisements
(D) enterprises

26 (A) contract
(C) franchise
(B) entrepreneur
(D) headquarters

27 (A) There are no more tickets available for this event.
(B) Tickets will be issued in the week before the Trade Fair.
(C) You'll receive credits each time you click on an ad.
(D) The brainstorming session is open to everyone.

Part 7: Reading Comprehension

Directions:

In this part you will read a selection of texts, such as magazine and newspaper articles, e-mails, and instant messages. Each text is followed by several questions. Select the best answer for each question and circle the letter (A), (B), (C), or (D).

Questions 28-30 refer to the following direct marketing letter.

The Great Chariot Hotel
New York City, New York, USA

Dear Sir/Madam,

I am writing on behalf of Real Event Solutions Ltd. We are an established events company that has worked on projects ranging from high street retail store annual banquets to movie wrap-up parties. When it comes to production, there is no requirement that Real cannot meet, and we pride ourselves on our high levels of efficiency and professionalism.

Should you be interested in hiring us for your event, I would be delighted to come in and give you a short presentation, free of charge. You can also reach me at mick@realeventsolutions.com or on 0981 410 0150.

Please also visit our website, where you can learn more about our past projects, as well as read testimonials from previous clients we've collaborated with.

Thank you and I hope to hear from you at your earliest convenience.

Yours sincerely,

Mick Vance
Senior Marketing Executive
Real Event Solutions Ltd.

28 What is the purpose of this letter?

(A) To request product information (B) To follow up on a payment

(C) To promote a company (D) To apologize for an error

29 What does the writer offer to give the recipient?

(A) A free presentation

(B) A discount on equipment

(C) A free banquet

(D) An invitation to his store

30 The word "retail" in paragraph 1, line 2, is closest in meaning to

(A) franchise   (B) selling

(C) location   (D) session

Questions 31-33 refer to the following news report.

BLAZE DEMONSTRATES RECOVERY

This week, Blaze Electronics reported better than expected quarterly profits, surprising the analysts who predicted the collapse of the company. These profits are the ultimate proof that, after a difficult few years, the company is on the road to recovery. ---[1]--- Blaze, once one of the most profitable electronics manufacturers, has seen steady losses during the past few years due to increased competition from new markets. Their newly appointed CEO, John Mitchell, was hired with the hope that he could reverse the downward trend. ---[2]--- Certainly figures for this quarter seem to back up his optimism. Unfortunately, while Mitchell is working towards shifting the company in a profitable direction, many remain doubtful that it is possible in the long term. ---[3]--- Competitors in Asia, with low labor and manufacturing costs, are pushing more established firms out. Mitchell attributes recent profitability to the company's strategy of building on its long-standing reputation for quality. ---[4]--- He points out that, in the long term, consumers are more likely to choose quality over price.

③1 What is the purpose of the article?

(A) To report on why Asian businesses are thriving

(B) To report on the appointment of a new CEO

(C) To report on a company's recent success

(D) To report a company's quarterly losses

③2 Why does John Mitchell believe the company will continue to be successful?

(A) Because the company will build more factories in Asia

(B) Because people will ultimately choose quality products over cheap ones

(C) Because he will reduce the company's labor and manufacturing costs

(D) Because the company's quarterly profits are demonstrating a recovery

③3 In which of the positions marked [1], [2], [3], and [4] does the following sentence best belong?
"Bringing Mitchell on board seems to be paying off and he firmly believes that the company can succeed."

(A) [1]

(B) [2]

(C) [3]

(D) [4]

Unit 3 Personnel 人事

本主題涵蓋內容包括：

- recruiting 招募
- hiring 雇用
- retiring 退休
- salaries 薪資
- promotions 升遷
- pensions 退休金
- job applications 求職申請

WORD POWER

 TRACK 26

01 amend [ə`mɛnd] *v.* 修改

- Mr. Jones amended the business proposal before sending it to the head of the sales department.
  瓊斯先生修改了商業提案，然後才寄給業務部的主管。

🔄 alter、modify *v.*
改變；修正

🔧 amendment *n.*
修正；改善；（議案等的）修正案

---

02 annual leave 年假

- Many employees like to take their annual leave during the summer.
  有很多員工喜歡在夏天休年假。

說明 annual [`ænjʊəl] 指「每年的」。另外，「請假單」一般譯為 leave-taking form。

常見的各種假

maternity leave
產假

sick leave 病假

personal leave
事假

bereavement leave
喪假

---

03 apply [ə`plaɪ] *v.* 申請

- After graduating from university, Dolores applied for a job in a local bank.
  大學畢業之後，朵莉絲申請了一份當地銀行的工作。

- Darren loves to cook, so he plans to apply to a cooking school to become a chef.
  戴倫喜愛烹飪，所以他打算申請一所烹飪學校以便成為廚師。

🔧 application *n.* 申請

🔧 applicant *n.* 申請人

🔧 applied *adj.* 應用的

說明 指「申請（某事物）」時，介系詞用 for。指「向（某機構）申請」時，介系詞用 to。

常考片語 apply to 適用；應用

- These regulations apply to all new employees.
  這些規定適用於所有新進員工。

---

04 appraise [ə`prez] *v.* 評價；估計；估價

- You must thoroughly appraise the situation before coming up with a solution.
  在想出解決方式之前，你一定要先徹底評估情況。

🔄 evaluate、assess *v.*
評價；評估

05 background [ˋbæk͵graʊnd] *n.* 經歷；背景；幕後

- Pierre has an interesting cultural background because he grew up in India and France.

  皮耶爾有個有趣的文化背景，因為他是在印度與法國長大的。

常用詞彙 cultural/educational/academic/family background
文化／教育／學歷／家庭背景

06 candidate [ˋkændə͵dət] *n.* 申請人；應徵者；候選人

同 applicant *n.* 申請人

- Only one of the three candidates was suitable for the position.

  三位申請者中只有一位適合這個職缺。

07 career [kəˋrɪr] *n.* 職業；生涯

同 vocation、occupation *n.* 職業

- Mr. Jackson quit working after enjoying a long career as a lawyer.

  傑克森先生享受了一段悠長的律師職涯之後就退休了。

常用詞彙 career consultant 職業諮詢師（常指職業仲介公司人員）

08 compensate [ˋkɑmpən͵set] *v.* 補償；給予報酬

衍 compensation *n.* 補償；賠償金；【美】津貼

衍 compensatory *adj.* 補償的

- The injured employee was not fully compensated because he didn't follow the safety procedures.

  受傷的員工沒有領到全額補償，因為他並未遵守安全程序。

說明 用法為 compensate for sth. 或 compensate sb. for sth.。

09 cover letter 求職信

關 résumé *n.* 履歷表

- In your cover letter, you should include a brief introduction of yourself and your reason for applying for the job.

  你的求職信中應該要包含一段簡短的自我介紹與應徵這份工作的理由。

10 **employ** [ɪmˋplɔɪ] *v.* 雇用；運用

- The hotel chain employs hundreds of people in three countries in Asia.

  這間連鎖旅館在亞洲的三個國家中雇用了數百人。

- When writing a cover letter for a job application, you should employ formal English.

  寫求職信時，你應該要使用正式的英語。

衍 employee *n.* 雇員；員工

衍 employer *n.* 雇主

衍 employment *n.* 雇用；受雇

關 contract employee 約聘人員

---

11 **evaluate** [ɪˋvæljʊ͵et] *v.* 考核

- Your supervisor will evaluate your performance two or three times a year.

  你的主管每年會考核你的表現二至三次。

說明 公司一般都會定期對員工進行 performance review「績效考核」。

同 appraise *v.* 鑑定

衍 evaluation *n.* 評量

---

12 **example** [ɪgˋzɛmp!] *n.* 典範；範例

- During the interview, Brad was asked to give four examples of when he improved workplace productivity.

  面試時，布萊德被要求提供四個他改善工作生產力的例子。

衍 exemplary *adj.* 典範的；楷模的；有代表性的

---

13 **full-time** [ˋfʊl͵taɪm] *adj.* 全職的

- Janice is a student, so she is unable to do a full-time job at the moment.

  珍妮絲是個學生，所以她現在不能做全職的工作。

說明 「全職員工」是 full-timer 或 full-time employee/staff。work full-time with . . . 則指「在（某公司）擔任全職工作」。

反 part-time *adj.* 兼職的

---

14 **headhunter** [ˋhɛd͵hʌntə] *n.* 獵人頭公司；獵才人員

- A headhunter contacted Joe and offered him an attractive salary to join a rival firm.

  一間獵人頭公司聯絡喬，並提出要以誘人的薪資將他挖角到一間競爭對手的公司。

說明 獵人頭公司亦常稱為 human resource service company「人力資源公司」，通常提供的是 job placement service「職業仲介服務」。

衍 headhunting *n.* 獵人頭；人才挖角

15 hire [haɪr] *v.* 雇用；租借

- The fruit farmer will hire extra workers to help with the harvest.

  那位果農將雇用額外的工人來幫他採收。

  說明 hire 可作名詞指「雇用」，亦可指「租用；使用費；工資」，如：car hire「租車」。

回 employ、rent *v.* 雇用；租借

反 fire、dismiss、discharge、lay off 開除；解雇；裁員

16 human resources 人力資源（部）；人事

- Most of your first day in the office will be spent with human resources.

  你到職日那天大部分的時間都會花在人力資源部。

  說明 常簡稱為 HR。

回 personnel *n.* 人事部門

17 internship [ˋɪntɝnˌʃɪp] *n.* 實習工作

- Maggie completed a short but very useful internship with a Paris-based fashion designer.

  瑪姬在一家位於巴黎的時裝設計公司做過一段短暫但很實用的實習工作。

衍 intern *n.* 實習生

關 trainee *n.* 練習生

18 interviewee [ˌɪntɝvjuˋi] *n.* 面試者；受訪者

- The nervous interviewee took a sip of water before the interview started.

  那位緊張的面試者在面試開始之前喝了一口水。

衍 interviewer *n.* 面試官；面試他人者

19 job description 工作說明

- Explaining things on the menu is part of a waiter's job description.

  解釋菜單上的品項是服務生工作內容的一部分。

  說明 description [dɪˋskrɪpʃən] 指「描寫；敘述；說明書」。

回 position description 職務描述

20 job fair 徵才博覽會

- The focus of the annual job fair this year is careers in engineering.

  今年年度徵才博覽會的焦點是工程領域裡的職業生涯。

回 career fair、career expo 就業博覽會

21 job opening 工作職缺
- The job opening is for experienced applicants only.
  這個職缺只開放給有經驗的應徵者。

📄 job vacancy 工作職缺

---

22 lay off 解雇；裁員
- The economy is suffering and many people are being laid off.
  現在經濟不景氣，許多人都被裁員。

  說明 原本指因為經濟不景氣等緣故而暫時解雇員工，等將來景氣好轉之後再回聘，但如今已無此意，現今常譯為「解雇；裁員」。

衍 layoff *n.* 解雇；裁員

---

23 leave without pay 無薪假；留職停薪
- If you have no vacation days left, you will have to take leave without pay.
  如果你的有薪假用完了，就得要請不支薪的假了。

📄 unpaid leave 無薪假
反 paid leave 有薪假期

---

24 move up 提升；升職；提高地位
- You will be able to move up the corporate ladder if you meet your monthly targets.
  如果你達到每月的目標，在公司裡就能晉升。

  常考片語 move up the corporate ladder 升職；在企業內晉升

📄 get promoted 升職

---

25 multitasking [ˌmʌltɪˈtæskɪŋ] *n.* 多重任務處理；多重任務執行
- Alex is not very good at multitasking and prefers to do every task separately.
  艾力克斯不是很擅長同時處理多項任務，他偏好每件事情分開做。

衍 multitask *v.* 一次處理多項工作

---

26 occupation [ˌɑkjəˈpeʃən] *n.* 職業；占領
- The young girl wants to focus on an occupation that helps people, so she will study to be a nurse.
  這位年輕女性想要著重在一種能夠幫助人的職業，所以她會攻讀護理以便成為護理師。

衍 occupy *v.* 占用；占領

27 on board 上任；加入

- It is exciting that we have a Japanese design team on board.

  有一個日本的設計團隊加入了我們真令人興奮。

關 join *v.* 加入

關 take office 公職的就職或上任

28 on the road 在旅途中；到處奔走

- The businessman is on the road for an average of seven days per month.

  那位商務人士每個月平均有七天在外四處奔波。

關 business trip 出差；商務旅行

29 on-the-job training 在職訓練

- It's OK if you aren't familiar with the machinery because you will receive on-the-job training.

  你不熟悉這個機器沒關係，因為你將會接受在職訓練。

關 pre-employment training 職前訓練

說明 有規模的企業常會在人力資源部下設 training manager 「訓練經理」一職，負責員工的專業能力進修和訓練課程。

30 overtime [ˋovɚˌtaɪm] *n.* 加班

- If there is a big order to complete, everybody must do overtime.

  如果有一筆大訂單需要完成，那麼每個人都必須要加班。

說明 「申請加班」則可說 apply for overtime。

常用詞彙 overtime pay 加班費

常考片語 work overtime 加班
claim overtime 申請加班費

- We occasionally work overtime in order to meet deadlines.

  我們為了趕上截止期限偶爾會加班。

31 paid vacation 有薪年假

- Your annual paid vacation is four weeks, but you can only take 14 consecutive days off.

  你每年的有薪年假是四週，但你只能連續請十四天。

反 unpaid vacation/leave 無薪假

說明 consecutive [kənˋsɛkjətɪv] 指的是「連續而不中斷的」。

32 paycheck [ˋpeˏtʃɛk] *n.* 薪資支票

- You will receive your paycheck on the first day of every month.

  你會在每個月的第一天收到你的薪資支票。

  [說明] 現在發放薪資通常不用支票而是直接匯入銀行帳戶，但 paycheck 可用來泛指員工的薪資。而在美國或加拿大常採用 weekly/biweekly paycheck「週薪／雙週薪」。

同 salary、wage *n.* 薪資

33 pension [ˋpɛnʃən] *n.* 退休金；津貼；補助金

- Mr. Smith has a small pension, so he cannot purchase luxuries on a regular basis.

  史密斯先生的退休金不多，所以他不能經常購買奢侈品。

同 retirement benefits 退休金

34 personnel [ˏpɜsəˋnɛl] *n.* 人員；員工；人事部

- All personnel are forbidden from using social media during office hours.

  所有員工都不得在上班時間使用社交媒體。

- Please contact the personnel manager for information about benefits.

  關於福利方面的資訊，請與人事經理聯繫。

同 staff、employees *n.* 全體職員；員工

同 human resources 人力資源部；人事部

35 pink slip 解雇通知單

- The company has been losing money for months, so it is inevitable that pink slips will be given out soon.

  公司幾個月來都在虧錢，所以不可避免地即將會有解雇通知單被發出來。

  [說明] pink slip 字面指「粉紅色的紙條」。這個詞彙源自二十世紀初，在美國公司老闆若要解聘員工，會在放薪資的信封裡夾帶一張用粉紅紙條寫的解雇通知，發放給不獲續聘的員工。即便現在的解雇通知不一定是粉紅色的，但此語已約定俗成而成為解雇通知書的同義詞了。

同 walking papers 解雇通知

36 position [pəˋzɪʃən] *n.* 職務；職位

- This position is more suitable for a single person because it requires a lot of travel.

  這個職位比較適合單身的人，因為它需要經常出差。

  常用詞彙 management position 管理職務

同 post *n.* 職位

37 **postgraduate** [post`grædʒəwət] *adj.* **大學畢業後的；研究生的** *n.* **研究生**

- Bob will take a postgraduate business course to further his knowledge of international trade.
  鮑伯會去上研究所的商業課程，以便拓展他對國際貿易的知識。

- John stayed at college for an extra year as a postgraduate.
  約翰以研究生的身分在大學多待了一年。

同 graduate *v.* 畢業 *n.* 畢業生

關 graduate school 研究所

字首 **post-** 表示「之後；後面」

post（在……之後）✚ graduate（畢業）
⬇
postgraduate 大學畢業後的；研究生的

其他同字首單字
- postmodern 後現代的（post + modern「現代的」）
- postwar 戰後的（post + war「戰爭」）

---

38 **probationary period** 試用期

- Ivan decided the job was too demanding, and he quit at the end of the three-month probationary period.
  艾文決定這份工作還是太嚴苛了，所以在三個月的試用期結束時辭職了。

說明 probationary [pro`beʃənˏɛrɪ] 指「試用的」。也常說成 probation period。

---

39 **proficient** [prə`fɪʃənt] *adj.* 精通的

- Harold is proficient in fixing computer problems.
  哈洛德精通於處理電腦相關的問題。

常考片語 be proficient/skilled in . . . 精通……

衍 proficiency *n.* 精通；熟練

---

40 **profile** [`proˏfaɪl] *n.* 個人簡介；輪廓；外形

- According to the lady's profile, she set up an investment company in New York three years ago.
  根據這位女士的個人簡介，她三年前在紐約創立了一家投資公司。

說明 作動詞指「畫……的輪廓；寫……的簡介」。

衍 high-profile *adj.* 高姿態的；備受矚目的

衍 low-profile *adj.* 低姿態的；低調的

SECTION B　必備詞彙

UNIT **3** Personnel 人事

41 qualification [͵kwɑləfə`keʃən] *n.* 資格；資格證明；證照；條件

• You don't have the right qualifications for the job on offer.

你並不具備現有職缺的合適資格。

說明 指「資格」時，常見用法為 qualifications for sth. 或 qualifications to do sth.。

- 同 capability *n.* 能力
- 同 credentials *n.* 資格證明
- 衍 qualify *v.* 使具有資格；使合格
- 衍 qualified *adj.* 具資格的；有能力的
- 衍 unqualified *adj.* 不符資格的
- 衍 overqualified *adj.* 資格超過要求的

42 recruit [rɪ`krut] *v.* 招募；招收

• It took a few months for the newspaper to recruit a new reporter.

這份報社花了好幾個月才招募到一位新記者。

說明 recruit 當名詞指「新來的人；新兵」。

- 衍 recruitment *n.* 招募
- 衍 recruiter *n.* 招聘人員

43 resignation [͵rɛzɪg`neʃən] *n.* 辭職

• Martin took responsibility for the huge mistake and handed in his resignation.

馬汀扛下那個大錯的責任，遞出了辭呈。

常考片語 hand in one's resignation 遞交辭呈

- 衍 resign *v.* 辭職

44 résumé [`rɛzə͵me] *n.* 履歷表

• Barry sent his résumé to a company and was invited for an interview a few days later.

貝瑞將他的履歷表寄給一家公司，幾天後收到面試邀請。

說明 意思等同於英式用法的 curriculum vitae [kə`rɪkjələm] [`vi͵taɪ] (CV)。

45 **retire** [rɪ`taɪr] *v.* 退休;撤退

衍 **retired** *adj.* 退休的

衍 **retiree** *n.* 已退休的人

衍 **retirement** *n.* 退休

- The musician retired at the age of 40 after making millions from his albums.

  那位音樂家透過其專輯賺進了數百萬元後,在四十歲的時候退休了。

- The mayor announced that he would retire from politics at the end of his term.

  市長宣布他任期結束後就要從政界退休。

說明 retire from sth. 指「自某處退休」,retire as sth. 則指「擔任某職務時退休」。

46 **salary** [`sælərɪ] *n.* 薪水;薪資

同 **wage**、**pay** *n.* 薪水;工資

- Your salary will increase if you are given a promotion.

  如果你被升職,你的薪水就會變多。

常用詞彙 basic/base salary 底薪
  monthly salary 月薪
  annual/yearly salary 年薪

47 **take over** 接替;接管

同 **step into sb.'s shoes** 接替某人的職位

- Kevin will take over as head of the advertising department starting next week.

  凱文下週開始將接管廣告部主管的職務。

說明 「頂替;代替某人」可用 to cover for . . .。

48 **unemployment rate** 失業率

反 **employment rate** 就業率

- The unemployment rate is predicted to rise this year due to the collapse of the domestic car industry.

  由於國產車產業的衰敗,今年的失業率預計會提高。

說明 unemployment [ˌʌnɪm`plɔɪmənt] 指「失業狀態;失業人數」。

49 **wage** [wedʒ] *n.* 薪水;工資

同 **pay**、**payment** *n.* 工資

- David makes sure that he saves a portion of his wages every month.

  大衛每個月都確保會將薪水的一部分存起來。

常用詞彙 minimum wage 最低工資

SECTION B 必備詞彙

UNIT *3* Personnel 人事

115

PRACTICE TEST

Part 1: Photographs

 TRACK 27

Directions:

For each question in this part, you will hear four statements about a picture. When you hear the statements, you must select the one statement that best describes what you see in the picture. Then circle the letter (A), (B), (C), or (D). The statements will not be printed below and will be spoken only one time.

(A)　(B)　(C)　(D)

(A)　(B)　(C)　(D)

Part 2: Question and Response

 TRACK 28

Directions:

You will hear a question or statement and three responses spoken in English. They will be spoken only one time and will not be printed below. Select the best response to the question or statement and circle the letter (A), (B), or (C).

3 (A)　(B)　(C)

4 (A)　(B)　(C)

5 (A)　(B)　(C)

6 (A)　(B)　(C)

Part 3: Short Conversations

 TRACK 29

Directions:

You will hear some conversations between two or more people. You will be asked to answer three questions about what the speakers say in each conversation. Select the best response to each question and circle the letter (A), (B), (C), or (D). The conversation will be spoken only one time and will not be printed below.

7 What is this conversation mainly about?

(A) Where Core Tech have advertised their job openings

(B) How to contact human resources at Core Tech

(C) Whether the woman should apply for a job at Core Tech

(D) Whether the woman has the right qualifications for a vacancy

8 How does the woman feel about applying for a job at Core Tech?

(A) She's confident that she'll get the job.

(B) She doesn't want to apply.

(C) She'd like to check other positions first.

(D) She's unsure if she has the right background.

9 What is implied about Core Tech?

(A) The two men used to work there but quit.

(B) The woman has long wanted to work there.

(C) They don't have many employees.

(D) They only advertise on social media.

NAME #	NOTES
Paul Lee	Experienced but nervous
Jock Green	Doesn't have degree required
Evan Isaacs	Qualified but over-confident
Sarah McAdams	Recent graduate so no experience

10 What is the woman's likely occupation?

(A) Trainee   (B) Secretary
(C) Interviewee   (D) HR Manager

11 What are the speakers doing?

(A) Checking résumés   (B) Deciding who to hire
(C) Interviewing candidates   (D) Appraising staff

12 Look at the graphic. Which candidate will not be considered?

(A) Paul Lee   (B) Jock Green
(C) Evan Isaacs   (D) Sarah McAdams

Part 4: Short Talks

 TRACK 30

Directions:

You will hear some short talks given by a single speaker. You will be asked to answer three questions about what the speaker says in each talk. Select the best response to each question and circle the letter (A), (B), (C), or (D). The talks will be spoken only one time and will not be printed below.

13 What is the purpose of this talk?

(A) To say farewell to someone who is leaving the company
(B) To congratulate someone on a promotion
(C) To evaluate an employee's successes at the company
(D) To explain how an employee was able to get new customers

14 What is implied about Bob's position at the company?
(A) The job will no longer exist.
(B) It was a relatively new post.
(C) His track record wasn't good.
(D) It involved a lot of traveling.

15 What does the man mean when he says, "It's really going to be tough for someone else to fill his shoes"?
(A) Bob's coworkers won't be familiar with his replacement.
(B) It will be impossible to find a replacement for Bob.
(C) It will be difficult for a new person to do such a good job.
(D) The company will need to provide new shoes for Bob.

Name: Charles Marden		Title: Licensing Manager
Description	**Earnings** (USD)	**Deductions** (USD)
Basic Salary	3,000.00	
Medical Allowance	300.00	
Company Pension Contribution	300.00	
Transport Allowance	200.00	
Meal Allowance	100.00	
Tax		100.00
TOTAL	**3,800.00**	

16 Who is being addressed?
(A) An employee who is being laid off
(B) An employee who has finished their probation
(C) An employee who has been promoted
(D) A contract employee

17 What is implied about Charles Marden?
(A) He was the only candidate for the position.
(B) The company decided to give him another chance.
(C) He was much more suitable than the other candidates.
(D) He didn't need to have any evaluations.

18 Look at the graphic. What was the employee's basic salary before the promotion?
(A) 3,500USD
(B) 3,000USD
(C) 2,900USD
(D) 2,700USD

Part 5: Incomplete Sentences

Directions:

A word or phrase is missing in each of the sentences below. Four answer choices are given below each sentence. Select the best answer to complete the sentence. Then circle the letter (A), (B), (C), or (D).

19 Personnel should fill out the necessary form once they return from _____ sick leave.

(A) their   (B) they

(C) them   (D) those

20 Only three people _____ for the chef position, probably due to the long hours they would have to work.

(A) apply   (B) applying

(C) applied   (D) applies

21 The job description says that it requires someone who is good at _____, doesn't it?

(A) personnel   (B) multitasking

(C) probation   (D) resignation

22 For this job, you will need to be proficient in _____ Microsoft Office and Adobe Photoshop.

(A) neither   (B) both

(C) either   (D) not only

23 When you begin your internship, you will need to _____ Mr. Jenkins.

(A) retire from   (B) lay off

(C) compensate for   (D) report to

Part 6: Text Completion

Directions:

Read the text below. A word, phrase, or sentence is missing. For each empty space in the text, select the best answer to complete the text. Then circle the letter (A), (B), (C), or (D).

Questions 24-27 refer to the following advertisement.

JOB FAIR
August 10, 11, 12
The Convention Center

TAKE YOUR CAREER IN THE RIGHT DIRECTION

Would you like to have a new occupation? Are you looking for on-the-job training? Would you like to ---24--- a post with the best employers in your industry? ---25--- You will have the opportunity to connect with employers, recruiters, and ---26--- from at least 200 local and international companies. You will be able to communicate your career goals to potential employers and, in addition, you can sign up for workshops on career development, essential proficiencies for today's jobs market, and résumé-writing and interview skills.

Register online at mycityjobfair.com and don't forget ---27--- your professional profile summary, and copies of your résumé and cover letter.

24 (A) take up   (B) take down
   (C) take note   (D) take away

25 (A) How would you like to get a postgraduate degree?
   (B) Then don't miss this year's Job Fair!
   (C) Where will your next adventure take you?
   (D) Would you like to take early retirement?

26 (A) headquarters   (B) headcounts
   (C) headlines   (D) headhunters

27 (A) brought   (B) to bring
   (C) bringing   (D) have bring

Part 7: Reading Comprehension

Directions:

In this part you will read a selection of texts, such as magazine and newspaper articles, e-mails, and instant messages. Each text is followed by several questions. Select the best answer for each question and circle the letter (A), (B), (C), or (D).

Questions 28-30 refer to the following e-mail.

To:	kelly@scholarsnote.com
From:	james@scholarsnote.com
Re:	Intern

Dear Kelly,

This is a quick message about our intern, Jeremy. Jeremy has been doing fantastic work down in our department and has been an invaluable asset since Caitlyn went on maternity leave. He is very friendly and efficient in his work and his communication skills are excellent. I really feel that he is able to take over any tasks that come up at the last minute and he never complains about the low wage or long working hours. I wanted to ask you about the possibility of offering Jeremy full-time employment at our company once his internship is up. I would hate to lose such a great team player to another company. What do you think? Do we have the capacity to offer him something?

Would love to know your thoughts, so please get back to me as soon as you can!

Thanks,

James

28 What is the purpose of the e-mail?

(A) To ask for someone to be headhunted

(B) To offer someone leave without pay

(C) To discuss a potential job offer

(D) To communicate a salary decrease

29 What is NOT mentioned as being one of the intern's qualities?

(A) He is never sick.

(B) He never complains.

(C) He is good at communicating.

(D) He is efficient.

30 The word "up" in paragraph 1, line 7, is closest in meaning to

(A) awake

(B) started

(C) high

(D) completed

Questions 31-34 refer to the following online chat discussion.

Tom Draper [9:05 a.m]
Hi guys. It's so great to have you two on board! I hope you are settling in well.

Susan Hill [9:07 a.m]
So far, so good!

Andy Hall [9:10 a.m]
It's great to be here. Everyone has been very helpful.

Tom Draper [9:11 a.m]
Good to know. Just a reminder that you will both have a 3-month probation period. After that, the sky's the limit! It's not hard to move up in this company if you work hard.

Susan Hill [9:15 a.m]
Good to know. Will you be doing an evaluation once our trial period is up?

Tom Draper [9:20 a.m]
That will be done by your supervisor in your department. We have employed a lot of new staff recently, so it makes sense to do it within each department.

Andy Hall [9:22 a.m]
Got it! Thanks.

Tom Draper [9:25 a.m]
OK, I'll let you get on with your work now. Unless you have any other questions for me?

Andy Hall [9:27 a.m]
Just one thing. My supervisor says there will be a lot of overtime hours this month due to the deadline. Will we be compensated for extra hours?

Tom Draper [9:30 a.m]
Of course! In addition to overtime payment, you can apply for an extra paid vacation day.

Susan Hill [9:35 a.m]
That's awesome!

31 Why will there be a lot of extra work hours this month?
(A) Work has to be finished by a certain date.
(B) Because everyone wants to get paid more.
(C) Many people have gone on vacation.
(D) Someone has handed in their resignation.

32 Who will be responsible for evaluations?
(A) Tom Draper
(B) A person from HR
(C) A manager of a department
(D) The CEO

33 What does Tom Draper imply about the company?
(A) Many people have retired recently.
(B) There are different options for compensation.
(C) The company had trouble hiring people.
(D) The company is doing poorly.

34 At 9:11 a.m., what does Tom Draper mean when he writes "the sky's the limit"?
(A) Andy and Susan will have to fly a lot.
(B) The company's prospects are limited.
(C) It's hard to move up within the probation period.
(D) Anything is possible for the two newcomers.

Unit 4 Manufacturing 製造業

本主題涵蓋內容包括：

- plant management 工廠管理
- assembly lines 生產線
- quality control 品管

WORD POWER

 TRACK 31

---

01 assemble [əˋsɛmbḷ] *v.* 配裝；組裝
- It will take the workers a few days to assemble the vehicle by hand.
  工人手工組裝這台車輛將會需要好幾天的時間。

◉ put together 組合

---

02 assembly line 生產線
- People who work on the assembly line must wear a helmet and protective clothing.
  在生產線上工作的人一定要戴安全帽並穿防護衣。

◉ production line
生產線

---

03 automated [ˋɔtometɪd] *adj.* 自動化的
- Many people were laid off when the factory became automated.
  當工廠變成自動化，許多人就被裁員了。

常用詞彙 automated factory 自動化工廠

衍 automate *v.* 自動化；
自動作業

衍 automation *n.*
自動化

衍 automatic *adj.* 自動的

---

04 batch [bætʃ] *n.* 一批（生產量）
- An employee ordered an extra batch of new chips to meet the demand.
  有位員工訂了一批額外的新晶片來滿足需求。

說明 batch 常用來表示一批一批不同時間生產的產品，如：the third batch of goods「第三批貨」。

◉ set、pack *n.* 一批

---

05 component [kəmˋponənt] *n.* 零件；組件
- The components made in Vietnam are cheaper than the ones made in Japan.
  越南生產的零件比日本生產的零件便宜。

◉ element、part *n.*
零件

衍 compose *v.* 組成；
構成

---

06 conform [kənˋfɔrm] *v.* 符合；遵守（+ to）
- All the work done in here needs to conform to high standards.
  這裡完成的所有工作都必須符合高標準。
- If guests refuse to conform to the no-smoking rule, they will be asked to leave the restaurant.
  如果顧客拒絕遵守禁菸規定，他們將會被要求離開餐廳。

衍 conformity *n.* 遵從；
一致

---

07 conveyor belt（生產線、機場行李等的）輸送帶
- Machines cover the doughnuts with icing as they move along a conveyor belt.
  當甜甜圈在輸送帶上往前移動時，機器將它們覆蓋上糖霜。

08 customize [ˋkʌstəmˏaɪz] *v.* 訂做
- The factory can customize any of its products if a client has a specific request.
  如果客戶有特殊需求，該工廠可以將他們的任何一項產品客製化。

衍 customized *adj.* 訂做的

衍 customization *n.* 客製化服務（按照客戶的個別需要進行產品製造）

衍 custom-made *adj.* 訂製的；非現成的

09 defect [ˋdɪˏfɛkt] *n.* 缺陷；瑕疵；缺點
- Before purchasing the object, the customer checked carefully to make sure there were no defects.
  購買這個物品之前，顧客仔細地檢查確定沒有任何瑕疵。

同 fault、flaw、weakness *n.* 缺點；瑕疵

衍 defective *adj.* 有缺陷的

10 device [dɪˋvaɪs] *n.* 設備；儀器；裝置
- I need to replace the cracked screen on one of my mobile devices.
  我需要更換我其中一個行動裝置上碎裂的螢幕。

同 gear、equipment *n.* 設備；裝置

11 electronics [ˏɪlɛkˋtrɑnɪks] *n.* 電子產品
- The factory manufactures small parts to be used in electronics.
  該工廠生產用在電子產品中的小零件。

同 electronic product 電子產品

常用詞彙 consumer electronics 消費性電子產品
　　　　 electronics industry 電子產業

12 examine [ɪgˋzæmən] *v.* 仔細檢查；檢測；測驗
- Your main jobs are examining the apples and packing them into boxes.
  你們主要的工作是仔細檢查這些蘋果，然後把它們包裝好放進盒子裡。

同 inspect、analyze、check over 仔細檢查

衍 examination *n.* 檢查；檢測；考試；測驗

13 extensive [ɪk`stɛnsɪv] *adj.* 大規模的；廣泛的

- Mr. Martin did extensive research and decided to open a factory in Taiwan and not China.
  馬汀先生做了大規模的研究之後，決定在台灣而非中國設廠。

🔄 broad *adj.* 廣泛的

✍ extensively *adv.* 廣泛地

---

14 facility [fə`sɪlətɪ] *n.* 設備

- The corporation decided to relocate its production facilities closer to home.
  該企業決定將生產設備遷移至離本國較近的地方。

🔄 amenity、building、structure *n.* 設施；建築

---

15 gadget [`gædʒɪt] *n.* 小機件

- The advertising team has come up with a great way to promote the gadget.
  廣告團隊想出了一個絕佳的方式來推銷這個小器具。

🔄 tool、device、instrument、appliance *n.* 用具

---

16 glitch [glɪtʃ] *n.* （設備、機器等的）小故障；小毛病

- The appliance store will give a full refund if there is a glitch in any of its machines.
  如果他們的任何一種機器故障，這間電器行都會提供全額退款。

常考片語▸ fix/correct the glitch 修正缺失

- Our engineers have corrected the glitches that users complained about.
  我們的工程師已經修正了那些被客訴的小問題。

🔄 malfunction *n.* 發生故障

---

17 goods [gʊdz] *n.* 商品；貨物

- You are not allowed to bring certain goods into the country.
  你不得攜帶某些商品入境這個國家。

常用詞彙▸ finished goods 成品

🔄 merchandise、commodity、product、item *n.* 商品；貨物

---

18 identify [aɪ`dɛntə͵faɪ] *v.* 辨認；鑑定

- It is easy to identify the company's products because they have a unique logo on them.
  要辨識這家公司的商品很簡單，因為它們上面都有一個獨特的商標。

🔄 distinguish *v.* 辨別出

✍ identification *n.* 識別；辨識

✍ identity *n.* 身分

19 in-house [`ɪn͵haʊs] *adv.* 內部完成而不假外力地
adj. 內部的
- It'll cost us more money to find someone to do this job, so we'll just have to try and do it in-house.
  找人來完成這份工作會花我們更多錢，所以我們將得試著在內部完成。

🔄 internally *adv.* 內部地

🔄 internal *adj.* 內部的

20 inspect [ɪn`spɛkt] *v.* 仔細檢查；稽查
- The meat-processing factory is inspected by health officials once a month.
  那間肉品加工廠每個月被衛生官員稽查一次。

🔄 examine、probe *v.* 檢查

🔄 inspector *n.* 檢查員；稽查員

🔄 inspection *n.* 檢查；檢驗

21 install [ɪn`stɔl] *v.* 安裝；設置
- After the robbery, the owner of the restaurant installed a more advanced security system.
  發生過搶案之後，那位餐廳老闆安裝了更先進的保全系統。

🔄 establish、inaugurate、instate *v.* 建立；開始；安置

🔄 installation *n.* 安裝

22 inventory [`ɪnvən͵tɔrɪ] *n.* 庫存；存貨；物品清單
- A clerk checks the inventory on a regular basis to see if he needs to replace anything.
  一位店員定期檢查庫存，以便確認他是否需要替換哪些品項。

🔄 stock *n.* 存貨

說明 inventory 亦可當動詞，指「盤點；清點庫存」。

常用詞彙 inventory control 庫存管理

23 machinery [mə`ʃɪnərɪ] *n.* 機械裝置
- It is dangerous to operate heavy machinery if you are tired or if you have consumed alcohol.
  如果你很累或喝了酒，操作重型機械是很危險的。

🔄 machine *n.* 機器；機械

24 maintenance [ˋmentənəns] *n.* 維修;保養
- Regular maintenance is performed on the elevators in the office building.
  辦公大樓的電梯有接受定期維修。

📙 care、upkeep、preservation *n.* 保養;維修

📗 maintain *v.* 維持;維修;保養

---

25 malfunction [mælˋfʌŋʃən] *n./v.* 故障;機能失常
- The machine had a malfunction but we've called someone to deal with the problem.
  機器發生故障,但我們已找人來處理這個問題。

- The computer malfunctioned when it was connected to an incompatible device.
  電腦連接到一個不相容的裝置時就故障了。

說明 字首 mal- 表示「壞;惡;不良」。

📙 breakdown、fault、glitch *n.* 故障

---

26 manufacturer [͵mænjəˋfæktʃərə] *n.* 製造業者;廠商
- Many clothing manufacturers are moving their factories out of China to other Asian countries.
  許多成衣業者正陸續將其工廠撤出中國並移至亞洲其他國家。

📗 manufacture *v.* 製造

📗 manufacturing *n.* 製造(業)

---

27 mechanic [məˋkænɪk] *n.* 技工
- The mechanic checked the air in the tires after fixing the engine.
  那位技師修理好引擎之後,檢查輪胎的胎壓。

📙 machinist、technician、repairman *n.* 技工

---

28 model [ˋmɑdl̩] *n.* 模型;型號
- Excited people lined up outside the store to buy the latest model of smartphone.
  興奮的人們在店外排隊要購買最新款的智慧型手機。

📙 type、version、shape、design *n.* 樣式;版本

---

29 on-site [ɑnˋsaɪt] *adj./adv.* 在現場的(地)
- There is a doctor on-site at all times to ensure the safety of the workers.
  有一位醫師隨時在現場確保工人的安全。

📕 off-site *adj./adv.* 不在現場的(地)

30 output [ˈaʊtˏpʊt] *n.* 產量 *v.* 出產；生產

- The only way to increase output is by building a bigger factory.

  增加產量的唯一方式就是蓋一間更大的工廠。

- The printer will output some test documents to make sure it has installed correctly.

  印表機會產生一些測試文件，確保它已被正確安裝。

同 production、manufacturing *n.* 生產；製造

同 yield、crop *n.* 產量；（同時產出的）一批

反 input *n.* 投入 *v.*（將資料等）輸入電腦

31 outsource [ˈaʊtˏsɔrs] *v.* 外包

- It is common for companies in developed countries to outsource services to countries where labor is cheaper.

  已開發國家的公司把服務外包給勞力較低廉的國家是很常見的。

衍 outsourcing *n.* 工作委外；外包

32 packaging [ˈpækɪdʒɪŋ] *n.* 包裝（業）；包裝材料

- You will receive a discount if you bring your own packaging to the store.

  如果你攜帶自己的容器到店裡，你將能得到折扣。

衍 package *n.* 包裹 *v.* 包裝

33 patent [ˈpætn̩t] *n.* 專利；專利權

- The young inventor has patents on his designs, so nobody can use them without his permission.

  那位年輕發明家擁有其設計的專利，所以沒有人可以未經允許使用它們。

同 license *n.* 許可；認可

關 trademark *n.* 商標

關 copyright *n.* 版權

34 plant [plænt] *n.* 工廠

- The plant was fined for releasing chemicals into the nearby river.

  那座工廠因為把化學物質排放到附近的河裡而被罰款。

同 factory、mill *n.* 工廠

35 procedure [prəˈsidʒɚ] *n.* 程序；步驟

- There are many complicated procedures to go through to set up a business in a foreign country.

  在國外設立一家公司有許多複雜的程序要執行。

同 process、course、step *n.* 程序；步驟

常用詞彙 standard operating procedure（SOP）
標準作業程序

SECTION B 必備詞彙

UNIT 4 Manufacturing 製造業

36 **product line** 產品系列
- In order to meet the demands of modern society, the fast food company expanded its product line by introducing vegetarian options.

  為了滿足當代的社會需求，那間速食餐廳將素食選項加入了他們的系列產品之中。

同 merchandise、line of products 商品（系列）

關 mass production 量產

---

37 **production** [prəˋdʌkʃən] *n.* 生產；產量；產物
- The factory increased production of its well-known products ahead of the Lunar New Year.

  那家工廠在農曆春節前增加了他們知名產品的生產量。

常用詞彙 production line 生產線
production process 生產流程

同 manufacture *n.* 製造；產品

衍 produce *v.* 生產；製造

衍 overproduction *n.* 生產過剩

---

38 **quality control** 品質管理（簡稱品管）
- We need to improve quality control because we have received many customer complaints.

  我們需要加強品管，因為我們已收到了許多客訴。

說明 常簡稱為 QC，如 QC history 指「品管記錄」、QC procedure 指「品管流程」、QC controller 指「品管員」。

同 quality assurance 品質保證

---

39 **ratio** [ˋreʃo] *n.* 比率
- The electrical item has a good price-performance ratio.

  這個電子產品的 CP 值很高。

說明 price-performance ratio 指「性能價格比」，亦作 cost-performance ratio，俗稱 CP 值。

---

40 **raw material** 原料
- Russia exports many raw materials to countries around the world.

  俄羅斯出口許多原料到全球各地。

同 natural resource、substance 原料

41 recall [rɪˋkɔl] v. 回收；召回

同 withdraw、call back 收回

- The company recalled one of its products due to a faulty battery.

該公司因為電池有問題而回收了他們的其中一樣商品。

說明 亦可當作名詞，如 order/issue a recall of . . . 即指「回收某項產品」。

字首 re- 可表「再度；回復」

re（再度；回復）＋ call（呼叫；叫喊）

↓

recall 回收；召回（把東西再叫回來）

其他同字首單字

- replace 取代；替換（re ＋ place「置放」）
- reunion 團聚；結合（re ＋ union「結合」）
- renew 更新（re ＋ new「新的」）

---

42 revenue [ˋrɛvəˏnju] n. 收入；營收

同 earnings n. 收入；工作所得（複數名詞）

- If revenues don't increase in the next few quarters, we will go out of business.

如果營收在未來幾季沒有增加，我們就會倒閉了。

常用詞彙 tax revenue（國家的）稅收
revenue forecast 營收預測

---

43 shortage [ˋʃɔrtɪdʒ] n. 短缺

同 lack、deficiency n. 缺少

- There is a shortage of certain vegetables, so prices in the market are generally higher at the moment.

現在某些蔬菜短缺，所以市場裡的價格一般都較高。

---

44 shut down 停工；關閉（機器、公司等）

同 close up、close down 停業

反 open up 開啟

- Many family-run shops are shutting down due to competition from huge supermarkets.

由於大型超市帶來的競爭，許多家庭經營的商店都關閉了。

說明 shutdown 則為名詞，指「停止運作」。

45 sort [sɔrt] *v.* 把……分類;整理

• Please sort these tubes by separating the red ones from the black ones.

請將這些管子分類,把紅色的和黑色的分開。

常考片語▸ sort out 解決;應付

• We had to call a plumber to come over and sort out a leak in the factory.

我們需要找一個水電工過來解決工廠漏水的問題。

🔄 categorize *v.* 將……分類

---

46 strike [straɪk] *n./v.* 罷工

• The factory workers have been striking over low pay and long working hours.

這群工廠工人因低薪和高工時而持續罷工。

🔄 walkout *n.* 罷工

🔄 walk out 罷工

🔗 revolt *n.* 反抗;造反

---

47 subcontract [sʌb`kɑntrækt] *v.* 分包;轉包

• If you subcontract minor work to another firm, you can focus on more important tasks.

如果你把較次要工作分包給另一間公司,你就可以專注在更重要的任務上。

衍 subcontractor *n.* 轉包商;分包者

字首 **sub-** 可表「下方;附屬」

sub(下方;附屬)✚ contract(合約)

↓

subcontract 分包;轉包(把合約向下分給別人做)

其他同字首單字

• subway 地下道;地下鐵(sub + way「道路」)
• submarine 海底的;潛艇(sub + marine「海的」)

---

48 warehouse [`wɛr͵haʊs] *n.* 倉庫

• The manufacturing company stores finished products in a warehouse, before later sending them to stores.

那間製造公司將成品儲存在倉庫,稍後才運送至商店。

🔄 storehouse、depot、depository *n.* 倉庫

---

49 wholesale [`hol͵sel] *adj./n./v.* 批發(的);躉售

• The wholesale fruit and vegetable market opens around five a.m.

這個蔬果批發市場大約在清晨五點左右開市。

反 retail *adj./n./v.* 零售(的)

PRACTICE TEST

Part 1: Photographs

TRACK 32

Directions:

For each question in this part, you will hear four statements about a picture. When you hear the statements, you must select the one statement that best describes what you see in the picture. Then circle the letter (A), (B), (C), or (D). The statements will not be printed below and will be spoken only one time.

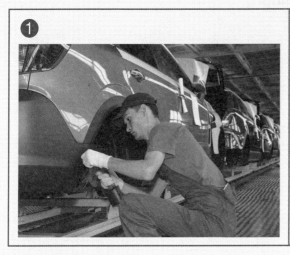

(A)   (B)   (C)   (D)   (A)   (B)   (C)   (D)

Part 2: Question and Response

TRACK 33

Directions:

You will hear a question or statement and three responses spoken in English. They will be spoken only one time and will not be printed below. Select the best response to the question or statement and circle the letter (A), (B), or (C).

 (A)   (B)   (C)

 (A)   (B)   (C)

❺ (A)   (B)   (C)

❻ (A)   (B)   (C)

Part 3: Short Conversations

 TRACK 34

Directions:

You will hear some conversations between two or more people. You will be asked to answer three questions about what the speakers say in each conversation. Select the best response to each question and circle the letter (A), (B), (C), or (D). The conversation will be spoken only one time and will not be printed below.

7 What are the speakers mainly discussing?

(A) Innovations in automation

(B) How to package goods

(C) Reducing their workforce

(D) Their factory's output

8 What does the woman suggest as a way to maintain output?

(A) Automating packaging

(B) Hiring more people

(C) Adding conveyor belts

(D) Laying people off

9 What is implied in the conversation?

(A) The company is facing a lot of competition.

(B) The workers in the factory are not happy.

(C) The assembly line employees are too slow.

(D) The company is struggling to make a profit.

REPORTED ISSUES	
Inspected by	**Issue found**
Tim Price	Paint peeling off
Greg Jones	Some scratches found
Alice Coulson	Size did not match standard
Peter Slane	Items damaged during packaging

10 What does the woman inform the man about?

(A) A list of quality control problems

(B) A list of new machinery to buy

(C) A list of damaged goods

(D) A list of quality control inspectors

11 What does the man think they should do?

(A) Run a quality control test

(B) Examine the machinery

(C) Change the packaging

(D) Speak to the team

12 Look at the graphic. Which inspector discovered the most serious problem?

(A) Alice Coulson

(B) Tim Price

(C) Greg Jones

(D) Peter Slane

Part 4: Short Talks

 TRACK 35

Directions:

You will hear some short talks given by a single speaker. You will be asked to answer three questions about what the speaker says in each talk. Select the best response to each question and circle the letter (A), (B), (C), or (D). The talks will be spoken only one time and will not be printed below.

13 What is the announcement about?

(A) An upcoming takeover

(B) The opening of a new plant

(C) A forthcoming merger

(D) The closure of the company

⓮ What does the speaker mean when she says, "this merger is in the best interest of our company"?

(A) It will benefit the company.　(B) It will be good for Global Toys.

(C) It will be interesting.　(D) It is not necessary.

⓯ Who most likely is the speaker?

(A) An assembly line worker　(B) A company director

(C) A mechanic　(D) A subcontractor

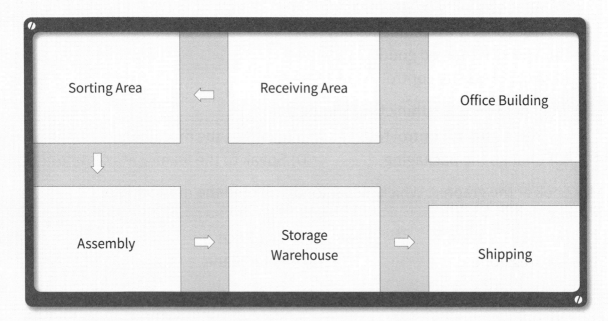

⓰ Who most likely are the listeners?

(A) Foreign tourists　(B) School students

(C) Potential clients　(D) Factory workers

⓱ What would the speaker like the listeners to do?

(A) Think about using this facility

(B) Make an appointment in the office

(C) Tour the plant by themselves

(D) Only visit the assembly line

⓲ Look at the graphic. Where will the listeners be unable to go today?

(A) The office building　(B) The receiving area

(C) The storage warehouse　(D) The sorting area

Part 5: Incomplete Sentences

Directions:

A word or phrase is missing in each of the sentences below. Four answer choices are given below each sentence. Select the best answer to complete the sentence. Then circle the letter (A), (B), (C), or (D).

19 The product was immediately recalled when it was discovered that babies could trap _____ fingers in it.

(A) them

(B) his

(C) its

(D) their

20 The new assembly line workers were shown how to _____ the products before they are packaged.

(A) put off

(B) put together

(C) put by

(D) put across

21 The manufacturing costs will largely depend on the size of the _____.

(A) shortage

(B) batch

(C) patent

(D) mechanic

22 A small factory was _____ to make some of the components for the production line.

(A) assembled

(B) customized

(C) subcontracted

(D) launched

23 This Indian company sells fabrics _____ to retailers, fashion designers, and other manufacturers.

(A) wholesale

(B) procedure

(C) maintenance

(D) industry

Part 6: Text Completion

Directions:

Read the text below. A word, phrase, or sentence is missing. For each empty space in the text, select the best answer to complete the text. Then circle the letter (A), (B), (C), or (D).

Questions 24-27 refer to the following article.

In a recent interview, Chief Operating Officer of GDE Manufacturing, Andrew Norwood, discussed how manufacturing businesses can use production data to improve operations. ---24--- The concept means that businesses ---25--- their production output in order to identify the batch with the highest quality and strongest cost-to-revenue ratio. Analyzing production data will reveal the factors that resulted in the "ideal batch". These could include materials, temperature, ---26--- speeds, most competent assembly line workers, etc. These insights can then ---27--- optimize production, which will improve efficiency, reduce costs, raise quality, and support ongoing improvements.

24 (A) Norwood has installed new software to analyze the data from his manufacturing plant.
   (B) Norwood believes that the concept of an "ideal batch" can be applied to most industries.
   (C) Norwood has decided to share his expertise on raw materials with other manufacturers.
   (D) Norwood believes that all assembly lines will be automated within the next ten years.

25 (A) examine   (B) assemble
   (C) install   (D) strike

26 (A) overproduction   (B) glitch
   (C) inventory   (D) machinery

27 (A) get used to   (B) be used to
   (C) used to   (D) use to

Part 7: Reading Comprehension

Directions:
In this part you will read a selection of texts, such as magazine and newspaper articles, e-mails, and instant messages. Each text is followed by several questions. Select the best answer for each question and circle the letter (A), (B), (C), or (D).

Questions 28-29 refer to the following press release.

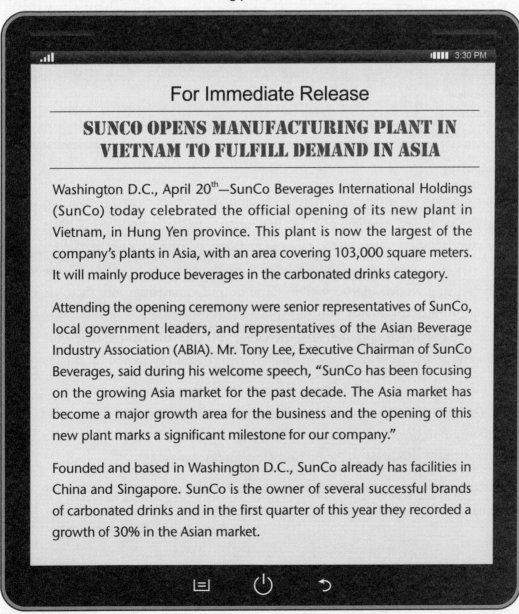

.ıll   ıllll 3:30 PM

For Immediate Release

SUNCO OPENS MANUFACTURING PLANT IN VIETNAM TO FULFILL DEMAND IN ASIA

Washington D.C., April 20th—SunCo Beverages International Holdings (SunCo) today celebrated the official opening of its new plant in Vietnam, in Hung Yen province. This plant is now the largest of the company's plants in Asia, with an area covering 103,000 square meters. It will mainly produce beverages in the carbonated drinks category.

Attending the opening ceremony were senior representatives of SunCo, local government leaders, and representatives of the Asian Beverage Industry Association (ABIA). Mr. Tony Lee, Executive Chairman of SunCo Beverages, said during his welcome speech, "SunCo has been focusing on the growing Asia market for the past decade. The Asia market has become a major growth area for the business and the opening of this new plant marks a significant milestone for our company."

Founded and based in Washington D.C., SunCo already has facilities in China and Singapore. SunCo is the owner of several successful brands of carbonated drinks and in the first quarter of this year they recorded a growth of 30% in the Asian market.

28 What is the purpose of this press release?

(A) To inform people of the expansion of an existing manufacturing plant

(B) To inform people of a company's decision to enter the Asian market

(C) To inform people of the opening of a new manufacturing facility

(D) To inform people of a speech made by the chairman of SunCo Beverages

29 Who was NOT mentioned as being present at this event?

(A) Local government leaders   (B) Local beverage suppliers

(C) Senior managers from SunCo   (D) ABIA representatives

Questions 30-34 refer to the following e-mail and production cost outline.

To:	Jack Greenfield
From:	Justin Moore
Subject:	Production cost outline

Dear Mr. Greenfield,

Following our meeting yesterday, I am hereby sending you the requested production cost outline. The proposed new line of in-ear headphones will be comprised of parts made in our own factories, unless stated otherwise. There is currently a big market for sports earphones and, as you know, our factories have the capacity to produce large batches that can ship worldwide. As well as large output capabilities, our factories also never compromise on quality and our quality control operations are some of the strictest in the manufacturing industry. Therefore, you can rest assured that what you are delivering to the consumer will adequately reflect your reputation for quality electronics.

Please note: Due to the fact that you are making a large order and in the hope we can do more business in future, I am pleased to inform you that I have lowered the cost per unit for each electronic component. Please see below for further details.

Please contact me once you have had a chance to review the cost outline and let me know if you have any questions.

Best Regards,

Justin Moore
Production Manager
LBJ Group Inc.

Planned Production Cost Outline for Elite Electronics	
Total Units: 10,000	

Cost Per Unit:

Plastic casing	$2.00/unit
Rubber ear buds	$1.50/unit
Electronic components (supplied by X-Electronics)	$5.00/unit
Wire	$1.00/unit
Packaging (supplied by Excel Cardboard)	$0.20/unit
In-house labor (0.25 hours/unit)	$3.80/unit
Total Direct Cost/Unit	$13.50/unit
Direct Cost	$13.50/unit x 10,000 units = $135,000.00
	Tax = $13,500.00
	Total Production Costs = $148,500.00

30 What is the main purpose of Mr. Moore's e-mail?

(A) To state why the company should produce more earphones

(B) To provide a cost outline to a potential customer

(C) To invoice a customer for work that has been carried out

(D) To explain why some components cannot be made in-house

31 Why does Mr. Moore mention his company's ability to produce large batches?

(A) It is a cheaper way to manufacture electronics.

(B) Quality control is easier for large quantities.

(C) There is a big demand for sports headphones.

(D) Only large batches can be shipped worldwide.

32 How many units does Mr. Moore give Mr. Greenfield a quote for?

(A) 135,000

(B) 13,500

(C) 10,000

(D) 20,000

㉝ Which of the following components will not be made in-house at LBJ Group's factories?

(A) Plastic casing

(B) Rubber ear buds

(C) Wire

(D) Electronics

㉞ What was the original cost per unit price of the electronic components, before the adjustment?

(A) $5.25

(B) $5.00

(C) $3.80

(D) $2.00

Unit 5 Purchasing 採購

本主題涵蓋內容包括：

- shopping 採買
- ordering supplies 訂貨
- shipping 送貨
- invoices 發票

WORD POWER

 TRACK 36

01 abundant [ə`bʌndənt] *adj.* 大量的；豐富的
- That store offers an abundant selection of stationery and office supplies.

  那家店提供豐富的文具和辦公用品選擇。

同 plentiful、ample
adj. 豐富的；充裕的

衍 abundance *n.* 豐富；充裕

---

02 appliance [ə`plaɪəns] *n.* 器材；用具；設備
- If your appliance doesn't come with a manual, you can find it online.

  如果你的電器沒有附說明書，你可以在網路上找到。

同 device *n.* 設備

---

03 assure [ə`ʃur] *v.* 向⋯⋯保證；擔保
- The sales assistant assured the customer that the product was high quality.

  那名銷售助理向顧客保證商品是高品質的。

衍 assurance *n.* 保證

常考片語 assure sb. of sth. 向某人保證某事
- You won't find a better price on this. I can assure you of that.

  這個商品你找不到更好的價格了。我可以跟你保證。

---

04 carrier [`kærɪə] *n.* 運輸公司；運送者
- The carrier did not say why the order had been delayed.

  運輸公司並未說明為什麼訂單延遲送達。

同 shipper *n.* 運輸公司；運送者

---

05 catalog [`kætə‚lɔg] *n.* 目錄；型錄；清單
- You can see a full range of our products here in this catalog.

  你可以在這本型錄中的這裡看到我們產品的完整品項。

關 list *n.* 清單；目錄

說明 英式拼法為 catalogue。catalog 亦可當動詞，指「將⋯⋯編入目錄」。

常用詞彙 product catalog 產品目錄

06 clarify [ˈklærəˌfaɪ] *v.* 闡明；使清楚

- I'd like you to clarify some details about the product before I buy.

  在我購買之前，我想請你解釋一下這個產品的一些細節。

同 explain、elaborate on 解釋；闡明

---

07 commodity [kəˈmɑdətɪ] *n.* 商品

- A "buyer's market" is when the price is low because there is a large amount of a commodity available.

  買方市場指的是當有大量商品可供販售而使價格下降的時候。

同 merchandise、goods *n.* 商品

---

08 complaint [kəmˈplent] *n.* 抱怨

- I have a complaint about a product I bought which is not working properly.

  我要對一個我購入的商品提出客訴，它並未正常運作。

衍 complain *v.* 抱怨

常考片語 file a complaint 提出投訴／抱怨

- Several staff members filed complaints about the way they were treated.

  數名員工就他們所受到的待遇提出投訴。

---

09 coupon [ˈkupɑn] *n.* 折價券；優待券

- With this coupon, you can get buy-one-get-one-free on your next order with us.

  有了這張折價券，您下次於本店消費時就能享買一送一的優惠。

關 voucher *n.* 票券；（具貨幣價值的）商品券

常用詞彙 discount coupon 折價券

---

10 credit [ˈkrɛdɪt] *v.* 把⋯⋯記入（帳戶或貸方等）；把⋯⋯歸因於 *n.* 信用；信貸；賒欠（常用來指用信用卡付款）

- We have credited your account with money back. Please accept our apologies.

  我們已將退款記入您的戶頭。請接受我們的道歉。

- The bank checked Brian's credit history before giving him the loan.

  銀行在貸款給布萊恩之前先檢查了他的信用紀錄。

同 ascribe、attribute *v.* 把⋯⋯歸因於

說明 credit 作名詞指「信用」，作動詞可指「將某一金額加入某一帳戶中」，如銀行帳戶、公司往來的信用帳戶或顧客於某商店所開的個人消費帳戶等。

11 customer [ˋkʌstəmɚ] *n.* 顧客;客戶

- It seems like we can get more customers if we offer free giveaways outside the store.
  如果我們在店外提供贈品,似乎就可以招到更多顧客。

常用詞彙 customer service 客戶服務
　　　　regular/repeat customer 常客;老顧客

同 guest、patron、client *n.* 客人;客戶

關 consumer *n.* 消費者

---

12 delivery [dɪˋlɪvərɪ] *n.* 傳送;傳遞

- Your delivery will arrive between February 3 and February 7.
  您的貨運將會在二月三號至七號之間送達。

常用詞彙 delayed delivery 延期交貨
　　　　delivery date 交貨日期

同 shipping *n.* 運輸(業)

衍 deliver *v.* 傳送;傳遞

---

13 eligible [ˋɛlədʒəbəl] *adj.* 有資格的;合格的

- Congratulations! You are eligible for a 10% discount on your next order!
  恭喜!您符合下一筆消費享九折的優惠!

衍 eligibility *n.* 具資格

---

14 estimate [ˋɛstəmət] *n.* 估價(單)
　　　　　　[ˋɛstəˏmet] *v.* 估計;估量

- Bill, can you contact StarWood and ask them to give us an estimate on 500 chairs, please?
  比爾,能請你聯絡星木公司並請他們給我們五百張椅子的估價嗎?

- We estimate that the total will be around 10,000 US dollars, but we will let you know when we know the exact number.
  我們估計總額將會是一萬美元左右,但我們知道確切數字時會再告知您。

說明 作動詞時也可指「評價;判斷」。

常用詞彙 rough estimate 粗略估計
　　　　conservative estimate 保守估計

同 guesstimate *n./v.*【口】猜測;估計

15 expect [ɪk`spɛkt] *v.* 預期；期待

- Thank you for your interest in the product. We expect to hear from you shortly.

  謝謝您對此產品感興趣。我們期待很快就能收到您的消息。

衍 expectable *adj.*
可預期的

衍 expectation *n.*
預期；期望

衍 expectancy *n.*
期待；期望的事物

---

16 flaw [flɔ] *n.* 缺點；瑕疵 *v.* 使有缺陷

- If the product has a flaw, you may return it within 30 days and receive your money back.

  如果這個產品有瑕疵，您可以在三十天之內退還且收到退款。

- The boss rejected our plan, saying that it was flawed in a few key areas.

  老闆駁回了我們的計畫，說它在某些關鍵方面有瑕疵。

同 defect、crack、
fault *n.* 缺點

---

17 fluctuate [`flʌktʃʊ͵et] *v.* 波動；震盪

- Ice cream sales fluctuate according to the weather.

  冰淇淋的銷量隨著天氣而波動。

衍 vary *v.* 變化

衍 fluctuation *n.* 波動；
變動

---

18 freight [fret] *n.* 貨運；貨物；運費

- This aircraft company deals with freight only; it has no passenger service.

  這間飛航公司只處理貨運業務；它不提供客運服務。

常用詞彙 freight company 貨運公司

同 shipment *n.* 貨運

---

19 guarantee [͵gærən`ti] *v.*（商品）保固 *n.* 保證書

- The product is guaranteed for the first two years.

  該產品附有頭兩年的保固。

- This letter of credit serves as a guarantee that you will be paid.

  這張信用狀即為您會收到貨款的憑證。

說明 letter of credit「信用狀」可簡寫為 LOC、LC、L/C，是國際間重要的付款方式之一。在國際貿易中，由於買賣雙方對彼此了解不深，無法明確掌握對方的信用，故買方會主動請銀行開立付款文據，即「信用狀」，請開狀銀行擔保買方的信用。

常用詞彙 lifetime guarantee 終生保固
satisfaction guaranteed 保證滿意

同 warrant、promise
v. 保固；應允

同 warranty *n.* 保證書

20 **in bulk** 大量；大批

- We should buy in bulk because the price per unit will be cheaper.

  我們應該大量購買，因為每單位的價格會比較便宜。

  說明 「大宗買入／賣出」可說 to buy/sell in bulk。

圓 in great numbers 大量地；大批地

關 bulk order 大筆訂單

---

21 **invoice** [ˋɪnˏvɔɪs] *n.* 發票；發貨清單

- Please pay the final invoice within two weeks.

  請在兩週內支付最後的發票金額。

  說明 「開立發票」可用 make/write out an invoice。

  常用詞彙 invoice amount 發票金額
  invoice number 發票號碼

關 bill *n.* 票據；單據；帳單

---

22 **item** [ˋaɪtəm] *n.* 項目；品項

- Jill bought too many items to carry by herself, so she asked Jack to help her.

  吉爾一個人在超市買了太多東西，所以她請傑克來幫她。

  常用詞彙 collector's item 收藏品

圓 article、thing *n.* 物品

---

23 **lump sum** 一次付清（的款項）

- If you have enough money now, you can pay in one lump sum.

  如果你現在有足夠的錢，你可以一次付清。

  說明 lump 作形容詞有「整個的；總共的」之意。「整筆一次付清」是 pay in one lump sum，而 pay in installments 則是「分期付款」。

---

24 **minimize** [ˋmɪnəˏmaɪz] *v.* 使減到最少；使縮到最小

- We are trying to minimize the impact of price rises on our customers.

  我們正試著盡可能減少漲價對我們顧客的衝擊。

反 maximize *v.* 使增加到最大

衍 minimum *adj.* 最小的；最低的 *n.* 最小數；最低限度

衍 minimization *n.* 最小化

25 net weight 淨重

- Without the packaging, the net weight of these beans is 400 grams.

  不含包裝，這些豆子的淨重是四百克。

  說明 gross weight 則指「總重量」，一般譯為「毛重」，即貨物本身加上包裝材料的重量。

26 notify ［ˋnotəˏfaɪ］ v. 正式通知；告知

同 inform v. 通知；告知

衍 notification n. 通知；告知

- Please notify me of any changes to the delivery schedule.

  運送的時程若有任何更動請通知我。

  說明 常見的句型為 notify sb. of sth. 或 notify sb. + that 子句，表示「通知某人某事」。

27 open account 記帳交易

- We could accept open account payments to gain an advantage over the competition, but the risk is that clients won't pay.

  為了在市場競爭中取得優勢，我們接受記帳交易的付款方式，但風險就是客戶不付款。

  說明 常簡稱為 O/A。這種交易方式指的是出口商依照買賣雙方簽訂的契約把貨物交運後，賣方直接把貨運單據寄給進口商去提貨，等到約定的付款時間到了才交付貨款。

28 order ［ˋɔrdə］ n./v. 訂購；訂貨；點餐

- Your order has been received and payment accepted.

  我們已經收到您的訂單，也接受了您的付款。

  常考片語 place an order 下單；訂貨

- I will be able to offer a better deal if you place an order today.

  如果你今天下單，我可以提供更優惠的價格。

29 packing list 裝箱單；送貨明細

- When you receive your items, please check that the type and amount are the same as on the packing list.

  當你收到貨品時，請確認種類和數量都符合送貨明細上的資料。

  說明 指一批貨物裝運的明細表。

30 pallet [ˋpælɪt] *n.* （裝卸、搬運貨物用的）貨板

關 packing case 板條箱；裝貨箱

- Most companies ship their bulk orders on pallets, which makes storage, handling, and transportation easier.
  大部分的公司以貨板運送大筆訂單，這種方式讓倉儲、管理與運輸更為容易。

  說明 貨板一般為木製的，但也有用塑膠、金屬甚至是紙板做成的。

31 parcel [ˋpɑrs!] *n.* 包裹

同 package *n.* 包裹

- Harry wasn't at home, so I signed to receive his parcel.
  哈利那時不在家，所以我簽收了他的包裹。

32 partner [ˋpɑrtnɚ] *v.* 與……合作（或合夥）*n.* 合夥人

衍 partnership *n.* 合夥（或合作）關係

- Nike partners with famous basketball players to release special sneakers such as Air Jordan.
  耐吉與知名籃球員合作推出了特別版球鞋，如「飛人喬丹」系列。

- The agreement between the business partners is based on several conditions.
  這兩個商業夥伴之間的合約是奠基在幾個條件之上。

33 pay on/upon delivery 貨到付款

關 cash on delivery 貨到付現

- You have the option to pay either in cash or by card upon delivery.
  您可以選擇貨到時以現金或信用卡付款。

34 payment in advance 預先付款

關 deferred payment 延後付款

- In order to reduce risk, our company's policy is to only accept payments in advance.
  為了降低風險，我們公司的政策是只接受預先付款。

  說明 為國際貿易主要條款之一，其作法是：出口商交運貨物前，由進口商先付貨款予出口商。

35 payment terms 付款條件

關 payment method 付款方式

- Our payment terms state clearly when we expect to be paid by.
  我們的付款條件明確表明我們預期最晚在何時要收到款項。

36 procurement [proˋkjurmənt] *n.* 採購；取得　　衍 procure *v.* 取得
- The government is reported to have a large budget for the procurement of military supplies.
  根據報導政府擁有龐大的預算來採購軍用品。

37 purchase [ˋpɜtʃəs] *v./n.* 買；購買　　同 buy *v.* 買
- To save money, Bob and Jane decided not to make any more major purchases over the next six months.
  為了省錢，鮑伯和珍決定不在未來半年內做任何高額的採購。

常用詞彙 purchase order 訂購單

38 quantity [ˋkwɑntətɪ] *n.* 數量；數額　　同 amount *n.* 數量
- We make only a little profit on each item, but we plan to sell a high quantity.
  我們每個品項的獲利很低，但我們計畫大量銷售。

說明 in quantity 意思是「大量地」，而 in large/small quantities 則分別指「大／小量地」。

常用詞彙 maximum quantity 最大數量

39 rebate [ˋribet] *n.* 折扣；貼現；退還部分付款　　同 allowance、discount *n.* 津貼；折扣
- Visitors to the country can get a tax rebate at the airport.
  這個國家的遊客可以在機場申請退稅。

說明 國外商家常以 cash rebate 作為推銷商品的手法。消費者購物後可依商品之優惠內容獲得一小部分現金退還的折扣優惠。

40 receipt [rɪˋsit] *n.* 收據　　同 sales slip、proof of purchase 售貨憑證；購物證明
- Keep your receipt as proof of purchase.
  要保留您的收據作為購買證明。

關 invoice *n.* 發票

41 refund [ˋriˏfʌnd] *v./n.* （提供）退款　　衍 refundable *adj.* 可退錢的
- We will not refund you the price of the phone if the damage was caused by a person.
  如果是人為損害，我們不會退回手機的銷售金額。

SECTION B 必備詞彙 | UNIT 5 Purchasing 採購

42 restock [rìˋstɑk] *v.* 補貨；重新進貨

- We had to restock the shelves regularly due to high customer demand.

  因為消費者的大量需求，我們必須經常補貨上架。

🔵 replenish *v.* 把……再補足

---

43 rush order 緊急訂單；急件

- We will be charged more if we need it by Friday, as it would be a rush order.

  如果我們週五前就要，我們將被收取較高額的費用，因為那將是急件。

常考片語 place/take a rush order 下訂／接受急件訂單

- I placed a rush order so it will arrive tomorrow.

  我下訂了一份緊急訂單，所以貨明天就會送到了。

---

44 shipment [ˋʃɪpˏmənt] *n.* 貨運物；貨運

- The US sent a large shipment of urgent medical supplies to the country with the disease.

  美國運了大量緊急醫療用品到染上那種疾病的國家。

衍 ship *v.* 運送

衍 shipping *n.* 運輸（業）

說明 貨運業一般都會有貨運追蹤系統（shipment tracking system），客戶只須提供訂單號碼便可查詢貨物的配送狀況。

常用詞彙 shipment status 貨運狀況
shipping terms 運貨條件

---

45 subtract [səbˋtrækt] *v.* 減掉；扣掉

- To apologize for the misunderstanding, we subtracted the service charge from your meal.

  為了因之前的誤解致上歉意，我們扣除了您用餐的服務費。

🔵 deduct *v.* 扣除

反 add *v.* 加

衍 subtraction *n.* 減；減少

關 subtotal *n.* 小計

46 supply [sə`plaɪ] *v.* 供應

- The factory agreed a five-year deal to supply the computer company with screens.

  工廠同意簽署一份五年的合約，為該公司供應螢幕。

  說明 supply 作名詞時指「供給；供應量；存貨；補給品」，如：
  water supply「供水」、electricity supply「供電」。

  常用詞彙 supply and demand 供需（關係）

同 provide *v.* 提供；供應

衍 supplier *n.* 供應者；供應商

---

47 surcharge [`sɝˏtʃɑrdʒ] *n.* 額外費用 *v.* 對……收取附加費

- There is a surcharge for bringing overweight baggage on the plane.

  攜帶超重行李上飛機將產生額外費用。

- The ATM machine surcharges users $2 every time they take out money.

  自動提款機針對每筆提款向使用者收取兩塊美金的額外費用。

同 additional charge 額外費用

---

48 throw in 外加；額外贈送

- We'll throw in a free phone if you sign a contract today.

  如果您今天簽約，我們就會額外贈送一支手機。

  說明 「免費贈品」可用 complimentary gift。

同 add *v.* 增加

---

49 transfer inventory 調貨

- The transportation cost of transferring inventory from seller to buyer was significant.

  把商品從賣家調貨給買家所衍生的運輸成本是很可觀的。

  說明 inventory [`ɪnvənˏtorɪ] 指「存貨清單；存貨盤存」。

關 transfer *n.* 遷移；轉移

---

50 warranty [`wɔrəntɪ] *n.* 保證書；擔保

- The computer comes with a two-year warranty, meaning we'll repair it free of charge if any problems occur.

  這台電腦有附兩年保固，這表示如果發生任何問題，我們會免費修理。

同 guaranty *n.* 保證書；擔保

衍 warrant *v.* 向……保證；擔保

PRACTICE TEST

Part 1: Photographs

TRACK 37

Directions:

For each question in this part, you will hear four statements about a picture. When you hear the statements, you must select the one statement that best describes what you see in the picture. Then circle the letter (A), (B), (C), or (D). The statements will not be printed below and will be spoken only one time.

(A)   (B)   (C)   (D)   (A)   (B)   (C)   (D)

Part 2: Question and Response

TRACK 38

Directions:

You will hear a question or statement and three responses spoken in English. They will be spoken only one time and will not be printed below. Select the best response to the question or statement and circle the letter (A), (B), or (C).

❸ (A)   (B)   (C)

❹ (A)   (B)   (C)

❺ (A)   (B)   (C)

❻ (A)   (B)   (C)

Part 3: Short Conversations

 TRACK 39

Directions:

You will hear some conversations between two or more people. You will be asked to answer three questions about what the speakers say in each conversation. Select the best response to each question and circle the letter (A), (B), (C), or (D). The conversation will be spoken only one time and will not be printed below.

7 Why is the woman contacting the supplier?

    (A) To open an account

    (B) To clarify payment terms

    (C) To request a refund

    (D) To ask for an estimate

8 What is implied about the man's company?

    (A) It sells a wide range of food products.

    (B) It's currently having some problems.

    (C) Their main business is shipping.

    (D) They have enough desks for the woman.

9 What does the man mean when he says "get hold of"?

    (A) To succeed in getting something

    (B) To talk to somebody face to face

    (C) To talk to somebody on the phone

    (D) To test a product before buying it

10 What is the man buying?

(A) Christmas gifts for his kids   (B) Some gifts for his coworkers

(C) A Christmas tree for his family   (D) A gift for someone called Harry

11 How does the man pay?

(A) With coupons only   (B) By credit card and a coupon

(C) With credit card only   (D) By cash and with a coupon

12 Look at the graphic. What does the man buy?

(A) Dolls   (B) Toy cars

(C) Clothes   (D) Board games

Part 4: Short Talks

Directions:

You will hear some short talks given by a single speaker. You will be asked to answer three questions about what the speaker says in each talk. Select the best response to each question and circle the letter (A), (B), (C), or (D). The talks will be spoken only one time and will not be printed below.

13 What is the purpose of the talk?

(A) To educate staff on medical care procedures

(B) To teach staff about customer care

(C) To prepare actors for a movie about shopping

(D) To discuss methods of managing stress

⑭ Who is being addressed?

    (A) A company's VIP customers

    (B) Lawyers and accountants

    (C) A company's management team

    (D) Service staff

⑮ When does the speaker think you may not want to deal with a customer?

    (A) When you are having a bad day

    (B) When the customer is right and you're wrong

    (C) When you have problems with your boss

    (D) When you have forgotten their name

Items	Price
Calculator	$10
Pen (black/blue/red)	$0.99
Eraser	$0.49
Stapler (small/medium/large)	$3/5/8
Sticky Tape	$1.99

⑯ What was the problem that caused the woman to make the call?

    (A) She couldn't find the right number.

    (B) She couldn't make an order online.

    (C) She sent an e-mail that was rejected.

    (D) She made an order that wasn't delivered.

⑰ How can the woman pay?

    (A) Only in advance

    (B) Only upon delivery

    (C) Neither in advance nor on delivery

    (D) Both in advance and on delivery

⑱ Look at the graphic. What is the subtotal for the staplers?

    (A) $10   (B) $30

    (C) $50   (D) $80

Part 5: Incomplete Sentences

Directions:

A word or phrase is missing in each of the sentences below. Four answer choices are given below each sentence. Select the best answer to complete the sentence. Then circle the letter (A), (B), (C), or (D).

19 Regrettably, we have had to stop offering the _____ account option to all buyers, due to several late and missed payments.
(A) purchase
(B) payment
(C) closed
(D) open

20 Management feels we can improve our efficiency, so they are considering the _____ of a new software system.
(A) pallet
(B) partner
(C) procurement
(D) parcel

21 The advertised cost of the flight ticket is $419, but that will rise to $449 after _____ are added.
(A) lump sums
(B) invoices
(C) flaws
(D) surcharges

22 This particular hotel _____ an extra night for you if you choose to stay for three nights or longer.
(A) has thrown in
(B) will throw in
(C) would throw in
(D) would have thrown in

23 Computers bought within the last two years are still under _____ and are therefore eligible for free inspection and repairs if necessary.
(A) warranty
(B) rebate
(C) freight
(D) net weight

Part 6: Text Completion

Directions:

Read the text below. A word, phrase, or sentence is missing. For each empty space in the text, select the best answer to complete the text. Then circle the letter (A), (B), (C), or (D).

Questions 24-27 *refer to the following e-mail.*

To:	174 recipients
From:	paul.franks@mtla.com
Subject:	The 11th Annual Maryville Tech Manufacturing Trade Show (5/25)

Dear Manager/Owner,

Please make space in your calendar now for the tech manufacturing industry event of the year! The 11th Annual Maryville Tech Manufacturing Trade Show ---24--- on Tuesday, May 25th, from 9:30 a.m. – 3:30 p.m. at the Maryville Conference Center, at 49 Lindon Road, Maryville.

Invite employees to gain insightful information on the latest technology and network with major ---25--- in the industry. Expect more than 100 vendors to be on hand, showing off the latest exciting products. Educational sessions on current industry topics will also be offered free of charge during the event. ---26--- Everyone attending the event will be entered automatically into the competitions and has a chance to win. We ---27--- that this is an event you can't miss!

For more information, call Tiana Rhodes of the Maryville Tech Association at 504-334-0816, or e-mail t.rhodes@mtech.com.

Sincerely,

MTLA Tradeshow Committee

㉔ (A) will be held　　　　　(B) was held
　　(C) are held　　　　　　(D) has been held

㉕ (A) catalogs　　　　　　(B) appliances
　　(C) dealers　　　　　　(D) freights

㉖ (A) Get a first glimpse of technology no one has seen yet.
　　(B) What's more, there will be over $5,000 in cash prizes.
　　(C) Send us an e-mail or telephone us to find out more.
　　(D) But bringing your own lunch won't be necessary.

㉗ (A) deliver　　　　　　(B) fluctuate
　　(C) minimize　　　　　(D) guarantee

Part 7: Reading Comprehension

Directions:

In this part you will read a selection of texts, such as magazine and newspaper articles, e-mails, and instant messages. Each text is followed by several questions. Select the best answer for each question and circle the letter (A), (B), (C), or (D).

Questions 28-29 refer to the following text message chain.

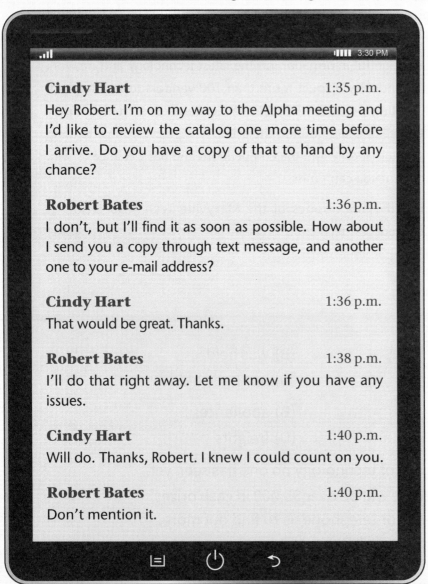

Cindy Hart   1:35 p.m.

Hey Robert. I'm on my way to the Alpha meeting and I'd like to review the catalog one more time before I arrive. Do you have a copy of that to hand by any chance?

Robert Bates   1:36 p.m.

I don't, but I'll find it as soon as possible. How about I send you a copy through text message, and another one to your e-mail address?

Cindy Hart   1:36 p.m.

That would be great. Thanks.

Robert Bates   1:38 p.m.

I'll do that right away. Let me know if you have any issues.

Cindy Hart   1:40 p.m.

Will do. Thanks, Robert. I knew I could count on you.

Robert Bates   1:40 p.m.

Don't mention it.

28 Where is Ms. Hart at the time of the conversation?

(A) In a meeting room (B) In her company's office

(C) On the way back to her office (D) On the way to a meeting

29 At 1:40 p.m., what does Ms. Hart mean when she tells Mr. Bates "I knew I could count on you"?

(A) She thinks Mr. Bates is good at math.

(B) She thinks Mr. Bates is easy to find.

(C) She thinks Mr. Bates is always reliable.

(D) She thinks Mr. Bates is very honest.

Questions 30-33 refer to the following purchase order.

Yellow Bus Stationery
1234 Main Street, Atlanta, GA

Tax Reg#: ABC 69786

PURCHASE ORDER

Purchase from	Deliver to	P.O.#	YB00010
WorkSmart	**Yellow Bus Stationery**	Date	Aug. 21
PO Box 8446	1234 Main Street	Your ref#	XY1234
Atlanta, GA	Atlanta, GA	Our ref#	YB00010-1234

Attention: Ms. Vanessa Villier

We are pleased to confirm our order of the following items:

	Product ID	Description	Quantity	Unit Price	Amount
1	P1001	Pencils HB	60	$1.00	$60.00
2	P1002	Pencils 2B	15	$1.00	$15.00
3	P1235	Paper – A4 Printer, 70 gram	10 packs	$3.00	$30.00
4	P1040	Paper – A4 Photocopier, 80 gram	15 packs	$3.50	$52.50
5	P2007	Pens – ball point, blue	10 boxes	$10.00	$100.00
6	P2009	Highlighters – 3 colors	8 sets	$6.00	$48.00

Comments:

Total before tax:	$305.50
Tax:	$0.00
Total After tax:	$305.50

TERMS & CONDITIONS

Delivery: All goods to be delivered within 14 days of PO

Condition: We reserve the right to reject goods that are not in good order or condition as determined by our quality control.

30 What is the name of the company placing the order?

(A) Worksmart

(B) Yellow Bus Stationery

(C) Atlanta, GA

(D) Vanessa Villier

31 How many packs of photocopier paper does the customer order?

(A) 10

(B) 15

(C) 30

(D) 60

32 The word "determined" in Terms & Conditions is closest in meaning to

(A) decided

(B) resolute

(C) chosen

(D) awarded

33 What will the buyer do if items are damaged upon delivery?

(A) They will fix the items on site.

(B) They will keep the items without paying.

(C) They will not accept the items.

(D) They will order replacements items.

Unit 6 Finance and Budgeting 金融／預算

本主題涵蓋內容包括：

- banking 銀行業務
- investments 投資
- taxes 稅務
- accounting 會計
- billing 帳單

WORD POWER

 TRACK 41

---

01 **account** [əˋkaʊnt] *n.* 帳戶；帳目；說明

- I can't use my bank card because there isn't enough money in my account.
  我無法使用我的金融卡，因為我的帳戶裡沒有足夠的錢。

說明 account 作名詞亦可指「（公司的）客戶」。

常用詞彙 account holder's name 帳戶名稱
account number 帳號
bank account 銀行帳戶
open an account 開設帳戶
joint account 聯合帳戶

衍 accounting *n.* 會計（學）；結帳

關 bookkeeper *n.* 簿記員

---

02 **activate** [ˋæktə͵vet] *v.* 啟用

- I just need you to fill in this form before I can active your account.
  只要您填寫好這張表格，我就能啟用您的帳戶了。

常考片語 activate a credit card 開卡

- Perhaps you should activate your new credit card before you destroy the old one.
  也許你該在新的信用卡完成開卡後再銷毀舊的卡。

反 deactivate *v.* 撤銷

衍 activation *n.* 啟動

---

03 **allowance** [əˋlaʊəns] *n.* 特別經費；零用錢；限額

- Many companies give their employees a travel allowance to cover business-related trips.
  許多公司提供員工旅遊津貼，補助與公事相關的出差行程。

常用詞彙 tax allowance 賦稅減免
baggage allowance 行李重量限制
budget allowance 預算限制

同 stipend *n.* 津貼

同 pocket money 零用錢

關 limitation *n.* 限制

---

04 **asset** [ˋæsɛt] *n.* 資產；財產；資源；優勢

- If you don't pay the bank back, they can take one of your assets.
  如果你不還錢給銀行，他們可以拿走你的一項資產。

常用詞彙 capital assets 資本資產（如機器、建築物等）
liquid assets 流動資產（容易換成現金的，如銀行存款、短期投資、應收帳款及存貨等）

關 holdings *n.* （持有）股份

關 resources *n.* 資源；物力；財力

關 capital *n.* 資本

05 ATM [ˏeˋtiˋɛm] *n.* 自動櫃員機

- I need to take some cash out of the ATM.
  我得去自動提款機領些現金。

  說明 ATM 是 automatic/automated teller machine 的縮寫。

  常用詞彙 ATM card 自動提款卡
  ATM transfer 自動櫃員機轉帳

同 cash machine 自動櫃員機

關 deposit *v.* 存款

關 withdraw *v.* 提款

關 transfer *v.* 轉帳

---

06 audit [ˋɔdɪt] *v./n.* 查帳；審計

- The company will be audited at the end of the financial year.
  公司在財政年度的尾聲會被查帳。

- An independent body will carry out an audit of the company's dealings.
  一個獨立組織會進行公司交易的審計作業。

衍 auditor *n.* 查帳員；審計師

衍 auditorial *adj.* 查帳的；稽查的

---

07 balance [ˋbæləns] *n.* 結餘；未付款項

- I want to check my bank balance on the ATM, but I don't want to take out money.
  我想要在自動提款機查詢餘額，但我不想提領現金。

反 liability *n.* 債務

關 surplus *n.* 餘額

關 balance sheet 資產負債表

---

08 bank statement 銀行對帳單

- You can get a printed bank statement that'll show you all the recent activity on your account.
  你可以拿一份紙本的銀行對帳單，它會顯示你近期的所有帳戶活動。

  說明 亦常直接說成 statement。

同 account statement 帳戶對帳單

---

09 bankbook [ˋbæŋkˏbʊk] *n.* 銀行存摺

- When you open a new account, the bank will give you a bankbook that records your activity.
  當你開立新戶頭時，銀行會給你一本存摺來記錄帳戶活動。

同 passbook *n.* 存款簿；銀行存摺

10 **bond** [bɑnd] *n.* 債券；公債；契約

關 stock、share *n.* 股票

- Pat chose to invest in government bonds in order to save for his retirement.

派特選擇投資攻府債券以便存退休後的老本。

常用詞彙 Treasury bond 美國政府公債

11 **budget** [ˋbʌdʒɪt] *v.* 編列預算 *n.* 預算

同 allocate *v.* 分配

同 allowance *n.* 分配額

- How much money should we budget for our vacation?

我們假期的預算應該要定為多少錢？

- We do not have the sufficient budget to purchase that machine.

我們沒有足夠的預算來購買那台機器。

說明 指「為……編列預算」，介系詞用 for。

常考片語 under/over budget 在預算之內／超出預算

12 **bullish** [ˋbʊlɪʃ] *adj.* （股市行情）看漲的；樂觀的

反 bearish *adj.* （股市行情）看跌的

- Following an unstable period, the market is starting to look bullish again.

經過一段不穩定的時期之後，股市開始再次看漲了。

- Investors seem to be bullish about the euro.

投資者對歐元的行情似乎很樂觀。

說明 bullish 引申自 bull market「牛市」，即「多頭市場」，形容股市行情看漲、買入動作熱絡。反之，bear market「熊市」則指行情看跌的「空頭市場」。股票漲跌常見說法：

上漲 ⇨	gain、rise、climb、increase
狂飆 ⇨	soar、surge、rocket
下跌 ⇨	fall、decline、drop
重挫 ⇨	sink、plunge、plummet、slump

13 **calculate** [ˋkælkjəˌlet] *v.* 計算；估計

同 estimate、figure、assess *v.* 估計；評估

- We should calculate how much the project will cost before we agree to it.

在我們同意之前，應該要先計算一下這個企劃會耗費多少錢。

衍 calculation *n.* 計算；深思熟慮；精打細算

衍 calculator *n.* 計算機

14 capital [ˈkæpət‖] *n.* 資金；資本；資方

- We have the chance to expand our business, but we must raise some capital first.

  我們有機會擴大企業規模，但我們一定得先募集到一些資金。

  說明 capital 亦可當形容詞，指「資本的；大寫字母的；重要的」。

同 funds、financing
n. 資金

關 labor *n.* 勞方

15 cash flow 現金流量

- If we increase our production then we can expect an increase in cash flow.

  如果我們增加產量，那我們就能預期現金流量也會有所增加。

  說明 常指某一會計期間，一家公司或機構的現金增減變動情形。

同 available funds
可用資金

16 cashier [kæˈʃɪr] *n.* 出納員

- We want all our cashiers to state the amount of change given back to the customer.

  我們要所有收銀員都對顧客說清楚找零的金額。

同 teller *n.* 銀行出納員

衍 cash *n.* 現金

17 certificate of deposit 定存；定期存款單

- A certificate of deposit is considered a relatively safe investment.

  定存被視為一種相對安全的投資。

  說明 常簡稱為 CD。certificate [səˈtɪfəkɪt] 指「憑證；單據」。

關 withdrawal slip
提款單

關 deposit slip 存款單

18 check [tʃɛk] *n.* 支票

- In the past, people used to write checks more often.

  以前人們比較常開支票。

  說明 「開支票」的動詞不可用 open，而要用 write 或 make。

  常考片語 make the check out to . . . 開支票給某人或某公司
  make the check out for . . . 支票開多少金額

- Please make the check out to Elite Incorporated. Make it out for $40,000.

  支票抬頭請寫伊利特公司。開四萬元。

關 money order 匯票

19 **checking account** 支票存款帳戶

- A checking account allows for easy access to your money and is commonly used for paying bills.
  支票存款帳戶讓你能輕易取用帳戶裡的錢，通常被用來支付帳單。

[說明] 赴美工作或留學到銀行開戶時，銀行通常會提供兩種帳戶的選擇，一種是 savings account，另一種是 checking account。savings account 顧名思義就是用來存款的帳戶（類似國內的活儲），其利率會比 checking account 高。而 checking account 的目的在於機動性地使用資金，例如用簽帳金融卡（debit card）提領現金、每個月的信用卡或水電帳單扣款、薪資的匯入或支票的扣款及入帳等。

🔗 savings account 儲蓄存款帳戶

---

20 **collateral** [kə`lætərəl] *n.* 抵押品；擔保品

- Property can be used as collateral when taking out a loan.
  申請貸款的時候，可以將房產用作抵押品。

[說明] 當客戶未償付帳款，經催收、寄出律師函等方法皆無效後，便得以將擔保品沒收。

🟰 security、pledge、guarantee *n.* 擔保品；抵押品

---

21 **currency** [`kɝənsɪ] *n.* 貨幣

- If you're going on vacation, you can exchange currency in a bank or airport.
  如果你要去度假，你可以在銀行或機場兌換貨幣。

[常用詞彙] foreign currency 外幣
hard currency 強勢貨幣

🟰 money、cash *n.* 貨幣；現金

---

22 **debit card** 簽帳金融卡

- You can use your debit card to pay in the store if you have money in your account.
  如果你的戶頭裡有錢，你就可以使用簽帳卡來支付店內的消費。

[說明] 即有信用卡功能的金融卡，但消費款項通常於三天內直接從銀行帳戶中扣除，而不像信用卡可隔月再繳納刷卡金額。

🔗 credit card 信用卡

---

23 **debt** [dɛt] *n.* 債；欠款

- Mike was advised by his wife not to buy any new things until they'd paid off their debts.
  麥克的太太建議麥克不要買任何新東西，直到他們還清所有債務。

[常用詞彙] debt collector 收帳人

🟰 liability *n.*
【會計】負債；債務

🔸 debtor *n.* 借方；債務人

24 **deduct** [dɪ`dʌkt] *v.* 扣除

- Income tax is automatically deducted from your salary every month.

  所得稅每個月會從你的薪資中被自動扣除。

衍 **deduction** *n.* 扣除；扣除額

衍 **deductible** *adj.* 可扣除的

---

25 **deposit** [dɪ`pɑzɪt] *n.* 保證金；存款 *v.* 存款；存放

- The hotel requires that all customers pay a deposit of 10% to secure a booking.

  這間飯店要求所有顧客支付一成的訂金來確保訂房。

- We should deposit that money in the bank and get some interest.

  我們應該把那筆錢存進銀行賺點利息。

常用詞彙 security deposit 保證金

反 **withdrawal** *n.* 提款

反 **withdraw** *v.* 提款

衍 **depositor** *n.* 存款人

---

26 **depression** [dɪ`prɛʃən] *n.* 蕭條；不景氣

- Many people lost their jobs during the depression of the 1930s.

  許多人在一九三〇年代的蕭條中失去了工作。

說明 depression 也可用來指「沮喪；憂鬱症」。

同 **recession** *n.* 經濟衰退；不景氣

衍 **depressing** *adj.* 令人沮喪的

衍 **depress** *v.* 使沮喪；使蕭條

---

27 **diversify** [daə`vɜsə͵faɪ] *v.* 使多樣化

- Most people agree that it's usually safer to diversify your investments.

  大部分的人同意分散投資通常比較安全。

衍 **diversity** *n.* 多樣化；多樣性

衍 **diversification** *n.* 分散經營

---

28 **dividend** [`dɪvə͵dɛnd] *n.* 股息；紅利

- The company pays dividends to its shareholders every three months.

  該公司每三個月支付股息給股東。

同 **bonus** *n.* 紅利；獎金

---

29 **down payment** （分期付款的）頭期款

- The down payment on the house was $80,000, and the rest will be paid over the coming years.

  這棟房子的頭期款是八萬美元，剩餘款項會在接下來幾年間付清。

同 **initial payment**、**first installment** 頭期款

30 **downturn** [ˈdaʊnˌtɝn] *n.* （經濟）衰退、下降　　🔄 decline *n.* 下降

- I didn't invest in any companies this year because of the economic downturn.
  因為經濟衰退，今年我沒有投資任何公司。

---

31 **equivalent** [ɪˈkwɪvələnt] *n.* 等同之物　*adj.* 等價的；等值的

- 1 USD is the equivalent of 30 TWD.
  一美元等於新台幣三十元。

- The cost of your ring is equivalent to three months of my salary!
  你的戒指等於我三個月的薪水！

- The judge told the politician that hiding these facts was equivalent to lying.
  法官告訴那個政治家說，隱蔽那些事實就等於是在撒謊。

說明 equivalent 當名詞是指「相對等之物」，the equivalent of sth. 就表示「相當於、等同於某事物」。equivalent 也可當形容詞「相對等的；等值、量的」，後面用介系詞 to 加上相比的事物或數值。

---

32 **expenditure** [ɪkˈspɛndɪtʃɚ] *n.* 消費；支出

- We need to increase expenditure if we want to increase revenue.
  我們如果想要增加營收，就需要增加支出。

🔄 cost、expense *n.* 開支

🔀 expend *v.* 消耗；花費

---

33 **financial statement** 財務報表

- Financial statements inform shareholders of everything they need to know about our finances.
  關於公司的財務狀況，財務報表讓股東們知道他們所須知道的一切細節。

🔄 financial report 財務報表

常用詞彙 常見的財務報表有：
balance sheet 資產負債表
income statement 損益表
cash flow statement 現金流量表

34 fiscal year 會計年度

- The taxman will check all the company's financial activity over the previous fiscal year.
  稅務人員會檢查公司在上一個會計年度的所有財務活動。

說明 fiscal 指「財政的；會計的」。

同 financial year 財政年度；會計年度

關 calendar year 曆年

35 forecast [ˈfɔrˌkæst] v./n. 預測；預報

- Share prices in AI companies are forecasted to increase this year.
  人工智慧公司的股價預估今年會上升。

- We might not be able to meet our profit forecast this year.
  今年我們可能無法達成獲利預測。

常用詞彙 profit forecast 獲利預測
sales forecast 銷售預測
revenue forecast 營收預測

同 prediction n. 預測

衍 forecaster n. 預測者

36 fund [fʌnd] n. 基金；專款；資金 v. 提供……資金

- The new company is still searching for investors to provide the necessary funds.
  這間新公司還在尋找投資者提供必要的資金。

- The whole project was funded by public donations.
  這整個案子是由大眾的捐款資助的。

常用詞彙 trust fund 信託基金
fund-raising 募款（活動）
mutual fund 共同基金

同 foundation、treasury n. 基金

37 in the red 負債

- My student loan left me 10,000 dollars in the red.
  我的就學貸款讓我負債一萬美元。

反 in the black 有盈餘

關 balance sheet 資產負債表

38 income statement 損益表

- The income statement showed that revenue had decreased by 17.5% in the third quarter.
  從損益表可以看出收益在第三季減少了百分之十七點五。

說明 為常見的財務報表（financial statement）之一。

同 profit and loss statement 損益表

關 annual report 年度報告

39 ## installment [ɪnˋstɔlmənt] *n.* 分期付款

- If you don't want to pay the whole $2,000 now, you can pay in installments over the next six months.
如果你現在不想付清兩千美元，你可以在未來六個月內分期付款。

說明 常用 in + 數字 + installments 表「分（幾）期付款」。

常用詞彙 installment plan 分期付款計畫

同 progressive payment、partial payment 分期付款

40 ## interest [ˋɪntrəst] *n.* 利息

- If you put your money in a savings account, you will earn extra money each year in interest.
如果你把錢放在存款帳戶裡，你每年會得到額外的利息。

說明 利息計算一般可分為：simple interest「單利」和 compound interest「複利」。

常用詞彙 interest rate 利率

關 principal *n.* 本金

41 ## invest [ɪnˋvɛst] *v.* 投資

- It is widely accepted that the best time to invest money is when a price is low.
人們普遍接受價格到達低點時就是投資的最佳時機。

- It is risky to invest in businesses that you are not familiar with.
投資你不熟悉的事業是有風險的。

說明 常見用法為 invest in sth.，表「投資某項目」。

衍 investment *n.* 投資
衍 investor *n.* 投資人

42 ## loan [lon] *n.* 貸款

- We took out a loan with the bank in order to buy a car.
我們為了買車向銀行辦了貸款。

常考片語 take out a loan 辦貸款；取得貸款
pay off / repay a loan 償還貸款

- Steve is 35 but he is still paying off loans from college.
史蒂夫三十五歲了，但他仍然在償還大學學貸。

衍 loanable *adj.* 可借貸的
衍 loanee *n.* 債務人
關 lender *n.* 貸方；出借人
關 security deposit 保證金

43 outstanding [ˋautˋstændɪŋ] *adj.* 未償付的；優秀的；出色的

- There is an outstanding payment on your account that was due three weeks ago.
  您帳戶中有一筆三週前就到期的未清償款項。

- Jacqueline won the annual award for outstanding performance.
  潔琪琳因為出色的表現而贏得年度大獎。

同 overdue *adj.* 過期的；遲到的；延誤的

同 exceptional *adj.* 傑出的；出類拔萃的

44 PIN [pɪn] *n.* 密碼；個人身分辨識碼

- You have to enter a PIN number every time you take out money from an ATM.
  你每一次從提款機領錢都必須輸入密碼。

[說明] PIN 是 personal identification number 的縮略詞。

同 password *n.* 密碼

關 confidential *adj.* 機密的

45 portfolio [portˋfolɪˏo] *n.* 投資組合；全部有價證券

- This portfolio lists all the investments you have made with us.
  這份投資組合列出了您跟我們購買的所有投資項目。

[說明] portfolio 也可指「作品集」，如：a portfolio of work。

關 stock *n.* 股票

關 bond *n.* 債券

46 profit [ˋprɑfɪt] *n.* 利潤 *v.* 有益於

- The company isn't making much profit because of a failed marketing campaign.
  因為一個失敗的行銷活動，該公司並未賺得多少利潤。

- It usually takes a while to profit from investments.
  從投資項目獲利通常需要一點時間。

反 debt *n.* 負債

反 lose *v.* 損失

衍 profitable *adj.* 有利的；營利的

衍 nonprofit *adj.* 非營利的

衍 profitably *adv.* 有利可圖地

47 ## reimburse [ˌriɪmˈbɝs] *v.* 償還；賠償

- The airline promised to reimburse all passengers whose flights had been canceled.
  這間航空公司保證會退款給所有航班被取消的乘客。

常考片語 reimburse sb. for sth. 因某事賠償某人

- The company reimbursed the customer for the faulty cell phone.
  該公司因為那支手機有瑕疵而賠償消費者。

同 repay、pay back
償還

衍 reimbursement *n.*
償還；補償

---

48 ## transaction [trænˈsækʃən] *n.* 交易；買賣；辦理商務往來

- Martha is very careful with her money and keeps a record of all her transactions.
  瑪莎對金錢很謹慎，每一筆交易都會記錄下來。

衍 transact *v.* 辦理；處理

---

49 ## transfer [trænsˈfɝ] / [ˈtrænsfɝ] *v./n.* 轉帳

- I always transfer my rent money to my landlord on the same day that I receive my salary.
  我總是在領到薪水的那一天把房租轉帳給房東。

- I can pay you in cash or via a bank transfer.
  我可以付現或從銀行轉帳給你。

常用詞彙 transfer slip 轉帳單；匯款單
automatic transfer service 自動轉帳服務

關 remit *v.* 匯款

---

50 ## withdraw [wɪθˈdrɔ] *v.* 提款

- I don't think that restaurant accepts credit cards, so I need to find an ATM to withdraw some cash.
  我想那間餐廳不能刷卡，所以我需要找一台提款機領一些現金。

反 deposit *v.* 存款

衍 withdrawal *n.* 提款

PRACTICE TEST

Part 1: Photographs

✎ TRACK 42

Directions:

For each question in this part, you will hear four statements about a picture. When you hear the statements, you must select the one statement that best describes what you see in the picture. Then circle the letter (A), (B), (C), or (D). The statements will not be printed below and will be spoken only one time.

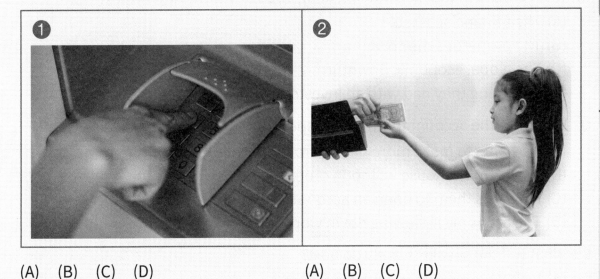

(A)   (B)   (C)   (D)   (A)   (B)   (C)   (D)

Part 2: Question and Response

✎ TRACK 43

Directions:

You will hear a question or statement and three responses spoken in English. They will be spoken only one time and will not be printed below. Select the best response to the question or statement and circle the letter (A), (B), or (C).

❸ (A)   (B)   (C)

❹ (A)   (B)   (C)

❺ (A)   (B)   (C)

❻ (A)   (B)   (C)

Part 3: Short Conversations

 TRACK 44

Directions:

You will hear some conversations between two or more people. You will be asked to answer three questions about what the speakers say in each conversation. Select the best response to each question and circle the letter (A), (B), (C), or (D). The conversation will be spoken only one time and will not be printed below.

7 What are the man and woman talking about?

(A) Their financial assets

(B) The properties they own

(C) The global economic downturn

(D) A meeting they had with an investor

8 Why does the accountant think the speakers should diversify their assets?

(A) He wants to make more money from the couple.

(B) Their current house will soon drop in value.

(C) He wants them to open an account at his bank.

(D) The economy is slowing down worldwide.

9 What will the speakers likely do next?

(A) Visit the accountant for more advice

(B) Go to a real estate agent to sell a property

(C) Consider other ways of investing their money

(D) Sell all of their investment bonds

Account Name	Interest Rate	Restrictions
Savings Deposit Account	0.01%	• Withdrawals limited to 5 per month
Savings Plus Account	0.10%	• Withdrawals limited to 12 per month • Minimum balance of $100,000
Certificate of Deposit Account	0.10%	• No withdrawals permitted for 5 years

10 Why does the man ask the woman if she has a savings goal?

  (A) To explain why she should save more

  (B) To discover how much money she has

  (C) To help her find the right account

  (D) To discover whether she is ambitious

11 Why does the woman have a large amount of money?

  (A) A family member left her some money when they died.

  (B) She won a lot of money gambling in Las Vegas.

  (C) She has saved all of her money for many years.

  (D) She made some wise investments in the past.

12 Look at the table. Which savings account is the most suitable for the woman?

  (A) None of them

  (B) Certificate of Deposit Account

  (C) Savings Deposit Account

  (D) Savings Plus Account

Part 4: Short Talks

 TRACK 45

Directions:

You will hear some short talks given by a single speaker. You will be asked to answer three questions about what the speaker says in each talk. Select the best response to each question and circle the letter (A), (B), (C), or (D). The talks will be spoken only one time and will not be printed below.

13 What is the purpose of the telephone message?

(A) To inform someone of a new way that they can repay a loan

(B) To tell someone that they are eligible for a loan from Capital Credit

(C) To notify someone that they have missed some payments

(D) To offer support to someone who is having cash flow problems

14 Who is Mr. Jones?

(A) Someone who would like to take out a loan

(B) Someone who has a loan with Capital Credit

(C) Someone who would like to make an investment

(D) Someone who would like to open an account

15 What does the speaker imply when he says, "there have been no recent transactions on your account"?

(A) There have been no deals closed recently.

(B) There have been no withdrawals.

(C) No new loans have been taken out.

(D) There have been no deposits made.

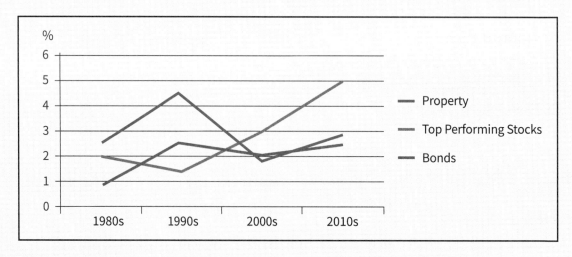

16 Who most likely is the speaker?

(A) A bank teller　　　　　　(B) An accountant

(C) A stock broker　　　　　(D) An investor

17 What is the purpose of the talk?

(A) To introduce investment basics　(B) To sell a particular stock

(C) To warn about risky stocks　　 (D) To entertain some clients

18 Look at the graphic. Which decade might the speaker be referring to when he gives the example?

(A) 1980s   (B) 1990s
(C) 2000s   (D) 2010s

Part 5: Incomplete Sentences

Directions:

A word or phrase is missing in each of the sentences below. Four answer choices are given below each sentence. Select the best answer to complete the sentence. Then circle the letter (A), (B), (C), or (D).

19 If you sign up for paperless bank statements, they will be sent to your e-mail account _____ through the mail.

(A) due to   (B) instead of
(C) more than   (D) as well

20 When Suzie goes to university, she will need to open a special student checking account, _____ she?

(A) will   (B) won't
(C) does   (D) isn't

21 People always used to use _____ when they went on vacation, but now people are more likely to use their credit card.

(A) cash flow   (B) down payments
(C) income statements   (D) traveler's checks

22 Being in debt is causing Jake a lot of stress and he will be much _____ once he pays off all of his loans.

(A) happiest   (B) happy
(C) happier   (D) the happier

23 Travelers are advised to change their _____ before leaving the airport, as they may not find a bank that will change money later.

(A) currency   (B) capital
(C) expenditure   (D) dividend

Part 6: Text Completion

Directions:

Read the text below. A word, phrase, or sentence is missing. For each empty space in the text, select the best answer to complete the text. Then circle the letter (A), (B), (C), or (D).

Questions 24-27 refer to the following letter.

Ms. S. Holmes
571 Kenwood Avenue
Boston, MA

FIRST CAPITAL BANK

Dear Ms. Holmes,

Thank you for ---**24**--- a new checking account with First Capital Bank. We are committed to providing the highest level of service to all of our customers. Please find enclosed your new debit card, bankbook, and a brochure with more information about your account.

Your ---**25**--- can be activated at any one of our bank's ATM machines around the city or by visiting the service counter at your local branch. Once activated, you will be able to use your card at any ATM, including overseas. Please note that for security reasons, your temporary PIN number will be sent separately. ---**26**---

Now that you have your new account, you will receive monthly ---**27**--- which will show all of your transactions for the previous month. In addition, we are pleased to be able to send you an annual financial statement. This will give you an overview of your savings and expenditures.

We are very pleased that you have decided to bank with us and hope you will take advantage of our wide variety of savings, investment, and loan products. More detailed information about our products and services can be found on our website at www.firstcapital.com.

Please do not hesitate to contact me should you have any questions.

Yours sincerely,

James Randolph
Branch Manager
First Capital Bank

---

24 (A) logging in (B) finding out
(C) setting up (D) pulling off

25 (A) bond (B) debit card
(C) transfer (D) budget

26 (A) It is a good idea to write down your PIN number somewhere where it can easily be found.

(B) You can rest assured that there is tight security at all of our bank branches.

(C) This will be your permanent PIN number, and it's important that you memorize it immediately.

(D) Once you receive your temporary PIN, you will be able to change it at any of our ATM machines.

27 (A) allowances

(B) profits

(C) bank statements

(D) down payments

Part 7: Reading Comprehension

Directions:

In this part you will read a selection of texts, such as magazine and newspaper articles, e-mails, and instant messages. Each text is followed by several questions. Select the best answer for each question and circle the letter (A), (B), (C), or (D).

Questions 28-29 refer to the following text message chain.

 Lisa [1:35 p.m.]
Hey James. What's our budget for our trip to Paris next week?

 James [1:36 p.m.]
Why do you ask?

 Lisa [1:38 p.m.]
I am going to go to the bank today to get some local currency.

 James [1:40 p.m.]
Great idea! Our hotel is paid for, but I think we will need at least €500 each for food. So you should exchange the equivalent of €1,000.

 Lisa [1:40 p.m.]
Will do.

 James [1:45 p.m.]
Don't forget the bank will deduct a fee for currency exchange, so you will need to calculate how much you need to exchange once you know what the bank charges.

 Lisa [1:46 p.m.]
Oh yeah. I hadn't thought of that!

28 Why has Lisa messaged James?

(A) She wants to know what the equivalent of € 1,000 is.

(B) She wants to ask him to go to the bank to change money.

(C) She wants to know how much money they need for their trip.

(D) She wants to know how much the bank charges to change money.

29 At 1:40 p.m., what does Lisa mean when she writes "Will do"?

(A) She will exchange an amount of her own currency equal to € 1,000.

(B) She will calculate the budget for the trip to Paris next week.

(C) She will transfer € 1,000 to pay for accommodation.

(D) She will calculate how much money she needs to exchange.

Questions 30-34 refer to the following advertisement, bill, and e-mail.

SureByte™
info@surebyte.com

Customer Name: DialonFire Inc.
Account Number: 1029384756

SureByte™ News:

Here at SureByte ™, we we are as dedicated to protecting the planet as we are to protecting your data. In keeping with this, we are offering a $0.50 discount to our monthly subscribers who switch to non-paper e-billing. If you'd like to know more, give us a call at 1-800-SUREBYTE, or e-mail us at ebilling@surebyte.com!

Monthly Statement Summary	
SureByte™ Diamond service	$16.95
Regional surcharge	$10.07
Total New Charges	**$27.02**

Thank you for being a valued SureByte™ customer!

To:	SureByte
From:	David Bright
Subject:	Canceling service

To SureByte Customer Service,

This is David Bright at DialonFire. We are looking to cancel our service with you. The issue is not with the service itself, which has been fine for the past ten years we've been with you. However, the extra charge pushes it a little out of our budget. If the total bill were a little cheaper, then I think we could keep the service. We are also not interested in switching to a lower package—we need the unlimited uploads and downloads. Unfortunately, we have no choice but to pursue other options.

Thank you,
David Bright

30 In the advertisement, the word "premier" in paragraph 1, line 1, is closest in meaning to

(A) earliest

(B) best

(C) last

(D) cheapest

31 What is suggested about DialonFire Inc.?

(A) The company is not in the US.

(B) The company is going out of business.

(C) The company has not been using SureByte™ for long.

(D) The company was previously using SureByte™ Sapphire.

32 How could DialonFire Inc. save some money on its bill?

(A) Switch to a lower-priced package

(B) Switch to electronic billing

(C) Put more data in CoolStore™

(D) Call for a discount

33 What problem does David mention in his e-mail?

(A) The service is too expensive.

(B) The service is too unreliable.

(C) They have not been using the service much.

(D) They no longer need the service.

34 Which service package does David say he needs?

(A) SureByte™ Emerald

(B) SureByte™ Sapphire

(C) SureByte™ Diamond

(D) A custom package

Unit 7 Corporate Development 企業發展

本主題涵蓋內容包括：

- **merger** 企業合併
- **research** 研究
- **product development** 產品研發

WORD POWER

 TRACK 46

01 **acquisition** [͵ækwə`zɪʃən] *n.* 收購（公司等）；獲得（物）

- The board of directors met to discuss the acquisition of a smaller rival company.
  董事會開會討論一家小型競爭對手的收購事宜。

🔵 obtainment *n.* 獲得

🔶 acquire *v.* 取得；獲得

---

02 **branch office** 分公司

- The company e-mailed the new policy to each of its twelve branch offices.
  該公司將新政策以電子郵件寄給它的十二家分公司。

[說明] 常可簡稱為 branch「分公司；分店；分部」。

🔴 main office、head office 總公司

---

03 **branch out** 擴充（業務）

- The clothing company decided to branch out into perfumes.
  那家服飾公司決定將業務拓展至香水產業。

🔵 expand *v.* 擴充

---

04 **breakthrough** [`brek͵θru] *n.* 突破

- We've just made a major breakthrough in securing permission to do business in Germany.
  我們剛剛確定獲得在德國經商的許可，達到了一個重大的突破。

[說明] 常以「a breakthrough in + 事物」表示「在……上有所突破」。

[常考片語] break through 突破

- There are still some barriers we need to break through as a foreign company in this country.
  在這個國家，我們作為一間外商公司還有一些障礙需要突破。

---

05 **cold call** 陌生電訪；主動以電話推銷商品

- We set up a team to make cold calls in order to find new clients.
  為了尋找新客戶，我們建立了一個團隊進行陌生電訪。

[說明] 除指電話推銷，亦可指實際的陌生推銷拜訪（visit）。

🔶 cold-call *v.* 陌生電訪

🔶 cold-calling *n.* 陌生電訪

06 company profile 公司概況

- Our company profile should introduce the functions of our business while highlighting our strengths.

  我們的公司概況中應該要介紹我們的企業功能並同時強調我們的優勢。

07 conducive [kən`djusɪv] *adj.* 有助的；有益的

- These are short-term solutions which are not conducive to long-term success.

  這些短期的治標辦法對長遠的成功而言是沒有幫助的。

同 helpful *adj.* 有助的

衍 conduce *v.* 有助於；導致

08 conduct [kən`dʌkt] *v.* 進行

- Either we conduct our own research into the market or we pay an agency to do the work for us.

  我們可以自己進行市場研究，或雇用代理機構來幫我們做。

常考片語 conduct a survey 進行調查

- The company conducted a survey to investigate consumer habits.

  公司進行了一項調查來研究消費者的習慣。

同 carry out 執行

衍 conductor *n.* 列車長；乘務員；車掌；（樂團）指揮

09 conglomerate [kən`glɑmərɪt] *n.* 企業集團

- The LVMH conglomerate owns 75 brands, all of which specialize in luxury products.

  路威酩軒集團擁有七十五個品牌，全部主打奢華品。

同 industry association、enterprise group 企業集團

10 core business 核心事業

- We should not move into new areas of business unless our core business is stable.

  除非我們的核心事業穩定下來，否則我們不該轉移到新的領域。

說明 有時會用 core activities/operations 來表示。

11 corner the market 壟斷市場

- Telecommunications companies rushed to make quick deals in order to corner the 5G market.

  電信公司為了壟斷 5G 市場而爭相快速簽定交易。

同 monopolize the market 壟斷市場

12 corporation [ˌkɔrpəˈreʃən] *n.* 公司；企業
- Three medium-sized companies joined to become one corporation.
  有三家中型的公司組成了一家企業。

說明 常指「財團法人」、「股份有限公司」等大型公司，縮寫為 Corp.。

同 industry、business、company、enterprise *n.* 公司；企業

關 trade、commerce *n.* 交易；商業

---

13 cutting-edge [ˈkʌtɪŋˌɛdʒ] *adj.* 尖端的；先進的
- The company is using cutting-edge AI technology to improve its golf clubs.
  那家公司運用尖端人工智慧改善他們的高爾夫俱樂部。

同 progressive、state-of-the-art *adj.* 先進的

---

14 demographic [ˌdɛməˈgræfɪk] *n.*（按性別、年齡、收入等區分的）人口統計資料；以市場作區隔的族群
- Video game developers mainly target the 18-29 demographic.
  電玩研發商主要將客群鎖定在十八至二十九歲的人口族群。

---

15 division [dəˈvɪʒən] *n.* 事業部；部門
- The company is looking for someone with English and Chinese language skills to manage its foreign division.
  該公司正在尋找精通中英文的人來管理國外的事業部。

說明 英文對於企業的編制單位稱呼沒有制式的規定，有些公司可能將部門稱為 division，有些則稱為 department。division 既可當「部門」，也可表示業務領域不同的各個「事業部」。

同 department、branch *n.* 部門

---

16 dominate [ˈdɑməˌnet] *v.* 支配；在……中占主要地位
- The subject of investor relations dominated the meeting.
  那場會議主要討論的主題是投資人關係。

同 rule、control、lead、command *v.* 控制

衍 dominance *n.* 支配

17 enduring [ɪnˋdjʊrɪŋ] *adj.* 持久的；長遠的

- The success of our leopard print skirts proves the enduring appeal of animal patterns in fashion.
  我們豹紋裙的成功證明了動物紋在時尚界長久不衰的吸引力。

- 同 lasting *adj.* 持續的
- 衍 endure *v.* 持續；忍受
- 衍 endurance *n.* 耐力

18 expertise [ˌɛkspɚˋtiz] *n.* 專門知識；專門技術

- Our new marketing manager brings with her an expertise in local markets.
  我們的新任行銷經理對當地市場具備專門的知識。

- 同 know-how *n.* 技術；技能
- 同 proficiency、mastery *n.* 精通；熟練
- 反 inability、incompetence *n.* 無能力
- 衍 expert *n.* 專家

19 feature [ˋfitʃɚ] *n.* （產品）特色 *v.* 以……為特色

- Ideally, we'd like to add a new feature to every new release of this product.
  理想情況下，我們想要為這個商品每一次的新發行加入一個新的產品特色。

- We're currently featuring a special offer on our website.
  目前在我們的網站上有特價優惠。

- 同 trait、characteristic *n.* 特色

20 foster [ˋfɔstɚ] *v.* 培養；促進

- The company made sure to foster good relationships with potential investors.
  這間公司確保與潛在投資人培養良好的關係。

- 同 cultivate *v.* 培育
- 反 discourage、frustrate *v.* 使受挫；勸阻

21 functionality [ˌfʌnkʃəˋnælətɪ] *n.* 功能

- Our new clothing line for physically disabled people aims to combine both fashion and functionality.
  我們為身障者推出的新服飾系列以結合時尚與功能性為目標。

- 同 use、capability *n.* 用途；功能；性能
- 衍 function *n.* 功能；作用
- 衍 functional *adj.* 起作用的

22 **generate** [ˈdʒɛnəˌret] *v.* 產生；引起
- Management called a meeting to discuss new strategies for generating income.

  管理階層召開了一個會議討論創造收入的新策略。

常用詞彙 computer-generated imagery 電腦合成影像（簡稱 CGI）

衍 generation *n.* 產生；發生；世代

---

23 **hands-on** [ˈhændzˈɑn] *adj.* 實際動手做的；親身投入的
- As the company grows, there is less need for the management to be so hands-on.

  隨著公司壯大，管理階層也較不需要如此事必躬親了。

反 hands-off *adj.* 不插手的；不介入的

---

24 **high-end** [ˈhaɪˌɛnd] *adj.* 高消費階層的；迎合高層次消費者的
- High-end fashion brands are popular across a wide range of ages.

  高階時尚品牌在廣泛的年齡層間受到歡迎。

反 low-end *adj.* 低消費階層的

---

25 **hostile takeover** 惡意併購
- Kraft Food Inc. bought UK chocolate brand, Cadbury, in a hostile takeover that forced the UK government to change its laws.

  卡夫食品在一次惡意併購中買下了英國的巧克力品牌吉百利，迫使英國政府修法。

說明 hostile [ˈhɑstɪl] 指「敵方的；懷敵意的；不友善的」。takeover 則指「接管；接收」。

關 acquirer *n.* 收購者

關 acquiree *n.* 被收購者

---

26 **incorporate** [ɪnˈkɔrpəˌret] *v.* 納入；併入；合併
- Manufacturing companies need to incorporate more environmentally friendly practices into business processes.

  製造公司需要將更環保的作法整合至他們的業務流程裡。

說明 常見用法為 incorporate A into/in B。

同 integrate、join、combine、unify、include *v.* 整合；包含；合併

衍 incorporation *n.* 結合；合併

衍 incorporated (Inc.) *adj.* 法人（公司）組織的

27 incubation [ˌɪnkjəˈbeʃən] *n.* 醞釀；逐漸發展

- If the incubation period for this fund goes well, we will launch the stock publicly.
  如果資金的醞釀階段進行得順利，我們就會公開發行這支股票。

衍 incubate *v.* 培育；醞釀

衍 incubator *n.* 孵化器（原指人工育化禽蛋的專門設備，引申指協助創新事業成長為成熟企業的一種經濟組織）

28 initiate [ɪˈnɪʃɪˌet] *v.* 發起；創始

- We've already initiated talks regarding the deal, and will continue talks next week.
  我們已經開始針對那項交易進行會談，下週還會繼續。

衍 initial *adj.* 最初的

衍 initiative *n.* 主動的行動；倡議

衍 initiator *n.* 創始者

29 innovation [ˌɪnəˈveʃən] *n.* 創新

- Successful technology companies must have a culture of innovation in order to stay competitive.
  為了維持競爭力，成功的科技公司一定要有創新的文化。

[說明] 亦常指創新或革新下的「產物」，如「新方法；新產品」等。

衍 innovate *v.* 創新；革新

衍 innovative *adj.* 創新的

30 intellectual property rights
智慧財產權

- We researched intellectual property rights laws in the region before deciding to expand there.
  我們研究了該地區的智慧財產權法後才決定將業務拓展到那裡。

[說明] intellectual [ˌɪntəˈlɛktʃul] 指「智力的；理智的」。

關 copyright *n.* 版權

關 patent *n.* 專利權

31 listed company 上市公司

- We've grown to the point where we can now consider becoming a publicly listed company.
  我們已發展到一個程度，現在可以考慮成為公開上市公司了。

[說明] 形容詞 listed 是指股票「掛牌上市的」。

反 unlisted company 未上市公司

32 market capitalization 市價總值；市值

（關）market value 市場價值

- The fact that we have one of the largest market capitalizations in our industry means we are a success.

  擁有業界最高市價總值之一的事實表示我們是一間成功的公司。

  說明 capitalization [ˌkæpətləˈzeʃən] 指「資本額」。常簡稱為 market cap，將公司所發行的「普通股數」乘以「市價」便可算出公司的市值。

---

33 market segmentation 市場區隔

- We use market segmentation in order to more accurately identify our target audience.

  我們運用市場區隔以便更準確地找出我們的目標觀眾。

  說明 segmentation [ˌsɛgmənˈteʃən] 指「分割；割斷」。

---

34 marketable [ˈmɑkɪtəbl] *adj.* 有銷路的；暢銷的；市場的

（同）merchantable、saleable *adj.* 有銷路的

- We have a very marketable product which a lot of people will be interested in.

  我們有一個銷路非常好的產品，許多人都會有興趣。

---

35 merger [ˈmɜdʒə] *n.* 合併

（衍）merge *v.* 合併

（衍）demerger *v.* 分拆（大公司分成若干小公司）

- The merger means that staff will have to get used to working with new people as well as new business practices.

  這起併購案意味著職員將得習慣與新的一群人共事，也要習慣新的經營方式。

  說明 merger「合併」通常指兩家公司會整合雙方的營運和管理；acquisition「收購」則是指一家公司買下另一家公司。

  常用詞彙 mergers and acquisitions 企業併購（簡稱 M&A）
  merger broker 合併經紀人（在可能成為合作夥伴的公司之間扮演中間人的角色，並安排合併事宜的個人或組織）

36 monopoly [mə`nɑpḷɪ] *n.* 獨占；專賣；壟斷

- If the biggest company in the industry buys the second biggest, they will have a monopoly on the market.

  如果業界最大的公司買下了第二大的公司，就會出現市場壟斷。

圐 corner *n.* 壟斷

衍 monopolize *v.*
壟斷；擁有……的專賣權

關 possession *n.* 擁有；
占有

 字首 **mono-** 表「一；單獨」

mono（一；單獨）＋ poly（販售） ↓ monopoly 獨占；專賣（市場上某產品幾乎都是某一家公司在賣）	其他同字首單字 • monologue 獨白；個人高談闊論（mono + logue「說話」） • monotonous 單調的；一成不變的（mono + ton「聲音；音調」+ ous「形容詞字尾」） • monorail 單軌鐵路（mono + rail「鐵道」）

37 overall [`ovɚ͵ɔl] *adj./adv.* 徹頭徹尾的（地）；整體的（地）

- This looks like an overall effective plan that I'm confident will succeed.

  這看起來是個完全有效的計畫，我有信心我們會成功。

- Jim had some good qualities, but overall he didn't meet expectations.

  吉姆有一些很好的資質，但整體而言他並未達到別人的期望。

圐 comprehensive
adj. 全面的；廣泛的

圐 altogether *adv.*
完全；全然

38 preliminary stage 初步階段

- Legal obstacles are keeping our new projects in the preliminary stages.

  法律方面的阻礙使我們的新企劃還維持在初步階段。

說明 preliminary [prɪ`lɪmə͵nɛrɪ] 指「預備的；初步的」。

反 final stage 最後階段

39 product development 產品開發；產品研發

- Due to a competitive market, we'll have to invest more in product development while cutting prices.

  因為市場競爭激烈，我們將得投資更多在產品開發上，同時把價格降低。

關 product testing
產品測試

SECTION B 必備詞彙

UNIT 7 Corporate Development 企業發展

40 prototype [ˈprotəˌtaɪp] *n.* 原型；標準；模範

回 model *n.* 原型；模範

- This prototype gives you a clear idea of how the product will look and feel.

  這個原型讓您對於此產品將呈現的外觀與感覺有清楚的概念。

41 research and development 研發

- The pills in this box are the end result of many years of research and development.

  盒子裡的藥丸是多年研發的最後成果。

說明 簡稱 R&D。

42 sector [ˈsɛktə] *n.* 產業；行業

關 industry *n.* 工業；行業

- Certain people choose to work in the public sector because they think it's more stable.

  有些人選擇在政府部門工作，因為他們認為比較穩定。

常用詞彙 public sector 公營經濟部門；政府部門
private sector 私營經濟部門；民營部門

43 simulation test 模擬測試

- The performance simulation tests are designed to make sure our products function well in real situations.

  這些成果模擬測試是設計用來確保我們的商品在真實情境中可以正常運作。

說明 simulation [ˌsɪmjəˈleʃən] 指「模擬」。做完模擬測試後，一般會進行 test analysis「測試分析」以改進產品瑕疵。

44 specs [spɛks] *n.* （產品）規格

關 description *n.* （物品）說明書

- Our smartphones have a wide range of capabilities and the specs match up against any of our competitors'.

  我們的智慧型手機有各式各樣的功能，規格足以和我們的任何一個競爭對手較量。

說明 specs 為 specifications [ˌspɛsəfəˈkeʃənz] 之縮略語。

45 telemarketing [ˌtɛləˋmɑrkɪtɪŋ] *n.* 電話行銷

- We train our telemarketing sales team in useful persuasion techniques when talking to strangers on the phone.

  我們訓練我們的電話行銷團隊在和陌生人講電話時，具備實用的說服技巧。

  說明 電話行銷是業者對消費者的一種 direct marketing「直效行銷」。

46 trial run 試用

- Sometimes, companies do trial runs of new products to test consumer demand.

  有時候，公司會做新產品的試用版來測試消費者的需求。

同 tryout、test run、practice run 試用

47 viable [ˋvaɪəbəl] *adj.* 可實行的

- It sounds like a good idea, but it may not be financially viable right now.

  這聽起來是個好點子，但就財務面來說目前可能行不通。

同 workable、feasible *adj.* 可行的

衍 viability *n.* 可行性

PRACTICE TEST

Part 1: Photographs

✎ TRACK 47

Directions:

For each question in this part, you will hear four statements about a picture. When you hear the statements, you must select the one statement that best describes what you see in the picture. Then circle the letter (A), (B), (C), or (D). The statements will not be printed below and will be spoken only one time.

(A)　(B)　(C)　(D)　　　　　(A)　(B)　(C)　(D)

Part 2: Question and Response

✎ TRACK 48

Directions:

You will hear a question or statement and three responses spoken in English. They will be spoken only one time and will not be printed below. Select the best response to the question or statement and circle the letter (A), (B), or (C).

❸ (A)　(B)　(C)

❹ (A)　(B)　(C)

❺ (A)　(B)　(C)

❻ (A)　(B)　(C)

Part 3: Short Conversations

 TRACK 49

Directions:

You will hear some conversations between two or more people. You will be asked to answer three questions about what the speakers say in each conversation. Select the best response to each question and circle the letter (A), (B), (C), or (D). The conversation will be spoken only one time and will not be printed below.

7 What type of company do the speakers work for?

(A) A web design company

(B) A telemarketing company

(C) An Internet service provider

(D) An advertising company

8 What does the company NOT want to do?

(A) Have telemarketers make cold calls

(B) Hire a telemarketing team

(C) Spend more money on advertising

(D) Have telemarketers call the existing customers

9 What does the woman mean when she says, "telemarketers are skilled at talking people into things"?

(A) They are good at telling people where to go.

(B) They can convince people to do something.

(C) They are good at getting customer feedback.

(D) They enjoy telling stories to customers.

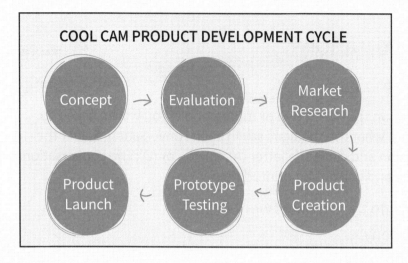

COOL CAM PRODUCT DEVELOPMENT CYCLE

Concept → Evaluation → Market Research

Product Launch ← Prototype Testing ← Product Creation

⑩ What is the man doing?

(A) Asking for information
(B) Explaining a concept
(C) Providing an update
(D) Conducting market research

⑪ What is implied about the market research?

(A) It will help the company to advertise its new wearable camera.
(B) It will be conducted using Internet surveys of consumers.
(C) The market research will only target certain people.
(D) It will help the company develop the product for particular consumers.

⑫ Look at the graphic. At which stage of the product development cycle is the company?

(A) Concept
(B) Prototype Testing
(C) Evaluation
(D) Market Research

Part 4: Short Talks

 TRACK 50

Directions:

You will hear some short talks given by a single speaker. You will be asked to answer three questions about what the speaker says in each talk. Select the best response to each question and circle the letter (A), (B), (C), or (D). The talks will be spoken only one time and will not be printed below.

⑬ Who is the audience for this talk?

(A) The media   (B) Employees

(C) Directors   (D) Teachers

⑭ What does the speaker say about the education sector?

(A) It is changing.   (B) It is profitable.

(C) It's their core business.   (D) It is traditional.

⑮ What will happen next?

(A) The merger will be publicized.   (B) Some employees will be laid off.

(C) Staff expertise will be evaluated.   (D) Smaller meetings will be held.

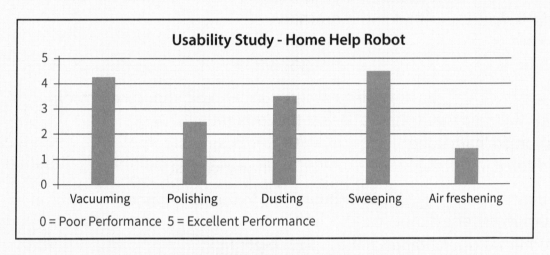

0 = Poor Performance 5 = Excellent Performance

⑯ What is the purpose of this talk?

(A) To launch a marketing campaign

(B) To discuss the results of some product testing

(C) To inform people how to use the home help robot

(D) To ask staff to clean the office

⑰ What does the speaker think about the research and development results?

(A) He thinks they were successful.

(B) He thinks they were a waste of time.

(C) He thinks they were not clear enough.

(D) He thinks they were surprising.

⑱ Look at the graphic. What problem area is going to be worked on first?

(A) Polishing functionality   (B) Vacuuming functionality

(C) Air freshening functionality   (D) Dusting functionality

Part 5: Incomplete Sentences

Directions:

A word or phrase is missing in each of the sentences below. Four answer choices are given below each sentence. Select the best answer to complete the sentence. Then circle the letter (A), (B), (C), or (D).

19 Please _____ our branch offices know that the prototypes will be delivered as early as next Monday.

(A) get (B) allow

(C) enable (D) let

20 All of the specs for this computer, as well as the software that comes pre-installed, _____ shown in this brochure.

(A) are (B) were

(C) be (D) has

21 There is a _____ on the website where you can read about the history, directors, and recent innovations of the corporation.

(A) preliminary stage (B) core business

(C) company profile (D) simulation test

22 Following the _____, it will be interesting to see what passengers think of the new driverless bus.

(A) market capitalization (B) trial run

(C) intellectual property (D) market segmentation

23 The training program gives students practical, _____ experience in product development and design.

(A) low-end (B) hands-off

(C) high-end (D) hands-on

Part 6: Text Completion

Directions:

Read the text below. A word, phrase, or sentence is missing. For each empty space in the text, select the best answer to complete the text. Then circle the letter (A), (B), (C), or (D).

Questions 24-27 refer to the following article.

Caledine Partners with High Schools for National STEM Week

Caledine Sydney, a ---24--- of The Caledine Group Inc., partnered with high schools in the Sydney area as part of the national STEM (Science Technology Engineering Math) Week. ---25--- Caledine organized tours of its branch offices and hands-on product development activities in its production facilities in the city. "Promoting interest in research and development, and fostering innovation in young people, is something that we take very seriously at Caledine," says Karen Young, Vice President of the ---26---. "We want to see the next generation enter the STEM fields in ---27--- numbers and come up with the cutting-edge designs that will make a difference in the future."

24 (A) division   (B) monopoly

   (C) resource   (D) demographic

25 (A) The idea is that students in high school will stay at home and study for their tests.

   (B) The week is forecast to be hot and humid, so people are advised to stay indoors.

   (C) The week is a government initiative that hopes to increase students' interest in these areas.

   (D) During certain weeks of the year, members of the public can visit Caledine's factory.

26 (A) acquisition   (B) resource

   (C) corporation   (D) merger

27 (A) equal   (B) sooner

   (C) lesser   (D) higher

Part 7: Reading Comprehension

Directions:

In this part you will read a selection of texts, such as magazine and newspaper articles, e-mails, and instant messages. Each text is followed by several questions. Select the best answer for each question and circle the letter (A), (B), (C), or (D).

Questions 28-30 refer to the following invitation.

Invitation for Submission of Proposals

Lea Valley Business Incubation—The Place to Grow your Business

The Lea Valley Enterprise Authority (LVEA) invites suitable manufacturing enterprises or individuals to the Lea Valley Business Incubator. The incubator provides a conducive environment for small to medium enterprises to grow and establish themselves as sustainable and commercially viable manufacturing enterprises. The program is expected to take a maximum period of 2 years, on a 1 year renewable lease.

Selected clients will benefit from the following resources and expertise:

- Research and Development units and office space at subsidized rates
- Hands-on business coaching and training
- Technology coaching and support
- Facilitation of market access
- Workshops on intellectual property rights
- Administration services such as Internet, photocopying, and printing

REQUIREMENTS

Eligible candidates should submit a business proposal which clearly outlines the following:

1. The core business and concept
2. The product development plan
3. Marketing plan and product line
4. Availability of funds to run the business
5. Historical and projected financials
6. Company documents

Candidates should submit relevant documents to:
The Selection Committee
Lea Valley Business Incubator
Post Office Box #339
Sacramento, CA

28 What is the purpose of this invitation?
  (A) To invite business people to lunch
  (B) To ask people to prepare some documents
  (C) To ask people to attend a meeting
  (D) To invite business proposals

29 What is NOT mentioned as a benefit of joining the business incubator?
  (A) Receiving coaching   (B) Making use of office space
  (C) Receiving funding   (D) Using administration services

30 The word "sustainable" in paragraph 1, line 4, is closest in meaning to
  (A) enduring   (B) environmental
  (C) temporary   (D) innovative

Questions 31-33 refer to the following meeting minutes.

MEETING MINUTES		
ITEM #	**Description**	**Status**
1.	Acquisition of Innovate Games by computer games conglomerate, InGames.	Talks are ongoing. --[1]-- No decisions have been made yet.
2.	Research and Development of WarQuest game.	Still in preliminary stage. Programmers and designers are still working on specs for new game. --[2]-- Marketing team to initiate market segmentation.
3.	Directors wish to branch out into games for stay-at-home mothers and fathers. They would like us to corner the market in this area.	Marketing looking into whether this is a marketable idea.
4.	A new telemarketing team is being trained by the Marketing Department to target users of the mobile gaming app. --[3]--	Training is due to be completed this week and new team will hopefully start generating new leads. --[4]--
5.	Decision was made to meet again when more is known about the acquisition.	A new meeting date will be sent to you.

㉛ What kind of work is being discussed in the meeting minutes?
(A) Teaching
(B) Telemarketing
(C) Games development
(D) Manufacturing

㉜ What type of customer would the company like to target next?
(A) Parents
(B) Kids
(C) Designers
(D) Business people

㉝ In which of the positions marked [1], [2], [3], and [4] does the following sentence best belong?
"This is to see if they would be interested in upgrading."
(A) [1]
(B) [2]
(C) [3]
(D) [4]

Unit 8 Technical Areas
技術層面

本主題涵蓋內容包括：

- electronics 電子

- technology 科技

- computers 電腦

- laboratories & related equipment 實驗室與相關器材

- technical specifications 技術規格

WORD POWER

 TRACK 51

---

01 **app** [æp] *n.* 應用程式；應用軟體 (= application)
- A number of educational apps use games to make learning more enjoyable.

  有很多教育方面的應用程式運用遊戲讓學習更有趣。

---

02 **back up** （檔案、資料等）備份

🔁 backup *n.* 備份

- We back up our work every day, because losing a day's work would be very costly for the company.

  我們每天備份工作，因為遺失一天份的工作內容對公司來說損失是很大的。

  說明 其名詞 backup 常可作形容詞用，如 backup file「備份檔案」、backup plan「備用計畫」、backup copy「備份拷貝」等。

---

03 **browse** [braʊz] *v.* 瀏覽

🔁 browser *n.* 瀏覽器

- In modern society, many people spend their free time browsing social media sites on their phones.

  在現代社會中，許多人花空閒時間在手機上瀏覽社群媒體網站。

---

04 **bug** [bʌg] *n.* （系統或程式的）瑕疵或錯誤

🔁 problem、error *n.* 問題；錯誤

- If the program contains a bug, you should delete it.

  如果那個軟體有程式錯誤，你應該把它刪除。

---

05 **capacity** [kəˋpæsətɪ] *n.* 容量；能力

🔁 capacious *adj.* 容量大的

🔁 capable *adj.* 有能力的

- Our computers' capacities don't need to be too large because most files are stored in another place.

  我們電腦的容量不需要很大，因為大部分的檔案都存在另一個地方。

---

06 **chip** [tʃɪp] *n.* 晶片；積體電路片

🔁 microchip *n.* 微晶片

- Our company manufactures chips that are used in computers and smartphones.

  我們公司生產用在電腦與智慧型手機中的晶片。

07 crash [kræʃ] *v.* 當機

- Save work regularly because you never know when your computer may crash.
  要定時存檔，因為你永遠不知道你的電腦什麼時候會當機。

  說明 要表「我的電腦當掉了。」除了說 My computer crashed. 之外，亦可說 My computer is down.。

同 freeze up 當機；停住

關 down、dead *adj.* 當機的；無法運作的

08 cyber [`saɪbɚ] *adj.* 電腦的；網際網路的

- The company pays another company $50 a month to protect against cyber attacks.
  公司每個月支付五十美元給另一間公司，以避免遭受網路攻擊。

衍 cyberspace *n.* 網際空間

衍 cybercafé *n.* 網路咖啡廳；網咖

09 database [`detə͵bes] *n.* 資料庫；數據庫

- If we can get new customers' e-mails in exchange for a free product, we can build a database.
  如果我們可以用一個免費商品換取新顧客的電子郵件地址，我們就可以建立起一個資料庫了。

同 data bank 資料庫

10 desktop [`dɛsktɑp] *n.* 桌上型電腦；桌面

- I have two computers; a desktop for my home, and a laptop that I can take to work with me.
  我有兩台電腦；一台家用的桌上型電腦以及一台我可以帶去上班的筆電。

- If you create a shortcut on your desktop, you will be able to access this folder faster in future.
  如果你在桌面建一個捷徑，以後就可以更快速地存取這個資料夾。

關 laptop *n.* 筆記型電腦

關 tablet *n.* 平板電腦

11 digital [`dɪdʒɪtḷ] *adj.* 數位的；數字的

- Sales of digital cameras have gone down since smartphones have become more popular.
  自從智慧型手機開始變得更普及，數位相機的銷量就下降了。

衍 digit *n.* 數字

12 **e-commerce** [ɪˋkɑmɝs] *n.* 電子商務
- Tom's e-commerce qualification has been very useful for him and his online business.

  湯姆在電子商務方面的資歷對他與他的網路事業都非常有幫助。

  說明 即 electronic commerce「電子商務」。

---

13 **familiarize** [fəˋmɪljə‚raɪz] *v.* 使熟悉
- We're buying new machines and we'll have a training day for staff to familiarize them with the new models.

  我們將要購入新機器，且會進行為期一天的員工訓練，使他們熟悉新的機型。

衍 familiar *adj.* 熟悉的

關 enlighten *v.* 啟發；啟迪

---

14 **filename** [ˋfaɪl‚nem] *n.* 檔名
- Save your work under a filename that is consistent with the style of other files in the folder.

  做好後請存檔，檔名要和該資料夾其他檔案的命名方式一致。

  說明 「為檔案命名／重新命名」是 to name/rename the file。

  常用詞彙 original filename 原檔名
  filename extension 副檔名（如 .txt、.exe 等）

衍 file *n.* 檔案

關 folder *n.* 資料夾

---

15 **get online** 連上網路
- You can buy a SIM card when you arrive at the airport to get online immediately.

  你到機場的時候可以買一張 SIM 卡，就能立即連上網路。

關 be off-line 在離線狀態

---

16 **hard drive** 硬碟
- We need to increase the hard drive speed so that the programs run faster.

  我們需要增加硬碟速度，好讓程式跑得更快。

  說明 全名為 hard disk drive，亦可簡稱為 hard disk。

關 storage *n.*【電腦】存儲器

關 storage capacity 儲存容量

關 CPU *n.* 中央處理器

17 headset [ˈhɛdˌsɛt] *n.* 頭戴式裝置；附麥克風的頭戴式耳機

- Each member of our telemarketing team wears 4G headsets to communicate with clients.

  我們電訪團隊的每一個成員都佩戴 4G 頭戴式耳機以便與客戶溝通。

---

18 icon [ˈaɪˌkɑn] *n.* 圖示；偶像

- Click on the icon at the top of the screen to open the program.

  點一下螢幕上方的圖示來開啟這個程式。

同 symbol *n.* 符號；象徵

衍 iconic *adj.* 具代表性的

---

19 infect [ɪnˈfɛkt] *v.* 感染（電腦病毒或疾病）；（電腦）中毒

- My computer got infected by a virus because I opened an e-mail attachment from an unknown sender.

  我打開一個來自某個不知名寄件者的郵件附加檔之後，我的電腦就中毒了。

衍 infection *n.* 傳染（病）；感染

---

20 instruction manual 說明書；使用手冊

- If you can't find the solution in the instruction manual, then call the company directly.

  如果你在說明書中找不到解決辦法，那就直接打給那家公司。

說明 常簡稱為 manual。

---

21 interactive [ˌɪntɚˈæktɪv] *adj.* 互動的

- Interactive learning apps are becoming more popular because they make education fun.

  互動式的學習應用程式變得較受歡迎了，因為它們把學習變有趣。

衍 interact *v.* 互動

衍 interaction *n.* 互動

衍 interactivity *n.* 互動性

---

22 interface [ˈɪntɚˌfes] *n.* 介面

- The interface of this smartphone is very user-friendly. It feels very easy to use.

  這支智慧型手機的介面很容易使用。操作起來感覺很簡單。

關 window *n.* 視窗

關 icon *n.* 圖示

關 menu *n.* 選單

---

23 ## Internet connection 網路連線
- Due to system maintenance, there will be no Internet connection between 10 a.m. and 10:15 a.m. today.
  因為系統維護，今天早上十點至十點十五分網路會斷線。

🔗 connected *adj.*（網路）連接的

🔗 disconnected *adj.*（網路）斷線的

🔗 connectivity *n.*（網路）連接

---

24 ## keyboard [ˈkiˌbɔrd] *n.* 鍵盤
- I knew Jim was busy because I could hear him tapping away energetically at his keyboard.
  我知道吉姆很忙，因為我可以聽到他大力敲打鍵盤的聲音。

  說明 tap away 為口語用法，指用鍵盤將資料輸入到電腦、手機等裝置中。

🔗 keypad *n.* 電腦小型鍵盤

---

25 ## laboratory [ˈlæbrəˌtorɪ] *n.* 實驗室；研究室
- After graduating from her science course, Kate got a job as an assistant in a research laboratory.
  凱特從科學課程畢業之後，在一間研究實驗室中找到了一份助理的工作。

  說明 常簡稱 lab。

🟰 testing room 實驗室

---

26 ## laptop [ˈlæptɑp] *n.* 筆記型電腦
- In order to save money on computers, the design company asked its workers to bring in their own laptops.
  為了在電腦方面省錢，那間設計公司要求員工帶自己的筆電來上班。

🟰 notebook *n.* 筆記型電腦

---

27 ## link [lɪŋk] *n.*（網站）連結 *v.* 連結
- The "contact" page was hard to find because the link was at the bottom of the page.
  「聯絡我們」的頁面很難找，因為連結在網頁的最下面。
- All the computers in the company are linked in order that information can be shared easily.
  公司裡的所有電腦都互相連結，好讓資訊可以被輕易分享。

衍 linkage *n.* 連結性

28 **log on** 登入

- Log on to the system using your ID number and password.

  用你的身分證字號和密碼登入系統。

  常考片語 log on to the system 登入系統

同 log/sign in 登入

反 log out、log off、sign out 登出

---

29 **memory** [ˈmɛmərɪ] *n.* 記憶體

- We should install more memory onto our computers. Then they can run multiple programs at the same time.

  我們應該要幫電腦安裝更大的記憶體。這樣它們就可以同時執行多個程式。

  常用詞彙 flash memory 快閃記憶體

關 RAM (Random Access Memory) 隨機存取記憶體

---

30 **monitor** [ˈmɑnətɚ] *n.* 螢幕 *v.* 監控；監測

- Graphic designers prefer to work with large monitors because they can see everything more clearly.

  平面設計師工作時偏好用比較大的螢幕，因為可以更清楚看到每個細節。

- Monitor the new trainee's performance and report back to me on her progress next week.

  密切觀察那名新受訓員工的表現，下週再跟我回報她的進步狀況。

同 watch、keep an eye on 監視；觀察

---

31 **network** [ˈnɛtˌwɝk] *n.* 網絡；網路；聯播網 *v.* 拓展人脈

- Please save that file on the network so that it can be accessed on other computers.

  請把檔案存在網絡上，讓其他台電腦也可以存取。

- In the business world, it is important to be able to network well.

  在商業圈裡，能有效拓展人脈是很重要的。

  常用詞彙 road/rail network 道路／鐵路網
  　　　　 local area network（電腦）區域網路

衍 networking *n.* 電腦系統連線作業

32 **operating system** 作業系統

- I downloaded the latest operating system and my computer ran a lot more smoothly.

  我下載了最新版本的作業系統，然後我的電腦就跑得順多了。

33 **platform** [ˈplæt͵fɔrm] *n.* 平台；月台

- These days, smartphone platforms such as iOS and Android have keyboards built in.

  現今的智慧型手機平台像是 iOS 和安卓都在軟體中內建鍵盤。

- The people stood on the platform waiting for the train to arrive.

  那群人站在月台上等火車抵達。

說明 作電腦用語時指一種作為基礎的軟體作業環境。亦可指（鐵路等的）月台。

常用詞彙 computing platform 系統平台（指在電腦裡讓軟體執行的系統環境，包括硬體環境與軟體環境）
hardware platform 硬體平台（指電腦系統建置所依據的標準。如工業標準的個人電腦，麥金塔、迷你電腦、主機電腦等平台）

34 **pop up** 突然出現；跳出來

- A new window will pop up on the screen if you click this link.

  如果你點擊這個連結，會有一個新的視窗跳出來。

衍 pop-up *adj.* 彈出式的；彈跳出的 *n.* 彈出式廣告

關 pop-up banner （網頁）彈出式橫幅廣告

35 **power button** 電源按鈕；電源鍵

- Hold down the power button for three seconds to turn the phone off.

  長按電源鍵三秒，就可以把手機關機。

同 power switch 電源開關

36 **search** [sɜtʃ] *n./v.* 搜尋
- If you're not sure about something, you can do a search on Google.
  如果你對某件事情不確定,你可以在谷歌上搜尋。
- Whenever I want to find out about something, I search for it online.
  每當我想要了解某件事情的時候,我就會上網搜尋。

說明 Google 原是熱門網路搜尋引擎的網站名稱,但因太常被大家當動詞使用,已成為「上網搜尋資料」的代名詞。

常用詞彙 search engine 搜尋引擎

同 hunt、quest *n.* 搜尋
同 seek、hunt *v.* 尋找

37 **security** [sɪˋkjʊrətɪ] *n.* 安全;防護(措施)
- Big companies pay a lot of money for security, to prevent the wrong people from accessing their systems.
  多家大公司在保安方面耗費大筆資金,就是為了防止不對的人進入他們的系統。

常用詞彙 for security purposes 安全起見
　　　　 security camera 保全攝影機

反 insecurity *n.* 不安全感;缺乏自信
衍 secure *adj.* 安全的;無危險的 *v.* 取得;獲得(地位、獎品等)
衍 insecure *adj.* 不安全的

38 **serial number** 序號
- I could give you this program, but you need a serial number to use it.
  我可以給你這個程式,但你需要一個序號才能使用它。

同 identification number 識別號碼

39 **server** [ˋsɜvɚ] *n.* 【電腦】伺服器
- The Internet has stopped working temporarily because the server is down.
  網路現在暫時斷線,因為伺服器掛掉了。

關 network *n.* 電腦網絡
關 file sharing 檔案分享

40 **software** [ˋsɔftˏwɛr] *n.* 軟體
- Our company uses advanced software programs to do these tasks.
  我們公司用高階軟體程式來進行這些任務。

常用詞彙 word-processing software 文字處理軟體
　　　　 design software 設計軟體
　　　　 anti-virus software 防毒軟體

關 hardware *n.* 硬體

41 **startup** [ˋstɑrtˌʌp] *n.* 新創公司
- Running a startup is high risk because the market is constantly changing.
  經營一家新創公司風險很高，因為市場不停在改變。

---

42 **technician** [tɛkˋnɪʃən] *n.* 技術人員；技師
- We didn't know what was wrong with the printer, so we had to call the technician.
  我們不知道印表機出了什麼問題，所以得打電話給技術人員。

衍 technical *adj.* 技術的；科技的

衍 technique *n.* 技術

---

43 **thoroughly** [ˋθɝolɪ] *adv.* 徹底地
- Instead of looking thoroughly through the database, it's much faster to use the "Quick Search" function.
  與其徹底檢視資料庫，使用「快速搜尋」功能快多了。

同 completely、fully *adv.* 完全地

衍 thorough *adj.* 徹底的

---

44 **top-of-the-line** [ˋtɑpəvðəˋlaɪn] *adj.* 頂級的；最先進的
- The car company uses top-of-the-line machines to build their cars.
  這家汽車製造公司使用最頂尖的機器建造他們的汽車。

同 top-notch、superb、state-of-the-art *adj.* 頂尖的；極好的

---

45 **update** [ˋʌpdet] *v./n.* 更新
- A pop-up will appear on your screen, asking you to update the software.
  你的螢幕會出現一個彈出式視窗，要求你更新這個軟體。
- Please wait while the computer installs updates.
  請耐心等待電腦安裝更新。

說明 軟體公司放在線上提供用戶下載的「更新軟體」可稱為 update software。

常用詞彙 automatic update 自動更新
　　　　 online update 線上更新

同 renew *v.* 更新

衍 updated *adj.* 已更新的

46 upgrade [ˋʌpˋgred] *v.* 升級 *n.* 最新版 　　　　反 **downgrade** *v.* 降級

- To use this software, you need to upgrade your hard drive.
  為了使用這個軟體，你需要把硬碟升級。

- The new computers are an upgrade on our old ones.
  這批新電腦是我們舊款的升級版。

---

47 user name 使用者名稱 　　　　關 **password** *n.* 密碼

- The user name you create must contain at least one capital letter and two numbers.
  你設的使用者名稱一定要包含最少一個大寫字母和兩個數字。

---

48 version [ˋvɝʒən] *n.* 版本

- My computer is downloading the newest version of the software, so I need to wait until it's finished.
  我的電腦正在下載這個軟體的最新版本，所以我必須等到下載完成。

常用詞彙 off-line version 離線版本

---

49 virus [ˋvaɪrəs] *n.* 病毒

- We can protect against viruses by using anti-virus software.
  我們可以用防毒軟體來保護電腦不被病毒攻擊。

說明 「中毒」是 be hit by 或 infected by/with a virus。其他與電腦侵害相關的名詞還有 worm「網蟲」、Trojan「木馬程式」、hacker「電腦駭客」等。

常用詞彙 anti-virus software/program 防毒軟體／程式
　　　　virus signature【電腦】病毒碼；病毒特徵

---

50 wireless [ˋwaɪrlɪs] *adj.* 無線的 　　　　反 **wired** *adj.* 有線的

- I can put my keyboard and mouse anywhere because they are both wireless.
  我可以把我的鍵盤和滑鼠放在任何地方，因為它們都是無線的。

PRACTICE TEST

Part 1: Photographs

TRACK 52

Directions:

For each question in this part, you will hear four statements about a picture. When you hear the statements, you must select the one statement that best describes what you see in the picture. Then circle the letter (A), (B), (C), or (D). The statements will not be printed below and will be spoken only one time.

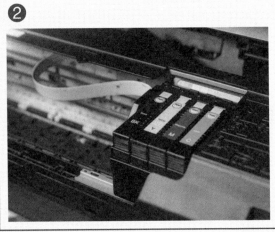

(A)   (B)   (C)   (D)   (A)   (B)   (C)   (D)

Part 2: Question and Response

TRACK 53

Directions:

You will hear a question or statement and three responses spoken in English. They will be spoken only one time and will not be printed below. Select the best response to the question or statement and circle the letter (A), (B), or (C).

3 (A)   (B)   (C)

4 (A)   (B)   (C)

5 (A)   (B)   (C)

6 (A)   (B)   (C)

Part 3: Short Conversations

Directions:

You will hear some conversations between two or more people. You will be asked to answer three questions about what the speakers say in each conversation. Select the best response to each question and circle the letter (A), (B), (C), or (D). The conversation will be spoken only one time and will not be printed below.

7 What does the caller need help with?

(A) An Internet connection

(B) E-commerce

(C) Some software

(D) An operating system

8 What does the technician offer to do?

(A) Send someone to explain later

(B) Come and visit the office himself

(C) Send the woman an instruction manual

(D) Provide advice over the phone

9 Why didn't the woman like the person that was sent last time?

(A) He arrived later than expected.

(B) He didn't understand the problem.

(C) He didn't appreciate the company.

(D) He wasn't good at explaining.

Laboratory	Conference Room
Control Room	Office
Observation Room	Break Room

Window

⑩ Why does the man want one-way glass?

(A) Because it will cost less money

(B) To make sure workers are not distracted

(C) Because lab workers have complained

(D) He doesn't want workers to see into his office.

⑪ What will the woman most probably do next?

(A) Contact a glass manufacturer   (B) Buy some tools

(C) Call a staff meeting   (D) Search the Internet

⑫ Look at the graphic. Where will the man's office be after the changes have been made?

(A) Next to the laboratory

(B) Between the control room and the lab

(C) Next to the observation room

(D) Between the lab and observation room

Part 4: Short Talks

 TRACK 55

Directions:

You will hear some short talks given by a single speaker. You will be asked to answer three questions about what the speaker says in each talk. Select the best response to each question and circle the letter (A), (B), (C), or (D). The talks will be spoken only one time and will not be printed below.

⑬ What is DateMarker?

   (A) A TV show about digital media   (B) An app for learning a language
   (C) A new online dating app   (D) An app for organizing your schedule

⑭ What does the speaker mean when she says, "Using DateMarker really is a walk in the park"?

   (A) DateMarker is very portable.   (B) It is easy to use DateMarker.
   (C) The app is good for dating.   (D) DateMarker plans activities.

⑮ What is a feature of DateMarker?

   (A) Traditional calendar   (B) Interesting pop-ups
   (C) User-friendly interface   (D) Advertisements

⑯ What is the main purpose of this talk?

   (A) To introduce a new system to staff
   (B) To help staff fix user problems
   (C) To explain how a website was designed
   (D) To tell staff how to change their password

⑰ Where can listeners find their usernames?

   (A) In the instructions   (B) In a link
   (C) On a piece of paper   (D) On their swipe card

⑱ Look at the graphic. Which of the following links is not currently accessible?

   (A) The "Home" section   (B) The "Upload" section
   (C) The "Help" section   (D) The "Edit Files" section

Part 5: Incomplete Sentences

Directions:

A word or phrase is missing in each of the sentences below. Four answer choices are given below each sentence. Select the best answer to complete the sentence. Then circle the letter (A), (B), (C), or (D).

⑲ The _____ inside the computer was damaged and had to be replaced.

(A) digital
(B) chip
(C) serial number
(D) access

⑳ The new computers we're buying _____ top-of-the-line ones, won't they?

(A) will be
(B) have been
(C) must be
(D) are

㉑ The search button can be found _____ the top of the page, beside the help button.

(A) above
(B) in
(C) at
(D) under

㉒ The operating system on this computer needs to be _____ because it is too old.

(A) logged on
(B) updated
(C) browsed
(D) accessed

㉓ I've _____ the computer several times already, but the problem persists.

(A) been trying to restarted
(B) tried to restarting
(C) restarted to try
(D) tried restarting

Part 6: Text Completion

Directions:

Read the text below. A word, phrase, or sentence is missing. For each empty space in the text, select the best answer to complete the text. Then circle the letter (A), (B), (C), or (D).

Questions 24-27 refer to the following online article.

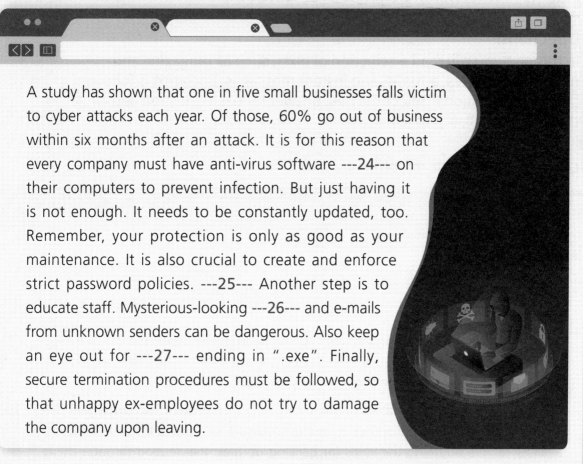

A study has shown that one in five small businesses falls victim to cyber attacks each year. Of those, 60% go out of business within six months after an attack. It is for this reason that every company must have anti-virus software ---**24**--- on their computers to prevent infection. But just having it is not enough. It needs to be constantly updated, too. Remember, your protection is only as good as your maintenance. It is also crucial to create and enforce strict password policies. ---**25**--- Another step is to educate staff. Mysterious-looking ---**26**--- and e-mails from unknown senders can be dangerous. Also keep an eye out for ---**27**--- ending in ".exe". Finally, secure termination procedures must be followed, so that unhappy ex-employees do not try to damage the company upon leaving.

㉔ (A) installing   (B) installation
    (C) installed   (D) install

㉕ (A) Good, difficult-to-guess passwords are essential to computer security.
    (B) Many companies have strict policies regarding lateness at work.
    (C) So don't forget to log out of the system every time you use it.
    (D) Viruses can cause a huge amount of damage to a company.

㉖ (A) linked   (B) links
    (C) link   (D) linking

㉗ (A) keyboards   (B) monitors
    (C) capacities   (D) filenames

Part 7: Reading Comprehension

Directions:

In this part you will read a selection of texts, such as magazine and newspaper articles, e-mails, and instant messages. Each text is followed by several questions. Select the best answer for each question and circle the letter (A), (B), (C), or (D).

Questions 28-29 refer to the following e-mail.

To:	all@alleviate.com
From:	palmer.greg@alleviate.com
Subject:	System update

📄 how-to.pdf   📄 System Differences.pdf

Dear Employees,

We are updating our operating system. As has been pointed out, the old one kept crashing. There were two reasons for this. Firstly, it had a lot of bugs. And secondly, it was not compatible with some of our newer software.

The new system will be installed by the technicians this weekend, so employees are hereby instructed to back up their own files to ensure nothing is lost. I've attached a "How to" file outlining the steps for backing up files. Please read through them carefully. Once you have backed everything up, tell Simon Jones, who will come and check that everything has been done correctly.

There are some differences between the new operating system and the old one. The second file I've attached explains these, so please read through these to familiarize yourself with everything. Again, for any questions about backing up files or using the new system, please speak to Simon.

Thank you and have a nice weekend.

Greg Palmer
CEO Alleviate Inc.

28 What most likely is Simon Jones's job?

(A) Software Salesman
(B) Data Entry Assistant
(C) CEO
(D) Technician

29 What is NOT something that employees are required to do?

(A) Back up files on their computer

(B) Read the attachments in the e-mail

(C) Install the new operating system

(D) Familiarize themselves with the new system

Questions 30-34 *refer to the following flyer and e-mail.*

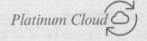

PLATINUM CLOUD STORAGE!

Creating and operating your own server requires time, space, effort, manpower, and most of all—money. And what happens if something goes wrong? Choosing to move your company's data to our server will save you a huge amount of time and money (no more need for backup!), while making your life a whole lot easier.

Why move to the cloud?

-Reduce costs

-Increase security

-Enhance flexibility

-Improve collaboration

-Remove need for daily backup

Why Platinum?

-Free consultation

-Free cancellation and removal

-Free data transfer (first 40TB)

-Only $0.01 per GB (all transfers after 40TB)

To: info@platinumcloud.com
From: ATaylor@astarweb.com
Subject: Cloud Storage

Dear Sir/Madam,

My company is going through a period of rapid growth. All our hard drives have reached capacity and we do not possess the resources to run our own server. It is for this reason that I read your flyer with great interest, as I have recently been considering moving my company's data to the cloud.

We are a one-year-old startup and we have 25TB of data that would require immediate transfer. Obviously, we expect that amount to increase over time as the company continues to grow.

I have very little idea of how cloud computing works, so the free meeting was of particular interest to me. What is the deal with this, exactly? Would you send a technician to my office or would I have to pay you guys a visit? Please supply me with as much information as possible and advise me on the next step.

Thank you.

Alan Taylor
(Owner of A-Star Web Design)

30 According to the flyer, what is the disadvantage of running your own server?

(A) A lot of things often go wrong.　(B) You need specialist knowledge.

(C) It requires a lot of resources.　(D) A personal server has limited capacity.

31 What is the purpose of the e-mail?

(A) To apologize for something　(B) To answer a customer's questions

(C) To make a direct order　(D) To state interest in a service

32 What kind of business is Mr. Taylor in?

(A) Internet banking　(B) Web design

(C) Online fashion　(D) Cloud storage

33 How much would Mr. Taylor have to pay for the first transfer?

(A) Nothing　(B) $0.01

(C) $0.40　(D) $100.00

34 Which part of the "Why Platinum?" section in the flyer is most appealing to Mr. Taylor?

(A) Free consultation　(B) Free cancellation and removal

(C) Free data transfer (up to 40TB)　(D) Only $0.01 per GB (after 40TB)

Unit 9 Housing & Corporate Property 房屋／公司地產

本主題涵蓋內容包括：

- **construction** 建築

- **specifications** 規格

- **buying and renting**
  購買和租賃

- **electric and gas services**
  電力瓦斯服務

WORD POWER

 TRACK 56

---

01 **amenity** [ə`mɛnətɪ] *n.* 便利設備；（環境等的）舒適

同 facility *n.* 設施

- We put all visiting partners in a local 4-star hotel that has lots of amenities such as a minibar and a jacuzzi.

  我們安排所有來訪的夥伴下榻當地的四星級飯店，那裡有很多便利設備，像是迷你吧檯與按摩浴缸。

  說明 作「便利設備」解時常用複數形。飯店設備中，amenity 通常指個人使用的東西，像是房間裡的煮水壺（kettle）、咖啡機、電視及按摩浴缸等這些較小型的便利設備。facility 通常則指可供飯店房客共同使用的較大型設施，如游泳池、健身房、網球場或水療館等。

---

02 **architecture** [`ɑrkə͵tɛktʃə] *n.* 建築物；建築構造

衍 architect *n.* 建築師
衍 architectural *adj.* 建築的；建築學的

- Our building is in the old downtown area that boasts mostly classic architecture.

  我們的大樓位在舊城區，那裡以多為復古建築而自豪。

---

03 **basement** [`besmənt] *n.* 地下室

同 cellar *n.* 地下室；地窖

- The company owns the first two floors, as well as the basement, which it uses for storage.

  一樓跟二樓是該公司所有，連同用作倉庫的地下室也是。

---

04 **block** [blɑk] *n.* 街區；區塊 *v.* 擋住；阻礙

- Our factory is only four blocks down from our main store.

  我們的工廠和主要店鋪之間只有四個街區的距離。

- Our plan to move to that site has been blocked by the local council.

  我們想要搬遷到那個地點的計畫被地方議會阻撓了。

---

05 **closet** [`klɑzɪt] *n.* 衣櫃；壁櫥

同 wardrobe *n.*（可搬移的）衣櫃
關 rack *n.* 掛物架
關 hanger *n.*（掛單件衣服的）衣架

- Our office has a closet for staff to put their coats in.

  我們辦公室裡有一個衣櫃，讓員工放大衣外套。

  說明 可走進的「大型衣櫃間」則稱為 walk-in closet。

06 condominium [ˋkɑndəˏmɪnɪəm] n.（各戶有獨立產權的）公寓大廈

• My boss owns a condominium in a new building by the lake.

我老闆在湖邊新建的公寓大廈擁有一戶產權。

說明 常簡稱為 condo。

常見的房屋種類

condominium 公寓大廈
每戶各自擁有產權，公共空間則為所有住戶共有，類似台灣的電梯華廈。

apartment 公寓
各戶分別出租，但整棟樓屬於單一產權，常由租賃公司統一管理。

house 獨棟房屋
通常有好幾個房間以及車庫、草坪和院子。

duplex 雙拼式房屋
兩間房子相連，共用一面牆，各有獨立門戶。

townhouse 多棟聯建住宅
多棟建築相連的透天住宅，多為二至三層樓。

studio 套房
臥房和客廳、廚房連在一起，除浴室外無其他隔間。

07 construction [kənˋstrʌkʃən] n. 建造；建設

• The design of the new office building has been approved by the government and construction will start soon.

新辦公大樓的設計已得到政府核准，很快就會開始興建。

常用詞彙 construction site 工地

常考片語 under construction 建構中

• Our new office building is currently under construction.

我們的新辦公大樓還在興建中。

衍 reconstruction n.
重建（物）

衍 constructional adj.
構造的；建造的

SECTION B 必備詞彙 ｜ UNIT 9 Housing & Corporate Property 房屋／公司地產

08　couch [kautʃ] *n.* 沙發

- At lunch time, employees from the office hurry to the café to grab a seat on one of the couches.

  午休時間時，辦公室的員工急忙趕到咖啡廳去占沙發區的座位。

常用詞彙 couch potato 電視迷（指不喜歡活動、整天躺在沙發上看電視的人）

圓 sofa *n.* 沙發

09　cupboard [ˋkʌbəd] *n.* 碗櫥

- If you need any bread, there's plenty in the cupboard.

  如果你想吃麵包的話，碗櫥裡面有很多。

圓 cabinet *n.* 櫥櫃

10　decoration [ˌdɛkəˋreʃən] *n.* 裝潢；裝飾

- We put up a tree and some decorations in our office every Christmas.

  每年聖誕節我們都會在辦公室裡立起一棵樹並放上一些裝飾品。

衍 decor *n.* 裝飾；室內裝潢

衍 decorate *v.* 裝飾；布置

11　district [ˋdɪstrɪkt] *n.* 行政區；特區

- We may have to move out of the business district in order to save money.

  為了省錢，我們也許得搬出商業區。

圓 area *n.* 地區

12　downtown [ˌdaʊnˋtaʊn] *n.* 市中心 *adj./adv.* 在市中心的（地）

- The restaurant is close to downtown so there might be some traffic.

  餐廳離市中心很近，所以可能會稍微塞車。

- Carl's office is downtown but he lives just outside the city.

  卡爾的公司在市中心，但是他住在市外。

反 uptown *n.* 非鬧區；住宅區 *adj./adv.* 在住宅區的（地）

13　elevator [ˋɛləˌvetə] *n.* 電梯

- There are four elevators that serve the 12 floors of this office building.

  這棟十二層樓的辦公大樓有四座電梯可供使用。

常用詞彙 elevator music【口】商店或公共場所播放的乏味音樂

衍 elevate *v.* 抬起；舉起；使上升

14 escalator [ˋɛskəˌletə] *n.* 電扶梯

- Department stores usually have escalators as well as elevators, to allow people to move around the building easily.

  百貨公司通常有電扶梯和電梯，讓人們可以輕易地在建築物裡四處移動。

衍 escalate *v.* 逐步上升

15 estate agent 房屋仲介

- Bob is an estate agent who specializes in corporate property rentals.

  鮑伯是一位房屋仲介，專門處理公司地產的租賃。

關 real estate agency 房仲公司

關 real estate 不動產；房地產

16 fire escape 逃生通道

- It is the law in this country that every office must have at least two fire escapes.

  這個國家的法律規定每間辦公室要有至少兩個逃生通道。

同 fire exit 逃生出口

17 foreman [ˋfɔrmən] *n.* 工頭；領班

- When the foreman left the company, Bill was the obvious replacement because he was the most experienced.

  當工頭離開公司後，比爾顯然是接班人，因為他最資深。

同 overseer *n.* 工頭

18 foundation [faʊnˋdeʃən] *n.* 地基；基礎

- The buildings in this country need to have very strong foundations because there are a lot of earthquakes.

  該國的建築需要有非常堅固的地基，因為那裡常有地震。

- The company's success is built on a foundation of good work ethics.

  該公司的成功建立在優良工作道德的基礎上。

同 base *n.* 基部

19 furnishings [ˋfɜnɪʃɪŋz] *n.* 室內陳設品；家飾（常用複數）

- Home furnishings are on the third floor next to the toy department.

  家飾區在三樓，就在玩具區旁邊。

衍 furnish *v.* 為（房間）配置家具

衍 furnished *adj.* 有配置家具的

SECTION B 必備詞彙

UNIT 9 Housing & Corporate Property 房屋／公司地產

20 **furniture** [ˈfɜnɪtʃə] *n.* (沙發、桌椅、床等大型實用的)家具

- The cleaner had to move some furniture in order to clean the office properly.
  清潔人員必須移動一些家具才能好好打掃辦公室。

---

21 **inherently** [ɪnˈhɪrəntlɪ] *adv.* 本質上；先天地

- Construction work is an inherently dangerous business.
  營造方面的工作本質上就具有危險性。

衍 inherent *adj.* 固有的；與生俱來的

---

22 **landlord** [ˈlændˌlɔrd] *n.* 房東

- The company moved out of their office because management had a bad relationship with the landlord.
  那間公司搬離了他們的辦公室，因為管理階層與房東的關係不好。

同 lessor *n.* 出租人

反 tenant *n.* 承租人；房客

---

23 **leak** [lik] *n.* 滲；漏 *v.* 洩漏(信息)

- Bill put a bucket on the floor because there was a leak coming from the ceiling.
  比爾在地上放了一個水桶，因為天花板在漏水。

- The employee who leaked important company data to the media has been fired.
  洩漏公司重要資料給媒體的那個員工被開除了。

衍 leaky *adj.* 有漏洞的

衍 leakage *n.* 滲漏量或物

---

24 **lease** [lis] *v.* 租用；出租 *n.* 租約；契約

- We need to decide whether to buy office space or to lease.
  我們需要決定辦公空間要用買的還是用租的。

- We signed a 4-year lease for our company headquarters.
  我們為總公司簽訂了為期四年的租約。

同 rent *v.* 租

衍 sublease *v.* 轉租；分租

25 location [loˋkeʃən] n. 場所；位置

- The restaurant had problems attracting customers due to its bad location.

  這間餐廳由於地點不佳，無法順利吸引顧客。

同 place、site、spot、position n. 地點

衍 locate v. 找出……的位置；設置

---

26 mortgage [ˋmɔrgɪdʒ] n. 房屋貸款；抵押；抵押單據

- The company couldn't afford the whole warehouse, so they took out a mortgage which allowed them to pay over many years.

  那間公司無法負擔整個倉庫的價格，所以他們申辦了房屋貸款，讓他們可以在未來幾年付完。

  說明 可用 take out a . . . mortgage 表示貸款的金額及期數，例如：take out a $50,000 mortgage 指「貸款五萬元」、take out a ten-year mortgage 則指「十年期貸款」。

  常用詞彙 mortgage broker 貸款經紀人

同 loan n. 貸款

關 monthly payment 月付額

---

27 neighborhood [ˋnebɚͺhud] n. 鄰近地區；社區

- The company provides many jobs for local people in the neighborhood.

  那間公司為社區當地人口提供了很多工作機會。

衍 neighbor n. 鄰居

衍 neighboring adj. 鄰近的

---

28 plumber [ˋplʌmɚ] n. 水管工

- We had to call a plumber because there was a leak in the bathroom.

  因為浴室漏水，我們必須打電話請水電工來一趟。

衍 plumbing n. 鉛管工的工作；建築配管工程

關 electrician n. 電工

---

29 porch [pɔrtʃ] n. 門廊；走廊

- We had to remove the porch when we turned the house into a store.

  我們把這房子改建成店鋪時，必須把門廊拆掉。

關 balcony n. 陽台

30 preferably [ˋprɛfərəblɪ] *adv.* 更好地；最好是

衍 preferable *adj.* 更好的

• We are looking for office space that can accommodate at least 50 employees, and preferably more.

我們正在尋找可以容納至少五十名員工的辦公室空間，最好是還可以容納更多人的。

---

31 property [ˋprɑpətɪ] *n.* 房產；地產；財產

同 estate *n.* 地產

• A security fence surrounds the property.

一道安全圍籬圍繞著這棟房產。

---

32 quote [kwot] *n.* 報價；開價

衍 quotation *n.* 引用；引文

• Our company plans to build a new headquarters and is already collecting quotes from land developers.

我們公司計畫建造一個新的總部，而且已經在向土地開發商收集報價了。

說明 quote 亦可作動詞表「引用；引述」之意。如 quote sb. as saying sth. 即指「引述某人的話說……」。

常考片語 give sb. a quote 提供報價給某人

• We asked several companies to give us a quote for the work.

我們請數家公司提供此工程的報價給我們。

---

33 raise [rez] *v.* 籌措；募集 *n.* 加薪

衍 fundraising *n.* 募款（也可拼成 fund-raising）

衍 fund-raiser *n.* 募款活動；募款人

• Following a successful year, the company has raised enough funds to open a new factory.

在成功的一年後，該公司已籌措足夠的資金來開設新工廠。

常考片語 give sb. a raise 給某人加薪

• Staff were not given a raise because the company has not made a profit this year.

員工並未被加薪，因為公司今年沒有獲利。

34 real estate 房地產；不動產

- We will contact a real estate agent to help us find a suitable location.

  我們會聯絡房屋仲介，請他幫我們找一個適合的地點。

  常用詞彙 real estate agent 房屋仲介；不動產經紀人

同 land、property *n.* 土地；地產

---

35 remodel [rɪ`mɑdl̩] *v.* 改建；重新塑造

- Staff were moved to a temporary location while the office was remodeled.

  辦公室整修的時候，員工們搬到一個臨時的地點上班。

同 renovate、remake *v.* 整修；改造

---

36 renovation [ˌrɛnə`veʃən] *n.* 整修

- The renovation of this building will be difficult because it's very old.

  這棟建築物的翻修作業將會很困難，因為它很舊了。

衍 renovate *v.* 整修

---

37 rent [rɛnt] *v.* 租用 *n.* 租金；出租的財產

- After the company got bigger, it stopped renting its offices and bought new ones.

  該公司的規模有所成長後，便不再租用辦公室，而是買下新的辦公室。

- The landlord wants to increase the rent on his apartments.

  房東想要漲公寓的租金。

  說明 名詞作「租金」解時亦可用 rental。

同 lease *v.* 租用；出租

關 rental contract 租賃合約

---

38 residence [`rɛzədəns] *n.* 住所；住宅；居住

- Luckily, my residence is within walking distance of my office.

  幸好我的房子就在我辦公室的步行距離內。

衍 resident *n.* 居民；定居者

衍 residential *adj.* 居住的；住宅區的

---

39 retrieve [rɪ`triv] *v.* 收回；取回

- We were not able to retrieve a full deposit when we moved out due to some damage that occurred.

  因為房子有一些毀損，所以我們搬走時無法拿回全額的押金。

同 reclaim *v.* 重新奪回

40 suburb [`sʌbɝb] *n.* （城市周圍的）郊區
- Buying office space in the suburbs instead of the city center will save us money.
  購買郊區而非市中心的辦公空間將會幫我們省下一筆錢。

- outskirts *n.* 郊外；郊區
- suburban *adj.* 郊區的；近郊的
- urban *adj.* 市區的

---

41 tenant [`tɛnənt] *n.* 房客；承租人
- In the rental contract, the company is referred to as "the tenant".
  在租賃合約中，公司被稱為「承租人」。

- renter *n.* 承租人
- landlord *n.* 房東

---

42 tile [taɪl] *n.* 磁磚
- Our office kitchen has tiles on the floor to make it easier to clean.
  我們公司廚房的地板鋪了磁磚，以便清潔。

- building/ construction materials 建材
- concrete *n.* 混凝土
- cement *n.* 水泥
- grout *n.* 水泥漿

---

43 urgency [`ɝdʒənsi] *n.* 緊急；迫切
- There was an urgency in the landlady's voice that suggested she wanted to sell the place quickly.
  女房東的聲音中帶著急迫感，暗示她想要迅速售出那個地點。

- urgent *adj.* 緊急的

---

44 utility [ju`tɪlətɪ] *n.* 公用事業
- Our rent does not include utilities such as water and electricity.
  我們房租的不包括水電等費用。

說明 多用複數 utilities 表示水電、瓦斯等費用。

- service *n.* 公共事業

---

45 venue [`vɛnju] *n.* 場所；會場
- We're looking for a 500 capacity venue to hold our annual company dinner.
  我們正在尋找一個能容納五百人的場地來舉辦公司年度晚宴。

常用詞彙 venue layout 場館配置圖

PRACTICE TEST

Part 1: Photographs

TRACK 57

Directions:

For each question in this part, you will hear four statements about a picture. When you hear the statements, you must select the one statement that best describes what you see in the picture. Then circle the letter (A), (B), (C), or (D). The statements will not be printed below and will be spoken only one time.

(A)　(B)　(C)　(D)　　　　　(A)　(B)　(C)　(D)

Part 2: Question and Response

TRACK 58

Directions:

You will hear a question or statement and three responses spoken in English. They will be spoken only one time and will not be printed below. Select the best response to the question or statement and circle the letter (A), (B), or (C).

3️⃣ (A)　(B)　(C)

4️⃣ (A)　(B)　(C)

5️⃣ (A)　(B)　(C)

6️⃣ (A)　(B)　(C)

Part 3: Short Conversations

✎ TRACK 59

Directions:

You will hear some conversations between two or more people. You will be asked to answer three questions about what the speakers say in each conversation. Select the best response to each question and circle the letter (A), (B), (C), or (D). The conversation will be spoken only one time and will not be printed below.

7 How does the man think the woman should feel about the leak?

(A) She should feel patient and relaxed.

(B) She should feel extremely angry.

(C) She should feel guilty and apologetic.

(D) She should feel a sense of urgency.

8 What does the woman mean when she says "for the time being"?

(A) Before they set up a warning sign

(B) Until a plumber comes to fix the leak

(C) While the plumber is fixing the leak

(D) Until the ceiling collapses

9 What does the woman tell the man to do?

(A) Make a sign

(B) Fix the ceiling

(C) Call a plumber

(D) Speak to staff

	Furniture	Washing Machine	Dryer	Air Conditioner
Property 1	✔	✔	✔	
Property 2		✔	✔	✔
Property 3	✔			✔
Property 4		✔		✔

10 What type of home is the man willing to consider?

(A) A house 　　　　　　　　　(B) An apartment

(C) A townhouse 　　　　　　　(D) Any type

11 What most likely is the woman's job?

(A) College student advisor 　　(B) Software programmer

(C) Bank clerk 　　　　　　　　(D) Estate agent

12 Look at the table. Which property is most suitable for the man?

(A) Property 1 　　　　　　　　(B) Property 2

(C) Property 3 　　　　　　　　(D) Property 4

Part 4: Short Talks

 TRACK 60

Directions:

You will hear some short talks given by a single speaker. You will be asked to answer three questions about what the speaker says in each talk. Select the best response to each question and circle the letter (A), (B), (C), or (D). The talks will be spoken only one time and will not be printed below.

13 Who is being addressed?

(A) Company staff 　　　　　　(B) CEO of a company

(C) Visitors to a company 　　　(D) Security staff

14 Why is the company moving to a new office building?

(A) The old office was badly damaged.

(B) The company is growing larger every day.

(C) It has newer and more impressive facilities.

(D) Access to the old office is temporarily blocked.

15 What is required to get into the main gate for the new office block?

(A) A signature 　　　　　　　(B) A swipe card

(C) An access code 　　　　　　(D) An ID card

FOR RENT! $150 p/month

Meeting Spaces

Conveniently located downtown
(near Central Station).

Spacious meeting room with tables
and chairs provided.

16 What is being promoted in the presentation?

(A) A company offering real estate lawyer services

(B) An online bank's mortgage service

(C) A furniture removals company promotion

(D) A website for renting out office space

17 Look at the graphic. How much money will the website keep from the listing of meeting spaces?

(A) Nothing. The entire rental fee is kept by the landlord.

(B) The website will keep $135 per month.

(C) The website will keep $15 per month.

(D) 100% of the rental fee is kept by the website.

18 What do the online forms make it easy for landlords to do?

(A) Set terms and conditions

(B) Buy or sell furniture

(C) Find new spaces to lease

(D) Contact potential tenants

Part 5: Incomplete Sentences

Directions:

A word or phrase is missing in each of the sentences below. Four answer choices are given below each sentence. Select the best answer to complete the sentence. Then circle the letter (A), (B), (C), or (D).

19 People who live in this _____ say they like it because it's very peaceful but also very convenient.

(A) neighborhood
(B) soil
(C) renovation
(D) tile

20 Outside the front of the house is a porch with some chairs _____ you can relax and get some fresh air.

(A) whose
(B) which
(C) where
(D) whom

21 All workers on this construction site, including the foreman, _____ by law to wear a hard hat.

(A) is requiring
(B) are required
(C) require
(D) required

22 We keep extra supplies, such as tissue paper and washing liquid, _____ the cabinet under the kitchen sink.

(A) by
(B) at
(C) on
(D) in

23 We still have another four months left on the lease, _____?

(A) don't we
(B) won't we
(C) do we
(D) will we

Part 6: Text Completion

Directions:

Read the text below. A word, phrase, or sentence is missing. For each empty space in the text, select the best answer to complete the text. Then circle the letter (A), (B), (C), or (D).

Questions 24-27 refer to the following notice.

CAUTION!

Dear All,

Due to recent issues with a couple of the elevators, a team of repairmen will be working on them ---24--- the next 2-3 days. ---25--- We understand and apologize for the inconvenience. The escalators from the first to the fifth floor are in perfect working order, so please use these and/or the stairs until the elevator system is up and running again. Please also make sure to stay clear of the areas in front of the elevators in order to ---26--- the repair workers to do their job. Thank you for your ---27--- during this time and we apologize once again for the inconvenience.

Security & Maintenance

The Elden Building

---

24 (A) over   (B) with

     (C) under   (D) by

25 (A) Unfortunately, we cannot say exactly when the escalators will be working again.

     (B) This is a modern system that has a reputation for never breaking down.

     (C) So until tomorrow, please use the stairs and/or escalators.

     (D) As a result of this, all elevators are out of order until further notice.

26 (A) make   (B) cause

     (C) allow   (D) force

27 (A) patient   (B) patience

     (C) patients   (D) patiently

Part 7: Reading Comprehension

Directions:

In this part you will read a selection of texts, such as magazine and newspaper articles, e-mails, and instant messages. Each text is followed by several questions. Select the best answer for each question and circle the letter (A), (B), (C), or (D).

Questions 28-30 refer to the following e-mail.

To: Adam Reynolds <a.reynolds@tmail.com>

From: Patricia Johnson <patricia@corpproperty.com>

Subject: Lionsdown Road

Dear Mr. Reynolds,

Thank you for expressing an interest in the property at 32A Lionsdown Road. ---[1]--- I will do my best to answer your questions as far as possible. First of all, yes, the property is still available at the price quoted. ---[2]--- And no, the property does not currently have a restaurant license but it would make a great venue for a restaurant. There are fire escapes on both floors, which make it legally possible to run a restaurant. ---[3]--- As far as the construction of a kitchen goes, there is a large area in the basement which may be suitable. As you know, it is located in the heart of a commercial district that is famous for its cuisine. ---[4]---

Give me a call if you have any further questions or would like to arrange a viewing.

Thank you,
Patricia Johnson

---

28 What is the purpose of the e-mail?

(A) To answer questions about food health and safety

(B) To persuade someone to open a specific business

(C) To answers questions from a potential buyer

(D) To find out information about a new venue

29 What is NOT listed as a reason why the venue would make a good restaurant?

(A) It already has a restaurant license.

(B) It has fire escapes on both floors.

(C) It has a basement that could fit a kitchen.

(D) It is in a good area for this kind of business.

30 In which of the positions marked [1], [2], [3], and [4] does the following sentence best belong?

"So local residents, as well as tourists, are used to dining out in the area."

(A) [1] (B) [2]

(C) [3] (D) [4]

Questions 31-35 refer to the following letter, enclosed map, and e-mail.

To the shareholders of RealGoods Inc.,

I am writing today to inform you of updates regarding the continued expansion of RealGoods Inc. In January's annual meeting, we reported on the wonderful progress being made at our new Beijing location. I'd like to update you on what is happening with our other enterprises: Tokyo and Delhi. Firstly, construction on the new factory and warehouse in Tokyo remains on track and we fully expect to meet our target opening date of November 30th.

With regards to the India project, our Delhi offices are finally up and running. However, we are still researching factory and warehouse sites that tick the right boxes, namely transport links and the availability of local skilled workers. Until we have laid the foundations for our own site, we will rent factory space in Delhi. Expansion can be one of the best ways to drive growth, but it is also inherently high-risk, so we are being as thorough as possible in gathering local knowledge for the Indian market.

We remain optimistic that expansion into the Japanese and Indian markets will be productive, and you can expect to see gains reflected in the next financial report. If all goes as well as forecast over the coming year, we will start looking more closely at the other locations on the enclosed map.

Yours faithfully,

Ron Williams
CEO
RealGoods Inc.

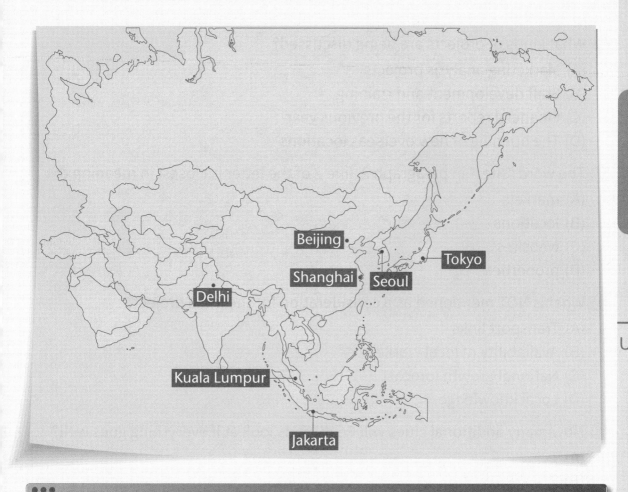

To: Ron Williams <rwilliams@realgoods.com>

From: Raju Singh <rjsingh@imail.com>

Subject: New Asia Locations

Dear Mr. Williams,

I read your recent letter with great interest. Not only have I held shares with RealGoods for almost ten years, but I am also originally from Delhi, India. I understand that good things take time and I am encouraged by your attention to detail in this matter. I think the idea to rent space until this is achieved is a good one, as it is important to get into the market as soon as possible. I do, however, have some concerns. It is always a delight when new buildings complement the local architecture instead of merely adding another "eyesore" to the skyline. So I would like to be forwarded any designs for new buildings when they come about. I also hope that a company as RealGoods would be aiming to continue its care in the community projects. As well as providing jobs and contributing to the economy, it is vitally important to help out local neighborhoods wherever possible. Can you tell me what the plans are with regards to this?

Thank you very much.

Sincerely,
Raju Singh

31 What kinds of projects are being discussed?
(A) Marketing analysis projects
(B) Staff development and training
(C) Financial reports for the previous year
(D) The opening of new overseas locations

32 The word "sites" in paragraph 2, line 2 of the letter is closest in meaning to
(A) markets
(B) locations
(C) websites
(D) properties

33 What is NOT mentioned as a consideration for the India project?
(A) Transport links
(B) Availability of local workers
(C) National growth forecast
(D) Local knowledge

34 How many additional cities will RealGoods look at if everything goes well?
(A) 1
(B) 2
(C) 3
(D) 4

35 What is Mr. Raju Singh referring to when he says, "I am encouraged by your attention to detail in this matter"?
(A) The company's investment in transportation
(B) The company's thorough research into locations
(C) The company's commitment to meeting deadlines
(D) The company's consideration of local architecture

Unit 10 Travel 旅遊

本主題涵蓋內容包括:

- trains 火車
- airplanes 飛機
- taxis 計程車
- buses 巴士
- ships 船隻
- ferries 渡輪
- tickets 票務
- schedules 時刻表
- station & airport announcements
  車站和機場廣播
- car rentals 租車
- hotels 飯店
- reservations 預訂
- delays & cancellations 航班／車次延誤與取消

WORD POWER

 TRACK 61

01 airline [ˈɛrˌlaɪn] *n.* 航空公司
- We always take business trips with the same airline because we trust their service.

  我們出差時總是搭乘同一家航空公司，因為我們信任他們的服務。

  常用詞彙 budget airline 廉價航空（亦可說 low-cost airline）

關 aircraft *n.* 飛機；航空器

02 announcement [əˈnaʊnsmənt] *n.* 公告；宣告
- Did you just hear that announcement? Our flight has been delayed.

  你聽到剛剛的公告了嗎？我們的航班延誤了。

衍 announce *v.* 宣布；公諸於眾

衍 announcer *n.*（廣播、電視的）播音員；播報員

03 bellhop [ˈbɛlˌhɑp] *n.* 行李員；侍者
- When you arrive at the hotel, a bellhop will be waiting to show you to your room.

  您抵達飯店時，會有一位行李員等著帶您到您的房間。

  說明 亦可說 bellboy。

關 luggage、baggage *n.* 行李

04 belongings [bəˈlɔŋɪŋz] *n.* 財產；攜帶物品
- I prefer to put valuable belongings in a small bag that I take onto the plane with me.

  我偏好把貴重的私人物品放在一個小包包裡隨身帶上飛機。

同 possession *n.* 擁有物；財產

關 belong to 屬於

05 boarding pass 登機證
- Have your boarding pass ready as you'll have to show it to airport staff when getting on the plane.

  準備好你的登機證，因為上飛機的時候你必須拿給機場的工作人員看。

衍 board *v.* 登上（車、船、飛機等）

同 boarding ticket 登機證

關 boarding gate 登機門

關 passport *n.* 護照

關 flight *n.* 航班

關 class *n.* 艙等

06 cabin ［ˋkæbɪn］ *n.* 機艙

- People on the plane lined up as they waited to exit the cabin.

  機上的人們排隊等待離開機艙。

關 cockpit *n.* 駕駛艙

07 captain ［ˋkæptən］ *n.* 機長；船長

- The captain announced that the plane was going to land in 15 minutes.

  機長公布說飛機將在十五分鐘內降落。

同 pilot *n.* 機長；駕駛員

關 copilot *n.* 副駕駛員；副機長

08 carry-on ［ˋkærɪˏɑn］ *adj.* 可隨身攜帶的 *n.*（帶進機艙的）隨身行李

- My bag weighed more than 7kg so the airline didn't let me bring it on the plane as carry-on luggage.

  我的包包重量超過七公斤，所以航空公司不讓我把它當隨身行李帶上飛機。

- This small bag is my carry-on.

  這個小袋子是我的隨身行李。

同 cabin baggage（帶進機艙的）隨身行李

關 check-in baggage 託運行李

09 check in （機場櫃檯）報到；登記入住（旅館）

- Travelers are required to check in for flights at least one hour before departure.

  旅客必須至少在起飛前一小時報到。

常用詞彙 check-in counter 報到櫃檯

反 check out（旅館）退房；結帳手續

10 claim ［klem］ *v.* 要求……的所有權；認領；宣稱

- It took a while to claim my luggage because mine was the last suitcase to come out.

  我等了很久才提領到行李，因為我的行李箱是最後一個出來的。

說明 claim 亦可作名詞，指「要求；索賠；宣言」。

常用詞彙 baggage claim (area) 行李提領處
baggage claim check 行李提領單

同 collect、take、call for 領取

同 declare *v.* 宣稱

關 carousel *n.* 行李轉盤

11 complimentary [ˌkɑmpləˋmɛntərɪ] *adj.*
【美】贈送的
- The airline offers complimentary water, tea, and coffee, but other items must be paid for.
  航空公司提供免費的水、茶與咖啡，但其他品項是要付費的。

⬛ free *adj.* 免費的

---

12 concierge [ˌkɑnsɪˋɛrʒ] *n.* 服務台職員
- The hotel concierge spoke good English and recommended some good local restaurants.
  飯店的服務台人員英文說得很棒，並推薦了當地一些不錯的餐廳。

關 clerk *n.* 辦事人員

關 receptionist *n.* 接待員

說明 大型飯店服務台通常會有 concierge 提供房客各項服務，包括旅遊諮詢、行程安排、活動訂票、接送機等。

---

13 consulate [ˋkɑnsələt] *n.* 領事館
- When we arrived in Hong Kong, we visited the British consulate for advice.
  當我們抵達香港的時候，我們造訪了英國駐香港總領事館尋求建議。

關 embassy *n.* 大使館

---

14 crew [kru] *n.*（飛機的）全體機員；空勤人員
- I tried getting the attention of the crew but no one noticed me.
  我試著引起機組人員的注意，但沒人注意到我。

關 flight attendant 空服員

常用詞彙 flight crew 機組人員

---

15 culinary [ˋkʌləˌnɛrɪ] *adj.* 烹飪的
- The culinary experience was a delight when we flew first class.
  我們搭頭等艙時享受到的料理體驗真是令人愉快。

說明 本字只能置於名詞前修飾。

常用詞彙 culinary skills 烹飪技巧
culinary delights 美食

⬛ cooking *adj.* 烹飪的

16 depart [dɪ`pɑrt] *v.* 啟程；出發

- The train departs in 10 minutes so we should hurry up.

  火車十分鐘後就要開了，所以我們應該快一點。

  常考片語 depart for (+ 地方) 前往……
  　　　　 depart from (+ 地方) 從……出發

- Your flight departs from JFK International Airport at 8:35 a.m.

  您的班機於早上八點三十五分從約翰・甘迺迪國際機場起飛。

同 leave、go、set off 離開；出發

反 arrive *v.* 抵達

衍 departure *n.* 出發

---

17 destination [ˌdɛstə`neʃən] *n.* 目的地；終點

- There was a problem with the station at our destination, so the train had to stop one station earlier.

  我們目的地的車站出了點問題，所以火車必須提早一站停靠。

  常用詞彙 tourist destination 觀光景點；度假景點

衍 destined *adj.* 注定的；（場所）預定的

---

18 dock [dɑk] *v.* 停靠碼頭；停泊

- The boat docked at its destination 10 minutes later than scheduled.

  該船比預定時間晚十分鐘停靠在它的目的地。

  說明 dock 作名詞用時則表示「船塢；碼頭」。

關 port、harbor *n.* 港口

---

19 drop-off service 異地還車服務

- Make use of our drop-off service and leave your car at any of our 25 drop-off locations around the city.

  利用我們的異地還車服務，可將車還到我們在市內的二十五個還車地點。

  說明 pick-up / drop-off service 則指「機場接送服務」。

關 car rental 租車

---

20 entrance [`ɛntrəns] *n.* 入口

- We were greeted by hotel staff at the entrance.

  我們在入口處受到飯店工作人員的歡迎。

同 gate *n.* 大門

同 doorway *n.* 門口；出入口

衍 enter *v.* 進入

SECTION B 必備詞彙

UNIT **10** Travel 旅遊

21 **express train** 高速列車

- There is an express train that runs from the airport to the city center.

  有一班高速列車從機場開往市中心。

  說明 常簡稱為 express。

🔗 local train 普通車

🔗 express *adj.* 迅捷的
   v. 表達

22 **fare** [fɛr] *n.* （公車、飛機、計程車等）費用

- The fare for the airport bus is just two dollars and fifty cents.

  機場巴士的車資只要二點五美元。

  常用詞彙 bus/train/cab fare 公車／火車／計程車費

🔗 half-fare *adj.* 半價的

🔗 full-fare *adj.* 全價的

23 **front desk** 櫃檯

- Can you call the front desk to ask if we can borrow an iron?

  你可不可以打電話給櫃檯問問看我們能不能借一個熨斗？

  常用詞彙 front-desk clerk 櫃檯人員

🔗 information desk 資訊櫃檯

24 **housekeeping (service)** 房間清潔（服務）

- Housekeeping will clean the room in the afternoon while the guests are out.

  飯店清潔人員會在下午房客出門時打掃房間。

🔗 housekeep *v.* 管家

🔗 housekeeper *n.* 管家；飯店打掃人員

25 **immigration** [ˌɪməˋgreʃən] *n.* 入境處；移民局；移民；入境檢查（不可數名詞）

- The lady at immigration asked me about my purpose for visiting the country.

  入境處的女士問我造訪這個國家的原因。

🔗 immigrate *v.* （從外國）移入；移居

🔗 emigration *n.* 移居；遷出

🔗 emigrate *v.* 移居國外

26 **itinerary** [aɪˋtɪnəˌrɛrɪ] *n.* 行程計畫

- I'll have a good look at the itinerary while I'm on the train.

  我在火車上會好好看一下行程表。

27 keycard [ˈki͵kɑrd] *n.* 房卡；鑰匙卡
- My keycard must've accidentally slipped out of my pocket in the taxi, so I couldn't get in the office.
  我在計程車上時，門禁卡一定是不小心從口袋裡滑出來了，所以我沒辦法進辦公室。

🔗 swipe card 刷卡卡片

28 laid-back [ˈledˋbæk] *adj.* 悠閒的；懶散的
- The airline crew's laid-back and friendly attitude helps travelers feel relaxed.
  航空機組人員悠然和善的態度幫助旅客放鬆。

🔵 mellow *adj.* 放鬆的；令人愉快的

🔴 uptight *adj.* 緊張的；焦慮不安的

29 landing [ˈlændɪŋ] *n.* 降落；登陸
- Airplane pilots take pride in making a smooth landing.
  飛機的駕駛員以能平穩降落而自豪。

🔴 takeoff *n.* 起飛（動詞為 take off）

30 landmark [ˈlænd͵mɑrk] *n.* 地標
- We told the travel agent which landmarks in the brochure we were interested in seeing.
  我們告訴旅行社專員我們想去這本小冊子中的哪些地標。

31 laundromat [ˈlɔndrəmæt] *n.* 自助洗衣店
- Our washing machine was broken, so we had to take our dirty clothes to the laundromat.
  我們的洗衣機壞掉了，所以我們必須把髒衣服拿到自助洗衣店洗。

🔵 laundry *n.* 洗衣店；洗衣間（可數）；待洗或剛洗好的衣物（不可數）

32 legroom [ˈlɛg͵rum] *n.* （與前排座位之間的）腿部空間
- If you ask to sit in the emergency exit seats, you will have more legroom.
  如果你要求坐靠近緊急逃生出口的座位，你就會有比較大的腿部伸展空間。

33 **luggage** [ˋlʌgɪdʒ] *n.* 行李 　　　　　　　　　　🔵 baggage *n.* 行李

- The airline lost my luggage, so I don't have any fresh
  clothes.
  航空公司把我的行李弄丟了，所以我沒有任何乾淨的衣物。

常用詞彙 luggage tag 行李標籤
　　　　luggage/baggage cart 行李推車（亦稱為 trolley）
　　　　luggage delivery service 行李運送服務
　　　　luggage deposit service 行李寄存服務
　　　　(free) baggage allowance 免費行李託運量；行李限額

34 **metropolis** [məˋtrɑpəlɪs] *n.* 大都市 　　🔵 metropolitan *adj.*
　　　　　　　　　　　　　　　　　　　　　　　　大都市的

- We wanted to get out of the busy metropolis and
  travel to the countryside for a nice, quiet weekend.
  我們想要遠離忙碌的城市，到郊外度過一個美好、安靜的週末。

　　　　　　　　　　　　　　　　　　　　　🔵 Metropolitan
　　　　　　　　　　　　　　　　　　　　　　 Museum of Art
　　　　　　　　　　　　　　　　　　　　　　 大都會藝術博物館（簡稱
　　　　　　　　　　　　　　　　　　　　　　 為 The Met，位於美國紐
　　　　　　　　　　　　　　　　　　　　　　 約中央公園旁，是世界上
　　　　　　　　　　　　　　　　　　　　　　 最大、參觀人數最多的藝
　　　　　　　　　　　　　　　　　　　　　　 術博物館之一）

35 **overhead compartment**（機艙座位上方　　🔵 overhead bin（機艙
的）置物櫃　　　　　　　　　　　　　　　　　　　 座位上方的）置物櫃

- The flight attendant helped me to put my bags into
  the overhead compartment.
  空服員幫我把我的包包放到上方的置物櫃裡。

說明 compartment [kəmˋpɑrtmənt] 指「隔間」。

36 **passenger** [ˋpæsənˌdʒɚ] *n.* 乘客；旅客 　　🔵 commuter *n.* 通勤者

- The pilot's announcement was intended to make the
  passengers feel calm.
  機長的公告是為了要讓乘客安心。

37 **refreshment** [rɪˋfrɛʃmənt] *n.* 茶點；便餐

- This is a budget airline, so they only sell basic
  refreshments.
  這是廉價航空，所以他們只販售基本的點心。

38 route map 路線圖

同 road map 路線圖

- The route map in the Tokyo train station was confusing because it had so many lines.

東京車站裡的路線圖令人困惑，因為路線太多了。

說明 route 可讀作 [rut] 或 [raut]，指「路線；路程；航線」。

39 shuttle bus 接駁車

衍 shuttle *n.* 短程交通工具 *v.*（短程）往返運送

- There is a shuttle bus which takes people from the airport to Main Station.

有一班接駁車從機場載送人們到火車總站。

40 standby [ˈstændˌbaɪ] *adv.* 候補

- I'm on standby, which means I can get on the flight if someone cancels.

我在後補機位的名單上，這表示如果有人取消訂位我就可以上飛機。

常用詞彙 standby ticket 候補票

41 suitable [ˈsutəbḷ] *adj.* 合適的；適宜的

衍 suit *v.* 適合；與……相稱

- Do you have a suitable car for me to rent?

你是否有適合我租借的車子呢？

常考片語 be suitable for 適合……

- Our smaller sized suitcases are suitable for business travelers.

我們尺寸較小的行李箱適合出差的商務人士使用。

42 suite [swit] *n.* 套房

關 single room 單人房

關 double room（一張大床的）雙人房

關 twin room（兩張小床的）雙人房

關 standard/deluxe room 標準房／豪華房

- The company arranges for its managers to stay in the business suite of hotels.

公司安排讓經理們住飯店的商務套房。

常用詞彙 presidential suite 總統套房
honeymoon suite 蜜月套房

✏️

43 **terminal** [ˋtɝmən!] *n.* 機場航廈；（火車、巴士等的）終站
- A small bus takes passengers from the plane to the airport terminal.
  一輛小巴士把乘客從飛機載往機場航廈。

🔗 arrival *n.* 入境
🔗 departure *n.* 出境

---

44 **timetable** [ˋtaɪm͵teb!] *n.* （公車、火車、航班等的）時刻表
- I'll check the timetable online and see which time would be most suitable.
  我會上網查時刻表看看什麼時間最適合。

🔄 schedule *n.* 時刻表

---

45 **tour guide** 導遊
- Our tour guide told us an interesting story about the Queen's palace.
  我們的導遊告訴我們一則關於女王宮殿的有趣故事。

🔗 travel agent 旅行社職員
🔗 travel agency 旅行社

---

46 **transit** [ˋtrænzɪt] *v.* 過境；運輸 *n.* 運送過程
- It's not a direct flight. We need to transit in Hong Kong.
  這不是直飛航班。我們需要過境香港。
- I asked for a refund because the product had been damaged in transit.
  我要求退款，因為商品在運送過程中損壞了。

説明 transit「過境」通常指搭機時中途在某地短暫停留（stopover），然後搭乘原班機繼續飛往目的地。transfer「轉機」則指航程中，旅客須在某地轉換不同班機或航空公司以便抵達目的地。

常用詞彙 public/mass transit 大眾運輸

🔀 transition *n.* 轉變；過渡期
🔀 transitional *adj.* 過渡性的；過渡時期的

---

47 **vacancy** [ˋvekənsɪ] *n.* 空房；空缺
- I called the hotel and they said they didn't have any vacancies. Do you want to try another one?
  我打電話給這間飯店，他們說沒有任何空房。你要問另一家嗎？

🔄 availability *n.* 可使用性
🔀 vacant *adj.* 空著的

---

48 **vibe** [vaɪb] *n.* 氣氛；情境（為 **vibration** 的口語用法）
- This city has a great vibe. I'd love to come back and enjoy it when I'm not on a business trip.
  這個城市的氛圍很棒。我想在不用出差的時候再回來享受一次。

🔄 atmosphere *n.* 氣氛
🔀 vibration *n.* 震動；顫動

PRACTICE TEST

Part 1: Photographs

TRACK 62

Directions:

For each question in this part, you will hear four statements about a picture. When you hear the statements, you must select the one statement that best describes what you see in the picture. Then circle the letter (A), (B), (C), or (D). The statements will not be printed below and will be spoken only one time.

(A) (B) (C) (D)   (A) (B) (C) (D)

Part 2: Question and Response

TRACK 63

Directions:

You will hear a question or statement and three responses spoken in English. They will be spoken only one time and will not be printed below. Select the best response to the question or statement and circle the letter (A), (B), or (C).

❸ (A)   (B)   (C)

❹ (A)   (B)   (C)

❺ (A)   (B)   (C)

❻ (A)   (B)   (C)

Part 3: Short Conversations

 TRACK 64

Directions:

You will hear some conversations between two or more people. You will be asked to answer three questions about what the speakers say in each conversation. Select the best response to each question and circle the letter (A), (B), (C), or (D). The conversation will be spoken only one time and will not be printed below.

7 What are the guests doing?

(A) Leaving their home

(B) Arriving at a hotel

(C) Getting on a plane

(D) Collecting luggage at an airport

8 What most likely is the man's job?

(A) Housekeeper

(B) Receptionist

(C) Concierge

(D) Bellhop

9 What do the guests say they want to do soon?

(A) They want to have dinner.

(B) They want to relax in the room.

(C) They want to go on a long trip.

(D) They want someone to pick them up.

Express Train		Shuttle Bus	
Train No.	Leaving Times	Bus No.	Leaving Times
41B	18:10	102	18:00
42A	18:40	104	19:00
43B	19:10	111	20:00
44A	19:40	118	21:00

10 Where most likely is the conversation taking place?

(A) In a restaurant

(B) In an airport

(C) On a train

(D) In a train station

11 What is the man's main concern when choosing how to travel?

(A) Convenience

(B) Money

(C) Time

(D) Comfort

12 Look at the graphic. Which train number does the man buy a ticket for?

(A) 42A

(B) 43B

(C) 44A

(D) 41B

Part 4: Short Talks

Directions:

You will hear some short talks given by a single speaker. You will be asked to answer three questions about what the speaker says in each talk. Select the best response to each question and circle the letter (A), (B), (C), or (D). The talks will be spoken only one time and will not be printed below.

13 What is being promoted in the advertisement?

(A) Personal security   (B) Travel luggage

(C) Transport rental   (D) Home storage

14 What does the speaker mean when he says, "look no further than BuzzCase"?

(A) Don't ask questions about BuzzCase.

(B) Don't consider other options besides BuzzCase.

(C) Don't travel too far without BuzzCase.

(D) It's not difficult to find a BuzzCase.

15 Who is being addressed?

(A) Cabin crew   (B) Business Travelers

(C) Suitcase manufacturers   (D) Vacationers

---

16 Why should the tour group look forward to visiting the harbor?

(A) Because the food there is delicious

(B) Because it offers a great sunset view

(C) Because they can use telescopes

(D) Because it has fascinating streets

Saint Martin's Church	11:00
Lunch	13:00
Dunphy's Bridge	15:30
The Old Streets	17:30
Dinner	19:30
Farnley's Lighthouse	21:00

17 What will the speaker do next?

(A) Take the group for a walk around the dock

(B) Show the group how to use a telescope

(C) Tell the group about the dock area

(D) Take the group to Saint Martin's Church

18 Look at the itinerary. When will the tour group eat dinner?

(A) 20:00   (B) 19:30

(C) 20:30   (D) 19:00

Part 5: Incomplete Sentences

Directions:

A word or phrase is missing in each of the sentences below. Four answer choices are given below each sentence. Select the best answer to complete the sentence. Then circle the letter (A), (B), (C), or (D).

19 I advised Jason to apply for this sales manager _____ at Thomson Airlines because I think he would be perfect for the job.

(A) captain   (B) landing

(C) vacancy   (D) crew

20 I _____ to over 30 countries, but I would like to go to Africa because I have never been there.

(A) have been   (B) have ever been

(C) haven't been   (D) haven't ever been

21 We will be departing _____ Port McArthur at 8 p.m., and arriving at Gray's Harbor at around 8:45 p.m.

(A) for   (B) from

(C) to   (D) at

22 The airline's new baggage _____ service will help travelers cut short waiting times at check-in counters.

(A) duty-free   (B) full-fare

(C) front-desk   (D) drop-off

23 This is an announcement by Southwest Trains: Please let passengers _____ off the train first before boarding.

(A) to get   (B) getting

(C) get   (D) gotten

Part 6: Text Completion

Directions:

Read the text below. A word, phrase, or sentence is missing. For each empty space in the text, select the best answer to complete the text. Then circle the letter (A), (B), (C), or (D).

Questions 24-27 refer to the following travel notice.

CONSULATE GENERAL OF INDIA

Travel Advisory Notice

For Indian Nationals Visiting Hong Kong

Please note that Indian nationals visiting Hong Kong are required to complete a Visitor Registration Card (VRC) before ---24--- flights. If VRC application is unsuccessful, applicants must apply for a VISA from the Hong Kong Immigration department at least two months prior to travel. ---25--- may be made on the Internet via the official Hong Kong Immigration website, or over the telephone, and are subject to a fee. If calling from overseas, please note that individuals may be subject to a higher rate. ---26---

For Indian Nationals Transiting through Hong Kong

Indian passport holders passing through Hong Kong for extensive periods of transit should note that ---27--- may not be permitted to leave Hong Kong airport and enter the city in absence of a valid Hong Kong VISA or VRC.

24 (A) landing   (B) booking   (C) docking   (D) claiming

25 (A) Applications   (B) Applicant   (C) Applicable   (D) Apply

26 (A) Upon completion of VRC, please make your way to the Immigration department.
     (B) All foreign nationals entering Hong Kong will be subject to a search upon arrival.
     (C) It is not possible to submit applications via the Hong Kong Immigration official website.
     (D) Further information regarding call fees and application fees can be found online.

27 (A) we   (B) it   (C) they   (D) she

Part 7: Reading Comprehension

Directions:

In this part you will read a selection of texts, such as magazine and newspaper articles, e-mails, and instant messages. Each text is followed by several questions. Select the best answer for each question and circle the letter (A), (B), (C), or (D).

Questions 28-30 refer to the following apartment rental listing.

California Apartment ($150 per night)

2 Bedrooms - PRIME LOCATION!
Apartment Listing by Jon Sanders

Entire apartment:
x5 guests
x2 bedrooms (3 beds)
x1 living room
x1 bathroom

2/5

A spacious apartment for rent, within five minutes' walk of the nearest subway station. Downtown location provides easy access to the city center, parks, restaurants, and plenty of art and culture. Apartment is suitable for all types of travelers, from couples, to solo adventurers, business travelers, families, and groups.

The space

A newly renovated space, fully furnished with new furniture, TV (100+ satellite stations + YouTube feature), and Wi-Fi access. Our space fits three people comfortably, and can sleep up to five people.

The services

A 24-hour security guard occupies the front desk in the lobby and housekeeping is included free of charge, once per day. There is a laundromat one block down from the apartment (2-3 minutes' walk).

28 What is implied about the apartment?

(A) It is not suitable for some travelers.

(B) It is in a new building.

(C) It is conveniently located.

(D) It is in a quiet and peaceful area.

29 What is the maximum number of people that can stay in the apartment?

(A) 2   (B) 3

(C) 5   (D) 6

30 Which service is NOT included in the apartment?

(A) Security   (B) Laundry

(C) Housekeeping   (D) Internet

Questions 31-34 refer to the following passage.

Visit the beating heart of Kansai, known as Osaka. ---[1]--- Second only to Tokyo in terms of population, and home to Japan's main port, the city is famous for its friendly citizens, laid-back vibe, and delicious cuisine. Here, you will find cultural and historical sites mixed with all the urban phenomena of a modern Japanese metropolis.

It is at night when Osaka really comes alive. Indeed, the Dotonbori district offers futuristic nightscapes, the likes of which you might expect to see in a science fiction movie—its flashing neon lights and audacious fashions providing a visual treat for the onlooker. ---[2]---

Of course, like everything the Japanese do, the food is exquisitely prepared. In addition to culinary delights, further highlights include Osaka Castle and its surrounding moats; Osaka Aquarium, famous for its giant whale shark; and a distinctive Open-Air Museum of Japanese Farmhouses. ---[3]--- It is a city to experience in its totality, and leisurely strolls through backstreets can be more rewarding than following the route map of an organized tour. ---[4]---

㉛ Where would this passage most likely appear?

(A) On a newspaper front page

(B) In a science-fiction novel

(C) In a travel brochure

(D) In a history book

㉜ The word "vibe" in paragraph 1, line 3, is closest in meaning to

(A) discussions

(B) atmosphere

(C) views

(D) appearance

㉝ What is NOT listed as a reason to visit Osaka?

(A) The nightlife

(B) Osaka Castle

(C) A unique museum

(D) An organized tour

㉞ In which of the positions marked [1], [2], [3], and [4] does the following sentence best belong?

"However, like Tokyo, Osaka has more to offer than just its sites."

(A) [1]

(B) [2]

(C) [3]

(D [4]

Unit 11 Dining Out 外食

本主題涵蓋內容包括：

- business & informal lunches 商務／非正式午餐
- banquets 宴會
- receptions 招待會
- restaurant reservations 餐廳訂位

WORD POWER

 TRACK 66

---

01 **alcohol** [ˈælkəˌhɔl] *n.* 酒精；含酒精的飲料
- In some cultures, it's normal to go to the pub and drink alcohol with coworkers after work.
  在某些文化中，下班後和同事去酒吧喝酒是很稀鬆平常的。

  說明 「含酒精飲料」亦可用 alcoholic drinks。

同 liquor *n.* 酒；含酒精的飲料

衍 alcoholic *n.* 酒精中毒的人 *adj.* 含酒精的

關 soft drinks 不含酒精的飲料

---

02 **atmosphere** [ˈætməˌsfɪr] *n.* 氣氛；大氣
- The atmosphere in the restaurant was very energetic and sociable.
  餐廳裡的氣氛充滿活力、適合交際。

  常用詞彙 restaurants with a romantic atmosphere 燈光美、氣氛佳的餐廳（通常是指裝潢奢華、價格昂貴的餐廳）

---

03 **banquet** [ˈbæŋˌkwɪt] *n.* 宴會
- Spouses were allowed to join the company end-of-year banquet.
  配偶可以參加公司的年終餐會。

同 feast *n.* 盛宴；筵席

關 reception *n.* 接待會；歡迎會；宴會

---

04 **barbecue** [ˈbɑrbɪkju] *n.* 烤肉
- The boss invited us to a barbecue in the summer.
  老闆夏天的時候邀我們去烤肉。

  常用詞彙 barbecue sauce 烤肉醬

---

05 **bartender** [ˈbɑrˌtɛndə] *n.* 酒吧的侍者；酒保
- The bartender made a nice drink that wasn't too strong.
  酒保調出了一種美味的酒，不會很烈。

同 barkeeper *n.* 酒保；酒吧老闆

---

06 **bistro** [ˈbistro] *n.* 小酒館；小飯館
- Cathy often eats lunch at a quiet, family-owned bistro just around the corner from her office.
  凱西經常去她公司轉角的一間安靜的家庭經營小飯館吃午餐。

關 eatery *n.*【口】（小）飯館

關 café *n.* 小餐館；咖啡廳

07　blend [blɛnd] *n./v.* 混合（物）

- This drink is a blend of orange juice and lemon juice.
  這杯飲品是柳橙汁與檸檬汁的混合。
- The sauce blends nicely with the pasta.
  這個醬汁和義大利麵完美地混合在一起。

(同) mixture、combination *n.* 混合

(衍) blender *n.* 混合器；果汁機

08　buffet [bəˋfe] *n.* 自助餐；吃到飽餐廳

- This restaurant serves a buffet, so you can eat as much as you want.
  這家餐廳供應自助餐點，所以你想吃多少就可以吃多少。

(關) cafeteria *n.* （常指學校或辦公大樓內的）自助餐廳

09　cater [ˋketɚ] *v.* 提供飲食；承辦宴席

- Our annual dinner was catered by a company that provided delicious food and excellent service.
  我們的年度晚宴是由一家供應美味餐點與絕佳服務的公司承辦。

常考片語 cater to 為……服務；迎合……

- The restaurant caters to students and faculty of the nearby university.
  這間餐廳為附近大學學生及教職員的餐飲需求提供服務。

(衍) catering *n.* 承辦酒席；提供飲食及服務

10　celebration [ˌsɛləˋbreʃən] *n.* 慶祝

- We had a big celebration by dining out at a famous restaurant in the town center.
  我們辦了一場盛大的慶祝會，在市中心一間有名的餐廳用餐。

(衍) celebrate *v.* 慶祝

11　champagne [ʃæmˋpen] *n.* 香檳

- At Tom and Mary's wedding banquet, we toasted the newly-married couple with champagne.
  在湯姆和瑪莉的婚宴上，我們以香檳舉杯慶祝這對新人的結合。

(同) bubbly *n.* 【英】【俚】香檳酒

(關) beer *n.* 啤酒

(關) wine *n.* 葡萄酒

SECTION B　必備詞彙

UNIT 11　Dining Out 外食

12 **chef** [ʃɛf] *n.* 主廚；廚師　　　　　　　　　　　回 cook *n.* 廚師
- Please tell the chef that we were very happy with the meal.
  請告訴主廚我們對這頓飯感到非常滿意。

  說明 「主廚」亦可用 head chef 表示。

13 **cocktail** [ˋkɑkˏtel] *n.*（西餐的）開胃品；水果雜拌；　　關 beverage *n.* 飲料
調酒
- Jenny had a cocktail which mixed many types of drinks together.
  珍妮點了一杯把許多種飲料混合在一起的雞尾酒。

14 **cuisine** [kwɪˋzin] *n.* 菜餚　　　　　　　　　　　回 food *n.* 餐點
- We enjoyed the cuisine in Barcelona, especially the fresh fish.
  我們很享受巴塞隆納的料理，特別是新鮮的魚。

15 **dessert** [dɪˋzɝt] *n.* 甜點；點心　　　　　　　　回 sweet *n.*【英】餐後
甜點
- The desserts look really good, but I'm too full from the main meal.
  甜點看起來真的很好吃，但我光吃主菜就太飽了。

16 **diet** [ˋdaɪət] *n.* 飲食；食物　　　　　　　　　　關 vegetarian *n.* 素食者
- In order to live a healthier life, Pam switched to a purely plant-based diet.
  為了過更健康的生活，潘轉為全以植物為基礎的飲食。

  說明 常用 on a diet 來指「節食；照規定飲食（如因糖尿病等疾病而限制食物）」。

17 **dining** [ˋdaɪnɪŋ] *n.* 進餐　　　　　　　　　　　衍 dine *v.* 進餐；用餐
- The dinner will be held in the hotel's main dining hall.
  晚餐會在飯店的主餐廳進行。

  常用詞彙 dining car 餐車
  　　　　dining table 餐桌
  　　　　dining room 飯廳；餐廳

18 **dish** [dɪʃ] *n.* 菜餚
- The man asked the waiter to suggest a salty meat dish for him.
  那個男子要求服務生為他建議一道重鹹的肉類料理。

🔗 fried rice with egg 蛋炒飯

🔗 macaroni and cheese 起司通心麵

🔗 fish and chips 炸魚薯條

19 **dressing** [ˈdrɛsɪŋ] *n.* （拌沙拉等用的）調料
- I want to order this salad but please don't put too much dressing on it.
  我想要點這道沙拉，但請不要放太多沙拉醬。

常用詞彙 Thousand Island dressing 千島沙拉醬
Japanese style dressing 和風醬
yogurt dressing 優格醬

20 **etiquette** [ˈɛtɪkət] *n.* 禮節
- It would be bad etiquette not to wear a tie at this event.
  在這個活動上，不打領帶是很失禮的。

同 manners *n.* 禮貌；風俗

21 **exquisite** [ˈɛkskwɪzɪt] *adj.* 精緻的
- The meal was exquisite! We will definitely come back!
  這裡的餐點好精緻喔！我們一定會再光顧的！

同 delicate *adj.* 微妙的；精緻的

22 **feast** [fist] *n.* 盛宴；（感官等方面的）享受
- My mother and grandmother prepared a huge feast for the whole family which we couldn't finish.
  我媽媽和祖母為全家人準備了一頓我們吃不完的大餐。

同 banquet *n.* 盛宴

🔗 treat *n.* 請客

23 **flavor** [ˈflevɚ] *n.* 口味；味道；香料；調味料
- The homemade tomato sauce added a rich flavor to the pizza.
  這種手工番茄醬為披薩增添了濃郁的風味。

同 taste *n.* 味道

說明 flavor 亦可作動詞，指「給……調味；為……增添風趣」。

24 foodie [ˈfudi] *n.* 【口】美食家
- I'm a real foodie, so I'll probably enjoy anything on the menu.
  我是個真正的吃貨，所以菜單上的每一道菜我大概都會喜歡。

---

25 foot the bill 付帳單
- The boss sometimes foots the bill when we have a business lunch.
  我們有商務午餐的時候，老闆有時候會幫我們買單。

  說明 foot 在此作動詞，指「付款」。加總後帳單的總金額通常會寫在帳單條的底部，即 foot of the bill，後來 foot 直接當作動詞，「付帳」也就演變成 foot the bill 了。

同 pick up the tab/ bill/check 付帳

---

26 fuss [fʌs] *n.* 大驚小怪；小題大作
- Why are those people lining up for that food? I've tried it and I don't understand what the fuss is about.
  為什麼那些人要為那道食物大排長龍？我吃過但不理解它是在紅什麼。

  常考片語 make a fuss 大吵大鬧；小題大作；過分激動
- Brenda's friends made a fuss over her new baby.
  布蘭達的朋友們因為她剛出生的寶寶而超級興奮的。

---

27 gourmet [ˈgurˌme] *n.* 美食家；老饕 *adj.* 美味佳餚的
- A gourmet like him always eats out in expensive restaurants.
  像他那樣的美食家總是在昂貴的餐廳用餐。

- Scarlett only eats gourmet food at fancy restaurants.
  史嘉莉只在高檔餐廳吃美食。

同 foodie *n.* 美食家

---

28 indulge [ɪnˈdʌldʒ] *v.* 沉溺於；盡情享受
- I indulge in delicious food on the weekends as a way to relax.
  我在週末時盡情享受美食，作為放鬆的一種方式。

  常考片語 indulge (oneself) in 縱情享受；沉溺

衍 indulgent *adj.* 溺愛的；放縱的

衍 self-indulgent、overindulgent *adj.* 自我放縱的

衍 overindulgence *n.* 放縱

29 ingredient [ɪn`grɪdɪənt] *n.* 成分；原料；因素

• The fast food company claims to use a secret ingredient that makes their chicken taste so good.
這家速食公司聲稱使用了一種祕密配方，讓他們的雞肉嚐起來如此美味。

🔄 element、component *n.* 成分

30 lean [lin] *adj.*（肉）無脂肪的；精瘦的 *v.* 傾向；傾身；屈身

• He ate a very lean steak with almost no fat on it.
他吃了一塊瘦肉很多的牛排，幾乎沒有脂肪。

• Tom leant impatiently against the wall as he waited for a seat.
湯姆等位子時，不耐煩地靠在牆上。

常用詞彙 lean meat 瘦肉

常考片語 lean toward（喜好、見解）傾向於

• You're right; the chicken does look good, but I'm leaning toward the duck.
沒錯；那道雞肉看起來的確很美味，但我傾向於點那道鴨肉。

31 luncheon [`lʌntʃən] *n.*（正式的）午餐

• My company is holding a luncheon event on Saturday.
我的公司要在週六舉辦正式的午餐聚會。

🔲 box lunch 盒餐
🔲 brunch *n.* 早午餐

32 main course 主菜

• I ordered the steak for my main course.
我主菜點了牛排。

說明 course 可指「一道菜」，如 first course 指「第一道菜」。
「主菜」亦常用 entrée [`ɑntre]。

🔲 appetizer *n.* 開胃菜
🔲 side dish 副餐

33 mayonnaise [`meə͵nez] *n.* 美乃滋

• I like to have mayonnaise in my chicken burger to give it some extra taste.
我喜歡在雞肉堡上加美乃滋，讓它增添更多風味。

🔲 ketchup *n.* 番茄醬
🔲 pesto *n.* 香蒜醬
🔲 gravy *n.* 肉汁

34 **mixture** [ˋmɪkstʃə] *n.* 混合物；混合料
- Pour the mixture into the pan and wait two minutes before turning the pancake over.
  把攪拌好的材料放進平底鍋，等兩分鐘後再把鬆餅翻面。

衍 mix *v.* （使）混合

---

35 **napkin** [ˋnæpkɪn] *n.* 餐巾
- Could I have another napkin, please? The sauce is dripping out of my burrito.
  可以請你再給我一張餐巾紙嗎？醬汁從我的捲餅裡滴出來了。

關 wet towel 濕紙巾

---

36 **occasion** [əˋkeʒən] *n.* 場合；活動
- It's a special occasion, so please wear smart clothes.
  這是個特殊場合，所以請穿整齊乾淨的服裝。

常考片語 on occasion 偶爾；有時
- Cindy drinks a glass of wine on occasion when she is having dinner.
  辛蒂在吃晚餐時偶爾會喝杯葡萄酒。

同 event *n.* 事件

衍 occasional *adj.* 特殊場合的

---

37 **produce** [ˋprodjus] *n.* 農產品
　　　　　　　[prəˋdjus] *v.* 生產；製造
- This restaurant uses only locally-sourced produce.
  這間餐廳只使用在地生產的農產品。
- The milk was cultured with special bacteria to produce cheese.
  這些牛奶以特殊菌種培養製作成起司。

衍 reproduce *v.* 繁殖；複製

衍 mass-produce *v.* 大量生產；量產

衍 production *n.* 製作

衍 product *n.* 產品

衍 by-product *n.* 副產品

---

38 **reception** [rɪˋsɛpʃən] *n.* 招待會；歡迎會；宴會
- After the wedding, we'll have a reception for all the guests.
  婚禮過後，我們會為所有賓客舉辦一個招待會。

同 party *n.* 聚會；派對

衍 receptionist *n.* 接待員

39 **recipe** [ˋrɛsəpɪ] *n.* 食譜;烹飪法　　　　 🔘 cookbook *n.* 烹飪手冊

- The chef is publishing a book in which you can learn how to make his famous recipes.

  這位主廚將出版一本書,你可以在書中學到如何烹煮他的名菜。

---

40 **recommend** [ˌrɛkəˋmɛnd] *v.* 推薦;介紹　　 🔘 recommendation *n.* 推薦

- I highly recommend using this food delivery service. They're reliable and the food is high quality.

  我強烈推薦使用這項食物外送服務。他們服務可靠且食物的品質很高。

- I recommend you take plenty of water with you as it's quite a tiring hike.

  因為這趟健行很累人,我建議你帶大量的水。

  說明 表「推薦某人嘗試某事物」,常用句型為 recommend + N./ V-ing 或 recommend + (that) S. + (should) V.,主詞後的動詞前省略了 should,故須用原形動詞。

---

41 **seafood** [ˋsiˌfud] *n.* 海鮮　　　　 🔘 meat *n.*（食用的）肉

- I don't eat seafood, so I have to avoid restaurants that have mainly fish dishes.

  我不吃海鮮,所以我得避免供應魚類料理為主的餐廳。

各種海鮮怎麼說

crab 蟹

prawn/shrimp 蝦

lobster 龍蝦

scallop 扇貝;干貝

mussel 淡菜;貽貝

salmon 鮭魚

42 seasonal [ˋsizn̩əl] *adj.* 季節性的；季節的

- The dish is served with seasonal vegetables such as carrots and red cabbage.

  這道菜會搭配時蔬，例如紅蘿蔔與紫高麗菜。

衍 season *n.* 季節

---

43 specialty [ˋspɛʃəltɪ] *n.* 特製品；特產；招牌菜

- You should try the mushroom pasta in this restaurant. It's their specialty.

  你應該試試這間餐廳的蘑菇義大利麵。這是它們的招牌菜。

衍 special *adj.* 特殊的

---

44 takeout [ˋtekˌaʊt] *n.* 外賣；外賣的餐館

- The restaurant doesn't have any available seating, but they said we could order takeout.

  這間餐廳現在沒有任何空位，但他們說我們可以外帶。

同 to go（餐點）外帶

反 for here 內用

關 for delivery（餐點等）外送

---

45 tender [ˋtɛndɚ] *adj.* 嫩的；柔軟的

- This steak is really tender. It's so easy to eat.

  這份牛排很軟嫩。非常好咬。

同 soft *adj.* 軟的

---

46 tip [tɪp] *v.* 給小費　*n.* 小費

- In the United States, it's unacceptable not to tip a waiter or waitress.

  在美國，不給服務生小費是令人無法接受的。

- The meal was fifty dollars, so a seven or eight dollar tip should be enough.

  那頓飯五十美元，所以給七或八元的小費應該就夠了。

同 gratuity *n.* 小費

47 top-notch [`tɑp`nɑtʃ] *adj.* 一流的；頂尖的

• That meal was top-notch. I really enjoyed it.

那道菜是一流的。我真的很享受。

說明 名詞 notch [nɑtʃ] 原指「鑿痕；刻痕」，也可指「等級」之意。

同 high-class、top-of-the-line、terrific *adj.* 高級的；一流的

反 low-end *adj.* 低水準的；便宜的

反 run-of-the-mill *adj.* 普通的

48 turnout [`tɜn͵aut] *n.* （集會等的）參加或出席人數

• We had a 100% turnout for the dinner, with everyone in the company coming to the restaurant.

我們晚餐的出席率是百分之百，公司的每個人都有來餐廳。

關 participant *n.* 參與者

49 vegetarian [͵vɛdʒə`tɛrɪən] *n./adj.* 素食主義者（的）；素菜（的）

• I decided to become a vegetarian for health reasons, and also because I love animals.

我基於健康因素決定成為一名素食者，也因為我熱愛動物。

• Even though the restaurant specializes in meat, it has recently added some vegetarian dishes to the menu.

雖然那家餐廳主打肉類料理，但他們最近也增加了一些素食菜餚到菜單中。

說明 vegan [`vigən] 則指不攝取奶製品與蛋製品的「嚴守素食主義者；吃全素的人」。

衍 vegetable *n./adj.* 蔬菜（的）

衍 vegetarianism *n.* 素食主義

50 well-done [`wɛl`dʌn] *adj.* （牛排）八分至全熟的；完全煮熟的

• I like my steak to be crispy and crunchy, so please cook it well-done.

我喜歡牛排吃起來酥酥脆脆的，所以請煮到全熟。

說明 其他牛排熟度的說法包括：rare「一～三分熟的」、medium-rare「三～四分熟的」、medium「五分熟的」、medium-well「六～七分熟的」。

關 steak *n.* 牛排

PRACTICE TEST

Part 1: Photographs

 TRACK 67

Directions:

For each question in this part, you will hear four statements about a picture. When you hear the statements, you must select the one statement that best describes what you see in the picture. Then circle the letter (A), (B), (C), or (D). The statements will not be printed below and will be spoken only one time.

(A)   (B)   (C)   (D)   (A)   (B)   (C)   (D)

Part 2: Question and Response

TRACK 68

Directions:

You will hear a question or statement and three responses spoken in English. They will be spoken only one time and will not be printed below. Select the best response to the question or statement and circle the letter (A), (B), or (C).

3 (A)   (B)   (C)

4 (A)   (B)   (C)

5 (A)   (B)   (C)

6 (A)   (B)   (C)

Part 3: Short Conversations

Directions:

You will hear some conversations between two or more people. You will be asked to answer three questions about what the speakers say in each conversation. Select the best response to each question and circle the letter (A), (B), (C), or (D). The conversation will be spoken only one time and will not be printed below.

7 When is Allison's birthday?
(A) In 14 days from now
(B) On the 14th day of this month
(C) 7 days from now
(D) In 40 days from now

8 What does the woman mean when she says, "I've been leaning towards the gourmet option"?
(A) She's been calling a number of gourmet restaurants.
(B) She thinks gourmet food would be the best choice.
(C) She'd prefer a restaurant with lean meats.
(D) She is not considering the gourmet food option.

9 How does the woman most probably feel about making the reservation?
(A) Bored
(B) Amused
(C) Annoyed
(D) Hurried

SECTION B 必備詞彙 | UNIT 11 Dining Out 外食

10 Why does the woman think the spring rolls were good?

(A) They had a high amount of fish in them.

(B) They seemed like they were handmade.

(C) The ingredients complemented each other well.

(D) The ingredients were most likely locally sourced.

11 Which of the following is the woman not impressed with?

(A) The pasta

(B) The decor

(C) The rugs and candles

(D) The service

Hua Binh Restaurant

Seafood Spring Rolls
$10

Rice Noodles
$8

Steak
$20

Grilled Chicken
$15

Chicken Pasta
$12

Vegetable Pasta
$10

12 Look at the graphic. What was the total cost of the meal?

(A) $30

(B) $40

(C) $47

(D) $52

Part 4: Short Talks

 TRACK 70

Directions:

You will hear some short talks given by a single speaker. You will be asked to answer three questions about what the speaker says in each talk. Select the best response to each question and circle the letter (A), (B), (C), or (D). The talks will be spoken only one time and will not be printed below.

13 Who most likely is the speaker?

(A) The head chef

(B) The restaurant manager

(C) A waiter

(D) A customer

14 How does Helen's Table guarantee the quality of its food?

(A) It works closely with local food producers.

(B) It inquires with guests about their experiences.

(C) It educates staff on the details of its policies.

(D) It imports quality produce from abroad.

15 What will the listeners do before Saturday?

    (A) Develop a plan   (B) Visit local farms

    (C) Read leaflets   (D) Make a peach pie

The Savoy Restaurant

Appetizers
Lamb Kebab w/ Cucumber Salad | Salmon Tartare | Nicoise Vegetables

Main Courses
Crispy Sea Bass | Beef Burgundy | Mushroom Risotto | Smoked Chicken Pasta

Desserts
Crème Brûlée | Iced Passion Fruit Mousse | Warm Banana Crumble

Drinks
Sparkling Water | Fresh Juice | English Tea | Americano Coffee | Espresso

Alcohol
Bottled Beer | Cocktails

16 What does the woman mean when she says, "you foot the bill" in the first sentence?

    (A) You have to tip the staff.   (B) You have to pay for the meal.

    (C) You should eat quickly.   (D) You collect everyone's money.

17 Look at the graphic. What does the speaker suggest avoiding on a short business lunch?

    (A) Smoked Chicken Pasta   (B) Iced Passion Fruit Mousse

    (C) Beef Burgundy   (D) Sparkling Water

18 Why should the host set a good example with his/her etiquette?

    (A) Because it will help guests feel more relaxed

    (B) Because it is required by the restaurant

    (C) Because business lunches are very formal

    (D) Because guests will be influenced by the host's actions

Part 5: Incomplete Sentences

Directions:

A word or phrase is missing in each of the sentences below. Four answer choices are given below each sentence. Select the best answer to complete the sentence. Then circle the letter (A), (B), (C), or (D).

19 Seeing as I don't eat meat, could you please tell me about your _____ options?

(A) tender

(B) lean

(C) vegetarian

(D) alcoholic

20 I've reserved a table _____ eight at 7:30 tonight, so make sure you're on time.

(A) for

(B) to

(C) about

(D) aside

21 This restaurant's menu contains a _____ of Thai and Cantonese cuisine.

(A) mixing

(B) mixture

(C) mixes

(D) mixed

22 Recently, the city's harbor area _____ and it now features a number of gourmet restaurants where you can experience fine dining.

(A) is going to develop

(B) was going to develop

(C) develops

(D) has been developed

23 You're on a diet, so you're not allowed to eat chocolate, _____ you?

(A) are

(B) aren't

(C) do

(D) don't

Part 6: Text Completion

Directions:

Read the text below. A word, phrase, or sentence is missing. For each empty space in the text, select the best answer to complete the text. Then circle the letter (A), (B), (C), or (D).

Questions 24-27 refer to the following e-mail.

To: jfarmar@tmail.com
From: terrypritchard@mandalin.com
Subject: About our banquet hall

Dear Mrs. Farmar,

In response to your e-mail with regard to our Banquet Hall, please be ---24--- as to the following:

The Banquet Hall hosts up to 200 seated guests, and has a standing ---25--- of 400 with the tables and chairs removed.

As per your inquiry regarding the possibility of utilizing the banquet hall for both a dinner function and a party function, the answer is yes. However, there is a more suitable option for this occasion.

The problems with using the same space for the after party are twofold. Firstly, the time it would take to remove the tables and chairs from the hall. Secondly, the issue of cleaning. ---26--- It is next to the Banquet Hall and boasts the following advantages:

-Large space (up to 600 guests)
-Performance stage
-State-of-the-art lighting and sound
-A beautiful art deco style cocktail bar

I can give you a 50% discount on the use of the Grand Hall, ---27--- that you are already booking the Banquet Hall. Please see the attached PDF file for more information.

Thank you for your interest in the Mandalin Hotel.

Yours sincerely,

Terry Pritchard
Senior Events Coordinator
The Mandalin Hotel Group

24 (A) advise   (B) advised   (C) advisable   (D) adviser

25 (A) capacity   (B) quality   (C) specialty   (D) durability

26 (A) It takes about fifteen minutes to remove all of the tables and chairs.
   (B) So when you finish having dinner, the staff will clean up the hall.
   (C) It is for these reasons that we advise using our Grand Hall for your after party.
   (D) We do, however, have a small hall that may be able to accommodate your party.

27 (A) given   (B) allowed   (C) including   (D) saying

Part 7: Reading Comprehension

Directions:

In this part you will read a selection of texts, such as magazine and newspaper articles, e-mails, and instant messages. Each text is followed by several questions. Select the best answer for each question and circle the letter (A), (B), (C), or (D).

Questions 28-30 refer to the following website review.

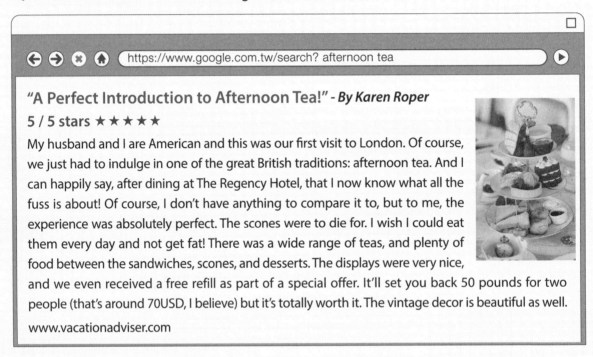

"A Perfect Introduction to Afternoon Tea!" *- By Karen Roper*

5 / 5 stars ★ ★ ★ ★ ★

My husband and I are American and this was our first visit to London. Of course, we just had to indulge in one of the great British traditions: afternoon tea. And I can happily say, after dining at The Regency Hotel, that I now know what all the fuss is about! Of course, I don't have anything to compare it to, but to me, the experience was absolutely perfect. The scones were to die for. I wish I could eat them every day and not get fat! There was a wide range of teas, and plenty of food between the sandwiches, scones, and desserts. The displays were very nice, and we even received a free refill as part of a special offer. It'll set you back 50 pounds for two people (that's around 70USD, I believe) but it's totally worth it. The vintage decor is beautiful as well.

www.vacationadviser.com

28 Why did the woman decide to try afternoon tea?

(A) Because she won't come to London again
(B) Because she'd heard it was good value for money
(C) Because she'd never tried it before
(D) Because she'd heard about a special offer

29 The word "fuss" in line 4 is closest in meaning to

(A) argument   (B) relaxation
(C) anger   (D) excitement

30 What does the writer mean when she says, "It'll set you back 50 pounds"?

(A) It's fairly cheap.   (B) It's a little expensive.
(C) It saves you fifty pounds.   (D) It's extremely heavy.

Questions 31-34 *refer to the following online chat discussion.*

Kristina [10:42 A.M.]
Hey all. I was thinking it might be nice to order takeout for lunch today. Would anyone like to join me?

Jamie [10:48 A.M.]
Great idea, Kristina. I was going to get seafood but I'm flexible.

Cathy [10:49 A.M.]
Me too. Did you have anything in mind, Kristina? I'm starving.

Kristina [10:50 A.M.]
I haven't had Mexican for ages. Are you guys into that?

Cathy [10:51 A.M.]
I love Mexican. And Jamie does, too. There are a few cool Mexican restaurants on the food app I use, DeliverU.

Jamie [10:53 A.M.]
I'm down for Mexican, although Cathy, the one you and I tried the other week from DeliverU wasn't all that. Shall we try another one this time?

Cathy [10:54 A.M.]
Agreed. The meat seemed old and wasn't tender at all. I'm just looking now. There's one called Jorge's Tex Mex. They have a nice mix of dishes and they even have some vegan options by the looks of it.

Kristina [10:55 A.M.]
Great! Could you order me a vegetarian burrito and I'll pay you the cash later?

Jamie [10:55 A.M.]
And I'll get the chicken tacos!

Cathy [10:55 A.M.]
Sure, I'll order for all three of us. We can go and sit in the break room. Speak soon!

31 What is the purpose of the conversation?

(A) To review a bad experience ordering online

(B) To arrange a restaurant visit for lunch

(C) To order food for a group lunch at work

(D) To discuss working part-time as a waitress

㉜ What will likely happen next?

(A) Cathy will order using the DeliverU app.

(B) Jamie will go to Jorge's Tex Mex.

(C) Kristina will make a call to order food.

(D) Cathy and Jamie will buy seafood.

㉝ What is Jamie going to eat for lunch?

(A) Seafood

(B) Tacos

(C) A burrito

(D) He is undecided.

㉞ At 10:53 a.m., what does Jamie mean when he writes, "the one you and I tried the other week from DeliverU wasn't all that"?

(A) He can't remember the name of the last place they went.

(B) The restaurant they bought from previously wasn't good.

(C) The place they went to before did not accept online orders.

(D) The Mexican food that they ate last time was delicious.

Unit 12 Entertainment 娛樂

本主題涵蓋內容包括：

- cinema/movies 電影
- theater 劇場
- music 音樂
- art 藝術
- exhibitions 展覽
- museums 博物館
- media 媒體

WORD POWER

 TRACK 71

01 album [ˈælbəm] *n.* 唱片專輯；相簿；集郵簿
- Stan can't wait for his favorite band to release their new album.
  史丹等不及他最愛的樂團發行他們的新專輯。

🔗 title song 主打歌
🔗 title track 專輯同名歌曲（常為專輯中的主打歌）

---

02 ancient [ˈenʃənt] *adj.* 古老的
- The tour guide took us to an ancient church that was over 500 years old.
  導遊帶我們到一座有五百多年歷史的古老教堂。

🟰 antique *adj.* 古老的

---

03 audience [ˈɔdɪəns] *n.* （電影、表演、演講等的）觀眾；聽眾
- Greg won two tickets to be in the audience for his favorite TV game show.
  克雷格贏得了兩張票，可以到他最喜歡的電視遊戲節目當觀眾。

🟰 spectators、viewers *n.* 觀眾
🟰 listeners *n.* 聽眾

說明 為集合名詞。如果要指「一位觀眾」則說 a member of the audience。另外，觀賞運動賽事的觀眾稱之為 spectators 或 the crowd。

---

04 audition [ɔˈdɪʃən] *v./n.* 甄選；試鏡
- Everyone must audition for a part in this play, including experienced actors.
  每個人都要通過試鏡才能在該劇中軋一角，包括資深演員在內。
- Ben had spent many weeks learning his lines for the big audition.
  班為了重要的試鏡花了好幾週的時間背台詞。

🔗 casting *n.* 選角

---

05 ballet [bæˈle] *n.* 芭蕾舞
- We went to the theater to see a famous ballet.
  我們去劇院看了一場有名的芭蕾舞劇。

衍 ballerina *n.* 芭蕾女演員
🔗 tutu *n.* 芭蕾舞裙

常用詞彙 ballet shoes 芭蕾舞鞋
ballet tights/costume 芭蕾（緊身）舞衣

06 boast [bost] *v.* 以擁有……自豪；以……感到光榮

- The show boasts a cast of more than 50 famous performers.
  該節目自豪其陣容有超過五十位知名表演者。

- Mike boasted that he was the best basketball player in the country.
  麥可對於他曾是國內最優秀的籃球選手而感到自豪。

- The museum boasts of having the largest collection of Van Gogh paintings in the world.
  這個博物館以擁有全世界最多的梵谷畫作收藏而自豪。

  說明 boast 可作及物或不及物動詞。作及物時，常用 boast + N. 或 boast that + S. + V. 的句型；作不及物時，則用 boast + of N./V-ing，均表「誇耀；以……自誇／自豪」。

圖 pride *v.* 使得意；以……自豪

---

07 box office 票房；（電影院、戲劇廳等的）售票處

- Journalists and industry experts loved the movie, but it was not a success at the box office.
  記者與同業的專家都熱愛這部電影，但是票房並不成功。

關 blockbuster *n.* 賣座電影

---

08 canvas [ˈkænvəs] *n.* 帆布；油畫布

- I visited the Fine Art Museum and saw a piece of art on a giant canvas that covered the whole wall.
  我參觀了美術館，看到一幅畫在巨大畫布上的作品，畫布覆蓋了整面牆。

關 oil painting 油畫

關 paintbrush *n.* 畫筆

---

09 chamber music 室內樂

- She has composed chamber music and operas and conducted her music in some of the world's greatest theaters.
  她創作過幾首室內樂曲與歌劇，也在全球幾個最大的劇院中指揮過她的音樂。

  說明 chamber [ˈtʃembɚ] 可指「室；房間；室內音樂的」。

關 symphonic music 交響樂

---

10 channel [ˈtʃænl] *n.* 頻道

- I browsed through the TV channels to find something interesting.
  我瀏覽電視頻道尋找有趣的東西。

圖 station *n.* 電視頻道

11 cinema [ˋsɪnəmə] *n.* 電影院；（總稱）電影；電影業；（一部）電影

- There were long lines at the cinema for Steven Spielberg's new movie last weekend.
  上個週末，電影院有大排長龍的人要看史蒂芬‧史匹柏的新電影。

- Bruce Lee is considered a legendary figure in martial arts cinema.
  李小龍被視為功夫電影的傳奇人物。

圓 movie theater、movie house 電影院

圓 movies *n.* 電影業

圓 film、motion picture 電影；影片

衍 cinematic *adj.* 電影的

---

12 contest [ˋkɑntɛst] *n.* 競賽；比賽

- The singing contest showcased the talents of several local artists.
  這場歌唱比賽展現了好幾位當地藝人的才華。

圓 competition、match、tournament *n.* 比賽

---

13 dialogue [ˋdaɪəˌlɔg] *n.* 對話；對白

- The movie was entertaining with some funny dialogue between the characters.
  這部電影因為角色之間有一些好笑的對話很有娛樂效果。

説明 亦常拼作 dialog。

常用詞彙 dialogue box（電腦）對話視窗

圓 talk、speech、conversation *n.* 對話；交談

反 monologue *n.* 獨白

---

14 drama [ˋdrɑmə] *n.* 劇情片；戲劇

- *Titanic* is a romantic drama which is based on a true story.
  《鐵達尼號》是一部根據真實事件改編的浪漫劇情片。

衍 dramatic *adj.* 戲劇性的；劇烈的

衍 dramatically *adv.* 劇烈地；急遽地

---

15 entertainment [ˌɛntəˋtenmənt] *n.* 娛樂；消遣

- Every year, the boss arranges a different form of entertainment for the company dinner.
  老闆每年都為公司晚宴安排不同型式的娛樂表演。

圓 amusement、recreation *n.* 休閒活動

衍 entertain *v.* 娛樂

衍 entertainer *n.* 藝人

衍 entertaining *adj.* 有娛樂效果的

16 episode [ˋɛpɪˏsod] *n.* （電視等的）連續劇的一集
- There are a total of 10 episodes in this TV series.
  這齣電視連續劇總共有十集。

17 exhibit [ɪgˋzɪbɪt] *v.* 展覽；展示 *n.* 展示品
- This gallery exhibits late 19ᵗʰ century to mid-20ᵗʰ century modern art.
  這間畫廊展示十九世紀晚期至二十世紀中期的現代藝術。
- The most popular exhibit in the museum is a giant dinosaur.
  那間博物館最受歡迎的展示品是一隻巨大的恐龍。

🔄 show、display、demonstrate *v.* 展覽；展示

🔀 exhibition *n.* 展覽

18 finalist [ˋfaɪnḷɪst] *n.* 決賽選手；最終候選者
- The two finalists played a great game, but there could be only one winner.
  兩位決賽選手打了精彩的一仗，但贏家只能有一位。
- The panel of judges nominated 12 finalists for the film competition.
  評審團在影片競賽中提名了十二位決賽入圍者。

🔀 final *n.* 決賽；期末考 *adj.* 最後的

🔀 semifinal *n.* 準決賽

19 gallery [ˋgælərɪ] *n.* 畫廊；美術館
- I suggested an art gallery that the client could visit on Sunday, as she's very interested in classic art.
  我建議了一間那位客戶星期天可以去參觀的畫廊，因為她對古典藝術很有興趣。

常用詞彙 art gallery 藝廊

🔗 museum *n.* 博物館

20 hit [hɪt] *n.* 成功而風行一時的事物；熱門金曲
- Michael Jackson had many hits in his long and successful career.
  麥可·傑克森在他漫長又成功的生涯中有過很多首熱門金曲。

常用詞彙 hit single 熱銷單曲
the greatest hits 精選輯

21 hype [haɪp] *v.* 大肆宣傳 *n.* 刺激；興奮

- The new smartphone was hyped by the company for many months before the official release.
  那款手機在正式上市之前，被公司大肆宣傳了好幾個月。

常考片語 live up to the hype 實至名歸；名實相符

- I want to know if that movie everyone's talking about really lives up to the hype.
  我很想知道大家正在討論的那部電影是不是真的那麼精彩。

衍 hyped *adj.* 過度渲染的；大肆宣傳的

衍 hyped-up *adj.* 興奮的

22 illustration [ˌɪləsˈtreʃən] *n.* 圖解；圖示

- It's hard to imagine what the meals look like because the menu doesn't have any photos or illustrations.
  因為菜單上沒有任何照片或圖示，所以很難想像餐點會是什麼樣子。

衍 illustrate *v.* （用圖、實例等）說明；插圖於（書籍等）

23 instrument [ˈɪnstrəmənt] *n.* 樂器；儀器；器具

- Did you know that the boss is also in a band and can play two instruments?
  你知道老闆也是某個樂團的一員，而且會彈奏兩種樂器嗎？

- Scientists use special instruments to find planets in the universe.
  科學家使用特殊的儀器來尋找宇宙中的行星。

衍 instrumental *adj.* 以樂器伴奏的；有幫助的

常用詞彙 string/woodwind/brass/percussion instrument
弦／木管／銅管／打擊樂器

常見樂器

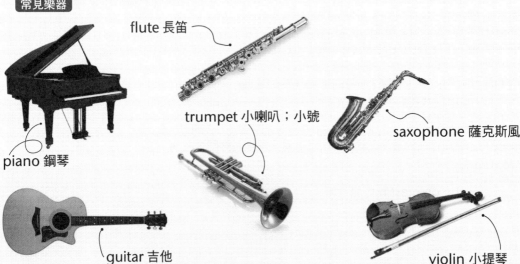

flute 長笛

piano 鋼琴

trumpet 小喇叭；小號

saxophone 薩克斯風

guitar 吉他

violin 小提琴

24 juggle [ˋdʒʌgəl] v. 拋接；玩雜耍；同時應付

- I can juggle with three balls, but when I use four balls I always end up dropping one.
  我可以同時拋接三顆球，但當我拋接四顆球的時候，總是會掉一顆。

- Tammy found it hard to juggle her job and raise kids at the same time.
  譚米覺得要同時應付工作和育兒很困難。

衍 juggler n. 耍把戲的人；變戲法的人

25 leaflet [ˋliflət] n. 傳單；單張印刷品

- The travel agent gave us a bunch of holiday leaflets.
  這位旅行社專員給了我們一堆度假傳單。

同 flyer n. 傳單

關 booklet、brochure n. 小冊子

26 leisure [ˋliʒɚ] n. 閒暇時間

- For leisure, I enjoy reading, and going skiing when I get the chance.
  閒暇時間我喜歡閱讀，而有機會的時候也喜歡去滑雪。

常考片語 at (one's) leisure 在（某人的）空閒時間；（某人）有空時

- I think it would be best for you to take these brochures home and look over them at your leisure.
  我想若您將這些小冊子帶回家在閒暇時瀏覽，是最好不過了。

衍 leisurely adj. 悠閒的

27 literature [ˋlɪtərətʃɚ] n. 文學作品

- Maggie likes reading classic British literature such as Shakespeare and Jane Austen.
  瑪姬喜歡閱讀經典英國文學，像是莎士比亞與珍・奧斯汀。

衍 literate adj. 識字的；能讀寫的

28 lyrics [ˋlɪrɪks] n. 歌詞（多以複數形呈現）

- John listens to classical music while working because he thinks lyrics would distract him.
  約翰工作的時候聽古典樂，因為他覺得歌詞會令他分心。

衍 lyricist n. 作詞家

關 composer n. 作曲者

SECTION B 必備詞彙

UNIT 12 Entertainment 娛樂

29 **musician** [mjuˋzɪʃən] *n.* 音樂家

- Ben is a talented guitar player, but he finds it hard to earn a good salary as a musician.

  班是一個天賦異稟的吉他手，但他覺得當音樂家很難賺大錢。

同 performer、player *n.* 表演者；演奏者

衍 music *n.* 音樂；樂曲；樂譜

衍 musical *adj.* 音樂的 *n.* 音樂劇

字尾 **-ian** 可表「……的人」

music（音樂）**+** ian（……的人）

⬇

musician 音樂家（創作或演奏音樂的人）

其他同字尾單字

- historian 歷史學家（histor(y)「歷史」+ ian）
- politician 政治家（politic(s)「政治」+ ian）

---

30 **painting** [ˋpentɪŋ] *n.* 圖畫；繪畫

- This gallery hosts a marvelous collection of paintings, mainly from 17th to 19th century European painters.

  這間畫廊擁有令人驚嘆的畫作收藏，主要來自十七至十九世紀的歐洲畫家。

同 picture、illustration *n.* 圖畫

關 canvas *n.* 油畫布

---

31 **plot** [plɑt] *n.* 情節；陰謀；（小塊）土地 *v.* 陰謀策畫；密謀

- The movie has an interesting plot about a relationship between a doctor and a student.

  這部電影的情節很有趣，是關於一個醫生與一個學生之間的感情。

- The team of criminals spent months working on a plot to rob a bank, but they still got caught by the police.

  這群罪犯花了好幾個月密謀搶銀行，但最後還是被警察抓了。

- My grandparents own a plot of land out in the countryside where they grow vegetables.

  我祖父母在鄉下有一小塊土地，他們在那裡種蔬菜。

- Tessa complained to the boss that a group of coworkers had been plotting against her.

  泰莎向老闆抱怨有一群同事一直在暗中陷害她。

同 scheme、conspiracy *n.* 計畫；陰謀

同 conspire *v.* 密謀

32 premiere [prɪ`mjɛr] *n.* 首映會；初次上演

- Tom Cruise arrived two hours early to the premiere of his new movie so that he could meet and greet fans.

  湯姆・克魯斯提早兩小時抵達他新電影的首映會，以便可以和粉絲見面打招呼。

關 debut *n.* 初次露面；初次登台

33 queue [kju] *n.* 行列（英式用法，相當於美語的 **line**） *v.* 排隊

- The queue to meet the famous singer went all around the block.

  要和那位知名歌手見面的隊伍占滿了這個街區。

同 line *n.*（排隊的）隊伍

衍 queue-jumping *n.* 插隊

常考片語 queue up 排隊等候

- I queued up for two hours to get tickets, but I'm sure the show will be worth it.

  我為了買票排了兩個小時的隊，但我確定那場表演值得我這麼做。

34 rehearse [rɪ`hɝs] *v.*（戲劇、音樂會等的）排練；排演；演練

- The piano player and drummer only arrived that night and did not have time to rehearse with the rest of the band.

  那位鋼琴手與鼓手當天上晚才抵達，沒有時間與樂團的其他成員彩排。

同 practice、train、drill *v.* 排練；練習

衍 rehearsal *n.* 排練；預演

35 relaxation [ˌrilæk`seʃən] *n.* 放鬆；娛樂；消遣

- My favorite type of relaxation is lying on a beach and reading a book.

  我最喜歡的放鬆方式是躺在海灘上讀一本書。

同 fun、recreation *n.* 娛樂；消遣

衍 relax *v.* 放鬆；使輕鬆

衍 relaxed *adj.* 輕鬆的；放鬆的

36 sculpture [`skʌlptʃɚ] *n.* 雕塑品；雕像

- Just in front of the palace there is a sculpture of a soldier on a horse.

  在那座宮殿的正前方有一座軍人騎著馬的雕像。

同 carve、shape *v.* 雕刻；雕塑

衍 sculpt *v.* 雕刻；雕塑

衍 sculptor *n.* 雕刻家

37 **sequel** [ˋsikwəl] *n.* 續集

反 **prequel** *n.* 前集；前傳

- The movie was so successful that the producers decided to make a sequel.

  那部電影是如此成功，以致於製片人員決定製作續集。

---

38 **series** [ˋsiriz] *n.* 連續；系列

- I stayed at home all weekend in order to watch a whole series of my favorite TV show.

  為了看完我最愛的電視節目的完整系列，我整個週末都待在家。

---

39 **sitcom** [ˋsɪtˏkɑm] *n.* 情境喜劇

關 **soap opera** 肥皂劇

- *Friends* was the most popular American sitcom of the 90s and one of the most successful of all time.

  《六人行》是九〇年代最受歡迎的美國情境喜劇，也是有史以來最成功的其中一部。

  說明 為 situation comedy 的簡稱，即國外常見的詼諧喜劇，如 *Friends*「六人行」、*Modern Family*「摩登家庭」等。

---

40 **soundtrack** [ˋsaundˏtræk] *n.* 原聲帶；配樂

- All the music on the soundtrack was created especially for this movie.

  這張原聲帶的所有音樂都是為了這部電影而特別創作的。

  說明 OST 即為 original soundtrack 的簡稱。

---

41 **stage** [stedʒ] *n.* 舞台；高台 *v.* 上演；籌劃

衍 **backstage** *adv.*
在後台地；幕後地

- The audience waited quietly for the singer to come on to the stage.

  觀眾們安靜地等待那位歌手走上舞台。

- The events company has staged many spectacular concerts with a variety of famous performers.

  那間活動策畫公司籌辦了許多由眾多知名表演者參與的精彩演唱會。

  常用詞彙 stage fright 怯場

42 stand-up comedy 單人脫口秀

- My brother was very brave to try stand-up comedy. He loves making people laugh.

  我哥哥很有勇氣，敢嘗試單人脫口秀。他喜歡逗人們笑。

衍 comedy *n.* 喜劇

衍 comedian *n.* 喜劇演員

43 stay tuned 請繼續收看（或收聽）；靜待後續消息

- The host of the TV show told the audience to stay tuned during the commercial break.

  電視節目的主持人告訴觀眾進廣告時不要轉台。

44 stream [strim] *v.* 在線收聽、收看；串流傳輸 *n.* 溪流

- The soccer game wasn't on television, so I streamed it on the Internet.

  電視沒播那場足球比賽，所以我從網路在線收看。

- Some of these villagers still wash their clothes in a nearby stream instead of at home.

  有些村民還是會在附近的一條小溪洗衣服，而不是在家裡洗。

常考片語 a stream of 一連串的

- A stream of news articles provided regular updates on the big news story.

  一連串的新聞報導為那則大新聞提供了定時更新。

常用詞彙 live streaming 直播
video-streaming service 影片串流服務

衍 mainstream *adj.* 主流的

45 subtitle [ˋsʌbˏtaɪt!] *n.* （電影等的）字幕；副標題

- Most movies are in English, but the most popular ones usually have Chinese subtitles.

  大部分的電影都是英文的，但最受歡迎的那幾部通常會有中文字幕。

- The subtitle of the book *Vanity Fair* by William Makepeace Thackeray is *A Novel Without a Hero*.

  威廉‧梅克比斯‧薩克萊的著作《浮華世界》的副標題是《一本沒有英雄的小說》。

46 thriller [ˋθrɪlɚ] *n.* 驚悚片

- I watched a crime thriller recently which had me on the edge of my seat throughout the whole movie.

  我最近看了一部犯罪驚悚片,從頭到尾都嚇得我差點從椅子上跌下來。

  說明 其他常見類型電影還有:comedy「喜劇」、action「動作片」、romance「愛情文藝片」、science fiction「科幻電影」、disaster「災難片」、animation「動畫片」、documentary「紀錄片」等。

衍 thrill *v.* 使緊張;感到毛骨悚然

關 horror *n.* 恐懼;恐怖片

關 suspense *n.* 懸疑;懸念

---

47 trailer [ˋtrelɚ] *n.* (電影的)預告片

- Before the movie started, we saw a few trailers of other films that were coming out soon.

  電影開始前,我們看了一些其他即將上映的電影的預告片。

同 preview *n.*【美】(電影、電視等的)預告片

---

48 witty [ˋwɪtɪ] *adj.* 機智的

- You can tell how witty Pete is because his replies are always quick and funny.

  你可以看出彼特多麼聰明,因為他的回答總是又快又有趣。

同 clever *adj.* 聰明的

衍 wit *n.* 機智;風趣

PRACTICE TEST

Part 1: Photographs

✎ **TRACK 72**

Directions:

For each question in this part, you will hear four statements about a picture. When you hear the statements, you must select the one statement that best describes what you see in the picture. Then circle the letter (A), (B), (C), or (D). The statements will not be printed below and will be spoken only one time.

(A) (B) (C) (D)   (A) (B) (C) (D)

Part 2: Question and Response

✎ **TRACK 73**

Directions:

You will hear a question or statement and three responses spoken in English. They will be spoken only one time and will not be printed below. Select the best response to the question or statement and circle the letter (A), (B), or (C).

❸ (A) (B) (C)

❹ (A) (B) (C)

❺ (A) (B) (C)

❻ (A) (B) (C)

Part 3: Short Conversations

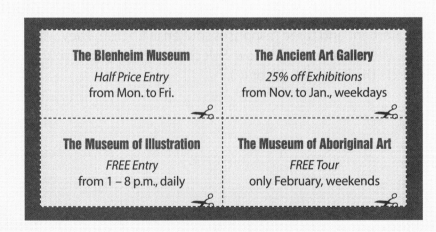 TRACK 74

Directions:

You will hear some conversations between two or more people. You will be asked to answer three questions about what the speakers say in each conversation. Select the best response to each question and circle the letter (A), (B), (C), or (D). The conversation will be spoken only one time and will not be printed below.

7 What does the woman mean when she says, "we've got a thousand dollars to play with"?
(A) The company has a budget of 1,000 dollars.
(B) They'll have a competition to win 1,000 dollars.
(C) They will still have 1,000 dollars extra after this.
(D) The boss doesn't mind if they spend more than 1,000 dollars.

8 Who may leave shortly after the dinner?
(A) The DJ
(B) The woman
(C) People with kids
(D) Younger employees

9 Why do the speakers decide to hire a magician?
(A) It will be more interactive.
(B) It will be cheaper.
(C) It's suitable for children.
(D) It will be expected.

The Blenheim Museum

Half Price Entry
from Mon. to Fri.

The Ancient Art Gallery

25% off Exhibitions
from Nov. to Jan., weekdays

The Museum of Illustration

FREE Entry
from 1 – 8 p.m., daily

The Museum of Aboriginal Art

FREE Tour
only February, weekends

10 Why can't they go to a museum in the morning?

    (A) They're not open in the morning.

    (B) There aren't any special deals.

    (C) The deals will have expired.

    (D) They've planned a sightseeing tour.

11 Which month is it now?

    (A) February   (B) January

    (C) December   (D) November

12 Look at the graphic. Which offer do the speakers decide to make use of?

    (A) Half Price Entry   (B) FREE Tour

    (C) 25% off Exhibitions   (D) FREE Entry

Part 4: Short Talks

 TRACK 75

Directions:

You will hear some short talks given by a single speaker. You will be asked to answer three questions about what the speaker says in each talk. Select the best response to each question and circle the letter (A), (B), (C), or (D). The talks will be spoken only one time and will not be printed below.

13 What does the speaker infer about what Johnny may have to do?

    (A) Deal with a problem by himself

    (B) Make sure to keep a secret

    (C) Find someone else to help him

    (D) Become friends with his neighbors

14 What is the name of the movie?

    (A) *The Watsons*   (B) *The Visitors*

    (C) *An Unlikely Discovery*   (D) *The New Neighbors*

15 Who most likely is the audience for this talk?

    (A) Fans of family movies   (B) Fans of classic music

    (C) Fans of horror movies   (D) Fans of historical movies

16 What is the speaker's occupation?

(A) Artist

(B) Taxi Driver

(C) Theater Attendant

(D) Tour Guide

ADMIT ONE

~The Marriage of Figaro~

| November 14th | Doors Open: 18:00 |

$100 USD

SEAT: **22A**

17 What was Queen Alexandria's main reason for building the Opera House?

(A) To make money

(B) To impress people

(C) To provide relaxation

(D) To host a variety of shows

18 Look at the graphic. What kind of seat has the ticket holder bought?

(A) A lower deck regular seat

(B) A lower deck box seat

(C) An upper deck regular seat

(D) An upper deck box seat

Part 5: Incomplete Sentences

Directions:

A word or phrase is missing in each of the sentences below. Four answer choices are given below each sentence. Select the best answer to complete the sentence. Then circle the letter (A), (B), (C), or (D).

19 The band's last _____ went straight to number one in the charts.

(A) canvas

(B) album

(C) literature

(D) illustration

20 I've just _____ two tickets to the premiere of the new Quentin Cornelese movie!

(A) winner

(B) winning

(C) win

(D) won

21 The judges felt that Judy's performance had been the most impressive _____ the nine finalists.

(A) of

(B) at

(C) for

(D) in

22 Do you agree that sequels are often not as _____ as the original?

  (A) well   (B) better

  (C) good   (D) best

23 1889 was the year _____ Dutch artist Vincent Van Gogh created his masterpiece, *Starry Night*.

  (A) who   (B) where

  (C) which   (D) when

Part 6: Text Completion

Directions:

Read the text below. A word, phrase, or sentence is missing. For each empty space in the text, select the best answer to complete the text. Then circle the letter (A), (B), (C), or (D).

Questions 24-27 refer to the following letter.

April 12

Dear Parents and Students,

Our year at Stratham Elementary School is drawing to a close. However, I am pleased to remind you that we do still have the annual talent ---24--- to look forward to, which will be held on the morning of May 27th.

Students are welcome to perform alone, or with a group of friends. I just need to know in advance. Talent acts must be tasteful, appropriate, and in line with school rules and expectations. Performances can be anything ---25--- singing, dancing, or playing an instrument, to magic tricks, juggling, karate, stand-up comedy, or anything else they are good at. I will be holding auditions over the next few weeks during music class. ---26---

There are a lot of talented kids at Stratham and I look forward to seeing what they can do! More details ---27--- provided at a later date.

Please let me know if you have any questions.

Sincerely,
Katherine Taylor
Music Teacher

24 (A) literature
(B) orchestra
(C) sitcom
(D) contest

25 (A) with
(B) from
(C) over
(D) for

26 (A) Let me take a moment to congratulate you on being chosen.
(B) I'll use this time to decide which acts are most suitable.
(C) Some light refreshments will be served between rounds.
(D) Your daughter was one of the most outstanding contestants.

27 (A) will be
(B) would be
(C) have been
(D) had been

Part 7: Reading Comprehension

Directions:
In this part you will read a selection of texts, such as magazine and newspaper articles, e-mails, and instant messages. Each text is followed by several questions. Select the best answer for each question and circle the letter (A), (B), (C), or (D).

TOP PICKS

The streaming giant, MotionPix, is gearing up for one of its biggest ever weeks. Returning are series favorites including Season 3 of *The Unexplained*, as well as drama *Court & Order*, sitcom *Bob & Jane* and the cartoon series, *The Magic Playground*. On the movie front, the pick of the bunch could be new MotionPix original, *The Stuntman*. This action movie is absolutely loaded with superstar talent, such as Jett Middler, Zoey Platt, Gwyneth Farlow and even performances from Christopher Dawkins, as well as basketball superstar, Magic Jordan. Yes, they've really pulled out the big guns and I, for one, can't wait to find out if *The Stuntman* is really worth the hype. After forming just four years ago, MotionPix cannot afford to take a backward step, with reports that rival services VidSnap and LightReel plan on spending big bucks to compete. Not to mention other established players in the industry desperate to claim a piece of the pie. What all this means, of course, is more choice for us, the audience! So which shows are you looking forward to this week? Leave a comment in the section below to let us know now.

28 What is the purpose of this article?

(A) To compare different streaming services

(B) To compare different kinds of shows

(C) To generate interest in MotionPix shows

(D) To explain why streaming TV is successful

29 What type of show is *The Magic Playground*?

(A) An animation   (B) A sitcom

(C) A talent show   (D) A drama

30 What is implied about MotionPix's competitors, VidSnap and LightReel?

(A) They provide more shows for their audiences.

(B) They are not very popular among audiences.

(C) They are more established in the industry.

(D) They're going to invest a lot of money.

SECTION B 必備詞彙

UNIT **12** Entertainment 娛樂

Questions 31-35 refer to the following advertisement and e-mail.

Director of Photography Wanted!

Volunteer work (expenses covered)

A chance to join an exciting film project by an independent crew of recent college graduates. The film is a thriller with a strong script which will be provided upon request. The candidate will be working with a talented set of very driven and passionate individuals taking their first steps in the industry. This is a two-week project and the short film will be 30 minutes long. It will be entered into a number of prestigious competitions, including the Royal Film Academy Shorts Competition later this year, so we expect it to get a lot of exposure within the industry. As stated, this is volunteer work, but we do cover all transport, food, and accommodation costs.

Ideal candidates will have:

- *Attention to detail and a commitment to excellence (required)*
- *Experience with the Canon C300 camera (preferred)*
- *Ability to record audio (preferred)*
- *Experience with editing software (preferred)*
- *Ability to thrive in a demanding, fast-paced environment (required)*
- *A flexible schedule including nights and weekends (required)*

Please forward a résumé and covering letter to janhawks954@vrzn.net.

* If you do not have one or more of the skills listed as *"required"* then please do not apply, as these are essential for the position.

To: janhawks954@vrzn.net

From: harrymyers@tmail.com

Subject: Applying for Director of Photography

Dear Jan,

I read your ad with enthusiasm, as I am keen to build up my experience, and the chance to be entered into the RFA Shorts Competition appealed to me. I graduated from the Marsden School of Arts three years ago and have been working on a number of projects as a DP since then.

As such, please accept this e-mail as a statement of my interest in the position of DP as advertised on jobs4everyone.com.

I take great pride in my work and am extremely thorough. I have extensive software editing experience, as well as a complete understanding of sound recording. I excel in a dynamic environment and currently have a schedule which is open during the period specified. Working late is not a problem for me.

With regard to the equipment side of things, the bulk of my experience is with Sony cameras such as Sony A6600. I do have some experience with the camera brand specified, but not that exact model. However, if awarded the position I would of course familiarize myself with this before shooting began.

Thank you and I hope to hear from you shortly.

Yours Sincerely,

Harry Myers

31 Why would someone apply for this job?

(A) To receive a highly competitive salary

(B) To work with experienced professionals

(C) To have work be seen by important people

(D) To be given a free camera

32 How long will the job last?

(A) Two days   (B) Two weeks

(C) 30 days   (D) 30 weeks

㉝ Which of the following is true of Harry's ability to meet the job requirements?

(A) He meets none of the essential requirements.

(B) He meets some essential requirements but not all.

(C) He meets most of the essential requirements.

(D) He meets all of the essential requirements.

㉞ In the e-mail, the word "bulk" in paragraph 4, line 1, is closest in meaning to

(A) Majority

(B) Collection

(C) Audience

(D) Trailer

㉟ What does Harry not have experience with?

(A) The Canon C300

(B) The Sony A6600

(C) Working as a DP

(D) Editing Software

Unit 13 Health 保健

本主題涵蓋內容包括：

- **medical insurance**
  醫藥保險

- **visiting doctors or dentists**
  看醫生或牙醫

- **going to the clinic or the hospital**
  去診所或醫院

WORD POWER

 TRACK 76

---

01 **antibiotic** [ˌæntɪbaɪˈɑtɪk] *n.* 抗生素 *adj.* 抗菌的

- Antibiotics are effective for treating throat infections.
  抗生素對於治療喉嚨發炎很有效。

- It is possible to get a natural antibiotic effect from eating certain plants.
  食用某些植物有可能產生天然的抗菌效果。

字首 anti- 表「對抗；反對」

anti（對抗；反對）＋ bio（生命）＋ tic（形容詞字尾）

⬇

antibiotic 抗生素；抗生的
（對抗會危害生命／健康安全的藥物）

其他同字首單字

- antiaging 抗老化的（anti + aging「衰老的」）
- antibody 抗體（anti + body「身體」）
- anti-virus 防毒；防電腦病毒（anti + virus「病毒」）

---

02 **bandage** [ˈbændɪdʒ] *n.* 繃帶

- Tom's mother gave him a bandage to cover the cut on his elbow.
  湯姆的媽媽給他一個繃帶來覆蓋他手肘上的傷口。

㊠ Band-Aid *n.*（包紮傷口的）透氣繃帶

---

03 **boost** [bust] *n./v.* 提升；增加

- Jane got a big boost when she received the news that her grandmother had made a full recovery.
  珍聽到祖母已完全康復的消息時，心情為之大振。

- Doctors say that drinking ginger tea can boost your health.
  醫生說喝薑茶可以促進健康。

㊟ booster *n.* 增強劑；推進器

常用詞彙 an adrenaline boost/rush 腎上腺素上升

---

04 **cast** [kæst] *n.*【醫】固定用敷料

- Everyone at school signed Jimmy's cast after he broke his leg.
  吉米摔斷腿後，學校裡的每個人都在他的石膏上簽名。

㊠ crutch *n.* 丁形枴杖

㊠ fracture *n.* 骨折；斷裂

---

05 checkup [ˈtʃɛkˌʌp] *n.* 身體檢查

- Gina goes to the dentist twice a year just for a checkup.

  吉娜一年看兩次牙醫接受檢查。

📖 physical examination 健康檢查

06 clinic [ˈklɪnɪk] *n.* 診所

- You can make an appointment with the doctor over the phone or by visiting the clinic.

  你可以透過電話或走一趟診所跟醫生約診。

衍 clinical *adj.* 臨床的；診所的

07 consult [kənˈsʌlt] *v.* 求教於；諮詢；查閱（字典、參考書等）

- You should consult a doctor about that cold you've had for the past week.

  你應該為了過去這一週的感冒去請教醫生。

- Tim consulted the dictionary to find out the meaning of a word.

  提姆查了字典，要找出某個字的定義。

說明 用法為 consult sb. about sth.，表示「就某事向某人商議／諮詢」。

衍 consulting *adj.* 提供諮詢的；顧問的

衍 consultation *n.* 請教；商議

衍 consultant *n.* 顧問

衍 consultancy *n.* 顧問公司

08 cough [kɔf] *v./n.* 咳嗽

- You should cover your mouth when you cough so that other people don't get infected.

  你咳嗽的時候應該要蓋住嘴吧，這樣其他人才不會被傳染。

- Smoking cigarettes is the reason why Ron always seems to have a bad cough.

  吸菸就是榮恩似乎總是咳個不停的原因。

常用詞彙 cough syrup 止咳糖漿

09 dental [ˈdɛntl̩] *adj.* 牙科的；牙齒的

- In many countries, basic dental costs are paid for by the government.

  在許多國家，基本的牙醫費用是由政府支付的。

常用詞彙 dental floss 牙線

衍 dentist *n.* 牙醫

10 **diabetes** [ˌdaɪə`bitiz] *n.* 糖尿病

- Despite learning that he has diabetes, Sean still eats a lot of sweets.
  即便知道有糖尿病，尚恩還是吃很多甜食。

衍 diabetic *n.* 糖尿病患者
關 insulin *n.* 胰島素

---

11 **diagnose** [`daɪəɡˌnoz] *v.* 診斷

- The doctor diagnosed Amy with a nut allergy.
  醫生診斷艾咪對堅果過敏。

說明 「診斷某人得某病」為 diagnose sb. with/as (having) sth.；「診斷某狀況為某病」則為 diagnose sth. as sth.。

衍 diagnosis *n.* 診斷
衍 diagnostic *adj.* 診斷的

---

12 **diarrhea** [ˌdaɪə`riə] *n.* 腹瀉

- The man thought his bad diarrhea must have been caused by something he ate.
  那男子覺得他嚴重的腹瀉一定是因為吃了某個東西導致的。

說明 「腹瀉」口語說法為 the runs，如 I've got the runs. 就是「我拉肚子了」。

---

13 **disease** [dɪ`ziz] *n.* 疾病；病痛

- A number of diseases cause millions of Africans to die each year.
  若干疾病導致一年有數百萬名非洲人死去。

同 illness *n.* 疾病

---

14 **dizzy** [`dɪzɪ] *adj.* 頭暈目眩的

- The winding road started to make Bobby feel dizzy.
  彎彎曲曲的道路開始讓鮑比覺得頭暈了。

同 light-headed、woozy *adj.* 頭昏眼花的

---

15 **emergency** [ɪ`mɜdʒənsɪ] *n.* 緊急狀況

- Frank realized it was an emergency when his son's friend called to say Ian had broken his leg.
  當他兒子的朋友打電話來說伊恩摔斷了腿，法蘭克理解到事態緊急。

常用詞彙 emergency room 急診室

同 crisis *n.* 危機

16 epidemic [ˌɛpəˈdɛmɪk] *n.* 傳染病；（疾病等）大流行 *adj.* 流行性疾病的

- The government closed many stores and told everyone to stay at home because of the epidemic.

由於大規模的傳染病，政府關閉了許多商店，並叫大家待在家裡。

常考片語 reach epidemic proportions 到達肆虐的程度

- The charity's goal is to reduce diseases that have reached epidemic proportions in Africa.

這家慈善機構的目標是要減少在非洲引起大流行的傳染病。

⟲ outbreak *n.* 爆發；暴動

⟲ plague *n.* 瘟疫

⟲ contagious *adj.* 感染性的；會蔓延的

關 endemic *adj.*（疾病）地方性的 *n.* 地方病

---

17 examination room 診療室

- The patient was asked to change clothes before entering the examination room.

那位病人被要求在進入診療室之前換衣服。

---

18 eye drops 眼藥水

- My doctor gave me some eye drops because I kept getting itchy eyes from my allergy.

我的醫生給了我一些眼藥水，因為我的眼睛過敏一直很癢。

說明 亦可拼為一個字 eyedrops。

衍 eyedropper *n.* 滴管

---

19 first-aid kit 急救箱

- Each classroom must have a first-aid kit in case of an emergency.

每一間教室一定要有一個急救箱以便應付緊急狀況。

衍 kit *n.* 工具組；成套用品

---

20 hygiene [ˈhaɪdʒin] *n.* 衛生

- You can improve your personal hygiene by washing regularly.

你可以藉由定時沐浴改善你的個人衛生。

⟲ sanitation *n.* 環境衛生；公共衛生

---

21 hypertension [ˌhaɪpəˈtɛnʃən] *n.* 高血壓

- Stress and smoking are two causes of hypertension.

壓力與抽菸是高血壓的兩個成因。

反 hypotension *n.* 低血壓

SECTION B 必備詞彙

UNIT **13** Health 保健

311

22 indigestion [ˌɪndəˋdʒɛstʃən] *n.* 消化不良
- Paul ate so fast that he accidentally gave himself indigestion.
  保羅吃東西吃得好快，導致他不小心害自己消化不良。

反 digestion *n.* 消化作用
衍 digest *v.* 消化

---

23 inflammation [ˌɪnfləˋmeʃən] *n.* 發炎；燃燒
- The virus had caused inflammation in my mouth, so the doctor gave me some pills.
  那個病毒導致我口內發炎，所以醫生開給我一些藥丸。

衍 anti-inflammatory *n.* 消炎藥
衍 inflame *v.* 發炎
衍 inflamed *adj.* 發炎的

---

24 insurance [ɪnˋʃurəns] *n.* 保險
- In some countries, the government provides free health insurance for all citizens.
  在某些國家，政府為全體國民提供免費的健康保險。

說明 「全額健保給付」則為 full-coverage health insurance。

衍 insure *v.* 投保
關 premium *n.* 保險費

---

25 medicine [ˋmɛdəsn̩] *n.* 藥；內服藥
- The doctor told me to take the medicine three times per day for five days.
  醫生叫我連續五天每天服藥三次。

衍 medical *adj.* 醫藥的；醫療的

---

26 nauseous [ˋnɔʃɪəs] *adj.* 噁心的；想吐的
- Ted doesn't like traveling by boat because it makes him feel nauseous.
  泰德不喜歡坐船旅行，因為那會讓他覺得噁心想吐。

同 sick、ill *adj.* 想吐的
衍 nausea *n.* 噁心；作嘔
關 vomit *v.* 嘔吐

---

27 nutrition [njuˋtrɪʃən] *n.* 營養
- You should try to get more nutrition in your meals by including a variety of vegetables.
  你應該試著在餐點中涵蓋更多種類的蔬菜，藉此攝取更多營養。

衍 nutritional *adj.* 營養的
衍 nutritious *adj.* 有營養的；營養價值高的
衍 nutrient *n.* 養分；營養物

28 obesity [oˋbisətɪ] *n.* 肥胖；過胖

- Obesity can lead to heart disorders and many other health problems such as diabetes.

  過胖可能導致心臟疾病與許多其他健康問題，像是糖尿病。

同 overweight *n.* 超重；過重 *adj.* 超重的；體重過重的

衍 obese *adj.* 肥胖的

---

29 ointment [ˋɔɪntmənt] *n.* 軟膏

- This herbal ointment will help your cut heal faster.

  這個草本軟膏可以幫助你的傷口更快癒合。

---

30 operate [ˋɑpəˏret] *v.* 開刀

- It took the doctor nine hours to operate on the man's heart.

  那個醫師花了九個小時幫那名男子開心臟手術。

衍 operation *n.* 手術

---

31 optical [ˋɑptɪkḷ] *adj.* 眼睛的；視力的；光學的

- Sam had an optical issue, so he went to see the eye doctor.

  山姆的眼睛有點問題，所以他去看眼科醫生。

- The software uses optical character recognition to scan handwritten documents into Microsoft Word.

  這個軟體使用光學字元辨識系統來將手寫文件掃描到微軟的 Word 中。

同 visual *adj.* 視力的；視覺的

衍 optic *adj.* 眼睛的；視力的；光學的

衍 optician *n.* 配鏡師；驗光師

---

32 outbreak [ˋautˏbrek] *n.*（疫情、事件）爆發；突然發生

- At the beginning of 2020, there was an outbreak of a virus called "Covid-19" which spread across the whole world.

  二〇二〇年年初，一種叫做「新型冠狀病毒」的病毒開始蔓延至全球各地。

常考片語 break out（事件、動作等）突然發生、爆發；（皮膚）冒痘子、疹子

- During the live TV debate, a big argument broke out between members of opposite groups.

  在現場直播的電視辯論會中，對立的兩個團體爆發嚴重的爭吵。

- After eating seafood, the skin on Theo's neck broke out in small red dots.

  吃了海鮮後，西歐脖子的皮膚冒出小紅點。

---

33 painkiller [ˈpenˌkɪlə] *n.* 止痛劑
- Take these painkillers three times a day to reduce your headache.
  每天服用這些止痛藥三次來緩解你的頭痛。

🔵 pain reliever 止痛劑
🔶 pain *n.* 疼痛

---

34 pharmacy [ˈfɑrməsɪ] *n.* 藥房；配藥學
- Take this paper to the pharmacy to collect your medicine.
  拿這張紙去藥房拿藥。

🔶 pharmacist *n.* 藥劑師
🟢 drugstore *n.*（常兼售化妝品、日用品等的）藥房；藥妝店

---

35 prescription [prɪˈskrɪpʃən] *n.* 處方箋；藥方
- The doctor gave me a prescription for some medicine because my stomach was hurting.
  醫生開給我一張領取藥品的處方籤，因為我的胃在痛。

🔶 prescribe *v.* 開（藥方）；為……開（藥）

---

36 side effect 副作用
- A side effect of this drug could be slight dizziness, so don't drive immediately after taking it.
  這款藥的副作用可能是輕微的頭暈，所以吃完藥不要馬上開車。

🔵 adverse effect 副作用

---

37 sneeze [sniz] *v.* 打噴嚏
- Derek sneezed into a tissue to prevent other people from catching his cold.
  德瑞克打噴嚏時用衛生紙摀住口鼻，以防其他人感染到他的感冒。

🟣 allergy *n.* 過敏
🟣 allergic *adj.* 過敏的

---

38 sore [sɔr] *adj.* 疼痛發炎的 *n.*（外部的）發炎酸痛
- I think I might have an infection because I'm getting a sore throat.
  我覺得我可能被傳染了，因為我喉嚨痛。
- The viral infection caused Linda to have sores in her mouth.
  病毒性感染導致琳達口腔發炎。

常用詞彙▸ sore throat 喉嚨痛

🔵 aching、hurting、painful *adj.* 疼痛的

39　stethoscope [ˋstɛθəˏskop] *n.* 聽診器

- The doctor listened to my heartbeat by putting a stethoscope against my chest.
　那位醫生把聽診器放在我的胸口，聽我的心跳聲。

40　stomachache [ˋstʌməkˏek] *n.* 胃痛；腹痛

- I ate a spicy curry earlier, which is probably why I've got a stomachache now.
　我稍早吃了很辣的咖哩，那可能就是我現在胃痛的原因。

　說明　ache 前面加名詞即指某處疼痛，如 backache「背痛」、toothache「牙痛」、headache「頭痛」等。

- 衍 stomach *n.* 胃；肚子
- 關 diarrhea *n.* 腹瀉
- 關 flatulence *n.* 腸胃脹氣
- 關 ulcer *n.* 潰瘍
- 關 (acid) reflux 胃酸逆流
- 關 cramp *n.* 痙攣

41　subside [səbˋsaɪd] *v.* 消退；平息

- If the pain doesn't subside, then you should see a doctor.
　如果疼痛沒有消退，那你應該去看醫生。

- 同 ease off 減緩；變小

42　surgeon [ˋsɝdʒən] *n.* 外科醫生

- It was difficult to find a surgeon who would agree to do the risky operation.
　很難找到一個同意執行這種高風險手術的外科醫生。

- 衍 surgery *n.* 外科；外科手術
- 關 physician *n.* 醫生；內科醫生
- 關 internal medicine 內科

43　symptom [ˋsɪmptəm] *n.* 症狀；徵候

- Muscle aches and pain can be symptoms of the flu.
　肌肉痠痛可能是流感的症狀。

- 關 runny nose 流鼻水
- 關 stuffy nose 鼻塞
- 關 headache *n.* 頭痛

44　tablet [ˋtæblɪt] *n.* 藥錠

- This bottle of medicine contains 40 tablets.
　這罐藥品含有四十顆藥錠。

- 同 pill *n.* 藥丸；藥片
- 關 caplet *n.* 膜衣錠
- 關 capsule *n.* 膠囊

45 **temperature** [ˈtɛmprətʃə] *n.* 體溫；氣溫

關 fever *n.* 發燒

- You should see a doctor if you have a temperature above 37 degrees.

  如果你體溫超過三十七度，就應該去看醫生。

常考片語 take sb.'s temperature 量體溫

- The doctor took Ben's temperature to find out if he had a fever.

  醫師量了班的體溫，要看他是不是有發燒。

---

46 **therapy** [ˈθɛrəpɪ] *n.* 治療；療法

衍 therapist *n.* 治療師

衍 aromatherapy *n.* 芳香療法

- Gavin decided to get therapy because he had been feeling depressed for a long time.

  蓋文決定接受治療，因為他長期以來感到憂鬱。

常用詞彙 physical therapy 物理治療

---

47 **thermometer** [θəˈmɑmətə] *n.* 溫度計

關 mercury *n.*（溫度計等的）水銀柱

- The thermometer showed that the temperature of the room was high.

  溫度計顯示房內的氣溫很高。

常用詞彙 forehead thermometer 額溫槍
ear thermometer 耳溫槍

---

48 **vaccine** [vækˈsin] *n.* 疫苗

衍 vaccinate *v.* 給……注射疫苗

衍 vaccination *n.* 接種疫苗；預防注射

- Scientists around the world were working day and night to develop a vaccine for the dangerous virus.

  全球科學家日以繼夜地想要研發那個危險病毒的疫苗。

---

49 **vomit** [ˈvɑmɪt] *v.* 嘔吐

同 spew、throw up、puke 嘔吐

- The food was so disgusting that I wanted to vomit.

  那食物好噁心，我都想要吐了。

50 # workout [ˋwɝkͺaʊt] *n.* 訓練；運動；體操

同 training *n.* 訓練

同 exercise *n.* 運動

- Just a five minute workout in the morning can improve your mood for the whole day.
  光是早晨五分鐘的運動就能改善你一整天的心情。

常考片語 work out 鍛鍊；健身；順利發展

- Ryan has a gym membership, but when it rains he usually works out at home.
  萊恩有一間健身房的會員身分，但下雨的時候他通常在家運動。

- Tina's new training schedule didn't work out as planned because she got an injury.
  蒂娜的新訓練計畫並未如期進行，因為她受傷了。

各種健身基本動作

stretch 伸展

squats 深蹲

sit-ups 仰臥起坐

push-ups 伏地挺身

jumping jacks 開合跳

cool down 緩和運動

high knees running in place
原地提膝踏步

PRACTICE TEST

Part 1: Photographs

TRACK 77

Directions:

For each question in this part, you will hear four statements about a picture. When you hear the statements, you must select the one statement that best describes what you see in the picture. Then circle the letter (A), (B), (C), or (D). The statements will not be printed below and will be spoken only one time.

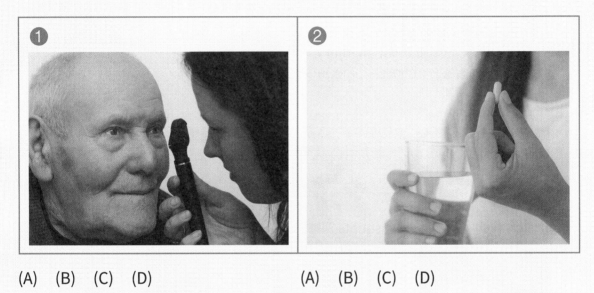

(A) (B) (C) (D)   (A) (B) (C) (D)

Part 2: Question and Response

TRACK 78

Directions:

You will hear a question or statement and three responses spoken in English. They will be spoken only one time and will not be printed below. Select the best response to the question or statement and circle the letter (A), (B), or (C).

3 (A) (B) (C)

4 (A) (B) (C)

5 (A) (B) (C)

6 (A) (B) (C)

Part 3: Short Conversations

Directions:

You will hear some conversations between two or more people. You will be asked to answer three questions about what the speakers say in each conversation. Select the best response to each question and circle the letter (A), (B), (C), or (D). The conversation will be spoken only one time and will not be printed below.

7 What are the speakers mainly discussing?

(A) A patient's medical history   (B) A patient's eating habits

(C) How to overcome heartburn   (D) A current medical issue

8 When has the patient felt the strongest pain?

(A) A few weeks ago   (B) In the morning

(C) After eating   (D) When sleeping

9 What will the patient most likely do next?

(A) Nothing   (B) Take medicine

(C) Eat something   (D) Have a scan

Monthly Plan Premiums	Rate (in dollars)
Self	9.50
Self + Spouse	19.50
Self + Child(ren)	12.50
Family	23.50

10 What was the woman's original plan?

(A) Self   (B) Self + Spouse

(C) Self + Child(ren)   (D) Family

11 Why does the woman want to change her private medical insurance plan?

(A) She is planning to retire.   (B) She has had a baby.

(C) She has recently gotten married.   (D) She can't afford her old plan.

12 Look at the graphic. How much more will the woman pay per month on her new plan?

(A) $3   (B) $7

(C) $9.50   (D) $12.50

Part 4: Short Talks

TRACK 80

Directions:

You will hear some short talks given by a single speaker. You will be asked to answer three questions about what the speaker says in each talk. Select the best response to each question and circle the letter (A), (B), (C), or (D). The talks will be spoken only one time and will not be printed below.

13 What is being advertised?

(A) A website about nutrition   (B) A new health food restaurant

(C) A food delivery service   (D) An ice cream delivery service

14 What does the speaker mean when he says, "That's where we come in"?

(A) EatWise makes you nauseous.

(B) EatWise helps organize your schedule.

(C) EatWise helps you switch to a vegan diet.

(D) EatWise helps you eat properly.

15 Who is the intended audience for this advertisement?

(A) People who don't have much free time

(B) People who enjoy cooking at home

(C) People who like eating "on the go"

(D) People who do a lot of exercise

BMI of Adults Aged 20 and Older

BMI	Classification
18.5 to 24.9	Normal weight
25 to 29.9	Overweight
30+	Obesity
40+	Extreme obesity

16 Look at the graphic. Which is most likely the BMI figure for one third of American adults aged 20 and older?

(A) under 18.5   (B) 18.5-24.9

(C) 25-29.9   (D) above 30

⑰ What is the purpose of this podcast?

(A) To promote exercise

(B) To sell health products

(C) To sell fitness equipment

(D) To compare health in different countries

⑱ Why is it good for employees to be physically active?

(A) Because they can make more money

(B) Because they enjoy it more than sitting down

(C) Because they can do less work this way

(D) Because it is natural for the human body

Part 5: Incomplete Sentences

Directions:

A word or phrase is missing in each of the sentences below. Four answer choices are given below each sentence. Select the best answer to complete the sentence. Then circle the letter (A), (B), (C), or (D).

⑲ Jenny's rash started _____ a few hours after she had applied ointment to it.

(A) to disappear   (B) disappear

(C) will disappear   (D) disappeared

⑳ In this first-aid kit, there are some _____ which can be used to treat cuts.

(A) thermometers   (B) pharmacies

(C) bandages   (D) eye drops

㉑ A sudden drop in blood pressure caused Karen to start feeling _____.

(A) allergic   (B) dizzy

(C) optic   (D) clinical

㉒ He's going to give himself indigestion if he keeps eating that quickly, _____?

(A) isn't he   (B) is he

(C) won't he   (D) doesn't he

㉓ _____ the surgeon is, I hope he or she is very well-qualified and experienced.

(A) Whenever   (B) Whatever

(C) Whichever   (D) Whoever

Part 6: Text Completion

Directions:

Read the text below. A word, phrase, or sentence is missing. For each empty space in the text, select the best answer to complete the text. Then circle the letter (A), (B), (C), or (D).

Questions 24-27 refer to the following website article.

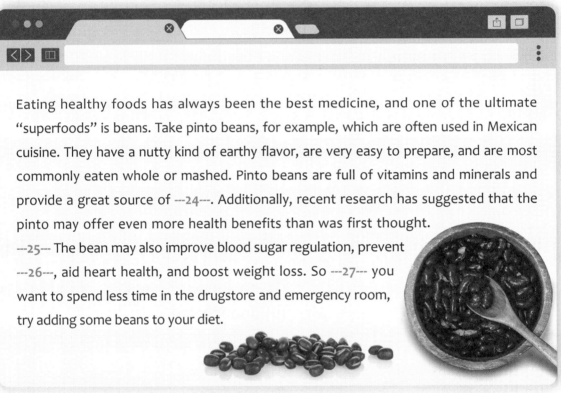

Eating healthy foods has always been the best medicine, and one of the ultimate "superfoods" is beans. Take pinto beans, for example, which are often used in Mexican cuisine. They have a nutty kind of earthy flavor, are very easy to prepare, and are most commonly eaten whole or mashed. Pinto beans are full of vitamins and minerals and provide a great source of ---24---. Additionally, recent research has suggested that the pinto may offer even more health benefits than was first thought. ---25--- The bean may also improve blood sugar regulation, prevent ---26---, aid heart health, and boost weight loss. So ---27--- you want to spend less time in the drugstore and emergency room, try adding some beans to your diet.

24 (A) energy
(C) energetic
(B) energize
(D) energetically

25 (A) One of the ways that pinto beans can be prepared is by mashing them into a paste.
(B) It is now believed that they may be associated with reduced inflammation.
(C) Indeed, pinto beans are the most popular type of bean eaten in the United States.
(D) Unfortunately, beans can lead to stomach cramping and flatulence.

26 (A) stethoscopes　(B) painkillers　(C) hygiene　(D) indigestion

27 (A) if　(B) until　(C) though　(D) while

Part 7: Reading Comprehension

Directions:

In this part you will read a selection of texts, such as magazine and newspaper articles, e-mails, and instant messages. Each text is followed by several questions. Select the best answer for each question and circle the letter (A), (B), (C), or (D).

Questions 28-29 refer to the following text message chain.

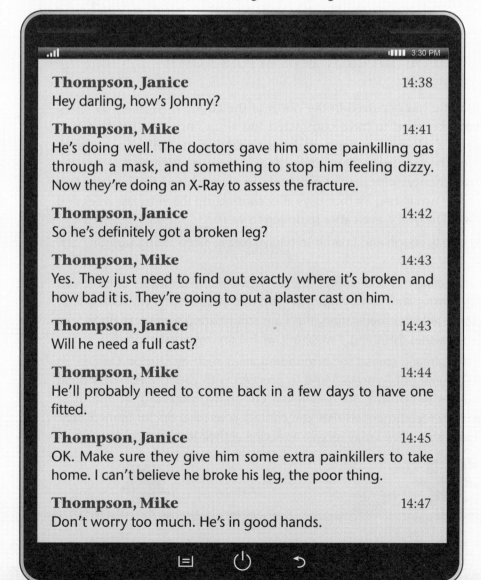

Thompson, Janice　14:38
Hey darling, how's Johnny?

Thompson, Mike　14:41
He's doing well. The doctors gave him some painkilling gas through a mask, and something to stop him feeling dizzy. Now they're doing an X-Ray to assess the fracture.

Thompson, Janice　14:42
So he's definitely got a broken leg?

Thompson, Mike　14:43
Yes. They just need to find out exactly where it's broken and how bad it is. They're going to put a plaster cast on him.

Thompson, Janice　14:43
Will he need a full cast?

Thompson, Mike　14:44
He'll probably need to come back in a few days to have one fitted.

Thompson, Janice　14:45
OK. Make sure they give him some extra painkillers to take home. I can't believe he broke his leg, the poor thing.

Thompson, Mike　14:47
Don't worry too much. He's in good hands.

㉘ How did the doctors make Johnny feel better?

(A) They did an X-Ray on him.   (B) They gave him special gas.

(C) They put a cast on him.   (D) They gave him some pills.

㉙ At 14:47, what does Mike Thompson mean when he writes, "He's in good hands"?

(A) His son has good parents who support him.

(B) His son doesn't feel any pain in his hands.

(C) The doctors taking care of his son are reliable.

(D) The doctors think his son is healthy.

Questions 30-34 refer to the following news article, memo, and schedule.

Flu Outbreak Sweeps Across North

An outbreak of the flu has occurred in the north of the country. As many as 2,000 people are already believed to have contracted the virus since the first case was identified last week. It is looking as if this epidemic could rival the last major outbreak that swept through the country in 2004. Over 1,000 of the cases identified so far have been in Morgrove County, with further outbreaks in Sheptan and Hollinsdale. Ann Wilson, of Morgrove, was in bed for four days after contracting the virus last week and has yet to make a full recovery, even after returning to work.

"I had this awful chesty cough and I had it so badly I had to sleep sitting upright," she said.

"I can't remember feeling this bad before," the forty-two-year-old mother of three was quoted as saying. "Fortunately, the symptoms started to subside after my local doctor prescribed me some antiviral medication. But I am still wearing a mask to make sure no one around me catches this thing. I wouldn't wish it on my worst enemy!"

The virus may have already spread to surrounding areas such as Murton-On-Sea, so members of the general public are advised to proceed with caution. For individuals experiencing flu-like symptoms, such as fever, coughing, sneezing, vomiting or diarrhea, it is strongly recommended that you contact your local doctor immediately. Those wishing to be immunized may receive a vaccine at their local health clinic.

Memo

Date: December 4th

Dear employees of Harwood Inc.,

As some of you may already be aware, in today's local news there is a report about a serious outbreak of the flu, with our area being the most at risk. It is for this reason that I am bringing forward the date of our annual Flu Vaccination Day. Normally, we hold vaccinations at the office somewhere around the middle of December but, with recent news in mind, I have deemed it necessary to take precautions earlier than scheduled.

I have attached a booking schedule to this memo for those wishing to get vaccinated on Wednesday. Vaccination times are grouped alphabetically according to surname. Please make a note. I will definitely be getting vaccinated myself and I strongly recommend all employees do the same.

For any questions, please contact Cathy Riley (wellness@harwoodinc.com).

Thank you,

Brian Harwood
Head of Human Resources

VACCINATION BOOKING SCHEDULE

I wish to be vaccinated on Wednesday, December 6th.

Group A (A-G) ☐   **Group B (H-P)** ☐   **Group C (Q-Z)** ☐
09:30-11:00   11:30-13:00   14:00-15:30

Employee Name (Print): _____

Employee ID Number: _____

Employee Signature: _____

30 What is the main purpose of the memo?

(A) To update staff on company news

(B) To tell staff when to visit a local health clinic

(C) To inform shareholders of a virus

(D) To inform staff of vaccinations

31 When was the current virus first detected?

(A) December 4th (B) December 6th

(C) Last week (D) Two days ago

32 Where is Harwood Inc. located?

(A) Morgrove (B) Sheptan

(C) Hollinsdale (D) Murton-On-Sea

33 In the second sentence of the memo, what does the phrase "bringing forward" mean?

(A) Changing to a later date

(B) Changing to an earlier date

(C) Drawing attention to something

(D) Analyzing something in more detail

34 What could be a possible time for the Head of Human Resources to get vaccinated?

(A) 10:45 (B) 11:45

(C) 13:45 (D) 14:45

Section C
多益全真模擬測驗

Section C 提供完整的 TOEIC 模擬測驗，以便準備應試的讀者練習考試速度的掌控並測試學習成效。

  TRACK 81 測驗時間：120 分鐘

LISTENING TEST

In the Listening test, you will be asked to demonstrate how well you understand spoken English. The entire listening test will last approximately 45 minutes. There are four parts, and directions are given for each part. You must mark your answers on the separate answer sheet. Do not write your answers in your test book.

PART 1

Directions: For each question in this part, you will hear four statements about a picture in your test book. When you hear the statements, you must select the one statement that best describes what you see in the picture. Then find the number of the question on your answer sheet and mark your answer. The statements will not be printed in your test book and will be spoken only one time.

Sample Answer
Ⓐ Ⓑ ● Ⓓ

Example

Statement (C), "The woman is holding a document," is the best description of the picture, so you should select answer (C) and mark it on your answer sheet.

1.

2.

Go on to the next page.

3.

4.

5.

6.

Go on to the next page.

PART 2

Directions: You will hear a question or statement and three responses spoken in English. They will not be printed in your test book and will be spoken only one time. Select the best response to the question or statement and mark the letter (A), (B), or (C) on your answer sheet.

Example

You will hear: What is the meeting about?

You will also hear: (A) He'll probably be late.

(B) Our new marketing plan.

(C) I have an interview.

The best response to the question "What is the meeting about?" is choice (B), "Our new marketing plan," so (B) is the correct answer. You should mark answer (B) on your answer sheet.

7. Mark your answer on your answer sheet.

8. Mark your answer on your answer sheet.

9. Mark your answer on your answer sheet.

10. Mark your answer on your answer sheet.

11. Mark your answer on your answer sheet.

12. Mark your answer on your answer sheet.

13. Mark your answer on your answer sheet.

14. Mark your answer on your answer sheet.

15. Mark your answer on your answer sheet.

16. Mark your answer on your answer sheet.

17. Mark your answer on your answer sheet.

18. Mark your answer on your answer sheet.

19. Mark your answer on your answer sheet.

20. Mark your answer on your answer sheet.

21. Mark your answer on your answer sheet.

22. Mark your answer on your answer sheet.

23. Mark your answer on your answer sheet.

24. Mark your answer on your answer sheet.

25. Mark your answer on your answer sheet.

26. Mark your answer on your answer sheet.

27. Mark your answer on your answer sheet.

28. Mark your answer on your answer sheet.

29. Mark your answer on your answer sheet.

30. Mark your answer on your answer sheet.

31. Mark your answer on your answer sheet.

PART 3

Directions: You will hear some conversations between two or more people. You will be asked to answer three questions about what the speakers say in each conversation. Select the best response to each question and mark the letter (A), (B), (C), or (D) on your answer sheet. The conversations will not be printed in your test book and will be spoken only one time.

32. Why does the woman have to schedule a new appointment?
    (A) She has to make an appointment for her son.
    (B) She missed her appointment last week.
    (C) She has new symptoms that concern her.
    (D) Dr. Goodwin asked her to schedule a new one.

33. What day is the woman calling on?
    (A) Friday   (B) Wednesday
    (C) Thursday   (D) Monday

34. What most likely is the man's job?
    (A) A doctor   (B) A nurse
    (C) A receptionist   (D) A dentist

35. What project are the speakers most likely talking about?
    (A) Constructing a new bedroom
    (B) Constructing a new bathroom
    (C) Making marble statues
    (D) Making new kitchen counters

36. What does the man want the woman to do?
    (A) Choose new materials
    (B) Use granite countertops
    (C) Call the manufacturer
    (D) Find a cheaper quote

37. What does the man suggest would be a better option for the client?
    (A) Using granite only
    (B) Combining granite and marble
    (C) Canceling the order
    (D) Putting the price up

38. What are the speakers concerned about?
    (A) They don't like working with a coworker.
    (B) They have been working overtime too often.
    (C) They haven't been paid for working overtime.
    (D) They don't want to train a new employee.

39. What does the woman think about working overtime again?
    (A) She feels like quitting.
    (B) The situation is out of control.
    (C) The company is acting illegally.
    (D) It's a good way to make extra money.

40. Why have the speakers been so busy recently?
    (A) The company fired a lot of employees.
    (B) The company accepted a lot of new orders.
    (C) They haven't been working efficiently.
    (D) They have been taking a lot of leave.

41. Why were the man's shipping costs higher?
    (A) He accidentally shipped the products to the wrong country.
    (B) He forgot to write an address when he made the order.
    (C) He shipped more items than usual to Australia.
    (D) He shipped fewer items to Canada than before.

42. What does the man mean when he says, "that's my bad"?
    (A) It's a bad order.
    (B) He's having a bad day.
    (C) He made a mistake.
    (D) The products are bad.

43. Where is the order being sent to?
    (A) Canada
    (B) Australia
    (C) The USA
    (D) The UK

44. What is the woman concerned about?
    (A) The salary
    (B) The benefits
    (C) Taking leave
    (D) The job description

45. What will happen during the first three months of her employment?
    (A) She will receive some training.
    (B) She will go on a business trip.
    (C) She will be training other employees.
    (D) She will not be paid.

46. When will the woman be able to start at the new company?
    (A) Right away
    (B) In a month
    (C) Next week
    (D) Tomorrow

Go on to the next page.

47. How many days does Janice want to take off?
    (A) Two weeks
    (B) Three days
    (C) One day
    (D) Four days

48. Why can Mr. Jeffreys not approve more leave days?
    (A) Janice has already taken too many days this quarter.
    (B) The company doesn't allow employees to take leave.
    (C) The company doesn't give bereavement leave.
    (D) Janice doesn't qualify for annual leave days.

49. Which of the following does the woman most likely have to give HR?
    (A) Her condolences
    (B) An job application
    (C) A death certificate
    (D) An airplane ticket

50. What position is the woman most likely starting?
    (A) Quality Control Assistant
    (B) Head of Quality Control
    (C) HR Manager
    (D) Personal Assistant

51. Who most likely is James Harris?
    (A) The CEO of the company
    (B) The HR manager
    (C) Head of Quality Control
    (D) An employee in the QC department

52. Why is James excited to have Ms. Grey on board?
    (A) She will make a lot of money.
    (B) She is very experienced.
    (C) She'll impress board members.
    (D) She might give him a raise.

53. When does John want to meet Mary?
    (A) At 11 a.m.
    (B) At 1 p.m.
    (C) At 1:30 p.m.
    (D) In 10 minutes

54. What can be inferred about the woman's job?
    (A) She has strict office hours.
    (B) Everyone takes lunch at the same time.
    (C) The office closes during lunch.
    (D) She can decide when to have lunch.

55. What type of restaurant is Mr. Toni's most likely?
    (A) A pizzeria
    (B) A fast-food place
    (C) A Chinese restaurant
    (D) A vegetarian restaurant

56. What most likely is the woman's job?
    (A) A store manager
    (B) A real estate agent
    (C) An office receptionist
    (D) A financial advisor

57. What is the man's concern about investing in new things?
    (A) He doesn't trust the stock market.
    (B) He prefers cryptocurrency.
    (C) He thinks it's too boring.
    (D) He doesn't have enough money.

58. What did the woman's firm do last year?
    (A) They started investing in the stock market.
    (B) They opened a department for cryptocurrency.
    (C) They created their own cryptocurrency.
    (D) They started advising the man.

Go on to the next page.

59. What are the speakers mainly discussing?
    (A) New products for potential customers
    (B) Necessary tools for a new product line
    (C) Marketing strategies for a new market
    (D) Marketing campaigns for a new product

60. What does the man mean when he says, "I'm not sure I follow"?
    (A) He doesn't want to follow someone.
    (B) He can't see where someone is going.
    (C) He's not sure he understands something.
    (D) He is lost and not sure where to go.

61. Why shouldn't they stay with current market strategies?
    (A) New strategies will definitely work in the new markets.
    (B) They definitely won't work in the new markets.
    (C) They may be lacking in important information.
    (D) Employees have complained about the old strategies.

62. What is special about this store?
    (A) They have just opened recently.
    (B) Their bathrooms have air conditioning.
    (C) The items are organized by season.
    (D) They are environmentally friendly.

63. Look at the graphic. How many items does the woman buy?
    (A) 1
    (B) 2
    (C) 3
    (D) 4

64. Where can the woman find a free item?
    (A) In the winter section
    (B) In the summer section
    (C) In the fall section
    (D) In the spring section

Nouveau Fashion

SPECIAL PROMOTION

➢ Buy 4 items from our Fall Collection and get a matching accessory free!
➢ Buy 3 items get 15% off
➢ Buy 2 items get 10% off

Only valid until 10th September

65. Where most likely are the speakers?
    (A) The MRT
    (B) A bus station
    (C) A train station
    (D) A ferry terminal

Due	Destination	Status	Platform
08:09	Stratford (London)	On time	1
08:10	Bishop's Stortford	On time	4
08:13	London Liverpool Street via Seven Sisters	On time	2
08:15	Hertford East	08:18 3 mins late	3
08:18	London Liverpool Street	On time	2

66. Look at the graphic. Where is the woman trying to go?
    (A) Stratford (London)
    (B) Bishop's Stortford
    (C) Hertford East
    (D) London Liverpool Street

67. What will the woman most likely do next?
    (A) Call the police
    (B) Buy a new ticket
    (C) Run to a platform
    (D) Choose another destination

68. What is Marlon Denning most concerned about?
    (A) The cast of the film
    (B) The cost of the film
    (C) The title of the film
    (D) The script of the film

69. Look at the graphic. What is the title of the woman's film?
    (A) Guinevere
    (B) The Pirate's Curse
    (C) Northwest Passage
    (D) A Night to Remember

70. Which most likely is Marlon Denning's profession?
    (A) A film editor
    (B) An actor
    (C) A director
    (D) An investor

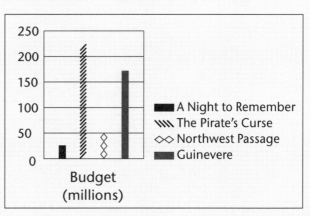

Go on to the next page.

PART 4

Directions: You will hear some talks given by a single speaker. You will be asked to answer three questions about what the speaker says in each talk. Select the best response to each question and mark the letter (A), (B), (C), or (D) on your answer sheet. The talks will not be printed in your test book and will be spoken only one time.

71. Who is Julie Brown most likely speaking to?
    (A) Potential customers
    (B) Fitness models
    (C) Potential investors
    (D) The bank loan manager

72. Why did the speaker and her team invent this vest?
    (A) There are many people who need to lose weight.
    (B) There are millions of people who want to exercise.
    (C) There are many people who can't leave the house.
    (D) There are many people who want to save money.

73. What is Julie Brown offering investors in return for their investment?
    (A) A guaranteed 30% interest
    (B) A 30% share in the company
    (C) 30% of the profits she makes
    (D) $300,000 per year

74. What most likely is the speaker's job?
    (A) A delivery man
    (B) A bank manager
    (C) A sales representative
    (D) A technician

75. What would the listener have to do first to start ordering from ElecCorp?
    (A) Pay for their full order in advance
    (B) Order products worth at least $20,000
    (C) Open a line of credit for $10,000
    (D) Pay a 50% deposit and the rest upon delivery

76. What would be the cheapest option to order from ElecCorp?
    (A) To pay over six months
    (B) To pay with a credit card
    (C) To pay in advance
    (D) To pay on delivery

77. When did Dave Smith become the CEO at ABC Inc.?
    (A) In 2006
    (B) In 2016
    (C) In 2015
    (D) In 2008

78. What does the speaker imply about Dave and John?
    (A) They are long-term friends.
    (B) They are rivals in the industry.
    (C) They will lead ABC Inc.
    (D) They went to the same college.

79. What is John Matthews' current position?
    (A) CEO of ABC Inc.
    (B) CEO of LiveNow
    (C) President and CEO of eDev
    (D) President at Dartmouth

Go on to the next page.

80. What has the government asked people to do?
    (A) Not go to school
    (B) Avoid driving on Friday
    (C) Use public transportation
    (D) Watch out for heavy winds

81. What most likely will highs on Friday be?
    (A) -5°C
    (B) -10°C
    (C) -12°C
    (D) -20°C

82. What is suggested about the weather?
    (A) Winter is ending.
    (B) It will likely force schools to close.
    (C) Things will return to normal next week.
    (D) Heavy snowfalls are expected on Sunday.

83. What two developments does the speaker mention?
    (A) An online platform and an app
    (B) A retail platform and a facilities app
    (C) A technology award and supply chain
    (D) New technology and traditional links

84. What does the speaker think the two developments show?
    (A) That retailers need to improve their channels
    (B) That the original supply chain still applies
    (C) That retailers need to help originators
    (D) That the grain industry has changed completely

85. What does the speaker suggest retailers do?
    (A) Create a lot of channels to sell their products
    (B) Pay suppliers more for their products
    (C) Sell more products to consumers
    (D) Use the same strategy on all their platforms

86. What kind of car will be discounted this weekend?
    (A) SUVs
    (B) All cars
    (C) Minivans
    (D) Convertibles

87. What does the speaker suggest listeners do on Saturday?
    (A) Bring a car to exchange
    (B) Pick up a coupon
    (C) Visit early in the morning
    (D) Use their employee discount

88. What does the speaker imply when he says, "cars will be driving themselves off the lot"?
    (A) They're moving the cars.
    (B) They're selling self-driving cars.
    (C) Cars in stock will be sold quickly.
    (D) They'll get a new shipment of cars.

89. Who is being addressed?
    (A) A captain in a plane
    (B) Flight attendants
    (C) Passengers in a plane
    (D) Travelers at an airport

90. What beverage is available for purchase only?
    (A) Tea
    (B) Soda
    (C) Wine
    (D) Coffee

91. When is the plane expected to land?
    (A) 5:15 a.m.
    (B) 5:15 p.m.
    (C) 8:00 a.m.
    (D) 8:00 p.m.

Go on to the next page.

92. Why does Patrick have to pay $200?
    (A) He has to pay the headhunter.
    (B) He has to pay a penalty.
    (C) He has to pay to work legally.
    (D) He has to pay to get a one-year license.

93. What position is Jane's company most likely offering Patrick?
    (A) An interpreter
    (B) An accountant
    (C) A management position
    (D) A government position

94. What should Patrick do next if he wants the job?
    (A) He should pay them $200.
    (B) He should go to the office on Tuesday.
    (C) He should call Janet before Monday.
    (D) He should quit his current job.

95. What will happen between 10 and 11 a.m.?
    (A) All the kids will get to meet Santa Claus.
    (B) Kids who missed their chance yesterday will meet Santa.
    (C) Kids who get there first will make their own Christmas decorations.
    (D) Kids who missed Santa will get a delicious meal.

96. Look at the graphic. On which floor is Santa's Work Station most likely located?
    (A) Ground Floor
    (B) First Floor
    (C) Second Floor
    (D) Basement

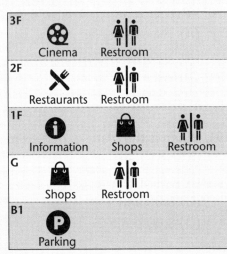

97. What can shoppers buy at Granny's Bakery?
    (A) Ingredients for their dinner
    (B) Ready-to-eat meals for dinner
    (C) A delicious brunch
    (D) Electronic devices

98. What was the company's main goal at the beginning of the year?
    (A) Increase web revenue as a share of total revenue
    (B) Decrease total revenue generated from web work
    (C) Expand into other areas of design for print
    (D) Design more web-related graphics and media

99. What does the speaker mean when he says, "We're over the moon"?
    (A) Management is very happy.
    (B) Management is surprised.
    (C) A difficult period has ended.
    (D) The year has come to an end.

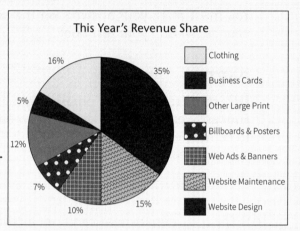

100. Look at the graphic. What percentage of revenue came from clothing designs in the year before this one?
    (A) 7%
    (B) 8%
    (C) 10.5%
    (D) 32%

Go on to the next page.

READING TEST

In the Reading test, you will read a variety of texts and answer several different types of reading comprehension questions. The entire Reading test will last 75 minutes. There are three parts, and directions are given for each part. You are encouraged to answer as many questions as possible within the time allowed.

You must mark your answers on the separate answer sheet. Do not write your answers in your test book.

PART 5

Directions: A word or phrase is missing in each of the sentences below. Four answer choices are given below each sentence. Select the best answer to complete the sentence. Then mark the letter (A), (B), (C), or (D) on your answer sheet.

101. The _____ department can't get all the products to the clients on time.
    (A) distribution
    (B) distributor
    (C) distribute
    (D) distributing

102. In many cultures, it is important to _____ eye contact when speaking to another person.
    (A) refrain
    (B) remain
    (C) explain
    (D) maintain

103. The person _____ donated this money prefers to remain anonymous.
    (A) who
    (B) which
    (C) whom
    (D) whose

104. Customer service representatives are always available to handle your concerns _____ your choice of e-mail, live chat, or social media.
    (A) above
    (B) through
    (C) since
    (D) until

105. Louis said he _____ hiking on Yangmingshan last weekend with friends.
    (A) went
    (B) will go
    (C) is going
    (D) will have gone

106. We have been in the _____ for three months; we'll have to close soon.
    (A) trouble
    (B) green
    (C) red
    (D) rise

107. Please _____ that you will need the booking reservation number to complete the transaction.
    (A) vary
    (B) affect
    (C) rent
    (D) note

108. The company _____ a new policy to ensure equal treatment of all its employees.
    (A) initiative
    (B) initiated
    (C) initiator
    (D) initial

109. Up next, we'll discuss the best marketing strategies with a leading _____ in the field.
    (A) directory
    (B) catalog
    (C) expert
    (D) period

Go on to the next page.

110. The boss was not satisfied with her employees' _____ for the last month.
     (A) procedure
     (B) patent
     (C) output
     (D) extension

111. The amount of time worked by the typical European each week is, on average, _____ that worked by the typical American.
     (A) less
     (B) least
     (C) far less
     (D) less than

112. With his _____ headset, Tim could continue the conversation anywhere in the house.
     (A) wireless
     (B) surrounding
     (C) relative
     (D) securing

113. The CEO was not worried about the sales figures, _____ they fluctuated during the last year.
     (A) as though
     (B) but also
     (C) even though
     (D) so that

114. You can welcome your family members home at the arrivals _____ of the airport.
     (A) departure
     (B) nation
     (C) terminal
     (D) citizen

115. Unfortunately, they could not publish the book because they felt it was not _____.
     (A) market
     (B) marketable
     (C) marketing
     (D) marketed

116. Many companies have had to downsize _____ the failing economy.
    (A) because
    (B) apart from
    (C) due to
    (D) except for

117. Mike is relieved that he made it through his _____ period.
    (A) frequent
    (B) indicative
    (C) probationary
    (D) comprehensive

118. Employees are _____ asked to work overtime and will be appropriately compensated according to the law.
    (A) exactly
    (B) extremely
    (C) particularly
    (D) occasionally

119. Sales tax and services charges _____ in the "new charges" section of each monthly bill.
    (A) includes
    (B) included
    (C) are included
    (D) are including

120. As the _____ shareholder, Mr. Musk is the primary decision-maker for the company.
    (A) former
    (B) majority
    (C) minority
    (D) minimum

121. Our last campaign did not _____ our target demographic, so we changed tack.
    (A) carry out
    (B) appeal to
    (C) tend to
    (D) set up

122. The end goal of the production process is to ＿＿ sufficient goods and services to satisfy consumer demand.
    (A) manufacture
    (B) manufacturing
    (C) manufactured
    (D) manufacturer

123. Enclosed you will find train tickets and a tentative ＿＿ for your upcoming trip.
    (A) candidate
    (B) franchise
    (C) billboard
    (D) itinerary

124. The airline will give you a ＿＿ meal voucher if you book your tickets today.
    (A) compliment
    (B) complimentary
    (C) complimenting
    (D) complimented

125. Many people believe it's better not to ＿＿, but to focus on one task at a time.
    (A) multitask
    (B) distinguish
    (C) influence
    (D) expose

126. Mr. Cage had the mechanic ＿＿ the car to find out what was making that horrible noise.
    (A) customize
    (B) strike
    (C) diagnose
    (D) inspect

127. Please inform all candidates that they are expected to show up early for ＿＿ group interview.
    (A) they
    (B) their
    (C) them
    (D) themselves

128. The scientists received a Nobel Prize for their _____ in the medical field.
- (A) estimate
- (B) breakthrough
- (C) hesitation
- (D) renovation

129. Your agreement with us is comprised of your filled-in and signed membership agreement form, these terms and conditions, and the terms of club use as outlined _____.
- (A) below
- (B) besides
- (C) behind
- (D) between

130. _____ you arrive more than 10 minutes after your booking time without informing us of the delay, you may lose your table to another group.
- (A) May
- (B) Have
- (C) Should
- (D) Could

PART 6

Directions: Read the texts that follow. A word, phrase, or sentence is missing in parts of each text. Four answer choices for each question are given below the text. Select the best answer to complete the text. Then mark the letter (A), (B), (C) or (D) on your answer sheet.

Questions 131-134 refer to the following website announcement.

Dear Valued Customers,

At Big Bucks Bank, not only do we aspire to help you achieve your financial goals, we pride ourselves on our solid track record of customer ---**131**---.

That's why we want to apologize for any difficulties you ---**132**--- during the launch of our new digital and mobile banking app yesterday. Please know that we designed our new platform with your convenience in mind, offering enhanced security, navigation, tools, and a modern look and feel. Unfortunately, we ran into some technical difficulties along the way, ---**133**--- we worked around the clock to resolve.

The last thing we want to do is disappoint you. That's why we're committed to making things right. If you have any questions about our new online banking experience or would like to see a video message, visit us <u>here</u>.

Thank you for being a part of the Big Bucks family. ---**134**---

Sincerely,
Sal Smitherson, Customer Service Director

131. (A) satisfy
    (C) satisfactory
    (B) satisfied
    (D) satisfaction

132. (A) encounter
    (C) will encounter
    (B) encountered
    (D) will be encountering

133. (A) that
    (C) which
    (B) what
    (D) how

134. (A) We are sorry you closed your account.
    (B) We will close early due to the holidays.
    (C) We will no longer offer online banking.
    (D) We are grateful for your continued loyalty.

Questions 135-138 *refer to the following e-mail.*

To:	macey@yaho.com
From:	res@hh.com
Subject:	Confirmation

Dear Macey,

---**135**--- We look forward to receiving you from October 28th to November 2nd. Please take note of the following:

1. Check-in time is at 2 p.m. and check-out time is at 11 a.m.

2. You can order breakfast the day before and enjoy it from 7 a.m. to 9 a.m.

3. There is a communal kitchen where you can cook your own lunch or dinner. ---**136**---, we can suggest some wonderful places very close to the hostel.

4. The communal living room has many books, board games, DVDs, etc. for you to enjoy with other guests.

5. Please keep the noise level down after 10 p.m. and be considerate of your fellow guests.

6. You can rent a towel and buy toiletries from our staff ---**137**--- you check in.

7. There is a self-service laundromat very close to the hostel.

8. Your 50% deposit is ---**138**--- until two weeks before your arrival date. After that, we will only refund 25% until two days before your trip. If you cancel two days before your trip, we will not refund your deposit.

Please let us know if you have any questions. We trust you will enjoy your stay with us!

Best,

HH

135. (A) Thank you for enquiring about our rooms.
   (B) Thank you for your recent booking at Happy Hostel in Oslo.
   (C) We apologize for the incorrect booking on our site.
   (D) We would like to offer you a discounted room.

136. (A) Impossibly   (B) Initially
   (C) Alternatively   (D) Defectively

137. (A) who   (B) when
   (C) which   (D) whose

138. (A) abundant   (B) commercial
   (C) optical   (D) refundable

Go on to the next page.

Questions 139-142 refer to the following notice.

Attention Members!

We would like to take this opportunity to express our gratitude to you, our valued customers, for your years of loyal patronage. As a token of our thanks, all frequent-flier members with at least one year under their belts will be awarded a bonus of 5,000 miles. Those with five to ten years will receive an additional 5,000 miles, ---**139**--- those with over ten years will see an additional 10,000 miles. They are valid from the time of this announcement and must be redeemed within the next two years. As always, they cannot be used in conjunction with any other ongoing airline ---**140**---.

Additionally, from now until this time next year, any miles accumulated through our domestic and international flights will be doubled. ---**141**--- As long as they are properly reported to our mileage program and received by midnight on this day a year from now, they ---**142**--- to your account. We hope you take full advantage of these free miles and continue to fly with us.

139. (A) hence
     (C) while
     (B) because
     (D) nor

140. (A) resignation
     (C) depression
     (B) promotion
     (D) malfunction

141. (A) They will stay frozen for an indefinite period of time.
     (B) There is no limit to the number of miles you can collect.
     (C) Once that happens, you will no longer be an active member.
     (D) After that, they will be halved again and again until nothing is left.

142. (A) credit
     (C) will be credited
     (B) is crediting
     (D) have been credited

Seeking Savvy Self-Starter!

Do you want to feel as ---**143**--- as you look? Are you seeking new opportunities for excellence? Contact me for a chance to work for yourself, as much or as little as you want. Leverage your networks and start making big money today!

Clary May Cosmetics beauty consultants buy their inventory from the Clary May wholesale division and sell it directly to customers at in-home parties and through personal websites. Similar to brick-and-mortar stores, consultants keep the difference ---**144**--- wholesale and market price.

Consultants desiring to earn a more full-time salary are encouraged to ---**145**---, manage and support a sales team of new consultants. We believe that encouraging consultants to form their own sales teams and rewarding them for sharing in each other's success builds a stronger sales force than one formed via more traditional management approaches. As your network grows, so does your business.

What are you waiting for? Seize this opportunity to become financially successful, and create new standards of personal excellence! ---**146**---

143. (A) success
    (C) successful
    (B) succeed
    (D) successfully

144. (A) between
    (C) besides
    (B) among
    (D) despite

145. (A) retire
    (C) recall
    (B) recruit
    (D) restock

146. (A) No purchase necessary to enter or win!
    (B) Helps control dandruff symptoms with regular use!
    (C) Special sales price available for a limited time only!
    (D) Contact us today and start living the life you deserve!

PART 7

Directions: In this part you will read a selection of texts, such as magazine and newspaper articles, e-mails, and instant messages. Each text or set of texts is followed by several questions. Select the best answer for each question and mark the letter (A), (B), (C), or (D) on your answer sheet.

Questions 147-148 refer to the following advertisement.

DATA ANALYST WANTED

BizGov is looking for a data analyst to join our team next year. We are a fast-growing, award-winning tech company, looking to expand into social media. But instead of copying or joining existing platforms, we want to create one that focuses on social awareness. We need your expertise to help us find our audience, reach them, and create the next trend in well-being. If you have proven experience in social media and references, we want to hear from you! We offer a competitive salary, remote work days, double the standard amount of paid leave, company trips, a great office environment, and skills development. Send your résumé to hr@bizgov.ca. We will send a short data test, followed by a short phone interview if you pass the test. After that, we'll set up an on-site interview and trial week.

---

147. What project is BizGov most likely working on currently?
    (A) Winning awards for technology
    (B) Copying a social media platform
    (C) Joining a social media platform
    (D) Trying to create social awareness

148. Which is NOT a benefit for employees at BizGov?
    (A) Well-being program
    (B) Working from home
    (C) Paid holidays
    (D) Company trips

Questions 149-150 refer to the following text message chain.

ABLE, TRAVEL REP 10:28 a.m.
Hi, Mark. Can I help you to book your next trip?

MARK JACKSON 10:30 a.m.
Yeah, sure. I want to go to Greece in June or July with my wife and kids.

ABLE, TRAVEL REP 10:32 a.m.
Wonderful idea! We have several tour packages for Greece. Here are the links:
http://www.travelgo.com/packages/greece-ruins/family
http://www.travelgo.com/packages/greece-athens/family
http://www.travelgo.com/packages/greece-islands/family

MARK JACKSON 10:35 a.m.
Thanks, but my kids are actually grown adults. I had a brief skim through your packages. Unfortunately, nothing quite fits our needs. We want a combination of your pensioner's package and the young backpacker's packages, if that's possible.

ABLE, TRAVEL REP 10:37 a.m.
Of course! Let me see what we can do for you. Could you give me your preferred dates and budget, please? Also an e-mail address for us to send the tailored packages to.

Aa [Send]

149. At 10:35, what does Mark Jackson mean when he writes "I had a brief skim through your packages"?
(A) He looked very carefully at some vacations.
(B) He discussed some ideas with the agent.
(C) He hasn't had the chance to go traveling.
(D) He looked very quickly at some trips.

150. What would Mark like Able to do?
(A) Send quotes for the packages
(B) Create a new package for them
(C) Give suggestions of locations
(D) Send him an e-mail about Greece

Go on to the next page.

Questions 151-152 refer to the following instructions.

Bernkitz Furniture Assembly Instructions

Pine Coffee Table

IMPORTANT
- Read the instructions carefully before starting assembly

Health and Safety
- DO NOT use this table if any parts are missing or broken
- DO NOT use this table if all fixings are not secure
- Only use on a level, even surface
- Recommended for two people to use and assemble

Care and Maintenance
- Do not place item in direct sunlight or next to a radiator. Heat could change the shape of the table.
- Do not place very cold or hot items directly on surface
- Use a duster or slightly damp cloth to clean
- Do not use soap and water or detergents
- You can treat the surface using fragrance-free block wax
- Check all screws and fixings regularly
- Keep sharp objects away from table

---

151. What is described in these instructions?
    (A) How to assemble the table
    (B) How to build a table
    (C) How to take care of the table
    (D) How to purchase a new table

152. Why should the user not put the table in sunlight?
    (A) It could change shape.
    (B) It will get stained in the sun.
    (C) It will break.
    (D) It will get too hot to touch.

Questions 153-154 *refer to the following memo.*

MEMO

Date: June 21

There have been a number of complaints recently about late deliveries and subsequent poor treatment from our representatives. We know that delivery delays are out of our control, but our treatment of clients is not.

Please keep the following tips in mind when dealing with a customer complaint:

- Stay calm and acknowledge the client's complaint. Even if the client is complaining about something that is outside of your control, still acknowledge that you understand their problem.

- Explain carefully that you do not have control over the deliveries as they go through a third party. But don't stop there! Offer to help the client follow up with the delivery company. You have two options to help them do this. The first option is to give them the contact details and necessary information regarding their order. The second option is to conference call the delivery company in on your current call with the client. This will take longer and may not be ideal, but it is an option especially when dealing with a difficult client.

- Don't promise to send the order again unless there's no way of getting the original order to the client.

- Don't get angry or hang up the phone. Clients can be difficult and demanding, but becoming angry yourself will only escalate the problem. If the call goes beyond five minutes without any resolution, transfer the call to your floor manager.

Thank you for your continued hard work and we hope this will help you.

153. What should representatives let unhappy clients know?
    (A) That they can't control the client
    (B) That they can't share contact details
    (C) That they can't help the client
    (D) That they understand the client's problem

154. What should representatives do to help clients?
    (A) Give the client a refund immediately
    (B) Get mad and hang up the phone
    (C) See if they can offer a better deal
    (D) Give them the details for the delivery company

Go on to the next page.

Questions 155-157 refer to the following news article.

Plain Retail Park is set to open next month near the National University's East Campus on Pine Road. —[1]—

The retail park, which is just under 3,000sq ft., will have student accommodation and academic buildings to one side and a shopping mall and gym on the other side. —[2]—

Macey Trent, Retail Operations Manager, said "Before we built this retail park, students had to cross a busy road to get to a store or gym. So this is much more convenient for them. And the student residences are just a short walk away so we are expecting to get a lot of business."

—[3]— The estate manager for Plain Park has confirmed that the rent will be controlled by an independent real estate agency. Students and potential buyers can contact park management to find out more. —[4]—

155. What will Plain Retail Park most likely NOT have?
   (A) Student dorms
   (B) A gym
   (C) A library
   (D) Clothing stores

156. What problem will the Retail Park most likely solve?
   (A) Students having to pass through traffic to reach a store
   (B) Students not having any accommodation
   (C) Students not having access to a gym
   (D) Students not being able to get to their classes on time

157. In which of the positions marked [1], [2], [3], and [4] does the following sentence best belong?
   "Most of the apartments have already been sold to local and international investors who will rent the properties to students."
   (A) [1]
   (B) [2]
   (C) [3]
   (D) [4]

Belmont Clinic
112 Main Road
Milkey City, CA 94966
www.blmclinic.org

30 November

Dear Mr. Gerton,

You had an appointment on Monday, 30 November at 11:30 a.m. with Dr. Pearson. Unfortunately, you did not cancel the appointment or notify us in advance that you needed to reschedule it. As such, your health insurance will be charged the full amount of the missed appointment.

Since this appointment was a follow-up on your blood tests from last week, we strongly urge you to schedule a new appointment as soon as possible. These results were part of your oncology treatment and are therefore very important for your future treatment. The doctor would like to discuss your test results and possible treatment plans.

It is a time-sensitive matter and the doctor would like to see you within the next two weeks. Please call our reception desk at 502-315-6480 to schedule a new appointment.

Yours in Health,
Belmont Clinic

---

158. Why is the Belmont clinic writing to Mr. Gerton?
(A) He missed an important meeting.
(B) He missed a doctor's appointment.
(C) He missed an important test.
(D) He needs to get blood tests done.

159. Why should Mr. Gerton make another appointment urgently?
(A) His medical insurance will be charged.
(B) The doctor wants to do blood tests.
(C) The doctor wants to give him test results.
(D) The doctor wants to discuss doing more tests.

160. What should Mr. Gerton do?
(A) He should request to be given a full refund.
(B) He should call his medical insurance.
(C) He should make an appointment to get tests done.
(D) He should make an appointment before December 14.

Questions 161-164 *refer to the following online chat discussion.*

Margo Diaz [7:18 a.m.]

Roll call! I want to know who's working the Bakersfield job next April. I'll be leading the project, and I'd like to start planning ASAP.

Tarik Smith [7:31 a.m.]

I don't know if I'm working Bakersfield or not. Have the assignment details been posted yet?

Margo Diaz [7:31 a.m.]

They haven't. Since planning isn't complete, there really aren't any details to post at this point. But you should have been informed if you're working the job.

Bev Maki [7:33 a.m.]

I was told that I'm being sent somewhere in April. I'm assuming it's Bakersfield? "You're going out on a job in April." That's what I was told.

Morris Yeun [7:34 a.m.]

Same here. I could really use a confirmation.

Margo Diaz [7:34 a.m.]

All right, I'll double-check regarding your placement. But for now, I'll tentatively mark you two down. I can also give you some very intial details. It's a factory-cleaning job in Bakersfield—a chocolate factory. Do you two have any experience with that?

Tarik Smith [7:35 a.m.]

I know you weren't asking me, but I actually have quite a bit of experience there. Back when I was in Ohio, I was assigned to a jam manufacturer pretty consistently. I cleaned the walls and the ventilation ducts.

Bev Maki [7:35 a.m.]

I don't have any experience with that.

Morris Yeun [7:35 a.m.]

Me neither.

Margo Diaz [7:36 a.m.]

OK. Tarik, I'm going to talk to Dave tomorrow and request that you come on this assignment too. I'll need your experience on this one. I'm also going to need you to help Bev and Morris get the hang of things.

161. Who most likely is Margo Diaz?

    (A) A custodian

    (B) A chocolatier

    (C) A project manager

    (D) A financial planner

162. What does the Bakersfield job entail?
    (A) Installing new ventilation ducts
    (B) Building new walls at a candy shop
    (C) Washing machinery at a jam manufacturer
    (D) Cleaning a chocolate factory

163. At 7:34 a.m., what does Morris mean when he writes, "I could really use a confirmation"?
    (A) He doesn't know anything about the job.
    (B) He was given the wrong information.
    (C) He's not sure if he's going on the job.
    (D) He would like more responsibilities.

164. What will mostly likely happen next in preparation for the Bakersfield job?
    (A) The team will go to Bakersfield.
    (B) Tarik will refuse to join the assignment.
    (C) Margo will ask that Tarik join the project.
    (D) Bev will study in order to get ready for the job.

Questions 165-168 refer to the following e-mail.

To:	maggie@mail.com
From:	johnmc@invest.co
Subject:	Financial Portfolio

Dear Ms. Jones,

Thank you for your inquiry about our financial services. Your e-mail didn't specify which products or services you might be interested in, so I will list the main ones here:

- Financial Portfolio: we can help to set up, maintain, or grow your financial portfolio through various products including bonds, dividends, investments, etc. To get started, we will need your current financial statements and monthly or yearly budget. From there, we will discuss your financial goals for the future and see how we can help you meet them. Contact finport@invest.co

- Tax Consultancy: should you need it, we offer comprehensive tax services. We can help you with individual or company taxes for the current or previous fiscal year. For taxes older than five years, we will need to work with our corporate office in New York. Contact taxcon@invest.co

- Retirement Planning: if your financial portfolio doesn't include a retirement plan, or if you would like an additional one, we can help you. We offer several different plans that start with a minimum contribution as low as $100 per month and can go as high as you would like. We also offer local and international investments at high, medium, or low risk. Contact retplan@invest. co

- Business Services: aside from our tax consultancy, we can also manage your company's finances for you. You don't have to hire a full-time accountant to do your books once a month. Instead, you can make use of our business services and only pay us for the time we spend on your company. We also offer financial advice and recommendations. We want to work with you to make your company a success. Contact busserv@invest.co

This is an overview of our main service areas. Please contact the relevant departments for more information. Or feel free to set up an appointment with me, if you are unsure of what you need or if you need more than one of these services.

We look forward to being of service to you.

Kind regards,

John McGuire
Financial Representative
Invest in Now

165. Why is Mr. McGuire writing to Ms. Jones?

(A) Ms. Jones is looking for a tax consultant.

(B) Ms. Jones wants to start saving for her retirement.

(C) Mr. McGuire wants to introduce himself.

(D) Ms. Jones asked about their services.

166. Which e-mail address should Ms. Jones write to if she wants individual tax consultancy, retirement planning, and an accountant for her company?

(A) finport@invest.co

(B) taxcon@invest.co

(C) johnmc@invest.co

(D) busserv@invest.co

167. Which financial service does Invest in Now NOT offer according to the e-mail?

(A) Monthly budgeting

(B) Saving for the future

(C) Managing finances

(D) Getting tax returns

168. Why would a business make use of Invest in Now's Business Services?

(A) To help them make more profits

(B) To help them find new clients

(C) To avoid hiring a full-time bookkeeper

(D) To avoid hiring full-time employees

Go on to the next page.

Questions **169-171** refer to the following online advertisement.

The Tuck Shop: A Taste of Back Home

Living out in Asia, we're lucky enough to be able to sample all kinds of wonderful cuisine. —[1]— However, every now and then, we yearn for a taste of back home, and there are some treats that are almost impossible to get your hands on.

When was the last time you had a Cadder's Cream Crunch or a Blaster Bar? How about a Big Forest Fudge or a Roly-Poly Surprise? —[2]— We're betting that the answer is a long time ago, unless you managed to get Mom to send you a package of some of these goodies.

We were sick and tired of having to wait on those packages too. That's exactly why we opened The Tuck Shop. Here in our little store, we have a massive selection of chocolate, candy, cookies, and other types of confectionery. —[3]—

So what are you waiting for? If you've got a sweet tooth and miss the tastes from when you were a youngster, get on down to The Tuck Shop now! —[4]—

169. The phrase "yearn for" in paragraph 1, line 2, is closest in meaning to
    (A) To intensely dislike
    (B) To strongly desire
    (C) To clearly remember
    (D) To amusingly observe

170. What does the advertisement say people have to do to get some items from back home?
    (A) Shop online
    (B) Get help from their parents
    (C) Have friends send them packages
    (D) Fly back home

171. In which of the positions marked [1], [2], [3], and [4] does the following sentence best belong?
    "If it's a popular treat back home, we've most likely got it."
    (A) [1]
    (B) [2]
    (C) [3]
    (D) [4]

Questions 172-175 *refer to the following article.*

Many people complain about a lack of energy in winter; a physical and emotional experience that feels like finding yourself weighed down by a heavy blanket. It's hard to get out of bed and easy to find reasons to take a nap. You crave carbohydrates and fats, and probably gain weight. You feel lazy and cancel social outings. In short, you behave like a bear ready for winter hibernation. In fact, nature may have written the same type of instincts into our genetic code.

This finding is important because it sheds light on the higher incidence of depression-like symptoms reported starting in the late fall. In other words, there is nothing wrong with us; we are just at the mercy of insufficient light and falling temperatures.

However, since humans are not bears and do not enjoy this experience, there are coping mechanisms to overcome the winter blues and keep your body and emotions running smoothly. Check the box of symptoms below and their corresponding remedies.

SYMPTOM	WE TEND TO	BETTER YET
Craving sweets	Have too many carbs, resulting in low energy	Skip the yo-yo feeling of sugar highs and crashes by loading up on high-nutrition-laden vegetables, and healthy proteins.
All-day sleepiness	Sleep in and then force ourselves awake with caffeine	Get up with your alarm and do some simple exercises. At lunchtime, go for a walk to soak up sunlight.
Feeling sad	Isolate ourselves	Join social events and stay in touch with friends or family for a natural boost to your mood.

172. Which would be a good title for the article?
  (A) Lessons from Bears
  (B) The Secret to Good Sleep
  (C) Reasons to Throw a Party
  (D) Shake Off the Winter Blues

173. What is compared to lying under a heavy blanket?
  (A) Getting sick
  (B) Experiencing tiredness
  (C) Feeling cold in the winter
  (D) Being controlled by the weather

174. According to the article, which illness can lack of energy in winter seem similar to?
  (A) Obesity
  (B) Depression
  (C) Social phobia
  (D) Muscle pain

175. What is recommended to combat wanting to sleep all the time?
  (A) Drinking coffee
  (B) Getting more rest
  (C) Pressing the snooze button on your alarm
  (D) Doing physical activity

Go on to the next page.

Questions 176-180 refer to the following e-mail and listings.

To:	john@stcloudreal.com
From:	barbwalsh@yakoo.com
Subject:	Real Estate Listings

Dear Mr. Cloud,

My husband and I just got married and we're looking for our first house. We are hoping to live in the downtown area near both our offices. Here is a list of our requirements:

• Quiet neighborhood, preferably with families
• A large porch at the front or back of the house
• Three bedrooms minimum, two bathrooms
• One floor with an open-plan living room and kitchen
• Old English architecture with brick face, not cement in front
• Close to schools, shops, and doctors

Ideally, we would like it to have a basement and double garage as well. We don't mind doing a bit of renovation ourselves. So feel free to send us any fixer-uppers that are cheaper. We have a meeting with our bank manager tomorrow to discuss mortgage rates and loans.

Please let me know if you have any listings that meet our needs. We could set up an appointment as early as next week to start looking at properties.

Kind regards,
Barbara Walsh

Stanley Cloud's Real Estate Listings	
SC-Portside-1001 • Two bedrooms • One bathroom • Large balcony • Two floors • Open-plan kitchen • Quiet neighborhood • Close to shops	**SC-Portside-1015** • Three bedrooms • One bathroom • Large front porch • Open-plan living room and kitchen • Quiet neighborhood • Close to schools and shops • Basement
SC-Portside-1020 • Four bedrooms • Two bathrooms • Large front porch • Brick-face • Quiet neighborhood • Close to shops and schools • Remodeling could create an open-floor kitchen and living room	**SC-Portside-1022** • Three bedrooms • Two bathrooms • Large porch • Open-plan kitchen • Close to shopping mall • Close to highway • Double garage • Needs renovation

176. What is the purpose of this e-mail?
    (A) To ask a landlord some questions
    (B) To complain about problems with a house
    (C) To inquire about finding a home
    (D) To inquire about cheap agents

177. Why would Mrs. Walsh need a mortgage or a loan?
    (A) She wants to build a house.
    (B) She wants to rent a house.
    (C) She wants to renovate their house.
    (D) She wants to buy a house.

178. What does Mrs. Walsh mean when she says, "So feel free to send us any fixer-uppers that are cheaper"?
    (A) They want to buy a house up the street.
    (B) They might buy a house that has been fixed.
    (C) They might buy a house that needs renovation.
    (D) They are not willing to do any work on the house.

179. What is wrong with SC-Portside-1022 according to Mrs. Walsh's requirements?
    (A) It has two bathrooms.
    (B) It doesn't have a living room.
    (C) It needs remodeling.
    (D) Nothing, it's perfect.

180. Which of the following would be most suitable for Mrs. Walsh?
    (A) SC-Portside-1015
    (B) SC-Portside-1001
    (C) SC-Portside-1022
    (D) SC-Portside-1020

Go on to the next page.

Questions 181-185 *refer to the following flyer and e-mail.*

TOUR CAPE TOWN!

Join us on our well-equipped, luxury tour bus, for an unforgettable tour of Cape Town!

Day 1: Arrive at Cape Town International Airport and travel to hotel via shuttle bus

Day 2: Explore the V&A waterfront and Table Mountain*

Day 3: Hout Bay and Boulders Beach to see penguins in their natural habitat[1]

Day 4: Wine and dine! We will visit the largest wine cellar in the world, KWV, to enjoy wine, brandy, and whisky tastings. After that we'll enjoy a fabulous dinner at La Colombe.

Day 5: Robben Island. We will return to the V&A Waterfront and take a ferry to the historical landmark of Nelson Mandela's prison on Robben Island.[2]

Day 6: Long Street and see ancient artifacts at the Iziko South African Museum.

* If the weather is unpleasant, we will return to Table Mountain on Day 5.

Optional extras:

1. The adventurous tourist can join a sea-kayaking trip to the penguin habitat on Boulders Beach.

2. You can include a trip to the Two Oceans Aquarium on this day as well.

Contact us at: info@greattours.com

To:	info@greattours.com
From:	mel345@homail.com
Subject:	Cape Town Tour

Dear Great Tours,

I am really interested in the tour of Cape Town, but I have a few questions.

1. What kind of accommodation do you provide? Can I book my own or stay with locals?

2. What are the costs for the optional extras on Days 3 and 5?

3. Do I need any experience for the optional extra activity on Day 3?

4. Are the tastings and meals included in the price on Day 4?

5. I'm not really interested in history. Could I skip those activities?

I look forward to your reply!

Kind regards,

Melanie

181. How will the tour participants get from the airport to the hotel?
    (A) They will take a tour bus.
    (B) They will take a ferry.
    (C) They will rent cars.
    (D) They'll take a shuttle bus.

182. What happens if the weather is bad on Day 2 of the tour?
    (A) They will stay at the hotel.
    (B) They will go to Hout Bay instead.
    (C) They will go back to the aquarium.
    (D) They will go to Table Mountain on Day 5.

183. What is implied about the sea-kayaking trip?
    (A) It's not for people who don't like adventure.
    (B) It's not recommended for tourists.
    (C) It's only recommended if you have experience.
    (D) It's a good activity for elderly people.

184. In the flyer, the phrase "wine and dine" on Day 4 is closest in meaning to
    (A) Tasting wine and other beverages
    (B) Drinking good wine and eating good food
    (C) Tasting food from different places
    (D) Making wine and cooking food

185. Which activities would Melanie most likely want to skip?
    (A) The V&A waterfront and Table Mountain
    (B) Long Street and Boulders Beach
    (C) The Iziko South African Museum and Robben Island
    (D) Two Oceans Aquarium and Hout Bay

Go on to the next page.

Questions 186-190 *refer to the following test results, patient information, and e-mail.*

Patient Code	Description	Value	Units	Range	Flag
TAY-12-001	White blood cell count	12.62	X10^9/L	3.0-10.0	High*
TAY-12-002	Red blood cell count	4.80	X10^12/L	4.4-5.8	
TAY-12-003	Lymphocytes	4.27	X10^9/L	1.2-3.65	High
TAY-12-004	HCT	0.439	L/L	0.37-0.50	

* Young or elderly patients should be careful if accompanied by high fever or vomiting.

Other Test Results

H1N1 virus: negative
Influenza A: negative

Patient Information	
Name: Patrick Taylor (TAY-12)	Date of Birth: 1945 – 05 – 30
Age: 75	Blood Type: A
Allergies: Peanuts	Address: 103 Main Road, Sherry Town, 116
Consultation Date: May 8	

Patient presented with flu-like symptoms: high fever, cough, blocked nose

Patient also complained of diarrhea and stomachaches

Diagnosis:

Blood and influenza tests ordered
Antibiotics and pain killers prescribed

To:	taylorpat@yadomail.com
From:	drb@medcare.com
Subject:	Blood Test Results

Dear Mr. Taylor,

The results of your blood test and influenza tests have arrived. Please see the results attached. Luckily you don't have to worry about the flu. But it does seem like you have an infection since your white blood cell count is high.

I suggest you get some rest over the next few days and drink a lot of water. Continue taking the Keflex until you finish all the pills. You can stop taking the ibu+ when your fever and pain goes away. I'd also recommend you stay away from coffee, spicy foods, and dairy for the next week. It will give your stomach time to recover.

If you are still feeling sick after two days, please come see me again. However, if your fever suddenly goes up or you start vomiting, please go to the emergency room immediately.

I hope you feel better soon.

Regards,
Dr. Bennison

186. Why did Mr. Taylor go to see Dr. Bennison?
    (A) Because his red blood cell count was high
    (B) Because he had many symptoms
    (C) Because he had H1N1 virus
    (D) Because he had influenza

187. Why does Dr. Bennison say that Mr. Taylor doesn't have to worry about the flu?
    (A) He doesn't have flu-like symptoms.
    (B) He has diarrhea instead.
    (C) His test results are negative.
    (D) His red blood cell count is high.

188. Why does Dr. Bennison think Mr. Taylor's stomach needs time to recover?
    (A) Mr. Taylor complained of diarrhea and stomachache.
    (B) Mr. Taylor has the H1N1 virus and needs to rest.
    (C) Mr. Taylor has been eating too much spicy food.
    (D) Mr. Taylor needs to recover after the flu tests.

189. What type of medicine is Keflex most likely?
    (A) A pain killer
    (B) An antibiotic
    (C) A pill for vomiting
    (D) A pill for blood tests

190. Why does Dr. Bennison advise Mr. Taylor to go to the emergency room if he starts vomiting?
    (A) Because the doctor's office isn't open
    (B) Because Mr. Taylor is older
    (C) Because he is very young
    (D) Because Mr. Taylor is allergic to peanuts

Go on to the next page.

Questions 191-195 *refer to the following letter, online review, and magazine article.*

On Body and Beauty

Dear valued customers,

New Product Line On Sale

We would like to announce an exciting new range of products, Liquify. These products will address a number of skin-care concerns such as sunburn, acne, dry or flaky skin, rashes, and oiliness. The range of products can be used safely on all areas of the body and for all ages, including infants and pregnant women. Over the next ten days, you will receive a 10% discount on all Liquify products as an introductory special. We trust you will love these products as much as we do!

Clearance Sale

We are also clearing out old stock this month. Enjoy products from BodyLove, Purify, and Lotioness at 50% off. Stocks are limited and we won't be ordering again, so don't miss out!

Blog Posts

This month's blog posts are all about ethical choices, from buying products to ordering a rideshare.

Recipe

Our recipe for this month is a dairy-free, meat-free lasagna that's better than the alternative!

We look forward to serving you in store. As always, feel free to stop by with any vegan-related problems or questions. Our staff members are well-informed on all the products we stock, as well as being familiar with a wide range of natural cures.

Yours in good health,

On Body and Beauty Management

Reviews

4.5 out of 5 ★★★★☆   **1,002** customers recommend On Body and Beauty
Mary-Anne Lewis recommends On Body and Beauty

1 day ago

"What a great store! The staff members really know their stuff and were very willing to help me, even if it meant recommending a product that they didn't currently have in stock. They went so far as to tell me where I could buy it, since it was an emergency. I browsed through most of their products and was impressed by the wide selection. I ended up buying a bottle of BodyLove's "Body4U" lotion for just $10 because it was on offer, and have loved it. I'd say about 70% of their brands have the Flying Rabbit logo which is way above other shops who also claim to stock ethical products."

Can cruelty-free be trusted?

A recent report in the *Bulk Times* has revealed that a number of companies that claim to produce cruelty-free products are actually not doing so.

Although they themselves don't test their end products on animals, the ingredients they buy from third-party suppliers do. This means that even though there is less animal-testing than with other companies, there is still more than people are led to believe. The companies range from herbal medicine giants like Pfiper to smaller local operations such as BodyLove Cosmetics.

Most of the companies did not respond to the allegations in the report. Two companies claim that they did not know about the animal testing, as their suppliers faked reports and data when they first agreed to order from them.

They now vow to find other suppliers who don't do any animal testing and bear the Flying Rabbit logo from Green Corp. This logo means that the product has been ethically sourced in every way possible. No slave labor, animal testing, or harmful chemicals were used during its production. Consumers can look for this logo to ensure their products really are cruelty-free.

As consumers become more aware of these breaches, companies will have to be more transparent about their entire operation. In a bid to improve customer relations, major cosmetic retailer, On Body and Beauty, is already making efforts to get rid of products that have been connected to animal cruelty. The hope is that more stores follow their lead.

191. Why might On Body and Beauty be selling all their BodyLove products?
    (A) Because of recent customer complaints
    (B) Because new products are cheaper
    (C) Because they want to get rid of some old stock
    (D) Because they have a bad relationship with BodyLove

192. What was the price of one bottle of Body4U before it was discounted?
    (A) $10   (B) $17   (C) $20   (D) $40

193. What is true about BodyLove?
    (A) It is an internationally established company.
    (B) It has only ever used ethically-sourced products.
    (C) It has received some negative publicity.
    (D) It doesn't want to change its prices.

194. Why does Mary-Anne mention the Flying Rabbit logo?
    (A) She likes the logo and thinks it's cute.
    (B) She only buys products with that logo.
    (C) She knows it means the company is ethical.
    (D) She thinks it's a good brand.

195. What does the article say companies have to start doing?
    (A) Offer better deals to customers
    (B) Be more honest about their production process
    (C) Put the Flying Rabbit logo on all products
    (D) Respond to allegations of unethical practices

Go on to the next page.

Questions 196-200 refer to the following job posting, e-mail, and response.

Digital media site looking for dynamic new hires

Copy Editor
- Candidate must have 1+ years' experience in Web content editing
- Must be familiar with *The Chicago Manual of Style*
- Must have background with a wide variety of content
- All articles written in American English
- Must know how to use the software package *NewLayout*
- Strong communication skills a must
- Competitive salary
- Contact tim_bendes@mediamate.com

To:	tim_bendes@mediamate.com
From:	jjenks@jmail.com
Subject:	Position of Copy Editor

To Whom It May Concern,

I am writing in connection with the position of copy editor that I saw advertised on the MediaMate site on Thursday. Attached is my CV. As you will see, it includes many years of experience at a variety of companies in traditional print and web media. My most recent role was at the Daily Scoop's website, where I was in charge of the sports desk.

Although most of my positions have been working for the sports sections of publications, I have also helped out in the business and politics departments from time to time, so I consider myself a jack-of-all-trades. In addition to my fine eye for detail and great copy editing skills, I am adept in a number of software packages, including the layout program InDesign.

I hope you will give my application some thought.

Best wishes,
Jez Jenkins

To:	jjenks@jmail.com
From:	vtomlinson@trendingdaily.com
Subject:	Copy Editor application

Dear Mr. Jenkins,

Many thanks for your application for the position of copy editor. Unfortunately, the role has already been filled, but we will keep your details on file.

I have a question: Are you from the UK? The reason I ask is that you use the word CV rather than résumé. Speaking of the résumé, it seems your eye for detail deserted you this time as you didn't attach it!

Anyway, thanks for your interest in the position and good luck with the job search.

Regards,
Vera Tomlinson

196. Which is a requirement in the job posting that Jez mentions in his e-mail?
    (A) Familiarity with *The Chicago Manual of Style*
    (B) Strong communication skills
    (C) Proficiency in required software programs
    (D) One or more years of experience in Web content editing

197. What is indicated about MediaMate?
    (A) It is a newspaper.
    (B) It is hiring a copy editor.
    (C) It helps people create résumés.
    (D) It forwards job applications to clients.

198. What is true of the job?
    (A) It is too difficult for Jez.
    (B) It is already taken.
    (C) It involves filing.
    (D) It would require relocating.

199. Which of the following skills does Jez NOT say he has?
    (A) Enough years of total job experience
    (B) Knowledge of the required software
    (C) A fine eye for detail
    (D) A background with a variety of content

200. What did Jez forget to do?
    (A) Write a résumé
    (B) Use correct English
    (C) Specify which role he wants
    (D) Attach a document

TOEIC 測驗成績計算方式

分別計算「聽力單元」與「閱讀單元」答對的題數，各單元答對的題數就是該單元的原始分數。將你的聽力及閱讀原始分數分別登記在以下欄位中，然後將你的原始分數範圍對照下表的評量分數範圍，並各自登記在聽力與閱讀單元的評量分數範圍欄位中。兩者相加即為多益總分範圍。

	原始分數	評量分數範圍
聽力單元		
閱讀單元		
總分範圍		

TOEIC 測驗分數換算對照表

聽力單元		閱讀單元	
原始分數範圍	評量分數範圍	原始分數範圍	評量分數範圍
96–100	485–495	96–100	455–495
91–95	445–495	91–95	410–490
86–90	400–475	86–90	380–455
81–85	360–450	81–85	350–430
76–80	330–420	76–80	315–405
71–75	300–385	71–75	290–380
66–70	265–355	66–70	260–355
61–65	235–330	61–65	235–325
56–60	210–305	56–60	205–300
51–55	185–275	51–55	175–270
46–50	165–250	46–50	155–235
41–45	140–225	41–45	125–205
36–40	115–195	36–40	105–170
31–35	95–165	31–35	85–140
26–30	80–135	26–30	65–115
21–25	65–110	21–25	55–90
16–20	35–90	16–20	45–75
11–15	10–70	11–15	30–55
6–10	5–60	6–10	10–45
1–5	5–50	1–5	5–30
0	5-35	0	5-15

TOEIC® 模擬測驗 答案紙

LISTENING SECTION

Part 1

No.	ANSWER
1	A B C D
2	A B C D
3	A B C D
4	A B C D
5	A B C D
6	A B C D
7	A B C D
8	A B C D
9	A B C D
10	A B C D

Part 2

No.	ANSWER	No.	ANSWER	No.	ANSWER
11	A B C D	21	A B C	31	A B C
12	A B C D	22	A B C D	32	A B C D
13	A B C D	23	A B C D	33	A B C D
14	A B C D	24	A B C D	34	A B C D
15	A B C D	25	A B C D	35	A B C D
16	A B C D	26	A B C D	36	A B C D
17	A B C D	27	A B C D	37	A B C D
18	A B C D	28	A B C D	38	A B C D
19	A B C D	29	A B C D	39	A B C D
20	A B C D	30	A B C D	40	A B C D

Part 3

No.	ANSWER	No.	ANSWER	No.	ANSWER
41	A B C D	51	A B C D	61	A B C D
42	A B C D	52	A B C D	62	A B C D
43	A B C D	53	A B C D	63	A B C D
44	A B C D	54	A B C D	64	A B C D
45	A B C D	55	A B C D	65	A B C D
46	A B C D	56	A B C D	66	A B C D
47	A B C D	57	A B C D	67	A B C D
48	A B C D	58	A B C D	68	A B C D
49	A B C D	59	A B C D	69	A B C D
50	A B C D	60	A B C D	70	A B C D

Part 4

No.	ANSWER	No.	ANSWER	No.	ANSWER
71	A B C D	81	A B C D	91	A B C D
72	A B C D	82	A B C D	92	A B C D
73	A B C D	83	A B C D	93	A B C D
74	A B C D	84	A B C D	94	A B C D
75	A B C D	85	A B C D	95	A B C D
76	A B C D	86	A B C D	96	A B C D
77	A B C D	87	A B C D	97	A B C D
78	A B C D	88	A B C D	98	A B C D
79	A B C D	89	A B C D	99	A B C D
80	A B C D	90	A B C D	100	A B C D

READING SECTION

Part 5

No.	ANSWER	No.	ANSWER
101	A B C D	111	A B C D
102	A B C D	112	A B C D
103	A B C D	113	A B C D
104	A B C D	114	A B C D
105	A B C D	115	A B C D
106	A B C D	116	A B C D
107	A B C D	117	A B C D
108	A B C D	118	A B C D
109	A B C D	119	A B C D
110	A B C D	120	A B C D

Part 6

No.	ANSWER
121	A B C D
122	A B C D
123	A B C D
124	A B C D
125	A B C D
126	A B C D
127	A B C D
128	A B C D
129	A B C D
130	A B C D
131	A B C D
132	A B C D
133	A B C D
134	A B C D
135	A B C D
136	A B C D
137	A B C D
138	A B C D
139	A B C D
140	A B C D

Part 7

No.	ANSWER	No.	ANSWER	No.	ANSWER	No.	ANSWER
141	A B C D	151	A B C D	161	A B C D	171	A B C D
142	A B C D	152	A B C D	162	A B C D	172	A B C D
143	A B C D	153	A B C D	163	A B C D	173	A B C D
144	A B C D	154	A B C D	164	A B C D	174	A B C D
145	A B C D	155	A B C D	165	A B C D	175	A B C D
146	A B C D	156	A B C D	166	A B C D	176	A B C D
147	A B C D	157	A B C D	167	A B C D	177	A B C D
148	A B C D	158	A B C D	168	A B C D	178	A B C D
149	A B C D	159	A B C D	169	A B C D	179	A B C D
150	A B C D	160	A B C D	170	A B C D	180	A B C D
						181	A B C D
						182	A B C D
						183	A B C D
						184	A B C D
						185	A B C D
						186	A B C D
						187	A B C D
						188	A B C D
						189	A B C D
						190	A B C D
						191	A B C D
						192	A B C D
						193	A B C D
						194	A B C D
						195	A B C D
						196	A B C D
						197	A B C D
						198	A B C D
						199	A B C D
						200	A B C D

TOEIC 全面備戰 7大題型應考策略＋13大情境必備詞彙

發 行 人　鄭俊琪

總 編 輯　陳豫弘

副總編輯　璩雅琪

編　　審　李建宏

英文編輯　Paul Duffy・Helen Gamble・Elene van Sandwyk

責任編輯　林怡君

中文編輯　莊琬茹・陳世弘・謝東翰・黃靖雯・張珮絹

英文錄音　Mike Tennant・Sarah Zittrer・Nick Wheeler・Niall Longobardi・
　　　　　Ashley Smith・Caitlin Hennegan・Meagunn Hart・Zach Mortimer

藝術總監　李尚竹

封面設計　王瑄晴

美術編輯　陳淑珍・黃郁臻

點讀製作　李明爵

出版發行　希伯崙股份有限公司

　　　　　105 台北市松山區八德路 3 段 32 號 12 樓

　　　　　電話：(02) 2578-7838

　　　　　傳真：(02) 2578-5800

　　　　　電子郵件：service@liveabc.com

法律顧問　朋博法律事務所

印　　刷　禹利電子分色有限公司

出版日期　2020 年 6 月 初版一刷

出版品預行編目資料

TOEIC全面備戰：7大題型應考策略+13大情境必備詞彙 /
陳豫弘總編輯. -- 初版.
-- 臺北市：希伯崙公司, 2020.06
　面；　公分
ISBN 978-986-441-389-8(平裝)

1.多益測驗　　　2.詞彙

805.1895　　　　　　　　109007535

《TOEIC 全面備戰 7 大題型應考策略 +13 大情境必備詞彙》讀者回函卡

謝謝您購買本書，請您填寫回函卡，提供您的寶貴建議。如果您願意收到 *LiveABC* 最新的出版資訊，請留下您的 e-mail，我們將寄送 e-DM 給您。

歡迎加入 *LiveABC* 互動英語粉絲團，天天互動學英語。請上 *FB* 搜尋「*LiveABC* 互動英語」，或是掃瞄 QR code。

姓名		性別 □男 □女

出生日期	年　月　日	聯絡電話

E-mail	□ 我願意收到 *LiveABC* 出版資訊的 e-DM

學歷	□國中以下　□國中　□高中 □大專及大學　□研究所

職業	□學生　□資訊業　□工　□商 □服務業　□軍警公教　□自由業及專業 □其他 _____

您以何種方式購得此書？

□書店　　□網路　　□其他 _____

您覺得本書的價格？

書名 □偏低　□合理　□偏高

您對本書的評價

	書名	封面	內容	編排	紙張
很滿意	□	□	□	□	□
還不錯	□	□	□	□	□
普通	□	□	□	□	□
不滿意	□	□	□	□	□
很後悔	□	□	□	□	□

您希望我們製作哪些學習主題？

您對我們的建議：

縣市

市區鄉鎮

村里　路街

段

鄰巷

手號

樓

室

1 0 5

希伯崙股份有限公司客戶服務部收

台北市松山區八德路三段32號12樓

英語數位學習第一品牌